THE
CONSPIRACY
CABAL

OTHER BOOKS BY DAVIE MAC

Too Young To Die
Taken And Afraid
Survival Of The Fittest
A Dangerous Environment

Davie Mac

The Conspiracy Cabal

A BLAKE MORAN NOVEL

Visit the author's website at www.daviemacbooks.com

The Conspiracy Cabal: A Blake Moran Novel

Copyright © 2024 David McAllister. All rights reserved. No part of this book may be reproduced or retransmitted in any form or by any means without the written permission of the publisher.

Published by K&D Publishing

Cover and interior design by Nicole Baron Designs

ISBN: 978-1-962947-01-5 (paperback)
ISBN: 978-1-962947-02-2 (e-book)
LCCN: 2024909428

The Conspiracy Cabal novel word count: 131,090

DEDICATION

To the Founding Fathers of this great Representative Republic, the United States of America. Their commitment, insight, wisdom, and love for this nation, and for God and His principles, provided the tools for our nation to truly be that "shining city on a hill". If only we as citizens will simply choose to continue the principles they established for us in our founding documents, we can once again be that great nation. They are worthy of both our respect and our ongoing fight for a truly free people and nation "under God".

Also, to each and every "patriot" who loves our nation as founded and wants only the best for her and her citizens. America has always needed a remnant of God-fearing men and women who refuse to give up on the ideals and foundation of our great nation. I hope and pray that you are one of those great patriots who is willing to stand up and fight—this is our time, this is our generation. And this book is for you!

DISCLAIMER

This is a work of fiction. Unless otherwise indicated, all the names, characters, businesses, places, events and incidents in this book are either the product of the author's imagination or used in a fictitious manner. Any resemblance to actual persons, living or dead, or actual events is purely coincidental.

PROLOGUE

His legs and arms were duct taped to the chair.

Senator Todd Ashford couldn't understand how this criminal had even gotten into the apartment, past his security detail—although when he thought about it, the intruder had clearly come in through a window he had left open.

But that window was seven stories above the ground, and the face of the building was smooth, so he had no idea how that was possible.

Todd was just trying to calm himself since he had a cloth stuffed into his mouth and could only breathe through his nose. He didn't know what this guy was looking for, but he was going through any and all papers he could find.

The unsettling thing was how calm the intruder was—that, and the fact he wasn't doing *anything* to hide his face from the Senator. After he got him secured to the chair, he took off the full-face mask and just looked at him for a moment.

Rule of thumb: if an intruder shows you their face, that's a bad sign—they're typically figuring they won't have to worry about you being around to describe them.

The dead eyes in his face were not reassuring either.

PROLOGUE

Todd was trying to find a way to alert his security team. He needed to make some noise that might bring them running, but he was back in the bedroom, and the plush carpet was not helping his cause.

He decided that if he could tip the chair over and make a loud enough thud when he fell, it just might be enough to cause them to investigate.

He started rocking the chair back and forth, but on the third one where he might have gone over, the intruder was there and stopped him.

He then calmly backhanded Todd so hard that he saw stars and felt like he might pass out.

Todd shook his head to try and clear it.

Todd realized the intruder didn't seem to care about anything but the papers he had in his briefcase and on his desk. That meant this wasn't some random burglary—this was targeted—it had to do with something he was working on.

Senator Ashford knew immediately what the intruder was looking for. There was only one piece of legislation he was proposing that the groups in power would be desperate to stop. That had to be it.

And all the paperwork was in his briefcase—but it was also on his laptop.

Maybe there was some hope. If he didn't think of the laptop, the information he'd been working on would be there for people to find.

His hopes were dashed when he saw the intruder find the laptop. He checked his watch, shook his head at something, paused for a moment, then walked into the kitchen area, out of sight.

Todd heard the water run for some time and then heard the splash. The intruder was frying the laptop by submerging it.

So much for that hope.

He looked around frantically to find some way to get out of this situation, but he wasn't seeing any options.

PROLOGUE

The intruder took the handful of papers, stuffed them into his jumpsuit and turned toward Senator Ashford.

As he walked toward Todd, he calmly pulled an ordinary plastic bag out of his pocket.

Senator Todd Ashford's eyes bugged out as he tried to thrash around, but the intruder just pulled the bag over Todd's head and duct taped it around his neck.

Todd struggled to breathe against the simple plastic bag, but he never stood a chance. He lost consciousness in a matter of seconds and died in just minutes; his last thoughts were of his wife and kids.

The intruder didn't even watch. He just looked around to make sure he didn't leave anything and pulled his full-face mask back over his head. He took one look back to make sure the Senator was dead, then walked to the window and glanced out to make sure everything was clear. He stepped back out of the window, seven floors above the ground—slid the window closed—and was gone.

THE CONSPIRACY CABAL

CHAPTER 1

My wife is HUGE!

Now undoubtedly, many of you are thinking the classic, *"Oh no, he didn't!"* and using your best twangy voice as you think it.

But I did.

You might also think I am seriously busted when my wife hears what I said—but believe it or not, she's actually OK with it.

In case you've missed my previous adventures and are just joining me, my name is Blake Moran. I'm a private investigator, formerly of Phoenix, Arizona, but now residing in Tucson, Arizona.

For the record, my tagline is, "We Find Stuff."

I know—it's good. What can I say? Thought it up all by myself. I'm just good at witticisms.

I was formerly a single man in my early thirties without much in the way of, shall we call them, resources.

Because of a series of events, I am now a married man who is a multi-millionaire with an estate the size of some palaces.

No, I did not marry into money—if that was your first guess.

And OK, "palace" might be a little bit of an exaggeration, but the house *is* over 15,000 square feet—so bigger than five large houses combined—so it is huge.

Which reminds me—we were talking about my wife—and her size.

My lovely wife was formerly Cindy Lou Rios, a detective with the Tucson Police Department—which affectionately referred to her as "Cindy Lou Who", which she hated. We met on a case I worked in Tucson, and I gradually wore her down till she decided I was OK.

I wore her down like a river carving a path through solid rock—isn't that *so* romantic?

We got married last January and had an amazing honeymoon in the best suite of rooms at an all-inclusive resort in Cancún, Mexico.

It was magical!

Some might contend it was a little *too* magical.

Which brings me back to the size of my wife.

Not only did we come home with an important case to work on together, we also brought something home from Cancún that we didn't plan on—which also resulted from us "working together."

Nope, it wasn't a set of towels from the resort, and it wasn't some sort of parasite—it was something we didn't even *know* we were bringing home.

It was a baby.

The little dickens hid from us for a few weeks, but he or she made themself very known when my bride started throwing up, sometimes right after kissing me. I've learned not to take it personally.

Real nice way to say "hello" to your mom and the world, future Moran kid!

Since that time, I've watched my bride go through sickness—the kind of sickness where just the smell of certain foods sent her running for the vaunted porcelain repository.

However, she got past that. The next thing I knew, I was watching my sweet, tiny little lady put away amounts of food that I couldn't imagine were possible.

If you've been with me on past adventures, you know that I like to eat, but I'd never challenge my wife to an eating contest when she's pregnant. I would lose in dramatic fashion if I did.

However, when I say that she is huge, I'm not sure that I'm doing her justice, cuz at about twenty weeks in, we went for an ultrasound and the OBGYN got a surprised look on her face and spoke some life-changing words to us.

"Oh—there are *two of them* in there!"

I once again needed a brown paper bag to breathe into—you might remember that Thurston had to get me one when I first saw Mr. Triplehorn's "stable of automobiles".

Cindy took it like a trouper—she actually seemed quite happy to hear it, but of course she cried, cuz she's a girl—it's what girls do. But they were happy tears.

So, it looked like ole Blake Moran threw a "double" in Cancún when he wasn't even batting for a "single". But, if you *saw* my wife in the Caribbean, in her bikini on our honeymoon, you would completely understand my happy helplessness to resist her.

I guess what I'm trying to say is that this current situation is actually *her* fault—if she's gonna look that good, I can't be blamed for simply taking the bait!

Once again, as you can tell, I'm a romantic at heart!

Wow! That look on your face pretty much says it all now, doesn't it? I'm gathering that you would have a different perspective?

CHAPTER 2

Any-who...

To continue our story, we now find ourselves a little over nine months since we got married, and my wife has been "eating for three" for quite some time now.

(Some might say she seems to be eating for *more* than three. *I'm* not saying that—I'm just reporting what "some" might say.)

So, this is why I can issue my topic sentence, "My wife is HUGE", and it's OK. Twins in one womb will do that to you. Cindy tells me how huge she is all the time.

Now, some might be thinking that it's OK if Cindy says it about herself, but I shouldn't confirm her suspicions. I will admit that there are times you are correct—times where Cindy would cry if I noted that she had, I don't know, gotten "a little bigger"—after all, Cindy is a girl, and she can get emotional at times.

However, for the most part, my girl is a trouper and just giggles about being so big with our children. She'll get out of the shower and just shake her head at the image staring back at her in the mirror. Cindy doesn't take herself too seriously—she's a fun and funny lady, and we love to tease each other. It just works.

It helps that Cindy looks absolutely adorable being "preggers". She is so beautiful—she kind of glows. I make sure she always hears *that part* of the equation too.

Women amaze me with all they will go through to bring a child into the world—and then they'll often even turn around and do it again!

Speaking for all humanity, if I might, we thank them, one and all, for providing the very survival and continuation of the human race.

Finally, in summary—my wife is HUGE!

"Blake, I'm stuck again!"

Cindy jarred me out of my intense pondering about how huge she was.

I could barely hear her. I'm a section or two over in the house, working in my office when she bellows.

I'm sorry—I should probably rephrase that—"when she calls".

I jumped up to go give her a hand.

"On my way," I yell. "Try not to eat anything else before I get there, OK?"

"You know someday I'm going to lose all this weight," she yelled back, "and then I'm going to kill you for comments like that!"

I finally rounded the corner and said, "I know you will, my little butterball."

She just shook her head and gave me the stink eye.

Cindy was sitting in one of our comfortable chairs that looked out toward the backyard and pool area, along with the Tucson Mountains at the back of our house.

These chairs pretty much "enveloped" you when you sunk into them, so they were very comfortable, but it wasn't all that easy to get out of them—especially if you're about to give birth to twins—and you're huge.

I had to stop and stare at Cindy for a moment.

"What's that grin for?" she asked.

"You are just so cute all snuggled up in that chair. I'm not sure that you could ever get out of there by yourself. It's like the chair swallowed you."

"That's why I'm yelling in such an unladylike way for my man, who for the record put me in this condition, for help. So, grab my hands and let's see if we can extract my sizable bottom from this form fitting chair."

I waited for a moment as we both stared at her tummy. We were at the point that any movement was clearly seen, and the boys were moving around right now.

Oh yeah, I forgot to mention, we're having two XYs—or boys, males, or penile-Americans, if you'd rather.

(Oh, come on, *that* was funny!)

Before Cindy got this big and things got so tight in there, there were some nights that we would lay in bed and just watch. It looked like the little dudes were sumo-wrestling in there. If you'd set a glass of water on her tummy, it might just spill.

We might be headed for quite the rambunctious boys.

I was still chuckling about Cindy's "sizable bottom" comment when I took her hands, braced myself and pulled. The chair provided some resistance, but eventually, we won the battle, and my bride was vertical.

"Thank you, kind sir, you shall be appropriately rewarded," and then she kissed me.

I kissed her back and then some.

"Hey, hey," she said, "that's what got us into this situation!"

"Well, you can't get any *more* pregnant."

"You always have an angle, don't you Mr. Moran?"

"I do, my love, I really do. What can I say? I will never get tired of loving you."

Cindy just kind of glowed at me.

"Oh, come here you little sweet talker."

And I did.

CHAPTER 3

It might not surprise you to know that my dear, sweet Cindy was counting down the days to her due date, which was almost here. There were multiple times when she was trying to lumber around the house to do things when I would hear her mutter, "I have got to get these babies out of me!"

It was stated with a fair amount of urgency.

Now, as you can imagine, being in the condition she was, she at times cursed the fact that our home was so large and spread out. The reality that "I left that in the bedroom" could bring her close to tears, because getting back to the bedroom felt like a three-day walk through the jungles of Borneo.

Fun Fact: the island of Borneo is the third largest island in the world, and the largest island in Asia. It is just south of China, across the South China Sea, and the island is divided into Malaysia and Brunei in the north, and Indonesia primarily in the south. It is just northwest of Australia, so it sits between China and Australia.

The island is divided almost in half by the equator, so, it can get pretty warm there. Borneo is surrounded by the South China Sea to the northwest, the Sulu Sea to the northeast, the Celebes Sea to the east (that's kind of fun to say—Celebes Sea, Celebes Sea—try it!), and the Java Sea to the south.

The warm climate makes it perfect for lots of foliage and specifically, jungles—thus my comment about "a three-day walk through the jungles of Borneo."

After that journey of words, I'm starting to feel "close to tears" myself, as I'm sure you are as well, so let's just agree to move on.

Having an estate this large requires procuring an estate manager—it's simply too much to handle for the owner, at least if you have a job.

Don't look at me like that; I have a job!

Sorta.

Any-who . . .

You might remember that my last adventure involved a young lady—fourteen-years old, named Isabella Maria Iglesias. I ended up saving her from a human trafficking, sex trade operation that was run by the Los Zetas Cartel. I was able to rescue her and six other young girls as well.

I asked Mr. Triplehorn, my favorite billionaire in the whole wide world, if he would fix all the immigration issues and get things settled for all the girls and their families.

He did that and then some! It's impressive what a man in his position—number twenty-third richest in the world—can do when he decides to.

I asked him if Isabella and her family could be placed in Tucson, and he made it happen. The whole process of saving Isabella had begun on our honeymoon in Cancún, when apparently, unbeknownst to me or her, I was impregnating Cindy.

(Pause in our story . . .)

Oh, sorry, my mind wandered back a little, but it was a really *happy* wander.

Consuela, Isabella's mother, figured out a way to talk to us about her abducted daughter, which started the whole process, so we felt especially connected to the Iglesias family.

Once they got here, it occurred to us that we couldn't manage a property this size ourselves, and we would need help. So, I sat down with Consuela and her husband, José, to see if they would manage the estate for us, which they gratefully agreed to do.

It was a "win-win" for everybody.

Which brings us back to the "three-day walk through the jungles of Borneo."

No, it's OK—I'm not going to tell you anymore about the island. You looked frightened there for a moment.

I'm just saying that Consuela has been so helpful to Cindy in these last few months when she needed something from the other side of "Borneo". (Insert smiley-face emoji here.)

Consuela had taken care of both the house and Cindy with great joy, clearly loving being a new American citizen and working for people who care about her.

José manages the estate, working hard every day, keeping this place looking like the day we bought it. He's a quiet man, but he takes great pride in his work, and now in his new country.

A real bonus is that Isabella comes around regularly and sees Cindy. If you were with us on our last adventure, you know that Cindy was a natural with the teenage girls I rescued, so she was enjoying being with Isabella some more. Cindy was like a big sister to her.

They are all going to be a great help once "thing one and thing two" decide to make their appearance.

Now, back to Borneo . . .

Relax, I was just funnin' you.

CHAPTER 4

"What's the status?"

He only knew him as the "Contractor", and he had been waiting for this call. He noted that the caller ID was blocked, which he appreciated—good tradecraft was important in operations like this one.

"The target has been neutralized."

Well, that was a relief.

"Were you able to search the apartment?"

"Yes. It wasn't too difficult since the residence seemed to be used sparingly, just when he was in town."

"Did you find the documents that I requested?"

"Yes, I did. I also found his laptop."

"Did you take it as well?"

"No."

Frustration crept into his voice.

"And why not?" he demanded.

"My method of ingress and egress made that somewhat unmanageable. However, I took care of it."

"How did you do that?"

"I filled the kitchen sink with water and submerged the laptop for a few minutes, then I plugged it in while submerged and fried the whole system. Just to be sure, I then opened it and tried to fire it up and got nothing."

"Excellent," said his employer, clearly relieved to hear what he had done.

"What do you want me to do with the paperwork?" the murderer asked.

"Just bring it and hand deliver it to me."

"No, I can't do that. You can't meet me or see me—that's the rule. No one can have knowledge of who I am, at least not if you want to remain alive."

"Well, how am I supposed to get the papers then?"

"I'm assuming you don't want me to mail them or message them over to you?"

"Absolutely not!" he bellowed. "These are highly dangerous papers and cannot be handled by anyone else."

"Noted. Tomorrow in the mail, you will receive something that will only make sense if you think of me. When you get it, your path to this material will be clear, if you just think it through."

"Don't get all 'Mission Impossible' on me—you bring me those papers now!"

There was silence on the phone.

"You are to pay the amount agreed upon into the numbered account that I supplied you—and you are to do that *now*. The paperwork will be made available to you as I have just said. If you deviate from what I am saying, I'm afraid that I will have to eliminate you—and perhaps your family."

Now the silence came from his end of the call.

"Did you just threaten me?"

"I did—was I not clear enough? Given my history and talent, I would encourage you to listen and follow my expectations. I do not accept deviations, and I do not make idle threats."

He felt a wave of uneasiness run through him.

"Again, pay the agreed amount into my account immediately and watch your mail tomorrow—you can take it from there."

"Lastly, if I have to contact you about this again, understand that it will be your *final* call, and it will *not* end pleasantly for you."

He found himself unable to respond, but then he discovered he didn't need to—he was listening to a dead phone.

CHAPTER 5

It was the middle of the night when I felt Cindy tense and then sit up as she issued a loud, "Ow, ow, ow, OW, OW!"

"Honey, what's wrong?" I asked.

Cindy tried to catch her breath.

"I think our little boys are tired of playing inside and want to get some fresh air," she said with a grimace.

"Is it time?" I asked.

Cindy looked over and slowly shook her head at me.

"Your ability to grasp the obvious amazes me, Mr. Moran."

"I know, right? It's why I'm such a good investigator, babe. But enough about how awesome I am, let's focus on you."

"I wasn't serious, Blake. I was *mocking* you," Cindy said through clinched teeth.

"I know, I was just having fun with you—and I thought I should let you have that one since it's highly probable that you're about to hate me just a little bit, since I'm the one who got you in this predicament."

Cindy chuckled.

"Yeah, I guess you'd better give me that one. Now, let's get our 'go bag' and *go* to the hospital!"

I started to say something funny when another contraction hit Cindy, so I just jumped up, got dressed and helped Cindy do the same between contractions.

I ran out to our six-bay garage and grabbed the clicker for Cindy's USSV Rhino GX. If you weren't with us on our last adventure, you should look it up—the only way to describe this vehicle is that it's the dictionary definition for "beast-mode"!

The bad guy named Santiago drove one, and Cindy decided that it was the perfect vehicle to safely tool around Tucson when the Moran twins decided to make their appearance.

It set me back over three-hundred-thousand-dollars, but I had the money, and it is an awesome beast to drive.

Any-who, I opened the garage door and drove the Rhino up the drive and over to the front door. I left it running and ran inside to help my bride waddle out and get in.

We might want to keep it just between us that I used the word "waddle" there, but I'm sorry, that's how my sweet Cindy had to walk right now. The boys were having their way with her balance, center of gravity, and equilibrium at the moment.

We had to pause on the way when another contraction started. Cindy just leaned into me and hung onto me with her arms around my neck and tried to relax.

In case you haven't been with me before, I tend to deal with stress with humor, and a number of funny comments came into my mind while Cindy hung onto me, but I restrained myself.

Wow, maybe becoming a dad is causing me to grow and mature as a man.

Let's sincerely hope *that's* not the case!

After basically lifting her into the passenger seat, I got her secured with the seatbelt—which was tough—and we were off to the Northwest Medical Center, or what they used to call a "hospital".

It was baby birthing time—time to meet our two new little dudes!

CHAPTER 6

It was a long night and even longer morning—but more for Cindy than for me.

(I thought I'd better add that before the mothers in the audience lovingly tie me to a stake and burn me. Wow, that ended up being unnecessarily violent!)

Cindy was working away all night and morning, the contractions getting closer and harder as the hours went by.

As for me, she was squeezing my hand really hard, and it hurt! But don't worry; I'm hanging in there—maybe I'll suck on some ice chips—thanks for your concern.

Speaking of which, my whole job was to keep the ice chips coming and to remind Cindy how to breathe—you know, the whole Lamaze thing?

This was our first go-around, but come on—we had to look a little crazy holding hands, staring into each other's eyes, and doing our "sound-breath" together through the contractions. It was really weird, but it did seem to work extremely well for Cindy, so, there ya go.

I kept telling her to just view the pain as "work", just like they taught us in class, fully expecting Cindy to crack me in the jaw at some point, while she encouraged *me* to try to view *that* pain as "work".

But she didn't.

It seemed like that mindset really helped her focus her energies toward letting her body do its thing—that "thing" being shooting two rambunctious baby boys out of the "exit", which I sincerely hoped was clearly marked!

Since Cindy was having twins, that moved her toward the "high-risk" side of the equation, so, about seven in the morning, they put the epidural into her spine which started giving her some help with the pain.

That helped her mood considerably.

"Wow," she joked, "we should have just had them put the epidural in around the eighth month!"

The process for placing the epidural was a little freaky though.

Cindy had to curl up in a ball—kind of the fetal position—and then was sternly told, "Now, don't move!"

They then had to insert this large needle past her spine and into the small space around her spinal nerves known as the epidural space. This enables them to give the medicine that "chills" the nerves and lessens the pain.

So, they had to place this *just right* into the space around the spinal cord, thus the command, "don't move!"

You really don't want to "miss" when you're that close around the spinal cord!

I was praying pretty hard around that time—my wife's future was on the line.

It all went well, and Cindy was almost euphoric in just a few minutes. Apparently, this stuff was magic. She could still feel the pressure of the contractions, but not so much the pain.

The anesthesiologist Doc told me that the real trick was giving Cindy just enough of the medication to help control the pain, but not so much that she can't push when it was time to.

If she got too much, get ready for a Cesarean section, cuz momma is just too loopy to help.

I decided to quit talking to him at that point so that he could concentrate on getting my wife and babies safely to our side of the equation.

It was mid-morning by the time they started telling Cindy to push. My lovely wife started giving her all to get the first little dude out. It took about fifteen minutes for the newest little Moran to join the world, and he did so with some degree of loud crying—for a brand-new baby.

One nurse held him while the OBGYN turned her attention to contestant number two.

That's when things got a little scary. Apparently, the little dude who got to the exit first caused his brother to get turned the wrong way—and you're not supposed to enter the world feet first. From what I could gather, trying to pull the head out last, with only that little, delicate neck supporting it, was a "no-can-do".

Things got real serious, real fast, in the room, and Cindy and I had tears in our eyes as we watched and waited.

Our Doc actually reached up inside of my wife and started carefully working the little dude around. Little by little, she moved him into the right position, now having the room since contestant number one had already exited, stage left.

The Doc then discovered that little dude two had also gotten his umbilical cord around his neck, so that took some more time for her to carefully move that around, and then off his neck.

Our tears were now falling fast as we watched this woman reaching up into my wife's womb to save our son's life.

Those may well have been the longest ten minutes of our lives.

Finally, the doctor said, "OK, I think I've got it—time to push."

I was tempted to speak up and say, "Ya think?" but it seemed like I needed to just keep that to myself.

Just three minutes later, little dude number two decided to grace us with his presence.

And then the tears came stronger, but they were all tears of joy at that point.

CHAPTER
—7—

Our new little boys were both placed up on Cindy's chest so that she could cuddle with her new sons.

We both started the counting, and sure enough, we found there was the correct number—which in our case, the magic number was forty.

Ten fingers, ten toes, and then multiply that by two. Forty.

The boys were all covered in a creamy, white, waxy substance they called vernix, which the nurses told us protects them from the amniotic fluid while they were in utero.

What's wild is that they said it didn't just protect the skin—it dampened noise in the womb, insulated the baby's body and acted as a lubricant for the wild "flume ride" down the chute toward the exit sign at the end.

They were wiping the boys off when our OBGYN asked me if I wanted to "cut the cord", or in this case, cords.

I most certainly did.

It's interesting that identical twins can share the same amniotic sac, but it's better if they have their own, which our boys did. But I gotta tell you—cutting the boys' umbilical cords was a trip!

Why, you may ask? Well, first of all, these cords are coming out of my wife, which is just weird no matter how you look at it—if you choose to look at it. Secondly, it is shocking how *thick* these bad boys are! The doctor put clamps on either side of where I was to cut and then handled me these industrial looking scissors. I started gnawing away at the cord and had to put my all into it.

"Have you sharpened these lately?" I asked the Doc.

She laughed and assured me they were sharp, then told me that the cords are just that tough.

Both cords were like that, but I finally worked my way through them.

"Whoa, that was tough!" I told Cindy.

"Oh, was that hard to do, Blake?" she asked me.

"Yeah, that cord is surprisingly . . ."

I cut off my words in mid-sentence when I saw the look on her face.

I realized that my bride was being sarcastic with me, clearly comparing my cutting the cords with all her effort in giving birth to our boys.

"Yes, it was very difficult," I finished, "but I don't expect that you can understand since you've never been through it, and you've just been lounging around for hours."

My teasing smile said it all.

Cindy just shook her tired head at me.

"I love you, Mrs. Moran—now 'mom'."

She laughed.

"I love you too, Mr. Moran—now 'dad'."

CHAPTER
— 8 —

Everyone around us was doing their thing, and now that the boys had been "released" from Cindy's body, they took them, cleaned them up and gave the boys their first sponge bath.

They weighed them first, although "thing number two" decided to pee right as they were getting ready to weigh him.

That probably cost him a few ounces.

And of course I had to say, "that's my boy!"

The first baby out of the chute weighed in at five pounds, nine ounces. Our trouble-maker—both getting out of the womb and being a "little squirt" after getting out—clocked in at five pounds, seven ounces.

That little potty break may have cost him those two ounces his brother had on him.

So, that added up to a total of eleven pounds of baby that my wife brought into the world—and a baby that size would have to be named "Bubba"!

That kind of poundage was also clear justification for my bride being "huge", as was previously described.

Getting back to names, Cindy and I had a lot of fun tossing ideas around. Actually, I probably had more fun than her, since much of her responses to me was just to shake her head or roll her eyes.

Sometimes both.

I came up with some great possibilities for our new little rugrats, but Cindy wasn't buying it. However, maybe she just wasn't seeing the genius in them, so tell me what you think.

Let's see . . . Mutt and Jeff, Bert and Ernie, Amos and Andy, Cuff and Link, a nod to the Rocky franchise, Butch and Sundance, Ping and Pong, Turner and Hooch, Tweedledee and Tweedledum (those two made Cindy laugh out loud), Slice and Dice (those two scared her a little), Marco and Polo, Biscuit and Gravy, Humpty and Dumpty, Tom and Jerry, Ruff and Tuff, Alpha and Beta, Tigger and Pooh, Razzle and Dazzle, Shake and Bake, Nick and Nack, Chip and Dale, Zig and Zag, Cheech and Chong, and Rock and Roll.

Now after hearing my list, apparently, I'm "immature" and wasn't taking this "seriously", so I'll just leave it to you to decide for yourself. After her harsh evaluation of my efforts, I offered Knucklehead and Chucklehead as another option, but she laughingly said that those wouldn't work either because they both already applied to me.

I guessed I should quit while I was behind.

She also said I was no longer allowed to weigh in on the names of our children.

I simply replied, "Through the ears, right to the feelings," putting my hands over my heart.

So, having rejected all my ideas, we rolled up our sleeves and tried to find some real names for our boys.

We finally settled on Nicholas, or Nic, for the first one out, and Lincoln, or Linc, for the second one out—in this case, also known as our "little squirt".

So, Nicholas Moran and Lincoln Moran—Nic and Linc it was.

Just looking at how little they were, all swaddled up, those seemed like pretty big handles for such little dudes.

I wasn't worried—they would grow into them.

CHAPTER
—— 9 ——

It was mid-afternoon when our friends, Brian and Kristi, stopped by the hospital to see our new additions.

In case you're just joining us, Brian is the Senior Pastor at our church, Desert Christian, and his wife Kristi is Cindy's best friend.

"How's the little family doing?" asked Brian when they walked in.

We both looked up. Cindy had Linc, and I was holding Nic.

"Hey guys, welcome," I said. "Come meet our new little rugrats."

Kristi went over to Cindy and gave her a hug.

"Who is this handsome guy?" she asked.

I cut in. "Please Kristi, this isn't about me—let's try to focus on the new babies now."

Cindy just slowly shook her head at me as Kristi and Brian laughed.

"This is Lincoln," Cindy said, "and the funny man over there is holding Nicholas."

They spent some time admiring our little boys and each took turns holding them. Linc ended up filling his diaper while Brian was holding him.

"Here you go, champ," Brian said, holding him out to me. "I already paid my dues over the years, so I'm tapping you in."

"Oh yeah, Brian," said Kristi, "you changed *so many* dirty diapers, didn't you?"

He smiled at her. He was still holding Linc out to me.

I looked back at him.

"Are you sure you don't want to give it a go—just for old time's sake?" I tried.

Brian shook his head slowly.

"Sorry dude, you inadvertently made this mess, so it's your job to clean it up."

They all laughed as I got my son and took my first shot at trying to win the "Battle of the Poo".

It wasn't pretty, but I basically got it done.

I added some commentary with, "That was disgusting!"

Kristi just looked at Cindy and shook her head. "Men," she said.

"Yep," replied Cindy, nodding.

After they had been there for a while, Kristi looked at her watch and said they were going to have to get going.

"They're having me fill in as anchor tonight," she said happily, telling us her good news.

Kristi had previously worked in TV news before she and Brian married and had their family. Now that the kids were older and most had moved out on their own, Kristi had gone back to work at the CBS affiliate in town—KOLD. She typically did remote reporting or field work for them now, so getting to fill in as anchor was extra fun for her.

"How exciting," said Cindy. "We'll make sure to watch. Are you doing both the 5:00 p.m. and the 10:00 p.m.?"

"Yeah," said Kristi.

"OK—well have fun, and we'll be watching."

"Thanks, and congratulations to both of you—you've just started a whole new adventure. Your lives will never be the same now that Nic and Linc are here."

"We're both excited for you," added Brian.

"Thanks guys—and thanks for coming to see our new little dudes," I said. "Although, it would've meant so much more if you'd changed that diaper, Brian, so, big miss on your part! Linc is going to hold it against you someday."

We all laughed at that.

CHAPTER
— 10 —

When the mail came the next day, he was there to get it. He wasn't trusting anyone else to fulfill this important task.

There was a small package he didn't recognize. That must be it.

He had done what the murderer said—he had paid the numbered account immediately. Honestly, the guy kind of scared him—actually *really* scared him—which was a new feeling for him that he didn't like.

He took the small package to his office to open it.

Inside was a locker key. There was a locker number stamped on the key, and it clearly said "Union Station" on it.

Clever.

He had left the material in a small locker at Union Station for him to pick up, using this key. That way, there was no interaction necessary or chance that he might see the murderer.

He was relieved. He had a feeling that even if he accidentally saw him, it wouldn't end well for him. This guy was intense, and he was happy to be done with him.

He called his driver and told him to bring the car around. This was something that you didn't send anyone else to do, and the trip to Union Station would take only about twenty minutes.

He looked around the area as they got closer to their destination. This wasn't the kind of place he would generally be around, but it was midday, so he felt he'd be relatively safe.

After the driver pulled up to the entrance and ran around to open the door, he told him to just wait there with the car because he wouldn't be that long.

He hoped that was true.

He walked briskly, his head on a swivel, keeping his eyes open for any sign of problems. It took him a moment to find the lockers, and then to find the specific one that he needed.

He took the key out of his pocket and put it into the lock. After he turned the lock, the key remained locked in the keyhole until the next person paid to use it.

He opened the locker and there lay a manila envelope that clearly had evidence of some paperwork inside. He looked both ways to make sure he was safe and then took the envelope out. He quickly opened it and took a look at the papers. Satisfied that it was what he hoped it would be, he closed the envelope and tucked it inside his jacket. He then carefully closed the locker, wiped off the key and latch where he had touched them, and headed out of the station with confidence.

The Contractor had come through and eliminated the threat. He was glad it was all over now.

CHAPTER —11—

Say what you will about the healthcare system—and I do—but they can really be efficient when they want you *out* of their hospital! Since everything was good with Cindy and the boys, it turns out that we were on a twenty-four-hour clock, meaning that twenty-four hours from when we checked in, we were outta there!

I asked the nurse if we got twenty-four-hours times two since we had twins, but I guess she wasn't in a laughing mood, cuz she didn't—which I realize is just one explanation.

We decided to settle in and enjoy the last few hours of our time. Even though we could technically stay till the early hours of the morning, we were going to cut and run in the evening hours so that we could get settled at home and get some sleep overnight.

Yeah, RIGHT!

OK, it was an optimistic hope, but optimism springs *eternal*!

Now, you might respond that the *reality* of having two brand new twin boys does *not* let you sleep, and the night will actually *feel* like an eternity—but how about you quit raining on our parade? We're new parents, so we know virtually nothing.

Any-who . . . before we headed home, we settled in with the boys—Cindy was feeding Nic, while I held Linc, who was having a little more trouble "latching on".

Who comes up with these terms?

We turned on the TV to watch Kristi anchor the KOLD newscast. We were a little nervous for her, but there was no need—the girl was a professional and nailed it from the beginning.

She ended up getting quite the significant news night to be the stand-in anchor because of the lead story—one of national importance.

"Good evening, I'm Kristi Jackson sitting in for Andrea Hernandez—here's our top story."

"She looks great, doesn't she?" asked Cindy.

"Yeah, she's got the look and the cadence down pat—so far, so good," I replied.

"From our national desk, there has been a significant development in Washington, D.C., from the horrific murder of a sitting California senator, Senator Todd Ashford."

Cindy and I looked over at each other. This was a big story which we hadn't heard since we'd been busy having our kids—a sitting U.S. Senator getting murdered.

"While the details are still coming in, we currently know that Senator Ashford was targeted in his seventh story apartment late last night by an intruder, was murdered, the perpetrator then escaping and being at large at the time of this broadcast. The specifics are unclear as to how the murderer was able to access the senator's home and avoid his security team, but the investigation is ongoing."

"Senator Ashford was a conservative senator, championing the right side of the political aisle throughout his career, which was at odds with the current administration."

"The White House has responded to this crime by saying that the President feels great sorrow over the loss of Senator Ashford and the loss to his family and the country."

"Senator Todd Ashford leaves behind his wife and four children."

"A great deal of praise has come in regarding Senator Ashford from the right side of the political aisle, as he was one of the major leaders of the conservative caucus."

"We will continue to update you as more information becomes available."

"On to more local and state news . . ."

Kristi went on with the newscast and Cindy and I looked over at each other.

"Wow!" I said. "Somebody offed a sitting United States Senator—and a conservative leader, at that. You gotta wonder what's going on with this."

Cindy nodded.

"Yeah, you can't help but wonder if something bigger is going on when a major player like this gets taken out."

Cindy was burping Nicholas and the lad let out an impressive belch.

"That's my boy!" I said proudly.

Cindy just shook her head at me.

"What am I going to do with three of you in the house now?" she lamented.

"Don't they call that 'livin' la Vida Loca'?" I asked. "What does that mean, by the way, oh Spanish translator wife of mine?"

"It means living the crazy life, oh he who cannot speak Spanish, yet lives in the southwest, husband of mine."

I laughed and got up and gave her Lincoln and took the now full Nicholas. Cindy started working on getting him to "latch on".

"Well, wouldn't you say that "livin' la Vida Loca' is probably a pretty good description of what our life will be like now?"

Cindy nodded.

"Yes dear, I would. And if I might get in an early request—could you please make the next one a girl? I'm going to need some female reinforcements with all this testosterone running around our house."

"I will do my best to accommodate you my dear by throwing an XX chromosome your way, which means that there's basically nothing I can do to fulfill that request. However, I will do my best to practice, practice, and yet even more practice—I will humbly do my part."

Cindy looked at me with a hard stare.

"You heard the doctor, Blake—nothing for you for a month. You heard that, right?"

"Oh, I heard her joking around about that—she is *such* a cut-up! You didn't think she really meant that, did you?"

"Blake Winchester Moran—if you come close to me with those intentions any time soon, I swear I will break it off!"

"Wow, that quickly became unnecessarily violent and graphic!"

"No, it quickly became *necessarily* violent and graphic—ask any woman on the planet!"

I chuckled.

"OK, but all I have to say is good luck being able to keep your hands off of me for an entire month—I just don't see you being able to do it."

Cindy laughed.

"It's becoming easier and easier, the more you talk."

I stood up and walked toward the window.

"How about now, after seeing my derrière walking away from you? Feelings changing a little now? Maybe I'll just let my body do the talking."

Cindy just shook her head and laughed.

"Good luck with that. But you do look good."

"And the seduction begins . . ."

CHAPTER
— 12 —

That first night at home was *a long one.*

We got the boys in the USSV Rhino GX, while accepting lots of compliments on our fancy vehicle from the hospital staff. I had already secured the two baby seats in the backseat—which practically required an engineering degree, but I got it done. The boys looked tiny in the seats, but to be fair, the boys *were* tiny. The seats were equipped to hold little babies, so they worked well—it just looked funny, so it was picture time.

I may have driven more carefully than at any other time in my life, although in this beast, if we had hit anything, we would just destroy it.

It was late evening by the time we got home, so we got the boys into their nursery and tried to get settled ourselves.

It was surprising how tired we were just from that little adventure, but this was new to us. I got why Cindy was so tired—she did all the work, but I was exhausted too.

Weird.

We thought we'd get some sleep, but Linc woke us up just two hours later, and of course that meant that Nic was now up too.

Oh dear, they were already teaming up against us.

Cindy fed Linc first, who was finally getting the hang of breast-feeding. I burped him while Cindy fed Nic. Once we got that done, we fell into bed exhausted.

They woke up three hours later.

We did the whole song and dance again—along with some diaper duty—and hit the hay again.

They woke up again around five in the morning and we both felt ready to give up. But as you probably know, giving up is apparently not one of the options in parenthood.

We could hardly see straight by now, and Cindy fell asleep nursing Linc, and I fell asleep holding Nic.

That's how José and Consuela found us just before eight o'clock.

José didn't say much; he just beamed at us. Consuela scooped Nic from me and talked non-stop to Cindy in Spanish. I'm not sure what she said, but the next thing I knew, she had herded us into our bedroom, taken both the boys and kept repeating "vete a dormir".

My bride looked at me with exhausted eyes and translated for me.

"She said to go to sleep—she's going to take care of the babies for a while."

Consuela immediately became an angel sent from heaven to both of us. We almost wept in gratitude.

Then we both slept.

CHAPTER 13

It was almost noon when I heard Cindy sit up in bed and look at the clock. Her eyes bugged out when she saw the time. Next thing I knew, she jumped out of bed and went out the door like a shot.

I didn't move as quickly, but I knew she was freaking out about the boys.

I found both Consuela and José holding the boys and talking quietly. Cindy was just standing back and watching them with tears in her eyes.

"You OK, babe?" I asked.

"Yeah, I just got startled when I saw what time it was, and then touched when I saw this picture. What wonderful people the Iglesias' are. Look at them with the boys—they're great."

"Yeah, they are, especially when you consider it's been a while since their kids were babies. It looks like they are having fun too."

José and Consuela finally saw us.

There was a stream of Spanish and then some laughter as Cindy went to say hello to each of the boys.

Cindy filled me in.

"They said that they gave the boys a little supplemental formula, and they were not amused. They took it, but they clearly didn't like it. Consuela said they were already spoiled on 'mama's milk'."

It was funny, but Cindy said that last part with a little bit of pride. "Mama" was getting the hang of this.

The women started talking, each of them holding one of the boys, so José signaled me, and we walked out onto one of the porches that overlooked the backyard and pool.

José was getting better at English, and I was trying to get better at Spanish too. I think he was winning.

In halting English, he asked me about a couple of projects that he was working on around the estate and how I wanted him to do them. José was a master of metallurgy, which is a fancy way to say he knew metals and how to cut and mold them to make them look awesome. When he wasn't doing upkeep on the estate, he was using his talents to make some beautiful additions to our property.

We talked for a while and then he went off to get started. I went back in to see how the women were doing.

The boys were now in their basinets, and Cindy was sitting and rocking them while Consuela cooked up some breakfast—or I supposed that by this time, it was more breakfast for lunch.

I hadn't realized how hungry I was until I smelled the bacon and eggs cooking. Thankfully she had made a lot because I dug in as soon as they were ready. She had added some of her homemade salsa to the table, which was surprisingly delicious on eggs.

Cindy must have been just as hungry because she was eagerly eating too.

Dang, taking care of kiddos could really make you exhausted and hungry. Who knew?

CHAPTER 14

The word got back to him that someone was putting out feelers and asking questions about Ashford's murder—someone other than your typical law enforcement, which they had been able to control.

Who is this person? What do they think they're doing?

He sat in the darkened room, surrounded by the tall ceilings and the solid wood-paneled walls. There were rows of expensive books which lined the bookcases. The smell of cigar and pipe smoke lingered in the air—not an unpleasant smell.

As he sipped on his Woodford Reserve Bourbon Whiskey, he studied the flash report in his hand, a sole reading light being the only light in the room. He would periodically take a draw on his Cuban cigar and savor the flavor.

Whoever this was, they were starting to get into some of the darker, more secret parts of their plan. They hadn't gotten very far, but if they dug too deep, they would find some of the threads that could lead them to the things they'd done to get here.

They couldn't allow that.

If they tugged at those threads too much, it could ruin the "Grand Plan", as they liked to call it. And it could put a bunch of them in prison—or worse. If the wrong person found out that they might be exposed, they might decide it was time to silence the major players and run for cover to fight another day.

That wouldn't be good for his health.

He took another sip.

Why won't these peons just leave us alone and let us formulate the world as it should be?

There was a knock on the door.

"Yes?"

His steward stepped in.

"Sir, just a reminder that you have a video conference with the President's chief of staff at one o'clock."

He nodded slightly and the steward vanished quietly.

He couldn't believe he had to talk to that moron again. It was inconceivable to him the level of incompetence that existed among the supposed leaders of this country—or even of the world, for that matter. He supposed he should be glad about this, since it made them easier to control, but he was still annoyed to have to interact with unqualified buffoons, all the while pretending they were important.

He sighed and shifted his attention back to the flash report.

We need to find out who is looking into our operation—it seems like they are starting to get close to the damning stuff.

I'll just get my best guys on it.

And when we find them, I'll have them killed.

He set the flash report down and started trying to decide what he wanted to have for dinner tonight.

CHAPTER 15

The first week of Nic's and Linc's lives kind of flew by. We had some of Cindy's family come to see us, and then some of mine showed up too. Thankfully, since our home was so big now, we just put them in different "wings" and had plenty of room for everyone, and lots of room left over.

Consuela was just loving the experience—she was a little more "in her element", with extended family all over the place. All the family and laughter and excessive loving on the babies—it was pretty cool. Good family can really be awesome.

Consuela's daughter, Isabella, was just a joy to have around. She was now almost fifteen-years-old, and absolutely loved the babies. Since we had such a history with Isabella, after saving her from human trafficking, she was extra special to us, again, like a little sister to Cindy.

On a side note, we had insisted that the Iglesias family allow us to host Isabella's upcoming quinceañera. The word is derived from the Spanish for fifteen and is a big celebration for a Mexican girl as she becomes a woman. That party would be in about a month, and we were planning quite the blowout.

Any-who, we all played some volleyball in the pool and barbecued out most nights. The boys got handed around to person after person, but they seemed to be fine with it—they were little troupers.

Cindy got stronger every day and was clearly heading back to herself again. She was thrilled to be rid of much of that extra fifty pounds of baby weight and was already starting to talk about getting back into her workout schedule to get rid of the rest.

We had notified all our closest friends about the boys' arrival. It was fun to have "Uncle Trent" stop by to see the boys. Trent was the detective who had been Cindy's partner at the Tucson Police Department. Blake and Cindy both felt close to Trent, so it was good to see him and watch him hold the boys.

"Ya did good kid," he said to Cindy.

Cindy just beamed.

Linc promptly spit up on Uncle Trent's tie, which Trent thought was hilarious. Cindy cleaned it off, but Trent always had stains on his tie, so whatcha gonna do?

Cindy and I were caught off-guard a couple of days after the boys were born when a whole bunch of cool toys and presents arrived for the newborns. There were so many, it took the UPS driver twenty minutes to unload all of them.

It all made sense when we saw that it was all from our favorite billionaire, Mr. Triplehorn, and his daughter, Susan.

I made a mental note to give Mr. T a call and thank him for his thoughtful gifts.

However, Mr. T beat me to the punch the next day.

"Hey Blake," said Mr. Triplehorn.

"Hey Mr. T, how are you and Susan doing?"

"We're well. How about you two—or I guess it's now you *four*?" he said laughing.

"Yeah, we're doing great. I was going to call you and thank you and Susan for all the gifts—you didn't really have to do that, sir."

"I didn't, Blake; that was all Susan. I wouldn't have the first clue what to get for newborns—I've been out of that game for way too long."

"Well, thank you, to both of you from us."

"Sure. Blake, I was wondering if Susan and I could fly down and see you and your new little family?"

Blake was surprised.

"Well, of course sir; we would love to have you."

"Don't worry; we'll get a place. We would just like to see you, and I also wanted to talk to you about something."

"Please Mr. T, don't get a place—stay with us. While it's not Triplehorn Mansion here, it is quite a place, and that's because of you. We would love to have you stay with us."

"Oh, we couldn't do that, Blake."

"Please sir, I won't hear the end of it from Cindy if you don't."

Mr. T laughed.

"Well, we can't make the new momma unhappy. OK, if you're sure, Susan and I will fly down tomorrow and stay with you at Moran Manor."

Hmmm. I liked the sound of that. I might have to try that out on Cindy. Maybe I'll get José to start on some metal art depicting that for our front gates.

"Alright sir, we'll look forward to it. See you then."

CHAPTER
— 16 —

Cindy was really excited to hear that Mr. Triplehorn and Susan were coming to see us—she had become quite fond of both of them, Susan feeling like yet another little sister to Cindy.

And this affection was not just cuz they gave us millions of dollars in payment for work I did for them.

They called us from their Gulfstream G650, a nice jet to have around if you can spare the sixty-million-dollar price tag. They let us know that they were arriving at Tucson International Airport and would be heading our direction after that.

We were both excited for Araby and Susan to see our new home—a home that we could have only because of Mr. T's great generosity for my efforts in saving his daughter, the city of San Francisco, and the nation from a perverted serial killer.

OK, maybe the "nation" is a little far-fetched, but it fits better into my superhero view of myself, so how about you just give me that one?

Cindy and I were out on one of the patios, each holding one of the boys, when they arrived.

It was a fun reunion. We hadn't seen them since our wedding—so almost a year—and getting to show them around the house was super fun.

Susan made a big fuss over the babies, wanting to hold them both, while Mr. T just smiled and declared them to both be handsome boys.

Classic man response.

They got to meet José and Consuela—which was one of the seven families that I had been able to save from the Los Zetas Cartel and potential retribution. Mr. Triplehorn had graciously played a huge part in getting the families' citizenship and in relocating them.

They both treated Mr. T with reverential respect, which made him quite uncomfortable.

I didn't even try and save him—he deserved their respect and love, so he was on his own.

Besides, it was funny to watch one of the most powerful men in the world, who was used to dealing with heads of state and who owned numerous large corporations, not knowing where to look as they thanked him profusely.

Later, as we sat out back on one of the patios, he commented on my lack of help.

"Thanks so much for bailing me out of the awkwardness back there with the Iglesias family, Blake."

"My pleasure, sir."

"My thanks was *not* sincere, Blake."

"Oh, but my pleasure was," I said laughing. "I've never seen you that uncomfortable, sir, but I'm sorry—if you're going to be that wonderful, you deserve what you get. This one is really on you, sir."

Mr. T just shook his head and chuckled.

CHAPTER

— 17 —

After staring at the mountains for a moment, Mr. T started a new conversation.

"Blake, I wanted to see you and Cindy and the boys, but I also had another reason for visiting you."

"I was guessing that sir, when you said you had something you wanted to talk to me about. I can only assume you want my opinion on a multi-national merger, or perhaps some advice about taking over a new nation that you've just purchased. I stand at the ready with my insight and deep wisdom, sir."

Mr. Triplehorn laughed.

"Well, oddly enough, I did want to talk to you about something regarding our national interest, so that was actually pretty close."

Now he really had my attention.

"Are you currently in the middle of any cases?"

"I have a few smaller things that I'm working on, but I purposely kept the caseload down so we could do the whole birth and settling in together."

"Why sir, what did you have in mind?"

"Did you hear about the murder of U.S. Senator Todd Ashford?"

"I did, sir. Our friend Kristi Jackson, our pastor's wife, was anchoring the news broadcast that night and reported on it. Do you remember them from the wedding?"

"I do. I didn't know she was a TV reporter, but I can sure see how she would be good in that position."

"Well, you probably heard that he was from California. He was someone I really believed in and someone whom I was planning on backing in the future for higher office."

"He was a really good man, Blake, not like the other guy whom I was so wrong about," he said, referring to a bad man from Tucson, whom I had put away for murder.

I nodded.

"I counted him as a friend, and he wasn't a typical politician, so his death was a shock and hit me hard."

"I'm sorry, sir."

"Thanks. The reason that I wanted to talk to you Blake is because I believe in you and your abilities, and I'm just not sure that his death is going to be investigated thoroughly. I'm convinced that this was a hit put on Todd because he was getting in some bad people's way."

"Wow. That's quite a statement sir, although Cindy and I wondered about that a little when we first saw the reporting. When a U.S. Senator is murdered, you can't help but wonder if politics had something to do with it."

Mr. T was nodding.

"There are some bad things happening in our political arena right now—and since I see a lot of what happens among lots of nations, I'm not just some run-of-the-mill conspiracy theorist. Anyone with eyes can see the mess our country is in right now. I sincerely wonder if there is a cabal of evil that is undermining our system of government, and just maybe Todd was getting too close and ended up stepping on the wrong toes."

"I've personally been using my connections and looking for some answers since Todd was murdered, but I haven't had much success, and I've run out of ideas. This isn't what I do, Blake, but it is what you do."

"I know what I'm good at and when I'm out of my depth. I tried to look into this and quickly learned that I don't know what I'm doing."

I thought about that.

"What do you want me to do, sir?"

"Well, I would need you to first research what our system of government is supposed to be—how it was all established—we can't put it back on the foundation unless we have a clear view of what that foundation was in the beginning. Then, I would want you to look into the murder and all the relevant things Todd was doing, to try and see if maybe my concerns might be valid. Hopefully, if there is a cabal, I would hope you could help me expose it and destroy it."

"Well, as long as you're not asking for much, sir."

Mr. Triplehorn laughed.

"I know it's a lot, Blake, but I'm really fearful for our country. We are spiraling down as a country, and all this money I have doesn't really matter if there is no good country left for Susan, or for Nicholas and Lincoln, to grow up in. I know there are powers behind every government, but this is starting to feel like an insidious evil is controlling ours, and I want it to stop—while we still have a country."

"What do you think, Blake—you want to put your tights and cape back on and save the world again?"

Wow, this man knew me! Evoking my superhero persona was a masterful move.

Although I'm not sure about the "tights" comment—Cindy would have a field-day with that picture.

CHAPTER
—18—

After I agreed that I would like to help, Mr. Triplehorn and I talked for some time about what he knew about the case so far, which wasn't all that much. He then broached another issue.

"I would think that you would know this, but I'll say it anyway—this is a paying job, Blake."

I shook my head.

"Mr. T, look around. Everything you see here is because of your generosity. I'm more than happy to help you with this investigation—you've already done plenty for me."

Mr. Triplehorn just stared at me for a moment.

"Blake, I love you, but you're going to have to learn to be a better businessman than that. When people achieve wealth, they tend to raise their standard of living, which means that they probably need to keep earning money. So, I say right back to you, 'look around'. Where we're sitting costs money to upkeep, so you need to keep providing for your family."

"In addition to that, I didn't just 'give' you the money—in my book, you more than earned it. You saved my daughter and my city."

"And the nation," I muttered under my breath.

"What?"

"Oh, nothing," I quickly said.

"So, while that money was a very large amount to you, from my perspective, it was a very fair amount."

"Lastly, how weird would it be if I expected that you were now forevermore on my payroll, and need to just drop everything you're doing when I call, based on the money I paid you for the last investigation?"

Blake looked at him.

"So weird, Mr. T—so weird!"

Mr. Triplehorn laughed.

"Anyway, this is a paying job, and that's non-negotiable, Blake."

"Well, if I'm going to be better at business, I guess I need to ask you how I know that you're good for it, sir?"

Mr. T just shook his head at me and laughed.

Mr. Triplehorn was spared having to respond to that when Cindy and Susan came walking up with the boys, and right behind them was Isabella.

We both stood up, and I made the introductions.

"Mr. Triplehorn, this beautiful young lady is Isabella Maria Iglesias, one of the girls you helped me save."

Isabella didn't even hesitate. She walked right up to Mr. T, threw her arms around him, and hugged him, with tears streaming down her face, saying "Gracias" over and over.

Mr. Triplehorn was fighting for some control himself—the old softy—and I could tell that the moment was extremely meaningful to him.

Finally, Isabella let him go, and he held her at arm's length and said, "It is very nice to meet you, Isabella."

Isabella just nodded back at him and then gave Susan the same, tearful, big hug too.

Susan didn't try to keep control in the least, she just tearfully hugged Isabella right back.

CHAPTER
—19—

We all had a great evening with the Triplehorns that night. Susan just couldn't get enough of holding Nic and Linc. She was going to be a great mom someday. She was such an awesome young lady—it was going to take quite the young man to be good enough for her.

And that's *before* you factor in that she was the daughter of the twenty-third wealthiest man on the planet. There's no way *that* might cause some issues with the future "Mr. Susan".

Cindy insisted Araby hold the boys. After he got over the awkwardness that comes from not doing it for so many years, he really settled in and thoroughly enjoyed them both.

The Triplehorns left the next morning, and we started trying to get our home down to some semblance of a schedule.

Cindy was feeling like a million bucks now that she was free from carrying thing-one and thing-two inside her body. She was working out daily and loving the physical activity—getting stronger each day.

And every time I started kissing on her, she reminded me of the doctor's one month prohibition of sex.

Seriously—every single time! Isn't that just like a woman? Always thinking that everything has to be about sex!

I'm just funnin' you—the girl knows her man and was preemptively fending off the full attack mode that was just about to commence.

So, since I had all this extra time on my hands, at least for a month, I turned my attentions to the murder case of Senator Todd Ashford.

THE CONSPIRACY CABAL

Mr. Triplehorn had used a couple words that I wanted to fully understand, so while I knew them, I took the time to look them up anyway.

The first one was *conspiracy*. Here's what I found.

Conspiracy: 1) A secret plan by two or more people to do something that is harmful or illegal. 2) An evil, unlawful, treacherous, or surreptitious plan formulated in secret by two or more persons.

OK, I see absolutely no reason they had to use the word "surreptitious" in that definition—it basically just means to try and avoid notice—so secretly. It might just be me, but I think someone was just showing off.

However, I will admit that it's a fun word to say: surreptitious. Try it, it's fun—surreptitious.

The second word was *cabal*. Here's what I found.

Cabal: 1) A cabal is a group of people who are united in some close design, usually to promote their private views or interests in an ideology, a state, or another community, often by intrigue and usually unbeknownst to those who are outside their group. The use of this term usually carries negative connotations of political purpose, conspiracy, and secrecy. It can also refer to a secret plot. 2) The contrived schemes of a group of people secretly united in a plot (as to overturn a government).

OK, I don't mean to harp on this, but did they really have to use "unbeknownst"? I mean, come on! Were they feeling whimsically archaic? All I can think is—if they lost a stick, I'm pretty sure I know where they can find it!

Now, if you were paying attention, you might point out that earlier I said, "unbeknownst to me or Cindy", I was getting her pregnant in Cancún while on our honeymoon. You might then ask *me* if I had found *my* lost stick yet. However, the difference was that when I said that, I *was* feeling whimsically archaic, so I had a reason—ergo, no stick to find.

Any-who . . .

Based on these two definitions, I'm going to go out on a limb and say that a conspiracy cabal is a *BAD* thing.

Genius, I know. I don't know how I do it, or how to explain it to you, but remember, I'm a professional, so please, don't try this at home.

CHAPTER
— **20** —

As I tried to consider what Mr. Triplehorn wanted me to do, I realized that I needed some clear information about American history and our form of government.

So, I asked Cindy a question and then made my next best move—I called my friend, Pastor Brian.

Now, I see the confused look on your face, but I'm telling you, this *was* my best move.

I don't know what your pastor is like—or if you even have a pastor—but my pastor is a *beast*! Based on the way he approaches ministry, he knows *so much stuff*, and he's done seminars on most of it—because he sees how God's stuff relates in the real world. That's a major reason we go to Desert Christian—it is so practical and applicable to living out a Christian life in the real world.

Pastor Brian had been a *huge* help on a number of my past cases, cuz this dude knows "stuff". I might "find stuff", but this dude "knows stuff". And it wasn't just stuff about the Bible, but other things and how they related to that.

Pastor Brian believed he needed to be able to confront the issues in our world—the things that become direct attacks on God. Because of this, he had done seminars on a wide variety of things that related to this.

For instance, he knew the world tried to say religion was existential, meaning it was *not* true in and of itself, but it could be "true" to you, if you just wanted to "make it your truth" and choose to believe it.

I had learned from him that existentialism starts with the premise that *nothing* is true, so everybody just chooses to believe whatever they want, and somehow magically, this supposedly makes it "true" to them.

So, Pastor Brian put together a seminar on the "Facts Behind the Faith" to prove God, Jesus, and the Bible, specifically showing Christianity as the *only* religion that could prove itself to be true. Now that might sound crazy, but it's actually what God says right in the Bible! Did you know that God actually *mocks* other religions because they aren't true? Yep, He does, right in the Bible. If that sounds "intolerant" in our day and age, that's only because it *IS intolerant*—by God's DESIGN! God has never been afraid of being labeled "intolerant", cuz He says clearly that He is the *only* God—and all others are fakes and phonies—again, right in the Bible.

Pastor Brian destroyed the whole concept of an existential approach to life and truth, cuz existentialism tried to destroy God and the idea of absolute truth.

It was pretty clear that Pastor Brian seemed to take that kind of attack personally—on God's behalf.

He also took on a major issue that people want to know about. It usually goes like this: "If God is supposedly a God of love, then why is there so much evil in the world?"

Good question. Fair question.

Pastor Brian provided a great answer in his seminar, "Why Bad Things Happen to Good People". The whole answer just blew my mind! And it made so much sense. It was an amazing help to some people I was helping in Florida.

And honestly, closer to home, it was revolutionary for my then girlfriend, Cindy Rios. Cindy had been raped when she was young, and when she needed some real answers about that, it blew her mind what she learned. And it changed everything for her.

Pastor Brian didn't stop there. Since Darwinian Macro-evolution is purposely a direct attack on the reality and existence of God, Brian put together a four-hour seminar using science, that totally *destroys* the whole concept of Darwinian Macro-evolution. It really is just awesome! And Susan Triplehorn used it in her psychology class at Berkeley to dismantle all comers—especially the "science majors". It was a beautiful thing to behold.

Each one of these seminars had ended up being shockingly helpful in my major cases of late, so I naturally thought of Brian as I faced this new challenge.

That brings us back to my topic sentence—I called my friend, Pastor Brian.

"Hey Blake, how are things going? You guys getting any sleep?"

I laughed.

"I'm getting more sleep than Cindy, but that seems to be because the boys don't seem nearly as interested in me when it's time to eat as they do her. Go figure."

Brian laughed.

"Yeah, there is that. What can I do for you?"

"Cindy and I were wondering if you and Kristi would be able to come over for dinner tonight. We know it short notice, but we thought we'd give it a try anyway."

"I don't know—let me check."

I waited.

Brian was back in about a minute.

"It looks like our social calendar is clear for tonight according to the keeper of the calendar. We'll be there. I've been instructed to ask if we can bring anything."

"Nope, we'll grill some steaks and stare at some babies—it should be a magical evening."

He laughed, and I gave him the time for dinner.

"Alright, see you tonight."

CHAPTER
—21—

Pastor Brian and Kristi did not show up that night empty handed—they had purchased "onesies" for the boys that said, "I'm with him", and arrows pointing opposite directions.

We were laughing about having to make sure the boys were placed right so the arrows would be pointing the right direction.

"Thanks for running right out and getting these, Brian," I said.

He chuckled.

"I didn't even know we got them until you opened them just now."

"OK, then you get to keep your 'man-card'," I said.

Our wives just looked at each other, shook their heads, and rolled their eyes.

Kristi started to make over the little guys, so I invited Brian to head out with me to one of the grills on our property.

If you just found yourself rolling your eyes at that last "one of the grills on our property" comment, that's only because it was clearly an "ostentatious" statement. I looked the word up to make sure I had it right, and it said, "characterized by a vulgar or pretentious display; designed to impress or attract notice".

Yep, that's clearly what that was, so I formally apologize for my clearly "ostentatious comment". Please forgive me—I will try to avoid ostentatious displays in the future.

As a side note, ostentatious is kind of fun to say.

Now, back to our unfolding story, already in progress.

Brian and I got settled out in the backyard cooking the steaks and just relaxed into the setting.

"This is quite a place you have here, Blake. You've come a long way from when I first met you."

"Yeah, apparently it really pays to work for the twenty-third richest man in the world."

We looked out at the expanse of the backyard and down at the pool, then up toward the mountains.

"I'm really happy for you and Cindy, Blake. You have a great future ahead of you."

"Thanks Brian, we are very thankful for all of it."

"Listen, I was wondering if I could ask you a few things. I'm on this new case for Mr. Triplehorn, and I think you could be helpful to get me started."

"Seriously? You brought me here to work? What's the consulting fee?"

I laughed.

"I'm going to serve you a really good steak."

"OK, but I brought you two "onesies", so I think I probably already covered the steaks."

We both laughed.

"Alright you little mooch, what do you need?"

"I need a broader understanding of our country and its founding, and our governmental system."

"Oh, is that all?" asked Brian dryly.

"Yep, and if you could explain all that to me before these steaks are done, that would be really helpful."

Brian just shook his head and chuckled.

"Well, if you want a full version of this, you can check out my 'Real American History' seminar—but I can give you the 'Cliff Notes' version if you want."

"I want. Can I first of all ask you why a pastor would even have a seminar like that?"

"Sure. America was unique in its founding as a Christian nation. That founding enabled us to experience amazing success as a nation.

However, each time we've stepped away from our foundation of God and His principles, our nation has decayed and failed. And that's not just some pastor talking—you can literally see the receipts if you just look back at history."

"OK," I said.

"I've always thought it was fascinating that God actually provides a basis for a standard of what we would call 'patriotism' for His people, regardless of what country they inhabit. Jeremiah 29:7 tells us to do the best for whatever country where we're 'planted', if you will, for in that nation's success is our success."

"And the fascinating thing about this, is that this was stated to God's people while they were living as captives in the very pagan world of the Babylonians. If they were supposed to do their best there, then we have the same responsibility in our culture."

"Since the actual history of our nation is so often garbled or flat out lied about, I felt that setting the record straight was my responsibility as a pastor."

"OK. Then what's the 'real history' you're talking about?" I asked.

CHAPTER
— 22 —

Pastor Brian continued.

"Well, the first correction is that this nation was most certainly founded as a Christian nation. The historical revisionist tries to say that the founders weren't Christians—and some of them weren't—but *all* of them understood the necessity of a nation founded on God and His principles for us to survive and succeed."

"I start off in the seminar by spending some time reading quote after quote from our founders about the centrality of God in our nation if we had any hope of success."

"For instance, Patrick Henry wrote: *'It cannot be emphasized too strongly or too often that this great Nation was founded not by religionists, but by Christians; not on religions, but on the Gospel of Jesus Christ. For that reason alone, people of other faiths have been afforded freedom of worship here.'*"

"Whoa, that's quite a quote!" Blake said.

"Isn't it? There are many of those quotes from our founders, and yet our historians don't tell us things like that because if it doesn't fit their narrative—the bizarre idea that our founders wanted religion to stay *out* of anything government related—they just don't report it."

"Check this one out; the second president of our nation, John Adams, said, *'Our Constitution was made only for a moral and religious people. It is wholly inadequate to the government of any other.'*"

"I wholeheartedly agree with that statement, and it's why I researched and did the seminar. If you look around, I think we've proven that statement to be true by trying to get rid of God and still have a nation that works—we keep failing miserably."

"Listen, there's a reason that the Declaration of Independence begins with, *'We hold these truths to be self-evident, that all men are created equal, that they are endowed by their Creator with certain unalienable Rights, that among these are Life, Liberty and the pursuit of Happiness.'*"

"You see, the founders of our nation studied many different ways and methods of government, looking for one that would work in the real world. Where they ended up after all that study, was to create a very unique formation of a country that had never been tried before."

"From the very beginning of our new nation, our founders understood that a key would be *God* being the foundation of everything, while *limiting* everything that groups of *people* touched—specifically called government."

"They understood that people working together had a tendency to gum up the works and snatch defeat from the jaws of victory—over and over."

Blake thought about that and laughed.

"It sounds like the founders might have agreed with something Albert Einstein reportedly said."

"What was that?" asked Brian.

"Oh, Ole Al said, *'Two things are infinite: the universe and human stupidity. And I'm not sure about the universe.'*"

Brian laughed.

"I'm not sure they were quite that cynical, but at least when it came to focusing on 'groupthink' over the individual person—yeah, they agreed."

"So, you're saying that they prioritized the individual and his or her potential over the collective group?" asked Blake.

"Well, honestly, not in the beginning—they had to learn a lesson first."

"What lesson?" Blake asked.

Brian shook his head.

"The first year they were in America, the settlers read something in the book of Acts, chapter four, and decided that they should practice Socialism as a country."

"Seriously?"

"Yep. When the first church started, they had a short period of time when travelers were stuck in Jerusalem, because they needed to learn more about Jesus and Christianity before returning back to their homes. So, the church all chipped in and helped everyone for that brief time. The New World settlers read that as 'all for one and one for all', and they set up almost a commune style of Socialism the first year—everybody getting an equal share out of one pot, regardless of each one's effort."

"What happened?" Blake asked.

Brian chuckled.

"What *always* happens when Fascism, Socialism, or Communism is tried—total, flat-out failure. Half of the settlers died that first year. Their 'everybody in this together' provided no income because people had no incentive to work. Governor William Bradford said in his History of Plymouth that many kept faking sickness and injury since they would get their part regardless of whether they worked or not.

So, after that abject failure, they went back to the Bible and read places like I Timothy 5 about each person having the responsibility to care for their own family. And then, they found the big one in II Thessalonians 3:10: *'He who will not work, neither let him eat.'* That changed everything for them. So, this time, they gave each family some land and told them it was up to them and their effort to succeed with their own possessions."

"And?" asked Blake.

"They quickly became the most effective and prosperous form of government in the English system—and they were all able to quickly repay the loans they had taken out to get to the New World. They became firm believers in what we call capitalism, and the success of that system has played out over our history."

"It cemented their view that the individual person, motivated to do the best for themselves and their family, was the key to corporate greatness as a nation."

"And big government was the danger and the enemy?" asked Blake.

Brian just nodded.

CHAPTER 23

It was mid-afternoon by the time he got back to his mansion. He left instructions with his staff to not disturb him, and he went into his study.

He went around and shuttered all the large windows that looked over his expansive property, making it dark inside the room.

He then walked over to the bar and poured himself some expensive whiskey. He stood there, letting the alcohol burn down his throat, while savoring the smoky taste and the hint of vanilla and oak.

He had some trepidation about reading what was in the package he had retrieved from Union Station. He had only been given hints about what Senator Ashford had uncovered in his search. What he was told was enough to make his mouth go dry and his heart race.

Also, what he'd been told was enough for him to hire the Contractor, at a substantial cost, to end Senator Todd Ashford's life.

That was not a small matter—to end the life of a sitting United States Senator—but their plan was little by little being put together, and they couldn't afford to have it exposed. Honestly, if all this had been exposed, he would have been one of the many who the Cabal would have called someone like the Contractor to eliminate.

In a real sense, it was either him or Senator Ashford.

That was an easy decision.

They would all just lay low during the fallout from his death. Then they would simply create a different news story and get the public focused on that instead. When you could control the narrative like they could, you could sell about anything.

The public had a notoriously short attention span anyway.

He walked over to his large desk where he had placed the manilla envelope. He turned on the desk lamp, which created a circle of light in the middle of the dark room.

He walked over to make sure that the doors were all locked, and then he sat in his desk chair and took a deep breath.

He then took out the papers and began to read.

CHAPTER

— 24 —

"What do you mean they '*limited* everything that *people* touched'?" I asked.

Brian looked over with a knowing look.

"Have you ever noticed that people have a capacity to really mess things up?"

"I have," I responded, laughing.

"Our founders had figured that out too. In addition to that, since they were trying to follow God's lead here, they recognized that people were 'fallen by nature', therefore sinful. The obvious conclusion to that is people mess things up—especially when it came to people in power."

"OK, but nations have to have people—even some in power—so what was their solution?" I asked.

"Have you ever read the Constitution of the United States?"

Now I don't know about you, but that is one of those questions that comes at you out of nowhere, that you *really* want to be able to say "of course" to. To answer any other way would make you seem uneducated, ill-bred and a bit of a rube.

"Um," was the best I could do.

Brian laughed.

"Don't worry, you ill-bred hick, lots of people haven't read it."

See! I told you! Ill-bred hick indeed!

"What you find in the Constitution is significant *limitations* on the powerful—on government—and great *freedom* for the individual. For the first time ever, we had a country focused on the freedom of, and belief in, the individual *citizen*, while having huge distrust of government and therefore limiting its power and scope."

"They even installed a thing called 'Federalism', which put the individual *states* in the place of power, while limiting the *federal* government in what they could do. They did this because the people had more control over their state—they were closer to it—than some overarching federal government of the 'powerful'. So, once again they emphasized the individual citizen over the powerful."

"They even designed the federal government to create gridlock so that it couldn't accomplish much."

"What do you mean?" I asked.

"Are you familiar with the three branches of government?"

This one I knew.

"Yes! The executive, the legislative and the judicial," I said proudly.

"Nicely done. Those are called the 'three equal branches of government' for the express purpose of creating gridlock. Our founders knew that by making them all equal, there would be very little they could all agree on enough to legislate—ergo, gridlock. Any changes they would be able to agree on would be small by definition. Our founders did not want our federal government to do much—they were staunch believers in 'limited government'."

"Wow, that sure didn't work out," I said.

"But look how right they were. The bigger our federal government has become the worse things have gotten. They were right—limited government, with an emphasis on the individual citizen's rights, was the key. When that gets violated, it fails every time."

"There's a story told, that when exiting the Constitutional Convention, Benjamin Franklin was approached by a group of citizens asking what sort of government the delegates had created. With no hesitation, Franklin responded, *"A republic, if you can keep it."* This exchange was recorded by Constitution signer James McHenry in a diary entry that was later reproduced in the 1906 American Historical Review."

"Why did Franklin say that?" I asked.

"Because he was a very smart man and knew human nature. Being able to keep the powerful pull of large government at bay, while instead keeping the focus on the individual citizen and limited governmental power, would be a herculean task. Spoiler alert; people want power."

"Yeah," I said, nodding.

Pastor Brian went on.

"President Ronald Reagan once said in a speech, *'The nine most terrifying words in the English language are, I'm from the government, and I'm here to help.'*"

"Wow, that's funny!" I said.

"And do you know *why* it's funny? Cuz we all know that it is totally *true*—big government just isn't very good at very many things. Our founders knew this and did all they could to design a limited government. Whenever we've violated this principle and set up bigger government, we've paid for it dearly as a country."

CHAPTER
— 25 —

I went to check on the steaks, flipped them over, and turned the flame down a little—then I was back.

"So, you were saying they set up limited government," I said.

"Yeah. Honestly, that's pretty evident if you look at the next thing they did after the Constitution. The Constitution was established in 1787, and already by 1791, they had decided that even more needed to be done to protect the citizens from the government. Notice their view—the citizens needed to be *protected from* the government. That year, they added ten amendments to the Constitution, with a total of twenty-seven finally being added in the ensuing years. The first ten of those amendments are called the *'Bill of Rights'*."

"Do you see how serious they were about keeping government *out* of our lives?" Brian asked.

"Yeah, I guess so."

"Just think what that *'Bill of Rights'* contains—a bunch of 'rights' of the individual, that the government is not allowed to infringe upon. Freedom of religion, speech, press, assembly, keeping and bearing arms, protection from unreasonable search and seizure, a citizen doesn't have to incriminate themselves, a fair and speedy jury trial, protection from cruel and unusual punishment—and on it goes."

"The Ninth Amendment even says the people may have even *more* rights that are not listed in the Constitution, and the Tenth says that if the Constitution doesn't specifically give the federal government some power, it *automatically belongs* to the state or the people."

I was quiet for a moment.

"How on earth did we get here then?" I asked quietly, a little confused. "Our government is huge and seems to be into virtually everything."

"Yep. It's fair to say that Benjamin Franklin's comment about *'a Republic, if you can keep it'* was an accurate concern."

"Right around the Great Depression, FDR, or President Franklin Delano Roosevelt, instituted what they called the *'New Deal'*, supposedly to deal with some of the issues surrounding the Depression. This was a Democratic Party plan that was the start of Social Security which everyone pays into—a huge government program."

"Yeah, I pay a lot of money into that," I said.

Brian nodded.

"Yes, you do, and that money is supposed to be in the Social Security 'Asset Reserve account'. Did you know that account has been empty since 1982?"

"What?" I asked, incredulous.

"Yep. So, for the last four decades, all the money getting paid out in excess of Social Security payments that comes in, has just been added to our huge national debt."

"See what I mean about big government? Failure."

I nodded.

"After that, LBJ, or President Lyndon Baines Johnson, instituted what they called the *'Great Society'*, supposedly to deal with the issues of poverty. The Democratic Party plan here led to the huge Welfare program that we see today."

"And do you want to know something that will blow your mind?" asked Brian.

"OK."

"The whole point of this Welfare program was to reduce poverty in the lower class—right?"

"Yeah."

"Well, check this out: *without* big government intervention—just people working hard—the poverty rate *fell by half* between 1950 and 1965."

"Wow—that's amazing," I said.

"Well, it gets more amazing. Since big government involvement with LBJ's Great Society, starting in 1965, the U.S. government has spent *more than $23 trillion* on what they called *'the War on Poverty'*—that's trillion with a 'T' by the way—and the poverty rate in that time has *remained unchanged*."

"What?" I asked, shocked.

"Yep, $23 trillion gone, and literally nothing to show for it—yet another example of the worthlessness of big government and another reminder of how smart our founders were to both fear big government and try to derail it."

"Oh, and just a reminder—the government does not have any money, they can only pick-pocket it from their citizens—so that $23 trillion that has been and continues to be wasted in this proven farse of *'the War on Poverty'*, is coming right out of our pockets—and is accomplishing absolutely nothing!"

I thought of the millions of dollars I had just paid in federal taxes.

"Wow, that is horrifying," I said, shaking my head.

"It's what big government does—not just in America, everywhere. Freedom of a people who have a foundation in God is the key to making all this work."

"Unfortunately, the bad news with the *'Great Society'* doesn't stop there."

"What else did it do?" I asked, getting frustrated.

"The whole plan they put in place ended up undermining the family structure in the inner city too."

"How so?" I asked.

"Well, with this infusion of support from the federal taxpayers, men in the inner city had no incentive to stay with their family and take care of them—Uncle Sam was now footing the bill. They kept making babies, but they didn't stay around to raise them. The fatherless percentage now in the inner city is *over eighty percent!*"

"What? As in eight out of ten inner city homes don't have dads?"

"That's right. And the evils we see in the inner cities across our nation like high school-dropout rate, violence, gangs, drugs, unchecked sexual behavior, homosexual involvement and more, can all be traced right back to not having dads in the homes to raise and direct their kids."

"Seriously?" I asked.

"Yep, the facts prove it. Did you know that black families were actually statistically *more* intact, *more* religious, and all around *more* successful than other ethnic groups *before* this mess the government created by 'helping them'?"

"Are you serious?"

"Yep. Big government has *destroyed* the black family in America. Like I said—whenever we violate the founders' principles and give into big government, we suffer. Those men really knew what they were doing if we would just *listen* to them."

CHAPTER
—26—

He could feel the perspiration growing along his hair line and under his dress shirt and suit. His breath was coming a little quicker as he read.

This was bad—*really, really bad.*

Senator Ashford's proposed legislation was backed up by some very thorough research. He wasn't sure how he had found all this out, but the facts were staring back at him from the pages he held.

Numerous meetings were listed where some of the prominent leaders of the Cabal were mentioned by name, his name often included. There was then a linking of various groups and meetings and associations that tied the leaders together. There was even a list of what Senator Ashford called, "confirmed Cabal members", and it was entirely accurate.

The pages went on to detail the various plans of the Cabal to control and direct the various entities to their desired goals. It then itemized the numerous individuals they had been using to orchestrate their plans. It showed people they had elevated and those they had taken out—a number of them whom they had literally "taken out". It described some of the smear campaigns they had constructed and then used to undermine those who they wanted out of the picture.

Somehow, Ashford had even gotten ahold of some of the payoff documents that showed how they had hidden much of their own culpability and gotten people to say nothing about what they had done—much of it through coercion, blackmail, and outright payoffs.

There was even a section that showed a continuing investigation into a number of people they had killed. Thankfully, the list was not complete yet. It didn't have the specifics on how they had done it or who they had paid to do it, but clearly Ashford had been making progress even in this area. He wasn't too far from finding the evidence for a number of murders they'd committed.

And if they found out the truth, he was one of the culprits numerous times.

He shuddered and thought.

The Cabal had no idea that Senator Ashford had been this close in his investigation of them. Every indication here was that he was planning on revealing all of this conspiracy at the same time he introduced his damning legislation that would have stopped them.

He clearly had the Senator killed just in the nick of time.

CHAPTER
—27—

"**B**lake?"

Pastor Brian and I turned to see Cindy headed toward them.

"Yeah?"

"How much longer on the steaks?"

I got up and walked over to the grill.

"Looks like they're about done. Are you and Kristi getting hungry?"

"Sure, but I just didn't want to throw the salad together too soon. Kristi is playing with the boys, so I'm going to get started on the salad. What do you think? About ten minutes?"

I looked at the steaks again and turned one over.

"I would say they'll be sitting *on* the table in ten minutes."

"Oh, OK. I'll hurry up then."

———◆———

We all sat out in one of the back area dining rooms that was semi-open to the amazing view of the estate, the pool, and the Tucson Mountains.

After praying for the food, during which the boys helped by adding some coos and gurgles, we all began passing the food around and talking about how hungry we were.

After some small talk about the babies and how little sleep Cindy was getting at this point, Kristi commented on their new home.

"This place is an amazing home, you guys. How do you even keep track of each other—do you ever get lost?"

I laughed.

"To be honest, I did get turned around once or twice when we first moved here, but I think we've got it figured out now."

Nic, or Linc—one of the boys made a little squeal, and they all laughed.

"Can you imagine how much fun the boys are going to have hiding from us someday?" I asked.

Cindy just shook her head, already feeling tired at the thought.

"I already feel exhausted just thinking about having to chase boys with your genetic make-up around, while trying to keep them out of trouble," said Cindy.

"Thank you," I said lovingly.

"That wasn't a 'thank you' type comment, Blake. It was a frightened mother, full of foreboding."

Everybody had a good laugh at the truth behind that statement.

Cindy changed the subject.

"Kristi, how has it been going back to being on-air at KOLD? It seems like they've been using you quite a bit."

"It's been fun. I've been kind of surprised how much I had missed being able to do that. Once you get to do that, it really is a fun job. It's not always fun to report some of the things we have to work on, but it feels like I'm getting to perform a service for our city."

I turned the conversation to one of her recent stories.

"Hey, Mr. Triplehorn has me looking into Senator Ashford's murder—I'm going to have to head for D.C. soon. Have you guys had any more follow-up on his murder since that initial report?" I asked.

Kristi's face darkened and she gave a big sigh.

"That's been one of the 'not fun' ones to work on. I didn't know anything about this Senator, but it turns out that he was pretty awesome—and he was a great Christian man too. His murder left his wife and four children without him, and the facts sure seem to point to an outright assassination."

"Really? What facts?" I asked.

"Well, the first thing they are still trying to figure out is how the murderer even got to the Senator. He was seven stories up with security guarding all the ways to get to him. Apparently, he was the subject of a lot of threats."

"Hmmm," I thought, always the profound one.

"The murder was relatively low tech. After securing him to a chair, the murderer just put a plastic bag over the Senator's head and suffocated him."

We all pondered the horror of being offed like that.

"Did they ever find any specific motive?" I asked.

Kristi was shaking her head.

"His personal things had been rifled through—maybe something was taken—but the murderer did put his laptop into the kitchen sink and submerge it. He then plugged it in while submerged to fry it."

"Hmmm," I thought again, beginning to challenge the likes of Socrates, Plato, and Aristotle in my insightful inner musings.

Out loud, I said, "So, something on that laptop mattered and needed to be permanently erased—if I can find out what was on that laptop, I'll have a path to finding the motive and the murderer."

"But how would you do that?" asked Brian.

Kristi jumped in.

"There is always the chance that it was uploaded to the 'Cloud', but so far, that doesn't seem to be panning out. He could have had it backed up some other way, but they haven't had any luck on that yet either."

Kristi looked over at me.

"You'd better be careful, Blake," continued Kristi, glancing over at Cindy. "This murderer was able to get in and out of an apartment that was seven stories in the air, right under the nose of a security detachment, and kill a seated Senator of the United States, and then get away. Whoever did this is *very good* at being *very bad.*"

Cindy cut her eyes toward me at that comment.

I anticipated an *uncomfortable conversation* later.

CHAPTER
— 28 —

Cindy and Kristi were busying themselves with the clean-up, so after Brian and I helped to clear the table, the ladies shooed us away while they finished.

We headed out back and down to the pool area—the property was so large that it was a bit of a walk. We got settled on some of the lounges around the pool and enjoyed the scenery.

As Brian looked around, he sighed with contentment and said, "You have quite a place here, Blake—I never would've guessed you'd end up in a place like this."

"Yeah, me neither. Mr. Triplehorn really changed everything for us after the *'See Me Killer'* investigation. I figured I could do pretty well in P.I. work over time—you kind of keep your eye out for the big case with the payday—but I never envisioned this kind of payday."

"And now you're working for him again. What is his interest in all of this regarding Senator Ashford's murder?"

"Well, Mr. T deeply cares about our country, and wants great people leading it. Given his wealth and position, he has a chance to play a role in who that should be. He was a strong supporter of Senator Ashford—apparently, he was one of the good ones—and I don't have to tell you that in Washington, D.C., the 'good ones' tend to be pretty few and far between."

Brian chuckled.

"Yeah, politics doesn't have much of a history that includes the 'good ones.' It's been more scoundrels and scallywags historically."

I made a note to myself to use the terms "scoundrels and scallywags" more often in casual conversation.

"Hey, you were talking about big government before we ate dinner. You kept pointing out that it was the Democrat Party that was so pro big government. Does that mean that big government gets pared down when the Republicans take the reins?"

Brian laughed.

"I wish. That was the idea—the Republican Party is supposed to be focused on the founders and following the Constitution, so they should be the party of limited government. But often when they get into power, they just see it as their turn to run the behemoth that is big government."

"However, to be fair to them, there is an inherent problem that gets in anyone's way who wants to go back to limited government—the administrative state."

"What's that?" I asked.

"For an easy reference point, do you remember when Donald Trump ran for President the first time, promising to 'drain the swamp'?"

"Yeah."

"Well, the 'swamp' is the administrative state. It involves many, what they call 'alphabet soup' agencies, like the FBI, DOJ, CIA, DOE, HUD, SSA, SBA, GSA, USDA, DOT, the VA and more. All these agencies issue regulatory standards that citizens must follow, and by doing this create 'laws' that have to be obeyed. So, the environment, education, building requirements, on the job restrictions, housing requirements—and on and on it goes. These are unelected and unaccountable bureaucrats who are setting the rules for the whole nation, instead of Congress."

"How did they get all this power?" I asked.

"Well, Congress is supposed to be the power here, but instead of doing their job—and by the design of the founders, ending up most of the time in gridlock and doing very little—they have farmed their job out to these unelected bureaucrats to determine everything for Americans. And most of these unelected bureaucrats belong to the Executive branch, so it ends up giving a lot more power to the President than was ever intended."

"This is why you'll see the House of Representatives being presented with a document so large, it often requires it to be rolled in on a cart. The document is thousands of pages long, and the House is told they must pass it the next day, or our whole country will fall apart, which is *never* true. The spineless Republicans in Congress cave into the political pressure over and over, and they pass it *without reading it*—and lots of crazy stuff gets passed by the administrative state, not by the designated law makers."

"And the result is that government is injected into every part of our lives. What cars we can drive, what stoves we can use, what our children are taught, what we can say on social media and on and on—all by people—we—did—not—elect."

"It's a horrible situation and the exact opposite of what the founders wanted. President Trump was right to want to drain the swamp, but do you remember how attacked he was when he got into office?"

"Yeah, that was crazy—starting with the Russia Hoax, it was one hoax after another that he had to fight against, and then he had to deal with COVID-19 when it hit the nation in March of 2020," I said.

"Yep, that was the administrative state creating and pushing all those hoaxes—mostly the FBI and DOJ in his case. Big government likes their power, and they are not going to let it go without an intense fight. Personally, I think they need to fire about two-thirds of all personnel in all agencies—the top people first—and then the agencies need to be decentralized."

"Decentralized how?" I asked.

"Well, Washington, D.C. is its own little echo-chamber—the beltway actually believes that whatever the 'elites' say is true, *is true*. Get all these people spread out around the country where real Americans live and work and just watch them start to think like Americans instead of like 'elites'. Once they realize that the New York Times, the Washington

Post and often X or other social media platforms, don't reflect what is actually going on in real America, we might have some real hope for a return to sanity again."

"Any chance that might happen?" I asked.

"Some of the leaders have been talking about decentralization lately, so maybe. I mean, come on, what is the federal Department of Agriculture doing in Washington, D.C.? It should be in the heartland where all the agriculture is taking place."

"Good point," I conceded.

CHAPTER
— 29 —

Cindy and Kristi finished up in the kitchen and came down to the pool. They each had one of the babies snuggling in their arms, and joined us on the pool lounges, each snuggling into their husband.

We all sat there and enjoyed the quiet for a moment, the boys periodically making baby noises.

"So, what have you guys been talking about?" asked Kristi.

"Blake wanted a refresher on some American history, so he'd be better prepared to head for Washington, D.C., to investigate Senator Ashford's murder for Mr. Triplehorn," said Brian.

Kristi turned toward me.

"You're really going to take this case on?"

"Yeah, I'll have to head out soon and get on it."

"Hmmm," was all Kristi said.

"What did that thoughtful interjection mean, oh friend of mine?" asked Cindy.

Kristi collected her thoughts.

"This murder just seems to me to have all the hallmarks of a political assassination. If that is the case, it would mean that very powerful people wanted Senator Ashford taken off the board, because he was becoming extremely—let's call it 'inconvenient'. If I'm right, and he was moving things in such a way their power was in danger, or being threatened, then these same evil people will look at a real investigation of his murder in the same light."

Kristi took a deep breath.

"And given your track record of success in cracking big cases, and the national exposure you've received because of it—if you're seen as, let's say, a fly in their proverbial ointment—these same powerful and dangerous people might decide to try and take *you* off the board."

Wow, Kristi was really upping the chance of that "uncomfortable conversation" later.

"Well, aren't you just the 'party pooper'," I said, trying for my best Arnold Schwarzenegger imitation from "Kindergarten Cop".

I waited. No one laughed.

Whoa, tough crowd.

I looked around at everyone.

"Look, I'll be careful," I assured them.

I'm not certain they were assured.

Kristi craned her head around and looked at Brian.

"In your American history treatise, did you explain the Left's shocking ability to misdirect—making everyone else guilty for what they do?"

"No, I hadn't gotten to that yet."

Kristi turned back around.

"Well, you need to know this, Blake, if you hope to figure out this murder without becoming a casualty yourself. The Left has long mastered the control of the 'narrative', meaning that they figure out a way to spin the story, distorting the facts to make themselves the heroes instead of the villains they so often are."

"If you don't understand this mastery of manipulation, by the time you're done, you may discover that YOU were the one who killed Senator Ashford!"

Now that I might be the perpetrator in my own murder investigation, of a man I hadn't known or ever even met, she had my attention.

"How is it that they manipulate the facts and control the narrative?" I asked.

Kristi glanced back at Brian, so he weighed in.

"Well, the Left controls most major news networks, but it doesn't stop there. They have control of social media platforms, major corporations, education, entertainment and even many sports organizations. They work through all of these to censor what they don't like and don't want people to know about. It's a direct attack on our First Amendment right of freedom of speech, but they don't care about that."

Kristi jumped in.

"Just think of the whole COVID-19 mess back in 2020 and after. Do you realize that virtually every single thing that the 'overlords' deemed to be a 'lie' and a 'conspiracy theory' and shut people down for—sometimes even at the cost of their jobs—ended up being true? For instance, masks don't stop the virus—that's been proven true. The Cochrane Report, the gold standard of studies—provided definitive proof for that, including the vaunted N95 masks. COVID came from a lab in Wuhan, China—again, true. Standing six feet apart did absolutely nothing—true. The supposed 'vaccines' don't stop you from getting or transmitting the virus, i.e., don't work—true. It was never an 'epidemic of the unvaccinated'—true. The mRNA vaccines are untested and may well produce side effects—true. Shutting down our country and our economy won't stop the virus—true."

"It goes on and on. All things that were labeled 'conspiracy theories' at the time, have now been shown to be true the whole time. And for the record, if you try and do a search on these issues even today, the search engines, cooperating with the government party line, bury the real scientific facts as deep as they can to perpetuate the control of the government narrative."

Brian looked over at me.

"They wield huge power and control over what people get to see as 'the facts', which is why our founders put the First Amendment in place for the very purpose of stopping government from having this level of control over her citizens."

"But you'd better learn it now—the Left doesn't care about rules or allow any rules to stop them—they do whatever they want. And if you're not careful, they *will* do it to you."

CHAPTER
— 30 —

"Let me give you a present-day illustration of their control of the narrative," said Brian.

"Alright," I said.

"Did you know that the Democrat Party typically gets over ninety percent of the black vote?"

"I didn't."

"Are you aware that the Democrat Party regularly brands the Republican Party as the party of white racists who want to 'put you all back in chains', as Joe Biden claimed to a black audience while running for President?"

"That I knew," I said.

"Now listen to how they have controlled *this* narrative. The Republican Party started in the north with one of its stated purposes of seeking to *end slavery*. Their first presidential candidate, Abraham Lincoln, expressly pledged to end slavery, which he did in 1863 with the 'Emancipation Proclamation'."

"And *what* was he fighting against the whole time?" interjected Kristi.

Brian looked over at us.

"The *Democrat Party*—the party of slavery."

"Really?" said Cindy and I at the same time.

"Yep. It was the Democrats in the south who used all the slave labor and demanded to be able to keep it."

"The Civil War was fought for a number of reasons, but the fight over slavery was the prominent one. And the Democrats were fighting to *keep* slavery."

"Wow."

"And it didn't stop there. After over six-hundred-thousand Americans gave their lives in the Civil War to end slavery, it was the Democrat Party that kept fighting to keep black people down."

"How so?" asked Cindy.

"It was the southern Democrats who enacted the 'Jim Crow' laws that sought to keep black people separate from other Americans, with things like separate bathrooms and drinking fountains. In the 1890s, the primarily Democrat south averaged one-hundred and thirty lynchings a year—literally murdering black people for being black."

"In 1963, it was Democrat governor George Wallace who literally stood, blocking the door with other Democrats, to refuse to let black people into the University of Alabama. The National Guard had to be authorized to remove him."

"It was Democrats who staged the longest filibuster in American history—sixty plus days—to *stop* the Civil Rights Act of 1964. The Democrats fought it because it would greatly benefit black people through simple equal rights that they were entitled to like everyone else."

"The longest serving Democrat Senator was Robert Byrd from West Virginia—fifty-one years. This man had proudly been the 'Grand Cyclops' of the Ku Klux Klan, a group that used threats and violence against black people in the south. The August Senator actually stated that he would rather *'die a thousand times than see our beloved land degraded by the black race mongrels'*."

"He did not!" I exclaimed.

"Yep, he did," said Brian.

"Whoa," said Cindy.

"Yeah," chimed in Kristi, "and that horrible bigot was actually eulogized by President Obama at his funeral."

"You're kidding," I said.

"I kid you not," said Kristi.

Brian went on.

"It was the Democrats who fought against equality for the races in education when the court, in 'Brown vs. Board of Education', ruled that segregation of public schools was unconstitutional. Republican President Eisenhower had to send federal troops and the National Guard to protect the black students from Democrat protesters."

Kristi looked down at Nicholas sound asleep, and then over at Cindy holding Lincoln. It was hard to think of such ugliness while holding such precious little lives.

CHAPTER
— 31 —

After a beat, Kristi added another wrinkle into the story that was especially horrifying, holding Nic and Linc.

"You can't know the whole, hideous picture, without knowing the story of the founder of Planned Parenthood, Margaret Sanger—another Democrat—who will make your blood boil."

"What do you mean?" asked Cindy.

Kristi just shook her head.

"It's bad enough that Sanger introduced our society to the idea of killing our children in the womb, but her stated reason as to *why* she did it makes it even more appalling."

"What reason?" asked Cindy.

"Well, here are just a few: She said she wanted to destroy the 'mongrel races'—her words. She stated she wanted to 'exterminate the Negro population'. She referred to black people as mentally and physically defective. She advocated for people to be able to have children only if the government gave them a permit. She wanted to have black people sterilized, because only white people were the 'cleaner race'."

Cindy and I were breathless.

Brian chimed in.

"And for the record, do you find it odd that the bulk of Planned Parenthoods today are located around black neighborhoods? And how about the fact that the black population today makes up about twelve percent of the total population, yet almost forty percent of all abortions are of black babies?"

"This is hideous!" said Cindy, angrily.

"Yep," said Brian, "but don't forget where we began. With all that history and more, the Democrat government machine and its allies in the government media, have convinced the black population, and a fair amount of the white population—that the *Republicans*, specifically the *Conservatives*, are the horrible, racist bigots, while it was the Republicans who fought to save their ancestors from slavery. And since then, the Democrats have convinced over ninety percent of the black population to vote for them—the perpetrators of all that evil that was aimed right at them—and continues to be."

"Literally unbelievable!" I said.

Kristi turned toward me.

"And this is why we're saying that you need to be aware of the kind of power you're coming up against. When you can demand that obvious lies be accepted as truth—like the current stupidity that a boy can become a girl, or a girl can become a boy just because he or she "feels like it"—and get people to go along with that, you can pull off just about anything."

I just stared back at Brian and Kristi.

CHAPTER
— 32 —

After Brian and Kristi had taken off, Cindy and I enjoyed working together to give the boys a bath. At this point, we were using a little tub-like thing that sat in a sink to get the job done. It was a surprising amount of fun getting Nic and Linc shiny and clean.

It kind of freaked me out though cuz they were so slippery—like trying to hang onto a watermelon seed.

After Cindy got them in their onesies, we sat out on one of the back patios while she nursed them and looked out at our amazing view.

"So, Blake, are you concerned about this investigation you're going to be doing?"

Ah, the aforementioned "uncomfortable conversation" had just stepped into my personal space and was about to smack me around, courtesy of my lovely wife, Mrs. Cindy Lou.

"Whatever do you mean?" I asked with a smile.

My flippancy got me nothing but the evil eye from my lovely bride.

OK, I guess evasion, and an attempt at charm, wasn't going to work with this one.

Cindy handed me Nic and started feeding Linc. Once she got settled, she answered my question.

"Blake, look at that boy you're holding. Nic and Linc need their dad, and I need my husband. You're not some single, fly by the seat-of-his-pants private investigator anymore."

She looked around.

"Clearly we don't need the money—and I readily recognize and admit that this is all due to your great work in the past."

I mimicked a tip of the hat to her.

"But Blake, when you start talking about the kind of people you are looking to go up against, this is a different breed. Up to this point, you've been dealing with a bad guy—as in one bad dude doing bad things. I get that, I was a cop."

"This isn't that. When Kristi is talking about the sophisticated nature of this crime, that typically means a group of evil people, all working together to shape the course of events to benefit themselves."

"A Cabal," I said.

"Yes, a Cabal. That means a whole network of really evil, but really powerful people, all working together to try and accomplish some bad things. That reality changes the equation. The danger ratchets up in an exponential way."

I tried some levity.

"Now don't you start talking all sexy like that—you know how much I like that, and we're trying to have a serious conversation here."

It didn't land. Cindy just stared dead-eyed at me.

Linc even let out a little fart while he was eating. I laughed at that.

I was the only one laughing.

Wow, when a baby fart can't provide a little comic relief, you were really in the middle of something serious.

CHAPTER 33

I took a deep breath.

"OK, I get it—this will potentially be dangerous, but you know that all of my jobs have been dangerous. I remember one when I was cuffed and given my Miranda Rights by this totally hot chick cop."

Dead-eyes again.

Seriously? We can't even bond on the nostalgia?

I stayed quiet for a moment and collected my thoughts. OK—that was weird. It made me wonder if I might be coming down with something.

"Fine. Look—to be fair to me, this is not my first rodeo when it comes to cabals. Would you not agree that me taking on the Los Zetas Cartel would count toward this situation?"

I could see that I'd landed a blow with that one. Cindy was trying desperately to find a way it didn't count, but clearly it was virtually exactly the same.

I went on while I had a little momentum.

"No one would disagree that the cartels are quite evil groups of people, working together to accomplish some bad things—some would say worse things than this Cabal. And for the record—they were succeeding."

Cindy said nothing.

"Cindy, I beat them. At least in my one adventure against them, I took what they were doing wrong, and I brought good out of the middle of all their bad. Isabella, and the whole Iglesias family are a constant reminder of that."

"I realize that this is a different kind of power, but honestly, in many ways, evil power is simply evil power, regardless of how it's wielded."

"I know that we don't need the money, Cindy, but this isn't about money; this is what I do. 'I never asked you to stop being a woman, so please, I'm asking you please, don't ask me to stop being a man'."

Cindy just shook her head slowly at me.

"Please tell me that in the middle of a serious discussion you didn't just quote a line from Rocky Balboa to me."

"Well, to be precise, it was a classic line from Rocky II to Adrian. It really landed, didn't it?"

Cindy just stared at me, so I decided that meant, "yes dear, that really landed", and just went on.

"Also, the way that your 'seat-of-the-pants' husband is able to beat them is what makes the difference, as I fight for right against wrong and defend the American way."

Cindy rolled her eyes.

"Please tell me that you're not invoking your superhero persona as you 'fight for the American way' here."

"Ma'am, I only hope to make our way of life safe for those who can't do that for themselves," I said in my best superhero voice.

"You're an idiot."

"I've been thusly informed in the past—and after doing a thorough search of that possibility, I've rejected it, and chosen to believe that to be nothing more than a term of endearment, my love."

"Well, hear this 'my love'—my cop demand of the past still stands—'DON'T GET DEAD'! If this is just what you do, then do it with this beautiful little family on your mind, cuz you are essential to it."

"Are we clear?"

"Yes ma'am."

"Are we CLEAR?"

"Crystal."

We both laughed.

In case you missed it, that was a spot-on reenactment from the court scene in "A Few Good Men". Cindy was Jack Nicholson, and I was Tom Cruise.

All that was left for me to do was to trick Cindy into passionately admitting that she did in fact order the "Code Red".

I guess that would have to wait until we got the twins into bed for the night.

"You WANT me on the wall—you NEED me on that wall!"

Sorry, I was just getting warmed up for my part. Oh, wait, that *Cindy's* part—she's Nicholson.

Dang it! I really wanted to say that line. Oh well, As opposed to, "You CAN'T HANDLE the truth!", I'll just have to *accept* the truth.

CHAPTER
—34—

Cindy decided that she wanted to luxuriate in the Jacuzzi tub in our bathroom and just relax for a while before bed.

I figured I'd go relax a little too, but my way was a little different.

If you were with us last time, you know that Mr. Triplehorn gave us the very car I had to crash to stop the *"See Me Killer"* from killing more young women. It was a *Bugatti Centodieci*—an amazing car with a new car price of over nine-million-dollars, so as you can imagine, it was really a bummer to crash it.

However, as a wedding present, Mr. T gave us the car after it had been completely restored—it was quite the gift.

Cindy convinced me on our honeymoon in Cancún that this was a crazy, expensive car to be driving around Tucson, Arizona—especially since we could use the money from the sale to buy an awesome home, which we did.

As a bit of a side note, I had the auto broker let the potential buyers know that this very car was the one to stop the *"See Me Killer"* in San Fransisco; therefore, it was a part of some awesome history. Believe it or not, instead of the price dropping from it being in a crash, the price soared to eleven and a half million dollars!

Oh yeah, Blake Moran, wheeler-dealer!

Any-who . . . as a bit of a consolation prize, I bought myself the "King Kong" of the front engine Corvettes—a 2019 ZR1 supercharged superstar with a horsepower rating of seven-hundred and fifty-five "horsies"—the fastest, most powerful production Vette to ever scorch the pavement up to that year.

Its supercharged, 6.2-liter LT5 V-8 engine has a top speed in excess of two-hundred and ten miles per hour, and it can go 0-60 in a "hang on to your seat, what the heck just happened" 2.85 seconds!

It was even the "Sebring Orange" color that Chevrolet had introduced for the C7, with black accents. It had the 3ZR interior package—which was the top of the line and hadn't even been driven—a car dealer owned it, just to show it off in his showroom.

It is truly an all-American supercar.

So, my "relax" looked more like my walking out to my six-bay garage and getting behind the wheel of my lovely Corvette.

Pretty cool "consolation prize", huh?

As I drove out of my garage and down my long drive, I dialed in some jams on the top-of-the-line sound system and got ready to have some fun.

I made my way over to the I-10 and then headed toward Phoenix—it was a nice, open drive where you could just think.

Once I had the Corvette cruising down the interstate, I took a deep breath and started to think.

For all my talk to Cindy about taking on the Los Zetas Cartel, I was well aware that this was different. While it was true that the cartels had begun to behave more like a corporation than a terrorist group lately, they would still lack the sophistication of the people I was about to take on. These people would probably be both national and even worldwide leaders—possibly even well-known "movers and shakers".

Also, the Los Zetas Cartel was in Mexico, and I was in Dallas when I came after them, so it wasn't like I took them on face to face.

In the scenario I was heading into, I was effectively going to be behaving like the homeless in San Francisco—I was going to go right into their backyard and defecate on their carefully mowed lawn.

Boy, there's a picture I could've done without. I'm guessing you're with me on that.

However, it was pretty accurate, and there was a small chance that these very powerful people would not be amused by my efforts to expose them.

Cindy and Kristi were right—these people punched the ticket of a sitting United States Senator—they wouldn't think twice about ending the life of a private investigator from Arizona.

Even one who was clever enough to come up with the tagline, "We Find Stuff."

In one way, this would be like the Los Zetas operation; I would have to do this under the radar. If the wrong people became aware of my efforts before I was ready to expose them, I could end up in the Potomac, "swimming with the fishes".

Was that a little too gangster for you? Well, just maybe I was going to have to operate as the OG—the "original gangster"—just to get this job done.

I chuckled at the thought of my being the OG, then I put my foot down and let the power of the Corvette bleed away some of my stress.

CHAPTER
— 35 —

The six of them gathered in a backroom dining area at Bourbon Steak, a posh "power restaurant", located in the Four Seasons Hotel in Washington, D.C. The dark wood and muted lighting conveyed power and money—not necessarily in that order—which was a good description of this group.

Given that it was just down the road from the White House—even being on Pennsylvania Avenue, just like the White House—the location itself lent to the power image that each of these men valued.

They were all standing around with their drink of choice in hand, while they waited for the security team to conclude their sweep of the space to make sure that what they said in here would stay in here.

This was just part of the cost of doing business—specifically *their* kind of business.

Having been given the assurance that no one was listening in, they each found their seat around the large table and began to decide on what they would have for lunch.

They all knew each other well, but to a person, they also hated each other. Each one was a threat to their power, an adversary to be swept aside, so that they could move higher up on the power dynamic pyramid.

It never ended—that hatred—but they would work together to accomplish their common end result for even more power and even more wealth.

However, they never turned an exposed back to any of these men, lest they find the proverbial knife residing in said back.

But today, they had commonality.

Having ordered their ridiculously expensive food, they became quiet as they waited to find out just where they stood as a group.

Everyone focused their attention on Mercurius.

Some of those in the group thought it was dumb that they all had "special names" in the group—after all, they knew each other's *actual* names—they were all too rich not to be known. However, Mercurius and others in the hierarchy believed that these names conveyed the status and power that was represented in the group.

For instance, Mercurius was supposedly a Roman god of commerce, eloquence, travel, cunning, and theft who also served as messenger to the other gods. He is commonly linked with the Greek god Hermes.

Whatever, it just seemed stupid to most of them.

To some, it just felt like they were going back in time to play superhero with their friends and make stuff up.

Not that any of them would ever voice that thought to Mercurius or any of the other leaders. They preferred to keep their heads firmly attached to their bodies, and they were smart enough to know that angering any of them might significantly alter the nature of that current "attachment".

"So, I want to update all of you on what we have discovered from the Ashford Incident," began Mercurius.

The "Ashford Incident" was the term they used to describe the murder of a sitting U.S. Senator who was about to destroy their little cabal. They were all culpable in this "incident" and were well aware of that fact.

Mercurius began to itemize what he had found on the paperwork that was retrieved from Senator Ashford's apartment. As he walked them through the litany of what he found, each man found that his sphincter tightened significantly when he heard what Ashford knew about each of them.

Mercurius summarized.

"So, as you can see, he had discovered much of our interconnected business dealings, some of our internal communications with each other, much of the overall plan for domination, and quite a few of each of our illegal acts that we've been doing to accomplish our overall plan."

"We don't know how he discovered all these things, but he did. I must also emphasize that our assassin destroyed his laptop. I would have preferred it if he had downloaded everything on the computer first, so that we knew everything that Ashford knew, but he pointed out that it would have been password protected. Being able to get Ashford to give that password up would've taken time—a luxury that he didn't have if we expected him to complete the primary mission of destroying both Ashford and his information."

"We should have demanded that he complete that task as well," offered one of the six.

"Yeah, I'll let you be the one to tell the assassin that in person," Mercurius said dryly. "Once you get to look right into, what I can only guess, are dead eyes, devoid of conscience or fear, we'll see how 'demanding' *you* are."

Everybody got the memo—you don't mess with the assassin.

Mercurius continued.

"So, while we don't know the full scope of what he knew about us or our plans for this nation—and ultimately the world—we have neutralized the threat and should be able to move forward with our plans."

"What about the investigation into his murder?" asked another of the six. "Are they going to stand down, or do we need to do something?"

"Things have been and are being done to both slow down the investigation and throw it off track. As you all know, we have deep tentacles into the various agencies, and we are using our power to bring the investigation to a speedy—and unsuccessful conclusion."

Mercurius looked around the room at the powerful men.

"It appears that we have eliminated the danger and should be able to get right back on track with our plan."

He said it with great confidence. He just hoped it was actually true.

CHAPTER
— 36 —

The next morning, Blake was up early to get everything set up—the flight out of Tucson International Airport and the hotel in Washington, D.C., where he would stay during the investigation.

He walked outside to one of the patio areas with his laptop so he wouldn't disturb his sleeping family and got to work.

Blake decided to fly into Dulles—it was further from D.C. than Reagan National by quite a lot, but he was going to rent a car anyway, and he figured the drive into the city could help him get the lay of the land.

He couldn't find a non-stop from Tucson—oh the joy of living in a smaller city than Phoenix—but he could get just one stop and a less than seven-hour trip, so he took an American Airlines flight later that day.

He also paid over $1,000 for first class, a habit he had developed after becoming a multi-millionaire.

Yep, he was becoming "that guy," while trying to pretend it could never happen to such a one as himself.

However, for the record, Mr. Triplehorn would be paying the freight on this, so it wasn't quite as big of a decision. Mr. T wouldn't mind his upgrade.

Blake wasn't exactly the "Super 8 Hotel" type of guy anymore either. He'd found out that hotels could be awesome, so now he looked for an awesome one.

There were a lot to choose from, but one kind of jumped out at him—the Waldorf Astoria. If you've ever seen it, it looks kind of like a castle or a fortress with its huge clock tower as its signature feature.

Its location at the corner of 12th Street and Pennsylvania—1100 Pennsylvania Avenue to be exact, might sound a little familiar to you.

Many people know perhaps the most famous address in the world—the White House—at 1600 Pennsylvania Avenue.

So, the Waldorf would put Blake about five blocks from the White House, just a nice little walk on a Washington, D.C. day. That would be helpful in case Blake needed to stop in and hobnob with the President about something while he was there.

Blake chuckled at that. He had a vague idea of what Mr. Triplehorn would think about him stopping by to "shoot the breeze" with the President.

In addition to being close, the Waldorf had some amazing accommodations to choose from. Blake looked at their different offerings and settled on the Junior Suite with the King bed. It was almost seven-hundred square feet of luxury, had an extra seating area for meetings, an office area with a desk that overlooked the city, and an impressive bathroom all done in marble and tile, with a walk-in steam shower and a Jacuzzi bathtub.

All that for just $1,275 a night!

That made Blake swallow hard, but he reminded himself that he had the big bucks now and the comfort would help him focus better on the case—at least that's what he was telling himself.

As hard as he tried, that just wasn't working for him, but then he reminded himself that *Mr. Triplehorn* was paying the freight for this investigation, and he had *really* big bucks. That *did* work for him.

He then noted something else. It might sound crazy but check this out: the Waldorf had a Bi-level Loft with Library for $2,720 a night. They had the Franklin One Bedroom Suite for $8,500 a night. The President One Bedroom Suite was $17,000 a night. And finally, the Waldorf Townhouse Two Bedroom Bi-level was $25,500 a night!

You could basically spend one night—or buy a CAR!

Blake nodded to himself and would've patted himself on the back if he could reach it. Just *think* of all the money he was *saving* Mr. Triplehorn by spending *only* $1,275 a night!

He felt quite frugal and almost noble—which made him chuckle.

CHAPTER
—37—

Blake scheduled the flight for the next morning and then began some investigation into the city where he was headed—Washington, D.C.

Blake heard Cindy get up. Apparently, Nicholas and Lincoln had decided they'd had enough of this sleeping thing and were demanding mom's attention.

Blake went in and said good morning to Cindy and the boys. He helped out by changing Linc's diaper while Cindy worked on Nic, and then helped get the three of them all settled in for "breakfast".

Once Cindy was set up and didn't need Blake for anything else at the moment, he headed back out to the patio and his research.

Blake was initially finding some helpful information—things like the fact that Washington, D.C., is relatively flat and located four-hundred and ten feet above sea level at its highest point, and at sea level at its lowest point. It also turned out that the city was not actually built on a swamp, as some people think, those "some people" included Blake. Speaking of water, three waterways flowed through Washington, D.C.: the Potomac River, the Anacostia River and Rock Creek.

Washington, D.C., is located in the humid subtropical climate zone and has four distinct seasons. Its climate is typical of the South, with humid and hot summers and fairly cold winters with occasional snow and ice. Blake just shook his head—being from Arizona, he had no use for "seasons"—they just sounded like some useless hardships to him.

Blake discovered that the city of Washington, D.C. is divided into four quadrants: NW, NE, SW and SE, but the four quadrants are not

THE CONSPIRACY CABAL

equal in size. Numbered streets run east and west of North and South Capitol Streets. Lettered streets run north and south of the National Mall and East Capitol Street.

Blake was already confused.

It turned out that Washington, D.C. is sixty-eight square miles, and all that land was taken from Maryland when D.C. was set up as the seat of the federal government.

That was about as far as Blake got in his actual real research, because he happened on a list of some "unique" facts about D.C., and Blake just could not resist going down *that* rabbit hole.

For instance, he found out that even though they had all the "alphabet" streets, there is no "J" Street in D.C. It appears that this happened because in antiquated typeface, the "I" and the "J" looked so similar that it was confusing, so "J" took the hit and was left out. It seemed that "J" was the "loneliest *letter* that there ever was". (That's just a shoutout to all the Three Dog Night fans out there.)

Blake was guessing that "Jay-Z" would have some objection to rap about regarding "J" being tossed in D.C.

It also turns out that Washington, D.C. gets more rain than even soggy Seattle, Washington does. That made Blake wonder if just maybe Washington, D.C. really was a swamp after all.

There was more: Franciscan monks built a series of catacombs under the Franciscan Monastery of the Holy Land in America, which was located in Washington, D.C. Why? Because they couldn't afford to go to Europe to see the catacombs there.

Blake had to wonder if the huge cost of building those catacombs just might have been more than a couple plane tickets. He then took a quick look at when they were built—it turned out to be 1898—so "plane tickets" weren't an option for them. He guessed he'd have to strike that comment now.

Everybody has heard of the cherry blossom trees in Washington, D.C.—at the right time of the year, they are pretty remarkable. However,

Blake didn't know that one lady, Mrs. Eliza Scidmore, was credited with the idea of planting Japanese cherry trees in Washington, D.C. Blake couldn't help but wonder if just maybe she should have spent some of her time on something a little more pressing—say, trying to get her last name changed to virtually *anything* else!

Any-who . . .

Ole Eliza Scidmore finally enlisted the help of first lady, Mrs. Helen Taft, and the first cherry blossom trees arrived in Washington, D.C. in 1910, as a gift from the city of Tokyo. But check this out—those first trees were so infested with insects that they had to be destroyed! Thanks for nothing, Tokyo! Ole Scidmore must have been ticked!

However, in 1912, the mayor of Tokyo tried to make it right by sending the Capital three-thousand and twenty cherry trees to celebrate the friendship between the two countries. These arrived healthy, and over ten varieties of cherry trees were planted around the Tidal Basin and East Potomac Park.

The first Cherry Blossom Festival was celebrated in 1935, almost twenty-five years after the first trees were successfully planted.

So, we'll have to give props to Mayor Yukio Ozaki for saving the day and saving face for Tokyo.

BANZAI!

(Sorry, that was a throwback to The Karate Kid—and to be fair, Mr. Miyagi was from Okinawa, which is a thousand miles from Tokyo on an adjacent Japanese island—but it was still fun to say!)

Oh, check this out: in 1999, vandals were suspected of chopping down four D.C. cherry trees. However, it turned out that it was just a pair of *beavers*. What a couple of smart-aleck, punk-beavers!

CHAPTER

— 38 —

Blake took a breakfast break and played with the boys for a while. He told Cindy some of the facts he'd uncovered about their Capital.

You probably won't be surprised that he ended up focusing with Cindy on Mrs. Scidmore's unfortunate name, the diseased trees from Japan, a quick reference to "BANZAI!" and a couple of trouble-making beavers.

Short story, Cindy learned very little about Washington, D.C., but to be fair, she was used to this, and oddly amused by it. This was her life, and she had willingly chosen it.

Go figure.

Blake headed back to his "research".

The first one he happened on might actually come in handy—D.C. has the second busiest Amtrak Station in the United States, just after New York City. He might have to give that a try getting around the city, just for the experience.

It turned out that the steps used in the 1973 film, *The Exorcist*, are located in Georgetown. Wow, that just made his head spin! (Insert either laughing emoji or exasperated emoji here—your call.)

Well, this one explains a lot—Washington, D.C. residents consume more wine per capita than anywhere else in the country. Now the lack of effectiveness of our federal government is starting to make sense—they're all bombed!

More facts: the U.S. Capitol Building dome is made up of 8,909,200 pounds of cast iron. In addition to that startling factoid, the sculpted head of Darth Vader is located on the northwest tower of the Washington National Cathedral among the gargoyles, or "amongst" if you're feeling whimsically archaic.

Blake couldn't help but wonder how *that* got there! So, he looked it up. It turns out that in the 1980s, there was a competition for schoolchildren to design a sculpture to be added to the towers. A kid named Christopher Rader got his included in the renovation. So, you could say that Rader, got Darth "Vader", placed on the Cathedral.

Onward we go; there is a copy of the Constitution, a map of the city, a book of poems, a Bible, and daguerreotypes of George Washington and his mother buried under the Washington Monument.

For the record, a "daguerreotype" is a photograph taken by an early photographic process employing an iodine-sensitized silvered plate and mercury vapor.

And no, I did *not* have to look that up.

(Just between you, me, and the wall, I *did* have to look it up—both *what* it was and *how* to say it—but don't tell anyone.)

Washington, D.C. is named after both George Washington (the Washington part), and Christopher Columbus (D.C.—District of Columbia).

Did you know that George Washington has a crypt in Washington, D.C. under the U.S Capitol? He does. He's not actually buried there—he's buried at Mount Vernon with his family. So, his capital crypt is empty, but he does have one—just in case you're in the market.

CHAPTER

— 39 —

OK, this one made my eyes bug out a little.
There is a chair in a crypt in Oak Hill Cemetery. President Abraham Lincoln used to visit his son, Willie, who had tragically passed away, pulling him *out of his casket* to hold him and chat with him. Both creepy, and really sad, but true.

Woodrow Wilson is the only U.S. president buried in Washington, D.C. at the National Cathedral. Being one of our worst Presidents ever, and an avowed hater of any other race of people, maybe he just didn't have any friends or any other place to go.

Did you know that the White House was formerly called the President's Palace? Andrew Jackson was the first to call it the White House, and Theodore Roosevelt officially changed the name in 1901.

The White House has thirty-five bathrooms. Good to know if you're there and you really have to go.

The White House has a movie theater that was originally a coat room—which, if you think about it, must have been a *huge* coat room! As an aside to that, President Jimmy Carter watched more movies in the White House—a total of four-hundred-eighty—than any other president to date. Given how badly the country was doing under his administration, he might have done better to spend that time actually fixing things.

John Adams was the first president to live in the White House, not George Washington. The White House wasn't built until after Washington's presidency.

D.C. is home to the largest collection of information on William Shakespeare at the Folger Shakespeare Library. So, it would seem that when it comes to the library, "to go, or not to go – that is the question".

There I go, Ham-let-ing it up again. Get it? "Ham-let-ing?"

I was also guessing you would get a good complimentary "cup of joe" at this library, since a "Folger" built it. However, it turns out that it was built by Henry Clay Folger, a Standard Oil executive from New York, not the coffee Folgers. I hope they don't offer a cup of oil!

The Library of Congress is home to more than one-hundred and seventy-million items—much of which you can probably access online now.

In 1884, the Washington Monument was the tallest structure in the world, and it is still the tallest structure in Washington, D.C. at five-hundred and fifty-five feet.

Across from the White House, in Lafayette Square, you will find a statue of Andrew Jackson. The cool thing about it is that it is partially made from cannons from the War of 1812.

If you look carefully, you can find a typo at the Lincoln Memorial in the word "FUTURE" on the north wall. They put an "E" instead of an "F", to read EUTURE. How would you like to be the editor who missed *that* before they literally etched it into stone? Did he just say, "My bad!", and that was that?

I was getting tired from my "research", but I stumbled across a list of famous people *from* Washington, D.C. You know I was going to look at that! So, here ya go!

Bill Nye the Science Guy, Al Gore, J. Edgar Hoover (former head of the FBI), J.W. Marriott, Jr. (head of Marriott International), Duke Ellington (composer), Kevin Durant (basketball player), Marvin Gaye (singer), Dave Batista (pro-wrestler and actor), Goldie Hawn (actress), Samuel L. Jackson (actor), Katherine Heigl (actress), John Philip Sousa (composer), Connie Chung (TV reporter), Maury Povich (TV Host), Dave Chappelle (comedian), Bella Hadid (American model), Stephen

Colbert (comedian, writer and actor), Taraji P. Henson (actress), and you may have seen the movie associated with this one—Patch Adams (American physician, activist, diplomat, and author). Side note if you didn't: he was quite quirky and would also dress up like a clown to help sick children. He also founded the "Gesundheit! Institute" in 1971.

Or I suppose, as an alternative, one might just say, "God bless you!" Institute.

CHAPTER
— 40 —

I still hadn't learned much I could use from my "research", but it *had* been interesting.

I spent the rest of the day with Cindy and the boys, just being a family. I was going to miss them all, and this was a first for me, since I had never left the boys before.

However, Cindy and I believed in what I was doing and were committed to this case.

When Cindy and the boys went down for an afternoon nap, I resisted the urge to do the same, and instead went back out on one of the patios and sat down to call my favorite billionaire.

"Hey Blake," said Mr. Triplehorn.

"Hey, Mr. T. Do you have a moment?"

"Sure."

"I'm taking off tomorrow morning for Washington, D.C., and I wanted to check with you and make sure that you're all prepared to throw your, 'I'm so rich and powerful that you'd better not mess with me', weight around for me."

Mr. Triplehorn laughed.

"Yeah, I think I can do that for you. Do you already need me to call someone and lean on them?"

"You're starting to sound like a Mafia Don, Mr. T."

Araby laughed at that.

I went on.

"No, I don't know exactly who I'm going to be talking to just yet, but I plan on going straight to the lead law enforcement on the case, and I'll need access. Being that this is such a big and sensitive case, they are going to reflexively want to shut down the lowly private investigator. You'll probably have to come down on them pretty hard."

"No problem there. You know what? I'll go ahead and call some of the big players who are leading the investigation and set them straight on you before you even get there. That way you won't have to waste a bunch of time trying to do your job."

"That would be great, sir. In a case of this magnitude, there will probably be any number of law enforcement involved. How are you going to find out who is running the show?"

Mr. Triplehorn thought about that question.

"That's a good point. I'm not going to waste time—I'm just going to call the President and find out what I need to know and who I need to talk to."

I paused.

"Hmmm. That was going to be my first move when I got there, but I guess it's OK if you want to get a jump on that. It'll save me having to take the time to hobnob with the Pres.—I just hate all that political stuff."

Mr. T chuckled.

"I'm not sure that having you talk to the President of the United States is a good idea, Blake. By the time you're done, we might find ourselves in the middle of an international incident, perhaps even on the edge of World War Three."

"A distinct possibility, sir."

Well, I guess I now know *exactly* what Mr. Triplehorn thought of me hobnobbing with the President.

With that, Mr. T was off to talk with the Leader of the Free World, and I was off to change a poopy diaper.

I tried to avoid the idea that this might be a comparative metaphor for each of our lives.

CHAPTER
—41—

It was late—very late when the call came in.

He wasn't used to being awakened—major events typically just needed to wait for him.

But this call was important and concerning.

"Where did you get this information?" he asked.

The answer surprised him.

"And they definitely told you that someone new is looking into Senator Ashford's murder?"

"Yes."

"Is it a journalist? Are they foreign or domestic?"

"No. They said it's a private investigator."

That made him sit up in bed.

"A what?"

"Yeah. Some gumshoe is coming to D.C. to investigate the murder."

"You *idiot*—why didn't you tell me that in the first place? Who cares if some wanna-be, rent-a-cop is coming into our backyard? We'll chew him up and spit him out. He won't know what hit him."

There was an uncomfortable silence.

"What?"

"I don't know about that with this one. I looked into him, and he's good—really good. This is the guy who took down Nicholas Whitlock."

Shocked silence.

"Are you *serious*?"

"Yes."

This was not good. Nicholas Whitlock had been on the fast track to the Oval Office when he was brought down. He was personally part of the reason Whitlock was headed there—he'd put him there.

The source cleared his throat.

"He was also the guy who brought down the *'See Me Killer'* out in San Francisco. He also stopped a serial child molester and killer in Florida."

There was a pause. He'd heard about both cases.

"And for the record, in each of these cases, law enforcement was getting nowhere before he showed up, just like this case."

He felt a little fear streak through him, a sensation he did not like—nor was he used to.

"Well, I don't care. We'll just deny him access and cross him up at every step."

There was some more uncomfortable silence.

"There's more, I'm afraid—he has a 'rabbi'."

"What do you mean?"

"The guy bringing him in is Araby Triplehorn."

Now he was having trouble catching his breath. Triplehorn was one of the richest men in the world and could circumvent any roadblock they could throw against this guy.

And even worse, he was one of those "red, white and blue", apple pie, and the American way rah-rah patriots, who actually believed all that "Founding Fathers" claptrap.

He had come up against Triplehorn before, and since he was so much richer than any of those in the group, his power to make things happen was problematic—and that was putting it nicely.

The informant on the phone went on.

"It turns out that it was Triplehorn who brought this guy to San Fran to solve the *'See Me Killer'* case—which he did in an impressive way."

"I think we have a problem, boss—possibly a really significant one."

"Who is this guy?"

"His name is Blake Moran."

He could hear some papers shuffle.

"He's from Tucson, Arizona, and get this—it says that his tagline is *'We Find Stuff.'*"

"What? That's his tagline? He sounds like a moron, not a Moran!"

"Yeah, but the facts say that he's not, sir—this guy is good. The facts say that we have a real problem, and that problem is backed by one of the richest and most powerful people on the planet."

Mercurius just screamed and threw his phone.

CHAPTER 42

Blake got up early the next morning and grabbed his already packed carry-on and garment bag to head out on his trip.

It was really hard to leave his new little family. Everybody was sound asleep, so he kissed them all carefully, trying not to wake them.

He went outside and wished he could just climb into "Black Beauty", his lovely 4X4 truck, which was sitting in one of the bays of his garage, and head for Tucson International Airport. However, he didn't want to leave it sitting at the airport while he was gone. Even in long-term, covered parking—a necessity in the Tucson heat—it was still better off in his garage.

So, he climbed into the waiting Uber instead.

He wasn't checking anything through, so he was able to get there and had a very short wait. He went through security with his carry-on and garment bag, and headed onto the plane, getting to be first in line, since he was paying for the privilege of flying first-class.

The whole process was uneventful, including catching his connecting flight in Chicago. It was a two-hour wait, so he went ahead and got something to eat at O'Hare while he waited. He even took a little nap on the last flight into Dulles International.

The little hot towel they gave him to refresh himself was really *quite lovely*, thought Blake, in his most snooty thought process voice he could muster.

That made him chuckle to himself—it sounded like something Thurston Twelvetrees would say.

He missed that little dude.

Once he got into Dulles, he made a beeline for the rental car agency he'd set things up with. They had a brand-new, 2024 Dodge Challenger waiting for him. He had his choice between an off-red with black accents and a green with black accents.

He liked the red one better—it was awesome looking and just looked powerful. However, with the green one, he could pretend that he was the Green Hornet and do his superhero thing.

Wait, that wasn't going to work. The Green Hornet's car was actually called "Black Beauty", just like he called his truck, so it wasn't green.

Also, he just couldn't see the Green Hornet's sidekick, Kato, driving a green car—just because it had the right color on it.

He looked up and saw that the attendant was staring at him—just waiting with eyebrows raised—clearly concerned that it was taking this long to choose between a red or green car.

"I'll take the red one," Blake said, much to the relief of the desk dude.

When asked about the insurance, Blake said he'd better get that, which phrased that way brought more furrowed brow and concern into the attendant's eyes.

Blake decided not to explain himself any further. You see, people had a habit of trying to kill him. He tried not to take it personally, but it was getting harder to do since it kept happening over and over.

That was also why he needed a car with the power of the Dodge Challenger—there were times he needed to move *fast*, and move fast *now*, so some horses under the hood were sometimes necessary to the furtherment of his life.

Blake was pondering whether he should do a little more introspection on why people just kept trying to kill him. It was at that point that he realized that the desk dude was staring at him again, his hand extended, trying to give back his credit card and the key fob to the car— and doggone it if his eyebrows weren't in the *up* position yet again.

He smiled and took the items from him, nodding his thanks, then he quickly walked away to get this red Dodge Challenger. He hoped the desk dude wasn't calling security.

That interaction ended up being really awkward, and could have *definitely* gone better, thought Blake.

CHAPTER 43

When I set the GPS to get me to the Waldorf Astoria, I wondered if maybe I should have flown into Ronald Reagan Washington National Airport instead. It said that it was going to take me forty minutes to get there, and the path wasn't exactly a straight shot.

It took me east on the 267 until that ended at Interstate 66. That bad boy wound around, finally passing close to Arlington, where it then became a bridge over the famed Potomac River via Roosevelt Island. It then routed me onto Constitution Avenue, which put quite the view on my right; the Lincoln Memorial, the Vietnam, Korean and World War II Memorials, along with the Reflecting Pool. I then passed between the Washington Monument on my right and the White House on my left.

I was rubbernecking like there was no tomorrow!

The National Museum of African American History and Culture showed up on my right, while the World War I Memorial was on my left.

I had just passed the National Museum of American History and then the Smithsonian on the corner when my GPS shook me out of my reverie. It told me to turn left onto 12th Street NW, and that my destination was there on my right, on the corner of Pennsylvania Avenue and 12th Street.

Isn't that just like technology to horn in on a sublime historical moment!

I have to admit that I'd changed my mind about flying into Dulles—

that drive was a fast forty minutes, and the journey through our nation's history and monuments had been worth the time!

Yep, it was pretty cool to be in our nation's capital—Washington, D.C.

After getting the Challenger parked, I made it through the check-in process and headed up to the suite.

It did not disappoint.

Out of the 263 guest rooms at the Waldorf Astoria, I had scored a room on the seventh floor where the view through the large windows looked east, and there in the distance, I could see the United States Capitol building. I was guessing that the famous "dome" would be lit up brightly at night. I looked forward to seeing if that was the case.

The room was just as advertised for this five-star hotel: done up in lots of white with dark wood furniture, it was almost seven-hundred square feet of luxury, and if you remember, it had an extra seating area for meetings, an office area with a desk, and an impressive bathroom all done in marble and tile, complete with a walk-in steam shower and a Jacuzzi bathtub.

And again, all this for just $1,275 a night! What a bargain—for my billionaire buddy, Mr. Triplehorn!

Speaking of him, I needed to give him a call and see what paths he had cleared for me to begin. So, I unpacked the few items I'd brought, put my luggage away, and settled in on the couch to call Mr. T, while looking out at the great view.

Time to start finding a murderer.

CHAPTER 44

"Hey, Mr. T—how's things in San Fran?"

"Hey, Blake. Same-o', same-o'. Are you in D.C. yet?"

"I am currently ensconced at the Waldorf Astoria, looking out at the United States Capitol building, hoping my friend and benefactor, Mr. Triplehorn, has some good news for me from the President of the United States."

"So, basically, just another normal day in my life—I guess I could say same-o', same-o' too."

"You're staying at the *Waldorf*?" asked Araby, clearly not distracted by my witty banter. "Please tell me I'm not springing for the President One Suite. I don't need to be throwing almost twenty grand a night at your accommodations, even if I am a billionaire."

Doesn't that just figure that Mr. T would know all about the Waldorf?

"No sir, your lowly private investigator only got a Junior Suite. I couldn't help but notice all the money I was saving you when I booked it—so basically . . . you're welcome."

Araby chuckled.

"Yeah, your tastes in accommodations have gone up some from the old days—you're now a 'five-star hotel' sort of traveler, aren't you?"

"Well, sir, I wouldn't want you to be embarrassed if any of your other billionaire friends found out that *your* investigator was staying in anything less than *their* investigators."

That merited another chuckle from Mr. T.

"Well, we can't have that, now, can we?"

"Also, to be fair, this is quite a step down from staying at Triplehorn Mansion with Thurston in attendance, while driving your exotic, multi-million-dollar high performance sports cars."

"Basically, you spoiled me."

"So, I guess this is all my fault," said Araby dryly.

"Well, I didn't want to just come out and say it, sir, but I'm glad that you were able to get there."

I could almost *hear* Mr. T shaking his head and questioning his life choices as he chuckled.

"So, enough small talk, sir; I'm a busy man," I said to the multi-billionaire. "What does the Pres have for me?"

That merited another laugh.

"Well, the 'Pres' had a lot to say—not the least of which was that he'd rather I didn't do this."

"Really? That seems odd," I said.

"I thought so too. Since when do politicians *not want* billionaires to pay the freight for the job that they should be doing themselves, so that they can take all the credit once said billionaire's investigator solves the case?"

That was a really good point—and a very long sentence.

"What did you say to that?"

"I told him to stay in his lane and out of my way."

I waited for the punch line or the laugh.

There wasn't one.

"Wait—are you serious? You told the President of the United States to '*stay in his lane*'?"

"I did."

"And he took that?"

There was the laugh.

"Blake, I know you're not familiar with this world, but men with as much money and power as I have are simply *not* told no. Politicians tend to kiss the proverbial butt of rich guys because they all need money—lots of it. He would never take a chance of offending me, if nothing else because I move in a crowd of all the other 'movers and shakers', and he can't afford to be downgraded by me to them."

I thought about that.

"You're telling me that the President of the United States—the leader of the free world—is afraid of getting a bad *Yelp review from you?*"

Araby thought for a heartbeat and then laughed.

"In a nutshell, yes, that's exactly what he's afraid of. Pretty ugly, isn't it?"

"Yeah. Who woulda thunk politics was ugly?" I said in my best hick voice. "I guess there's a reason that politics comes from two words—*poly*, meaning many, and *tics*, meaning blood sucking insects."

I chuckled at my own humor—I do that sometimes. It helped that Mr. T was chuckling too.

"So, did he end up giving you what I need?" I asked.

"Yep, right after the 'stay in your lane' comment."

"I guess I'm just glad you're on my side, Mr. T. Give me the 'deets'."

And he did.

CHAPTER
— 45 —

It turns out that there were going to be a number of law enforcement agencies that I would have to deal with.

Oh boy!

In case you missed it, that was intended to be sarcasm. I'm *not* really excited about this. Sometimes my exclamations are pretty subtle, so I thought I'd make sure you got that.

Any-who . . .

When it comes to Washington D.C. proper, the city itself is watched over by the Metropolitan Police Department of the District of Columbia (MPDC), more commonly known as the Metropolitan Police Department (MPD), or the DC Police, and colloquially, the DCPD.

Is it just me, or do we need just a few *more* acronyms?

Again, sarcasm.

Let's go with the DC Police for brevity. They are the primary law enforcement agency for the District of Columbia. With approximately thirty-four-hundred officers and six-hundred civilian staff, it is the sixth-largest municipal police department in the United States. The department serves an area of sixty-eight square miles, and a population of over seven hundred thousand people.

Here's a little-known fact: established on August 6, 1861, the MPDC is one of the oldest police departments in the United States.

For the record, I didn't say it was an *interesting* fact—just little-known. Now it's a little better-known.

Now, you might think that this would be my primary go-to agency, but you'd be wrong—they are in the mix, but they are not primary.

There are two primary agencies to deal with, the first being the United States Capitol Police, which, you may be shocked to learn, also has an acronym: USCP.

So, why the Capitol Police, you ask?

What? You didn't ask? Oh. Could we pretend that you did? You know, just to move the story on?

OK, thanks.

Let's start with their very own statement about what they do:

The United States Capitol Police (USCP) safeguards the Congress, Members of Congress, employees, visitors, and Congressional buildings and grounds from crime, disruption, and terrorism. We protect and secure Congress so it can fulfill its constitutional and legislative responsibilities in a safe, secure, and open environment.

We protect the legislative process, the symbol of our democracy, the people who carry out the process, and the millions of visitors who travel here to see democracy in action. We also protect everyone who visits . . .

OK, that's enough.

Now, just as a reminder, our murder victim was *Senator* Todd Ashford, from the great state of California. OK, how about the "used to be" great state of California—does that work for you? OK.

Since it was a Senator who was murdered, the Capitol Police had primary jurisdiction over the local police.

As a side note, the Capitol Police are often seen as a sister agency of the United States Secret Service, which is tasked with protecting the President and Vice President, and their families.

Now, being the ever-vigilant reader that you are, I'm sure you remembered that I said there were *two* primary agencies with which I would have the joy of interacting. (Read as sarcastic "joy".)

Both of the agencies I've mentioned up to this point have been local,

THE CONSPIRACY CABAL

but you should never underestimate the ability of the *federal* government to jump into an investigation with both feet.

That is why you can add the FBI to my list of "Oh boy, I get to work with them too" excitement. And lest you think that the FBI stands for Female Body Inspector—like they did in the TV series, *Cobra Kai*—here's what the Federal Bureau of Investigation has to say about itself:

> *The FBI's investigative authority is the broadest of all federal law enforcement agencies. The FBI has divided its investigations into a number of programs, such as domestic and international terrorism, foreign counterintelligence, cyber-crime, public corruption, civil rights, organized crime/drugs, white-collar crime, violent crimes and major offenders, and applicant matters. The FBI's investigative philosophy emphasizes close relations and information sharing with other federal, state, local, and international law enforcement, and intelligence agencies. A significant number of FBI investigations are conducted in concert with other law enforcement agencies or as part of joint task forces.*

Ah, very good, Daniel-San, I think in my best Mr. Miyagi voice, as a nod to old-school *Karate Kid* and later to *Cobra Kai*.

So, they say they have the "broadest authority" to get involved and they work "in concert with" other law enforcement agencies, "as part of joint task forces".

Therein is the reason that the FBI will be a part of my upcoming great "opus". Since it's "in concert with", let's call it, "Mr. Moran's Opus".

Or not.

(Did you see *Mr. Holland's Opus*? I did. Honestly, not all that great of a movie. Sorry Dreyfuss.)

CHAPTER
— 46 —

So, *that* was a lot of information, simply to tell you where I was headed first—the Capitol Police Department. But hey, I enjoyed the extra time we got to spend together.

It probably won't surprise you to learn that the Capitol Police Department Headquarters was located just a handful of blocks away from the United States Capitol building—that thing I said I could see out of my hotel window. That seemed appropriate given that both the Senators and Representatives they were supposed to protect worked there. The Supreme Court was right there too.

I got into the red Challenger and headed east on Pennsylvania Avenue until I made a soft left onto Constitution Avenue. Then, passing the United States Capitol building on my right and seeing the Supreme Court up further, I headed north on Delaware Steet for two blocks, then turned right onto D Street, and a block and a half later, I was there.

When I saw the Capitol Police Headquarters, I guess I expected more of a building. However, after seeing it, it made some sense to me that it wasn't huge, because their mission or purview was somewhat limited too.

However, I wasn't going to mention any of that to them. I am *not* as dumb as I look!

There are over two-thousand police officers and civilian personnel who work for the Capitol Police. Now, when you consider that there are four-hundred and thirty-five Representatives in the House, and one-hundred Senators in the Senate, that protector to protectee ratio is pretty good.

Mr. Triplehorn told me that I was to talk to the top dog, the Chief of the Capitol Police himself, Raymond Ortez. It didn't surprise me that I would need to start there—after all, a United States Senator had been murdered on their watch—but I was guessing I would be quickly passed on to the lead detective who was doing the real work in the field.

The receptionist looked up when I walked in.

"May I help you?" she asked.

"Yes. I'm Blake Moran and I'm here to see Chief Ortez please."

"Do you have an appointment?"

"No, but I was told I should come and talk to him by the President of the United States."

Who's playing the big dog now?

That got her attention.

"Just a moment."

I'm guessing that she was calling Chief of Police, Raymond Ortez, and telling him what I just said.

Don't ask me how I do it—I'm just intuitive that way.

She got off the phone.

"Chief Ortez will see you now. If you'll head through security and then take the elevator to the top floor, you'll be guided to his office."

I nodded and did just that. Once upstairs, I was pointed to the big corner office and then asked by the Chief's executive assistant to wait for a moment.

That moment turned into twenty minutes, no surprise to me. The top dog was performing the proverbial "pissing competition", where he reminds me of how important he is and how unimportant I am, simply by making *me* wait for *him*.

I've learned to expect this from law enforcement, so I always make sure I am prepared to use that time well—I am a professional after all.

I played "Doodle Jump" on my phone.

CHAPTER
— 47 —

By the time the Chief had "put me in my place", I had almost achieved my highest score, so I was feeling pretty good.

"The Chief will see you now," said his assistant.

The Chief was a Hispanic man, which I was guessing when I heard "Ortez"—again, it's a gift—he was a man of about six feet tall, who clearly must love too many bean and cheese burritos with extra guacamole and sour cream.

All of that to say he was "portly".

That comment may well come off like a cheap shot, but he did keep me waiting for twenty minutes, so let's call it even.

I introduced myself and sat in one of the chairs in front of his desk.

He stared at me for a beat.

"I received calls from the Majority Leader in the Senate and the Speaker of the House regarding you. They said that the President had instructed them to tell me that we were to cooperate with you regarding your investigation into the murder of Senator Ashford."

I just nodded and stared back at the Chief. Everything he said sounded about right, so I had nothing to add, which doesn't happen often.

And yes, my silence was my own brand of "power move", back to the proverbial, "pissing contest".

When it was clear that I wasn't going to respond, he went on.

"Can you tell me why we should do this?" he asked.

"Sure."

When I didn't say anything more, he said, "Well?"

"Well, what?" I asked.

His eyebrows went up.

"Can you tell me?"

"Yes, I can."

More staring.

Finally, "Are you going to?"

"Oh, you want me to tell you now? OK. All you had to do was ask. The reason is cuz, 'the President SAID SO!"

I finished that sentence with quite the emphasis and flourish, in case you didn't notice.

Now, one might venture to say that I was acting like a petulant child, but that would only be because I *was*. You didn't really think I would *decline* the invitation to join the "proverbial pissing contest", did you?

He stared at me.

I stared at him.

Finally, I decided I was tired of this game, which was kind of a bummer, cuz that would mean that the moment I spoke, he officially won that round. I hate to admit it, but fair is fair, and that is how the game is played.

"Look, I'm sure you're busy—I mean, it took you twenty minutes just to see me. We both know that the real help I'm going to need will be your lead detective, so we're both just burning daylight hours here. Since the President, the Majority Leader, and the Speaker told you what you need to do, how about you just tell me the name of your lead detective, point me in the right direction, and we can both get back to our busy schedules."

After a little more staring, during which I was tempted to get back on my phone and work on my "Doodle Jump" score a little more, that's exactly what the Chief did.

CHAPTER
— 48 —

"He's here."

They were sitting on a bench at the National Mall, with the White House just to their right in the distance, the Washington Monument directly on their left, and the Reflecting Pool right in front of them. Beyond that was the Lincoln Memorial and the Potomac River.

Even though they were out in the open, they both had looked around carefully before they began to talk. With the existence of parabolic microphones, one had to take precautions, even out in the open like this.

So, they spoke quietly to each other.

"When did he get here?" asked Mercurius.

"Late this morning."

"Any idea what he's planning on doing?"

A look around.

"My source says that he's talking to the Capitol Police Chief right now, courtesy of an order from the President."

"Why would the President do that?"

"Triplehorn called."

There was frustrated silence while he fumed.

"Do we have anything in place that could stymy him?"

"We can use our leverage at certain points, but if Triplehorn continues to put the pressure on, it's going to be hard for even our contacts to refuse to cooperate."

He thought about that for a moment.

"Do we have our bases covered?"

His informant looked around.

"Look, as far as we know, we destroyed any of the evidence Ashford had that could expose us. As long as the laptop was the sole place he kept it, then we're golden."

"Did you search his office?"

"Of course we did," the frustration in the edge of his voice coming through.

"Anything?"

"No," he said as he thought what a stupid question that was.

"OK, then we should be safe."

They both sat there, pretending that they completely believed that last statement.

"What about this Moran guy? Do we have contingencies in place in the event he starts to get too close?"

The informant took another look around.

"I'm assuming you can engage the assassin again if we end up in a worst-case scenario?"

He looked around before he replied.

"I can if I have to, but I don't want to. When too many people show up dead, other people start asking more questions. And seriously, that guy is lethally dangerous—and not just to the mark. I get the distinct feeling that if anyone displeases him in any way, he just ends them without a second thought."

"That could easily become any one of us."

The informant nodded, recognizing that he just got added into the equation.

"But you can use him if we have to, right?"

Mercurius nodded.

"I can, but it will look really bad. The Senator is murdered, then the investigator is murdered. However, I'm starting to wonder if we might have to do it anyway. This guy has some real juice with Triplehorn backing him, and his track record is way too good for my comfort—he has too much "juice" of his own. If he starts to make any progress, I'll be forced to have him taken out."

The informant just nodded, and they both stared out toward the Reflecting Pool, neither one of them actually seeing it.

CHAPTER
— 49 —

Chief of Capitol Police, Raymond Ortez did more than give me the lead detective's name—he actually had the detective come and get me from his office—I'm assuming so I wouldn't just wander around his headquarters.

While the meeting hadn't gone all that well with the Chief, the lead detective didn't seem quite as adverse toward me as the Chief, which was right out of the starting blocks. His name was David Lee.

Now, I know what you're thinking—with that surname, we're probably talking about an oriental man. After all, Lee means "plum tree" in Chinese and was a royal surname during the Tang Dynasty.

(What? You *weren't* thinking that? Oh, my bad. Hmmm . . . well, if you don't mind, I'm just going to go on as though you were.)

In addition to that, someone like Bruce Lee comes to mind, one superbad dude who could throw down with anybody—even other karate dudes.

Now, to be accurate, I probably should note that Bruce Lee didn't technically use Karate. He started with *Tai Chi*, but quickly turned to *Wing Chun*, a soft form of *kung fu*. (Does Wing Chun sound like a popular side dish at an oriental buffalo wings restaurant to you? I mean, come on! Can you not *totally* hear someone say, "Yeah, I'd like a side of *Wing Chun* please." Me too—but I'm kind of hungry right now, so who knows?)

From *Wing Chun*, Bruce Lee then developed a martial art technique called *jeet kune do*, a blend of ancient kung fu, fencing, boxing, and philosophy, which he began teaching instead of traditional martial arts.

However, now I have a fear that you might consider me pedantic for noting that difference, and then judge me unfairly because of that, so maybe I won't note that.

Hmmm ... now I'm just concerned you're a little annoyed that I used the word "pedantic" and will think me to be uppity.

However, I have to admit that virtually *no one* has *ever come close* to thinking of *me* as "uppity"—it just doesn't fit my persona. However, I admit that I feel a certain attraction to being thought of that way, maybe just this once.

And as a side note, the fact that I just used "persona" might argue in favor of that description.

I paused for thought.

My *first* thought was to once again note that I'm a little hungry for oriental food—maybe a nice side of "Wing Chun" with some *jeet kune do* to dip it in? That made me laugh.

But my *second* thought was that somehow, I'd gotten off track—and for the life of me, I could *not* remember what I was talking about.

CHAPTER
— **50** —

I thought hard, and it took me a moment, but then I remembered—oh yeah, we were talking about Detective David Lee.

Well, it turns out that David Lee was *not* of oriental descent, but never fear! The surname "Lee" is also derived from Old English to mean "clearing" and is also an Irish surname meaning "a poem".

So, that means that there was always an option that he might *not* be oriental.

We could do a genealogical search of all his ancestors and try and figure out exactly where he hails from, OR I could just tell you that *I'm looking right at him right now*, and he is a pasty-white guy in a suit!

Yeah, let's save some time and just do that.

Do *you* feel like we just "saved some time"?

Yeah, me neither.

Any-who . . .

The Chief introduced me to Detective Lee, to whom I immediately did my best oriental bow (just messing with you—I shook his hand).

The Chief clearly wanted us to beat feet out of his office, so we did.

As we walked to the elevator, we got a little acquainted.

"How long have you been with the Capitol Police?" I asked.

"Almost ten years. Before that, I was in Baltimore as a beat cop with the police department there. Capitol offered me a detective assignment here, so I made the move."

"Do you like it?"

"It's alright. It moves slower than Baltimore PD did, but we get to deal with the 'movers and shakers' of the country, so that's interesting."

We got into the elevator, and he pushed the fifth-floor button.

"Interesting, good or interesting, bad?" I asked.

"Yes" was all he responded, and we both laughed.

Arriving on the fifth floor, we got out and walked through the bullpen area toward his office. I hadn't seen a "hoosegow" yet, but I was guessing it was probably on a lower floor.

Oh, in case that's a foreign term to you, you're not alone, cuz "hoosegow" actually came from a foreign term. The word has come to mean a jail, but it sprung up in the western United States in the early 1900s from the mispronunciation of the Mexican Spanish word, *juzgado*, which meant "tribunal or court".

So, to simplify things, I hadn't seen their jail yet.

Once again, I'm just *feeling* the time being *saved* and things being *simplified*!

When we got settled in Detective Lee's office, I was jolted by what was clearly a Samurai sword displayed on his wall. I did a quick visual check on my "pasty-white guy" appearance evaluation and questioned if just maybe I would have to reevaluate my genealogical math and maybe even show my work.

He clearly saw my reaction and glanced at the sword.

"Oh, the guys thought it was funny to get me a Samurai sword because of my last name. I ended up really liking the sword, so I put it on my wall."

"It's a pretty good conversation starter," he concluded.

I would have to admit that he was right. Case in point, we were currently conversing about it.

"Yeah, it's cool," was all I said, thankful that my genealogical math was safe.

CHAPTER
— 51 —

"So, you're from Arizona, huh? Have you worked on any cool cases lately?"

Now, you have to understand what was happening here. Detective David Lee was "detecting", trying to figure out just what he had been handed. Was I some wanna-be rent-a-cop who was just going to trip all over his investigation or could I possibly bring value to his case?

I get it—I'd do the same thing in his position.

So, I took a deep breath and clued him in.

"Well, a few years ago, I was the guy who brought down Nicholas Whitlock for murder."

David Lee tried his best to keep his cool, but his widened eyes completely gave him away. You have to understand that especially here in D.C., that had been a HUGE story, cuz ole Whitlock had been on his way to becoming everybody's boss as President, and everybody knew the plan.

At least that's what everybody thought until the "Blake-myster" stepped in and changed the course of the nation!

Did that sound arrogant? It felt arrogant when I said it. I'll have to ponder that later. Prideful jerks are just the *worst*.

I let that little factoid settle in with Detective Lee for a moment, then I went on.

"Then two years ago, I found and stopped a serial kidnapper, rapist, and killer of multiple preteen girls in Florida."

More staring.

"Then just last year I found and stopped the *'See Me Killer'* in San

Francisco—you may have heard about it—and then I ended up watching the fool die after he tried to run away and fell on his own knife."

"I have to say, it could not have happened to a more deserving guy."

"That was you?" croaked out Detective Lee, incredulity running wild in his mind.

"Yep. Fun side note to that story—I was working for billionaire Araby Triplehorn on that case, the same guy who hired me to investigate this case—and I ended up having to crash one of his many supercars—his nine-million-dollar *Bugatti Centodieci* to be exact—to stop the pervert."

Lee just stared.

"And here's the crazy thing—Mr. Triplehorn wasn't even upset about the car, cuz I also saved his daughter from this freak. But seriously, can you imagine not having to sweat the loss of a nine-million-dollar, high-performance supercar? What must *that* be like?"

Lee just shook his head; speech clearly having forsaken him at all these revelations.

In the silence, I felt like I should probably sum up.

"So, yeah, I've had some pretty cool cases lately."

I probably don't need to tell you this, but my "market-value" had just risen exponentially—like a rocket—among the Capitol Police department—cuz I can assure you that Detective David Lee was in no way going to keep this newly-acquired information to himself—everyone would soon know.

After all, they had a celebrity and celebrated crime solver amongst them—at least that's how I thought about it in my mind—which might beg the question earlier queried by myself about "arrogance".

Any-who . . . getting that "gravitas" with these boys in blue was my point in revealing it—not just arrogance.

We'll all work better together this way.

CHAPTER
— 52 —

While Detective Lee was still trying to wrap his head around my being anything but some wanna-be rent-a-cop, and all the "cool cases" I'd just listed off for him, I thought maybe I should move the conversation along.

"So, enough about me—can you tell me what you've learned so far about Senator Ashford's murder?" I asked. "I'm going to need to get up to speed pretty quickly."

That seemed to shake Detective Lee out of his reverie, and there was clearly a new respect in his tone as he began to fill me in on what the department had found.

"I'll tell you right up front that this is a really odd and difficult case. It's been especially hard on our force because not only did we fail in our primary mission of protecting an elected official, but Senator Ashford was also one of the good ones and was really well-liked by all of us."

"I probably don't have to tell you that a lot of the people we protect are not particularly nice people."

I nodded. I would have guessed that.

"So, you're saying that most politicians are jerks. Now, is that 'off the record', or can I call the New York Times and get the word out?"

Detective Lee laughed.

"Yeah, I know that it's not 'news at 10' material, but it is a real thing we deal with that most don't. Todd was a real and decent human being—the kind of guy that any of us were eager to protect."

"That's what made this so horrible for us."

"Was his security team with him?" I asked.

"Yeah, they were stationed out in the hallway at the time, which was understandable, since his apartment had been searched by them when they arrived—which is protocol—and it's on the seventh floor, so the door was the only access point."

"Or so we thought."

"A window?" I asked.

Detective Lee stared at me.

"Yeah," he said slowly, "how did you work that out?"

"I can't say that I actually 'worked it out', but when I looked at the facts of the case, I couldn't see any other options. It kind of comes down to the old Sherlock Holmes quote, *'When you have eliminated all which is impossible, then whatever remains, however improbable, must be the truth.'* Based on what I'd seen so far, the only possible answer I could see—even though highly improbable on the seventh floor—would be a window."

Detective Lee stared at me another beat.

"Well, it would seem that is the case, although we aren't sure exactly how he—or I suppose possibly she—could do that. The building is quite smooth on the outside, but honestly, it is the only option we can see."

"There had been two windows open for ventilation, but one was facing a busy street, so the other one makes more sense."

"OK."

"The weird thing is that the assassin made one mistake."

"What was that?" I asked.

"He actually took the time to slide the window shut when he left. That let us know that it had been used simply because we knew it had been opened."

"Couldn't Senator Ashford have closed it?" I asked.

"He could have, but he knew that he was to lock the window if he ever did that—it was just protocol."

"And the window wasn't locked?" I asked.

Detective Lee shook his head.

"It was not."

"The assassin sliding that window closed has been the main clue we were given to work with, so we simply have not had much to work with."

I thought about all that.

"How long are you thinking the assassin was in the apartment?"

Detective Lee thought about that.

"We're guessing probably less than fifteen minutes. He obviously had to be concerned that one of the Capitol Police could enter the residence at any moment, so, being that he was clearly a professional, he would have been extremely efficient."

"How does it appear he got the drop on the Senator without him yelling for help?"

Detective Lee considered that.

"From what we could tell, it appeared that Senator Ashford was working on his laptop, sitting on the couch. We think the assailant entered the apartment from the window in the other room, then came up behind Todd, got the drop on him, and then choked him out."

I had an *immediate* question when I heard that.

CHAPTER
—53—

"Was there petechial hemorrhaging?" I asked.

Detective Lee's face registered surprise.

"Dang, this guy really knows his stuff," thought Detective Lee.

"Yeah. There were numerous broken blood capillaries in the whites of his eyes, or petechiae, indicating he may have been choked out."

I thought about that, then I ventured a guess.

"There must have been something more. Since Senator Ashford was suffocated with a plastic bag taped around his neck—that could have produced the same result," I said, the question implied.

"Wow, this guy really doesn't miss much," thought Detective Lee.

"Yes, there were pressure marks found around his neck, and then some damage was found on his esophagus at the autopsy."

I was nodding, as Detective Lee continued.

"Senator Ashford probably came to, finding himself bound to the chair he was found in, with a gag stuffed into his mouth. There was a contusion on his face where it appeared that he'd been struck, prior to having the bag put over his head and taped around his neck."

We both took that statement to heart silently. It was not a pleasant, shared moment.

Detective Lee and I took a pause, looking out his window. A good man had been killed, we were guessing, for simply being a good man, and that reality was sobering.

I broke the silence.

"You had stated earlier 'or I suppose she', in your speculation. Wouldn't you agree that Senator Ashford being choked out and having to be carried as dead weight into the other room, would almost certainly rule out a woman?"

Detective Lee thought about that and nodded.

"Great, that narrows our suspect pool down by half."

I went on.

"Can I ask what the protocol is for me to get to take a look at Senator Ashford's apartment?"

"Well, given that every major player—including the President of the United States—has said we are to cooperate with you, the 'protocol' is pretty much you saying you want to."

I chuckled.

"Yeah, I know—I think it's weird how much power a billionaire like Mr. Triplehorn has too. But that doesn't mean I won't use it to get the job done."

"I would too. So, do you want to go take a look?"

"I do. Is that something you could assist me on or am I on my own—I could use the extra eyes if you can spare the time."

Detective Lee laughed.

"I am at your service, sir."

"Awesome, let's go."

———◆———

Detective Lee grabbed all the crime scene information that we would need, and we left.

After we walked out of the station, Detective Lee headed for his cruiser. I stopped him and asked him to step back into the station with me.

"Yeah?" He asked.

"Listen, I would appreciate your doing something for me."

"What's that?"

"Would you be willing to throw your jacket on to conceal your badge and firearm?"

Detective Lee squinted his eyes and made that little "V" between his eyebrows.

"OK, can I ask why?"

"Sure. We are dealing with some people here who have no compunction about killing a Senator of the United States. They are clearly powerful and in the know. While they might be less inclined to kill a police officer, they wouldn't think twice about icing a private investigator like me. I mean, come on, my infamous tagline is, *'We Find Stuff.'*"

"I would like to keep this as much on the down-low as I can, cuz I'd like to keep breathing."

Detective Lee was nodding, following my logic. He then went ahead and put on the jacket he'd been carrying.

"Can I ask you a question?" he asked.

"Sure."

"Did you really just use the word 'compunction'?"

"Yeah. It's a feeling of guilt or moral scruple that prevents or follows the doing of something bad—ergo, these dudes had 'no compunction' for killing."

"No, I'm fully aware of what the word means. It's just that you went on to tell me that your tagline is *'We Find Stuff.'* Do you see how those two pictures don't really line up?"

"And for the record, you just used 'ergo' as well."

I thought about that.

"So, are you saying that the two—or now, maybe three—don't seem to fit in juxtaposition?"

"Wow! Now let's go ahead and make it four that don't fit. You're getting in pretty deep here. If you're such a wordsmith, take a shot at explaining your tagline to me."

I looked at David Lee.

He looked back with lifted eyebrows, then said, "I'm waiting."
"I'll take the fifth."
David chuckled.
"Yeah, I bet you will."

CHAPTER 54

Now, with his jacket on, Detective Lee headed once again toward his cruiser.

"Um, at the risk of really annoying you, would it be OK if I drive?"

Detective Lee turned back toward him.

"What now?"

"Well, come on—one does not have to be so eloquent as to use compunction, ergo, and juxtaposition—to see that pulling up in a Capitol Police cruiser might just cause someone watching to notice an investigative presence. In addition to that, your cruiser can be tracked."

"Besides, I'm driving a red Challenger, so it's very understated and 'under the radar'."

David laughed.

"Alright professor, let's go in your subtle vehicle."

"Oh, it's 'professor' now, huh?" I laughed.

I then stopped again.

"Oh."

"How could there *possibly* be something else?" asked Detective Lee, very probably now in the aforementioned state of being "annoyed".

"Well, would you mind turning off the location service on your phone?"

"My what?"

"Your location services. It's under your privacy settings. If it's not shut off on your phone, it will tell anyone who might be looking, exactly where you are."

Detective Lee stood, staring at me.

"And why would anyone be 'looking'?" he asked.

I paused and considered how to answer that while not offending Detective Lee and his profession.

"Um," I began articulately.

David waited.

"Would you agree that the people who committed this murder are powerful and well-placed?" I asked.

"Yes, of course."

"Would you agree that it is at least possible that they might have well-placed moles in places of authority—even perhaps unknowing moles?"

I added that last "unknowing" part to avoid the possible offense I mentioned before.

Detective Lee considered that and then looked back at the Capitol Police Headquarters.

"You think someone in there might be keeping tabs on where we are and what we're doing—is that what you're saying?" asked Detective Lee.

I shook my head.

"I'm not *saying* they are—I'm asking you if you think it is *possible*, and that just the possibility itself is worth protecting against."

David looked at me a beat longer, glanced back at the building again, and then took out his phone and scrolled to the location services section.

CHAPTER
—— 55 ——

Firmly now ensconced in the red Challenger, as I drove, Detective Lee and I got to know each other a little better.

(For the record, you probably shouldn't tell David that I used the word "ensconced" in that last sentence—much more of this, and he's going to start to wonder if I'm just a little pretentious.)

(Oh, and don't tell him I used pretentious either. Let's go with "he'll wonder if I have a proverbial stick up my butt" instead. Yeah, that's good—it's dude worthy.)

It turns out that David was a little further along the family line than me, which made sense cuz he was about ten years older. He had three kids—two boys and a girl—two of whom were in elementary school, and one headed for preschool soon.

I told him about the honeymoon surprise of Nic and Linc and the recent havoc they were causing, just by being babies. He laughed and told me some of his stories about the kids when they were little and then growing up.

I have to say it was an interesting and even surreal experience to be having this discussion, and through it, bonding with another man. This was a first for me. I was now a "family man", and that brought with it different experiences and therefore different discussions with people. It felt so "grown-up" to me, which is not something that I had felt much in my life. Sitting here, swapping kid stories with this other family man was nice—and "adult", and I liked it.

(Having said that, you probably shouldn't mention my use of

"surreal" either. It might head back to that whole stick and butt issue again. I hope you're keeping a list at this point.)

David was giving me directions to the late Senator Ashford's apartment, since it wasn't all that easy to navigate around Washington.

In case you are unaware, the streets of the city of Washington, D.C., are laid out in a "spoke and wheel" pattern. If you look at it in a map search in the aerial mode, you can see it clearly—and it's a little crazy.

The history behind this is kind of interesting: this dude from France, Monsieur L'Enfant, is best known for designing the D.C. roadways of circles and spokes, a 1791 master plan that transformed a patch of swamp and farmland into the capital of the United States. Even today, much of Washington, D.C., with its wide boulevards and public squares follows L'Enfant's original concept.

I found this description:

"The historic plan of Washington, District of Columbia—the nation's capital—designed by Pierre L'Enfant in 1791 as the site of the Federal City, represents the sole American example of a comprehensive baroque city plan with a coordinated system of radiating avenues, parks, and vistas, laid over an orthogonal system. Influenced by the designs of several European cities and eighteenth-century gardens such as France's Palace of Versailles, the plan of Washington, D.C. was symbolic and innovative for the new nation. Existing colonial towns surely influenced L'Enfant's scheme, just as the plan of Washington, in turn, influenced subsequent American city planning. . . .

OK, I have to say a few things about that description. First of all, Pierre L'Enfant designed all of this, but never got to see it implemented—apparently, as a person, he was a bit of a pain in the butt who wouldn't compromise on anything, so nothing got done until after his demise.

Secondly, and the most obvious thing—I've always said that if it isn't "baroque", don't fix it!

Waiting . . . waiting . . .

Oh, come on! That was funny!

Really, nothing?

Yeah, I know it's a style of European architecture, art, and music from the seventeenth and eighteenth centuries—like the Palace of Versailles or Vivaldi, Bach, and Handel—but again, *if it isn't "baroque", don't fix it*!

Get it?

Oh, you get it—you just don't *want it*?

O . . . K . . . , moving on.

I have to admit that I had no idea what "orthogonal" meant—had to look it up. It means, "involving right angles".

Seriously? The dude couldn't have just said that?

Although, I suppose I don't really have any room to talk, given some of the words I've been using. That whole "kettle calling the pot black" comes to mind.

Any-who . . .

All that to say that navigating the streets of Washington, D.C. can be a little "wild and crazy", with the implied hat-tip to comedian, Steve Martin.

Hmmm . . . that really was a little more succinct way to say that.

(It probably goes without saying, but I'll say it anyway—don't mention that I used "succinct" to David, especially after what some might say was a less than succinct oration on the street pattern of D.C. Oh, and don't mention "oration" to him either.)

I may have a real problem here . . .

CHAPTER
— **56** —

It ended up that Senator Ashford's apartment had been just north of the campus of George Washington University, which means we got to drive north of the White House on our left, with the Washington Monument further off in the distance.

This place was so full of history—I made a note to myself that I really needed to get Cindy here with me so we could do the tourist thing together. That would be so fun!

Although, reflecting on our new "sitch", doing that with two twin babies might be a little bit of a challenge.

And of course, that was assuming horrible people didn't *kill* me during this investigation. Being killed could really be a serious buzzkill to a future fun vacation with my wife and kids.

Just sayin'.

So, we pulled up in front of the late Senator Ashford's apartment. I pulled into a parking space across the street, and we sat and looked at it.

The building had ten floors, so I counted the floors up to the seventh. It was high—which really wasn't any great private investigator insight, since everybody knows that approximately seventy feet in the air is "high".

Detective Lee and I got out of the car and crossed the street. David started to head into the building, but I motioned to him that I wanted to go down to the side of the building.

We got over to that side of the building, and I looked around. This street was very much a side street that was little used, which would have provided some privacy while you scaled a building to kill a U.S. Senator, I suppose.

"What time did the murder take place?" I asked Detective Lee.

"It was close to 9:00 p.m."

I looked across the side street at the buildings that were housing businesses. I was looking at the side of the buildings.

"Are these businesses closed at that time of night?" I asked.

Detective Lee nodded and said, "Yep."

I turned back toward the building.

"Which window was it?" I asked.

Detective Lee pointed up to the seventh floor and toward the front of the building.

I stared at the window. I took my gaze down the building for seven stories, and then I started at the window again and looked up at the additional three stories to the roof.

I looked over at David.

"So, he either scaled up the side of the building for seven stories, or he rappelled down from the roof for three stories."

"Yep."

"It would seem that rappelling makes more sense, especially with how flat these walls are—not all that much to hang onto when climbing. Also, you get the shortest path to the goal by rappelling. And rappelling would let gravity do the work for you on the way down and then you're just climbing a rope on the way up."

Detective Lee was nodding.

"Did you find anything on the ground or on the roof that led you either direction?"

Detective Lee was shaking his head.

"No. There were no distinct impressions in the grass that gave us any indications, but it hadn't rained in a few days, so the ground was pretty hard. On the roof, there were places he could have tied off a rope, but if he did, he didn't leave any scrape marks on the edge of the roof to indicate he'd done that."

I took a moment so I could think about that.

CHAPTER 57

"OK, so he could've used padding of some kind between the rope and roof edge to avoid the scrape marks on the roof," I said, really just thinking out loud.

David was nodding.

"Well, clearly there is easy 'ground access', but what about roof access?" I asked.

"There's a hatch that opens to the roof through a service area. The service area requires a simple passcode, but they're all the same throughout the building, so he could have observed any service personnel using the code to get it."

I thought about that theory and decided I didn't like it. Clearly this guy had worked hard for anonymity, and being around the building when others were around and could remember him would be putting that at risk.

"Have you talked to the building management company about that? Have you asked them if they have had any recent calls or requests for the code from any of their service providers who said they were doing routine maintenance?"

Detective Lee flipped through some notes.

"Nope, I don't see that here."

"OK, could you make a call and see if perhaps that happened? It would really help if we could determine whether we are dealing with some sort of freaky climber or simply a guy who knows how to rappel."

"OK," said Detective Lee as he stepped away to make the call.

While he was calling, I started looking at the lighting on the building. Since it was daytime, I could only see where the lights were placed, not what it would have looked like at night.

It appeared that the building had sconces at the top of the building that pointed down to create light paths that ran down the building. They were placed between the windows on the building, I was assuming they did that to avoid excessive light shining into the residents' windows at night from the outside lighting.

While I was studying this, Detective Lee came back from his call.

"Well, they said they didn't have anything out of the ordinary."

"Did the manager ask the secretaries?" I asked.

"What?"

"Oh, I guess I mean administrative assistants—did he ask them?"

"I don't think so. I talked to the head guy of the management company, and he just said there had been no such requests."

"Call and ask the secretaries."

"OK . . . why?"

"Cuz if I was this dude, I would be trying to keep as low of a profile as I could. I wouldn't be talking to the 'head guy'—too much exposure, and way too easy to remember."

"Call the front desk and ask if a service company called and said something like their regular guy was out sick or on vacation, but that a required service was due, so they needed the code. The front desk wouldn't bother the boss for that, they would just give it to him—it's not like they were giving away the U.S. nuclear launch codes."

Detective Lee stared at me.

"I'll be right back," he said.

CHAPTER 58

"You were right."

I stopped studying the building and looked over at Detective Lee.

"What did you find?"

"The front desk girl said that a few weeks ago, their HVAC company for this building called and asked for the code."

"Did he go for sick or vacation?"

"Neither. He said the regular guy had a family emergency and had to leave to take care of it suddenly, so now he had to step in and do the service. He said he could call the guy to get the code, but because of the emergency, he hated to bother him with this."

"She gave him the code."

I nodded.

"That's a good one—you add in a little sympathy while giving out the, 'I'm just the guy who's caught in the middle trying to do my job' vibe. It works."

"Just to make sure, could you call the HVAC company and check to find out if maybe this *was* a real thing? I'd hate to think we had our answer and start chasing this hard, only to find out this whole 'guy had an emergency' thing really did happen."

"Sure, I'll follow up on it now."

Detective Lee had the name of the company in his notes, so while we walked around the building, he called them.

This time, he just talked to the secretary since they tend to have all the information.

He ended the call.

"Nope, no family emergency that took anyone off the job. Also, I had her check, and there was no scheduled service for this building either."

"Good catch. So, the roof it is," I said. "Let's start there."

We took the elevator up to the top and then headed for the service area. Detective Lee had the code from when they had searched the roof before. The police had already dusted for prints, just in case the perp went this way, so we didn't have to bother being careful. We pulled the hatch stairs down and went up onto the roof.

Since the access was at the back of the building, we had to walk the length of the structure toward the front. As we did, both David and I were scanning the roof to see if anything jumped out at us. The investigation team had already done this, but it never hurt to have extra eyes on the scene.

Once we got to the area above Senator Ashford's apartment, I squatted down and studied the scene, doing my "think like the perp" thing.

Oddly enough, it appeared that the commercial HVAC unit would have been the key. There were units all around the roof, but they were all elevated and sitting on metal struts which were bolted into the roof.

"If it were me, I would have attached the rope to the struts under that HVAC unit—it's strong and would easily hold a man's weight."

Detective Lee agreed.

I stood up and we walked over to the edge of the building, which had a parapet wall. I looked over the edge and saw the light sconces I'd seen from the ground.

I turned to Detective Lee.

"Could you go down into the service room and see if you can find the outside roof sconces or light switches? I'm sure it's on a timer—or maybe light activated—but see if there is a switch you can just throw on."

"On it," he said.

As I continued to look around, the lights suddenly came on about two minutes later.

They all seemed to be on—specifically the ones I was looking for around Senator Ashford's window.

I admit that I was a little surprised. I figured the dude would have knocked them out somehow.

David was just coming back up on the roof, so I yelled, "OK, they are working. Could you turn them back off?"

He waved and went back down to do so.

Off they went.

Detective Lee was back.

We both stood there, thinking.

"The assassin takes an unnecessary risk by climbing down with those lights on, yet he didn't break them. Although, breaking them would cause a sound that might get unwanted attention too."

I thought some more. There had to be an answer.

CHAPTER 59

As I kept thinking, I walked over to the parapet wall, directly over the light closest to the front of the building. I lay down on the parapet wall and realized that I could reach the wall sconce.

I got back up.

"David, I want you to hang on to me. I need to lean over and see something. Can you do that?"

"Sure—just don't lean too far."

"OK."

I got my waist on the wall and Detective Lee put pressure on the back of my legs to hold me there.

It was a bit of a rush, dangling about one-hundred feet over the ground, but I just ignored the ground—I needed to see the light.

I was able to get my face under the sconce and look closely all around it. David and I then moved to the next one down and did the same thing.

I then surprised Detective Lee by going halfway down the building and doing the same thing on a sconce there. We even did the third one down the building.

After I was hauled back up, David wanted to know why.

"I needed to see a sconce that I was sure the assassin wouldn't need to mess with. It would be my 'control sconce'—if you will. As you can imagine, the control was covered with dust uniformly, from simply being out in the open and untouched."

"However, if you look at those first three, you'll see some of the dust is brushed off of each one of them. The dude just leaned over the edge and unscrewed them enough, so they didn't shine. I have to admit I'm surprised that he then actually took the time to screw them back in after he killed the Senator."

This assassin must have ice-water in his veins to hang around after a murder, screwing in lightbulbs.

"Are you saying he had an accomplice, since I had to hold your legs for you to do that?" asked David.

"No. He didn't have to lean as far as I did just now. I had to get my face in there to see—all he had to do was get his hand in there to unscrew the bulb. He could do that on his own."

"And that's what he did."

Now that we knew what the assassin had done, we went back to the supposed place of the rappelling. I had David stand over by the HVAC unit, while I looked at where Senator Ashford's window was to get the best line where the rope would've been.

Once we had determined that, he and I looked more closely at the parapet wall.

There was a metal facia on the top of the wall. As David had said, there were no scratches left by the assassin from the weight of him on the rope.

However, I wasn't looking for scratches, since I assumed he used padding around the rope to obscure what he was doing.

But there was still his weight to consider.

The average weight for an American male is almost two-hundred pounds. However, that's also with an average waist of over forty inches and an average height of only five feet, nine inches.

Having trouble picturing it? Think of the old TV commercial for trash bags—"Hefty, Hefty, HEFTY"!

You can thank America's commitment to fast food for those stats—however, if you've been with me for our other adventures, you know it would be both hypocritical and highly entertaining for *me* to rail against fast food.

I'm a bit of a fast-food enthusiast and aficionado.

OK, maybe more than "a bit".

But I'm not overweight!

Did I just hear you think, "Me thinks he dost protest too much"?

Even though you're talking smack about me with that comment, I do have to give you kudos for being knowledgeable about Shakespeare's Hamlet.

Any-who . . .

This dude probably wasn't "hefty". If nothing else, he would have to be in great physical shape, just to do his job. But even if he was a "hard body", say one-hundred-seventy pounds, that is still a lot of weight hanging over a parapet wall—especially one with a metal facia wrapping the top.

So, I found it—a dent.

The outside corner of the metal facia directly over Senator Ashford's window, had a dent where the rope had conveyed the weight of the assassin, through the padding, and into a bent "clue" for us.

The padded rope didn't change that basic law of physics.

Detective Lee came over and took some photos of the dent to add to his crime scene photos and then we headed down to the apartment itself.

CHAPTER

— **60** —

The seventh-floor apartment wasn't much except just that—an apartment. It was sparsely furnished with only the basic furniture. There were no pictures or knickknacks that a "home" would tend to have—this looked like a bachelor's pad—a place to basically "crash".

I said as much to Detective Lee.

"Yeah, we asked his security team about that. They said that this is pretty much just that—a place the Senator came to work a little and then sleep. They said that when he was in D.C., he was here to get his work done so he could get back to his family in California."

We walked around while Detective Lee showed me the rooms and described what they had pieced together about what had happened that night.

"We think that Senator Ashford was sitting on this couch, working on his laptop. The assailant entered through the window in the other room, then came up behind Todd and choked him out. When Todd came to, he found himself in that other room, taped to that chair and gagged."

"His briefcase had been rummaged through and his laptop had been fried, by being turned on and dumped into the kitchen sink which the assassin had filled with water."

"Senator Ashford was struck at some point, and then was suffocated with a common plastic bag, which the assassin taped around his neck."

"The killer then apparently climbed back up the rope, removed all remnants of his crime, and left the premises."

159

I considered all this, and then added, "But he closed the window—which was a mistake—and now we know he even bothered to screw the lights back into the sconces. He clearly wanted no record of his presence."

David nodded.

"Can I see the crime scene photos?" I asked.

"Sure," said Detective Lee.

He got the photos out and laid them across the kitchen island counter one by one. They showed the senator from various angles, first with the bag over his head, and then after the bag had been carefully removed by the crime scene team.

I studied the pics while glancing over at the chair where his body had been. I especially studied the ones where his face was visible.

Something stood out to me.

"You said that Todd had been struck—is this contusion on his face the reason you believe this?"

Detective Lee nodded and said, "Yes."

I kept studying it.

"Do you see that it is on the left side of the Senator's face?"

David nodded again.

"So, the Senator was taped into this chair," I said as I walked over to it, "and for some reason was struck by the assailant."

"Yes."

I mimicked the strike.

"Is it just me, or doesn't it make sense that if this grown man is strapped into this chair, hitting him with a full fist would be counterproductive, since it would most probably knock him over and make a thud when he hit the floor?"

Detective Lee considered that.

"Yeah, I think that does makes sense."

"So, if we accept that premise, that means that the assailant would not have struck him with his fist, but rather would have hit him in a more controlled way."

"He would have backhanded him."

We both looked closer at the pictures and the contusion. We then both nodded. The contusion fit that explanation better.

I looked over at Detective Lee.

"We just got another clue."

"We did?" he asked.

"Yeah. The assassin is most probably left-handed."

CHAPTER 61

"How did you get that?" asked Detective Lee.

"Well, unless the assailant is purposely trying to fool us, which isn't impossible—and he behaves like most human beings—he would have used his dominant hand to backhand the senator."

I went up to David to mimic the move.

"If he hit him on the left side of his face with a punch, that would be a right-handed man."

I did that move.

"But if he backhanded him with his dominant hand, then that left side of the face strike would demand a left-handed hit."

I illustrated it with David as I explained it.

David was nodding.

"Yeah, you're right—it would've been his left hand."

I nodded back.

"It takes some supposition, but if we're right, that narrows down our group of perpetrators significantly. Only about ten percent of the population are left-handed, with men statistically being more likely than women to both be left-handed and express their left-handedness more dominantly—just meaning that you can count on men to use their dominant hand more than women."

"Also, to be fair, about one percent of people are ambidextrous, using both hands equally well, but with that low of a percentage, I think it's fair to guess that our perp is a lefty."

Detective Lee was staring at me.

"How on earth do you know this stuff?" he asked.

"I don't know—stuff like this just sticks in my brain."

I went on.

"Now, since the U.S. population is about three-hundred-forty million people, that narrows it down to only about thirty-four million people, but with men about half of that number, we're now down to about seventeen million."

I looked over at David.

"So, we're almost there!" I said with a smile.

"However, if we make a few fair assumptions, we can get that number even lower."

"What assumptions?" asked David.

"Well, given the surveillance and planning that would be required to pull something like this off, I think we can both agree that a professional hitter was brought in for this murder."

David was nodding.

"Becoming that dude takes a little time and experience, so I think we can rule out babies, toddlers, school aged children, and probably even twenty-year old men."

Detective Lee thought about the last assertion.

"OK, I guess I can see that last one."

"Great. Now, given the physical nature of the operation with what the perp had to be able to do, it would seem that we could rule out senior citizens and probably even just men in their fifties."

David was nodding.

"So, that would bring our probable perp list down to left-handed men, in their thirties or forties."

I did some quick calculations in my head.

"With the demographics spread evenly across that seventeen million, that would mean that we are now down to *only* four to five-million left-handed men!"

I looked over at David.

"Hardly seems like much of a challenge at that point," I said dryly.

We both had a laugh over that statement.

I had a thought.

"Of course, all of this assumes that they hired a hitter from the U.S. If they hired one internationally, then our pool just became left-handed, thirty- or forty-year-old men—*in the world.*"

I looked over at Detective Lee.

"For the record, that *would* be a challenge," I acknowledged.

CHAPTER

— **62** —

The report came in right before noon.

"What do you have?" Mercurius asked in a gruff voice.

"The private investigator was here this morning and met with the Chief. That meeting didn't take very long. However, the Chief summoned the lead detective in the case, Detective David Lee, and he and the P.I. went to his office and talked for about a half an hour."

"Was that it?"

"No. After that, the two of them left the building together and went somewhere."

"What does 'went somewhere' mean? Where did they go?"

"I'm not sure."

"How can you not be sure? Just track his undercover cruiser and tell me where it is."

"I did that and discovered that it is still sitting out in the parking lot. They didn't go anywhere in Detective Lee's car."

He thought about the time.

"Is it possible that they just walked to somewhere around there to get an early lunch?"

The informant thought about that.

"It could be, but there's not all that much around here where they could go eat."

Mercurius thought.

"Well, ping his phone and find out where he is."

"OK, hang on."

It took a few minutes, but then the mole was back.

"Nothing."

"What do you mean, 'nothing'? His phone didn't show up? Is it possible he didn't take it?"

"No, he has to keep it on his person when he's on the job. It appears that he has turned off the location services on his phone."

Mercurius didn't like the sound of that at all.

"So, there is no way we can find him?"

"Hang on for a minute. Since his location services are off, I asked our guy to ping the towers to see if that will tell us anything. Let me see what he found."

A couple more minutes passed.

"OK, this isn't terribly helpful, but we at least know he's not around here having lunch. By triangulating his phone using cell towers, we know that he travelled somewhere northwest of the White House."

"I'm afraid that's as close as I can get to locating him."

Mercurius fumed as he paced in his office.

"Can you just call him and ask him where he is and what he is doing?"

"I could, but I don't actually know Detective Lee except in passing, so I don't know what my excuse would be."

"So, all you know is that the P.I. was there, talked to the Chief, talked to the lead detective, and then apparently left with the detective to some unknown destination?"

The man thought about that.

"Yeah—and are probably currently somewhere northwest of the White House, or at least passed by that direction."

Mercurius ended the call abruptly, picked up an expensive Waterford vase and threw it against the wall with all his might as he screamed.

That throw just cost him almost one thousand dollars, but he struggled with impulse control, and he could afford it.

CHAPTER
— **63** —

Having accomplished about everything we could at the Senator's apartment, Detective Lee and I climbed back into the red Challenger and headed for our next investigative location.

Something most people would just call "lunch".

Well, to be honest, lunch was just a stop *on the way* to the next investigative location—Senator Ashford's office.

Since his office was back toward where we'd come from, I asked Detective Lee to tell me a good place for us to get lunch.

If you've been with me on my former adventures, you know I've mentioned that cops always know the best places to eat in any city.

His response was pretty quick.

"Let's go to Tune Inn," he said.

"Let's go to tune into what?" I asked.

David laughed.

"No, Tune Inn—with two 'Ns'—it's Tune Inn Restaurant and Bar down on Pennsylvania Avenue. It's got some good food."

"OK—tell me how to get there."

And he did.

We made our way through the crazy "spoke and wheel" roads of D.C. again, around the White House. The fact that it is on Pennsylvania Avenue may once again remind you of the most famous address at 1600—the White House, but this isn't the Pennsylvania Avenue NW of that famous address, but rather the Pennsylvania Avenue SE!

Ah, conundrum averted!

This meant that we had to work our way around the U.S. Capitol Building, using a few of those crazy "round-abouts", hit Independence Avenue and then swing onto Pennsylvania Avenue SE.

Just a couple of blocks later, and there we were—the Tune Inn Restaurant and Bar.

There was some outside seating, but we decided to go inside. There were lots of booths available, so we grabbed one for ourselves and got settled into the leather.

I noticed that the menu pointed out that the Tune Inn had been a candy kitchen, then a "speak-easy" in the 1920s. Later, it was a men's tailor shop that catered to the gentlemen of the U.S. Congress. It wasn't until 1947 that Joe Nardelli acquired the building and named it The Tune Inn. They also pointed out their unique distinction of holding the second oldest liquor license in D.C. after the repeal of prohibition.

Hmmm. That's a brag, but it seemed like a bit of a weird brag to me.

After Joe Nardelli died, his son, Tony, took over the business and now Lisa Nardelli—Joe's granddaughter and Tony's daughter—is the owner and operator. That meant that the Tune Inn had been family owned and operated for over 70 years.

OK, that was just a lot of information for a dude who was just hoping the food was good.

I figured I should get something "healthful", since I knew that was what my sweet bride would want.

So, I started with an order of mozzarella sticks—and since the Tune Inn seemed known for their chili, I got a chili-cheese burger.

What? Don't look at me like that.

If you'll notice, I said I "should" get something "healthful"—go ahead, you can go back and see for yourself—I'll wait.

Told ya. Of course my sweet bride would *want* that, she wants me to live, after all. But sometimes you simply have to do more than just survive on this planet, you have to really *live* a little—maybe even a lot of the time.

Cindy will understand—plus, I'm not gonna tell her what I had for lunch. There's really no need for me to bother her with such pedestrian aspects of my day.

And the mozzarella sticks, and chili-cheese burger were SO good!

(Oh, and add "pedestrian" to your list of words I've used that you're *not* going to tell Detective Lee.)

CHAPTER
— 64 —

Sufficiently filled with delicious calories, Detective Lee and I wiped our faces and headed for the late Senator Ashford's office.

The office was only about one mile from the Tune Inn. We had to go past the British Museum—I had to wonder why we had that in America, since they're the ones we had to defeat to *become* America! We then passed the U.S. Supreme Court, with the U.S. Capitol Building in the distance on our left. After that, we were there—the Dirksen Senate Office Building.

Before we head into Senator Ashford's office, let me give you a little helpful background.

The congressional office buildings are used by the United States Congress, both the Senate and House, to help make up for the limited space in the United States Capitol building. The congressional office buildings are part of the Capitol Complex and are therefore under the authority of someone called the "Architect of the Capitol", and protected by the United States Capitol Police, which includes my new friend, Detective David Lee.

There are three primary office buildings for the U.S. Senate; Russell, Dirksen, and Hart, all of which are located on Constitution Avenue, to the northeast of the U.S. Capitol Building which houses the U.S. Senate.

The U.S. House of Representatives also has their own offices buildings; Rayburn, Cannon, Longworth, and Ford, all of which are located on Independence Avenue, which is to the south of the U.S. Capitol Building.

THE CONSPIRACY CABAL

People are often surprised to learn that the congressional office buildings are connected to the U.S. Capitol building by means of underground pedestrian tunnels, some of which are equipped with small railcars shuttling users to and from the Capitol, which together form the Capitol subway system.

So, that means there is a whole labyrinth of underground tunnels where our congressmen and women travel to get to their jobs. With most people's attitude toward politicians in general, the concept of them scurrying around underground would seem to make a lot of sense.

The United States Congress meets in the Capitol Building. Originally built in 1800, the Capitol Building stands prominently atop the famously named "Capitol Hill" on the eastern edge of the National Mall.

Both the Senate and House of Representatives, which together constitutes the full Congress, meet in separate, large "chambers" on the second floor of the Capitol Building. The House Chamber is located in the south wing, while the Senate Chamber is in the north wing, both of which explain the location of their respective offices—each being closest to where they meet.

So, this is the world in which Senator Todd Ashford lived during his tenure as a senator of the United States. As I mentioned, his office had been in the Dirksen Senate Office Building, so we found the parking lot off of Constitution Avenue, parked, and headed to investigate his office.

CHAPTER
— **65** —

It was just weird to be walking through these halls. To either side of us as we walked were the offices of senator after senator, some of whom I recognized.

There are only one-hundred senators in the United States Congress—two per state—so one hears some of those names in the news a little more often. The U.S. House of Representatives is parceled out proportionately by population statistics, so there are four-hundred and thirty-five of them—which makes getting your name out there a little more difficult.

As I glanced into the open doors, it appeared that most of the offices had reception areas for the citizenry peons to wait for the great man or woman to graciously grant them some of their valuable time.

That sentence may have given away my general attitude toward these politicians, but to be fair, that tends to be the general attitude of *most* of the American population—and typically for pretty good reasons.

As we kept walking, I pondered how my investigation was different. A man who I greatly admire and respect, Mr. Triplehorn, said that Senator Todd Ashford was one of the rare ones—a truly good and honorable man—trying to do his best for the country he loved. This was the kind of man who our founders knew would be essential to lead our country, if we had any hope of continuing to be that "shining city on a hill".

It was a fair assumption that this good man had been killed for being exactly that, a good man, simply trying to do the right thing. He was in the middle of a cesspool of people who were just going along with what the "powerful" people told them to do, for their own benefit.

Their job was to serve the American people and protect the U.S. Constitution's principles against all enemies, both foreign and domestic—it was right there in the oath they took. However, the level of corruption in any government is often astounding, and unfortunately, the United States government is no different.

As I walked these halls, I couldn't help but think about some movies that attacked this government corruption in such a powerful way. I don't know if you've seen the old Jimmy Stewart movie, *"Mr. Smith Goes to Washington"*. It's so old, it was in black and white. Jimmy Stewart was portrayed as basically a "boy scout", fighting the powerful, and winning. It was an awesome flick!

Or, how about *"Clear and Present Danger"*, where Jack Ryan, played by Harrison Ford, finds out the corruption goes all the way up to the President of the United States? When he confronts the President with his lawless actions, the corruption rears its ugly head when the President tells Ryan, "You got yourself a chip in the big game now", and that he can now play the game the way the powerful do too. The President refers to this corruption as "the old Potomac Two-Step, Jack", referring to the river that runs down the west side of D.C. Jack Ryan then delivers the line of the movie when he says, "I'm sorry Mr. President; *I don't dance.*"

Those movies and more were all produced because *everybody knows* this is the way Washington, D.C. works. How sad is that? If we're honest, we know we all hate it.

And Senator Todd Ashford died for trying to change that reality.

I simply cannot allow the death of this good man to be in vain.

So, let me just say, *"I don't dance!"*

CHAPTER 66

We finally came to Senator Ashford's office. There was crime tape guarding the door, but one side had been pulled back and was dangling.

I let Detective Lee take the lead here—after all, it was his police tape.

He checked the door and found it unlocked, which seemed odd to me, being it was considered a part of a crime scene investigation. Detective Lee pulled his gun from his side holster and carefully opened the door and ducked under the remaining tape.

I followed.

Inside the office was a reception area with some seating and bookshelves and official pictures scattered around the walls. It had three smaller desks, each of them with one side up against one of the walls, and then a larger desk at the back that was apparently the "keeper of the inner sanctum".

This must be the one who officially says, "None shall pass" to those who weren't welcome into the great man's office.

There was a woman seated at that desk, going through the various drawers, which might explain the unlocked door and the dangling crime tape.

I looked over at David to make sure this woman rummaging through drawers was allowed.

Detective Lee cleared his throat and the woman looked up. Her eyes were red, and she kept wiping her nose.

I was hoping it wasn't contagious.

She then looked alarmed when she saw David's gun in his hand. He slowly put it away.

"Excuse me, Ma'am, but these offices are sealed off for a police investigation. Can I ask what you are doing please?" said Detective Lee.

The woman wiped her nose again.

"I'm Denise Upton. I was Senator Ashford's executive secretary. I was told I could begin to consolidate his paperwork and prepare to evacuate his offices."

David nodded.

"Told by whom?"

"Senate Majority Leader Brooks called me and said that he had cleared this with the Chief of the Capitol Police—I think he said Chief Ortez—and that I should begin to get things packed up to be removed."

The annoyance that Detective Lee felt that Chief Ortez had overstepped into his investigation and released his crime scene without even consulting him, could be read from a mile away.

Once again, a political decision being made where it was an investigative issue, not political.

I tried to make myself invisible at this embarrassing turn of events for the detective.

"I'm afraid there's been a misunderstanding, Ms. Upton. We're not quite ready to release the scene just yet—we're actually here to do some follow-up investigation. I'm sorry to inconvenience you, but I'll have to ask you to wait to do this until after we've completed our investigation. I apologize for the mix-up."

Denise took a deep breath and let it out.

"That's OK—I really wasn't ready to do this yet—I was just told that I needed to by the Majority Leader. I'm still too emotional right now anyway."

Ah, the potential illness was actually just excess emotions. Probably not contagious.

Denise got up and grabbed her purse to leave.

"Could I ask you something?" I asked.

She looked at me, clearly a little confused as to *who* I was or *how* I fit into this scenario.

I didn't take the time to enlighten her.

"Was Senator Ashford involved in any major legislation or projects to your knowledge?"

Denise looked down.

"He had his hand in a number of things."

"Anything stand out in your mind?" I asked.

Denise thought.

"Well, we were all given certain responsibilities to help him get information on any number of tasks."

I saw a fleeting look pass over her face.

"What?" I asked.

"What—what?" she staggered back my question to me.

"It looked like you thought of something for just a moment."

She looked off to the side and took another deep breath, clearly trying to decide whether to fess up.

"I was just thinking of something that Senator Ashford seemed to be working on that the staff—including me—weren't involved with."

"What was that?" I asked.

"Honestly, I'm not sure. A couple times when I went into his office, the senator would close his laptop or put notes he was working on into his desk drawer. I asked him a couple different times if I could help him on that project, but he said it was too confidential for even his staff to be a part of."

"I have to say that it seemed like he was actually protecting us from something. I can't help but wonder if it didn't have something to do with his murder."

I looked at her.

"And you have no idea what he was working on?"

She shook her head.

"When it came to that project, he clearly was doing his own research and making his own calls—he didn't involve his team at all in that one—and he was spending a lot of time on it."

I stared at her for a beat.

"OK, thanks—that may be helpful."

She looked back at me.

"And you are?" she finally asked, seeking for the aforementioned enlightenment.

"Oh, sorry, I'm a private investigator from Arizona who has been brought in to augment the police investigation."

Her eyes welled up again and she nodded.

"Well, a very good man was murdered, so please, I'd like to request that you give 'em hell."

I looked back at her and nodded my agreement.

"I will do just that."

CHAPTER 67

Denise Upton got her effects together, leaving everything in the office just where it was, and made her exit.

Detective Lee and I waited patiently while she did.

After she was gone, we could talk freely.

"I like her—she seems like good people," I said.

"So, what all have you guys done up to this point?"

Detective Lee took a deep breath and let it out.

"Well, we've scoured both this office and the senator's office, looking for anything that might provide any clues as to what happened. And for the record, it hasn't just been us—we have the first pass, but the FBI came in right behind us and did it all again—and as you can imagine, the feds were pretty thorough too."

I nodded as I looked around.

I had a decision to make. I needed clues to continue the investigation, but two different bureaus had already thoroughly searched both offices and found nothing. Should I spend time going through it all again?

To be fair, they had both gone over the apartment building too, and yet I had found clues they had missed. So, that argued in favor of taking the next few days and plowing through everything in the offices.

Having thought that, I had to admit that the things they had missed were more "big picture" items. They were focused on the minutia of DNA and hair follicles and fingerprints—stuff like that.

I, on the other hand, was trying to think like the killer, and that had led me to my clues.

However, Senator Ashford's office was *not* the place to think like the killer—it was the place to try and think like Todd. Since the apartment was so barren, that was clearly no more than a crash pad for the senator. *This* was where Todd worked and almost lived when in D.C. This would tell me about him, and I needed his help in a way, if I had any hope of catching his killer and the cabal behind his murder.

That meant that this reception area office was *not* the key I needed, his personal office was. I needed to see through Todd's eyes, and his "space" might get me some "big picture" clues to seeing that.

"Yep," I thought, as I glanced around the reception office, "the key, if there was one, would be in the next room, not this one."

I suddenly realized that Detective Lee was staring at me. How long had I been gone in my little internal monologue? Was it long enough for him to notice?

"Are you OK, Blake?"

Yep, it had been long enough for him to notice.

"Yeah, sorry, I was kind of lost in thought."

"Do you do this often?" he asked.

"No."

"Well—yes," I said with a sheepish grin, throwing my own brand of a hail Mary to honesty.

CHAPTER
— **68** —

"Well, I want to thank you for the second-thought honesty—I'll consider myself warned," laughed Detective Lee. "Did you have any epiphanies while you were gone, or was this more like a mental coffee break?"

I smiled.

"For the record, you can have epiphanies while on a coffee break, but yes, I had a thought. Since you guys have done such a thorough job on all the searches through documents, I think I'll do better to just take in a bit more of a 'bird's-eye view' and see if anything jumps out at me."

That comment made me think of something. I shifted my stance and leaned against Denise's desk.

"Speaking of a 'bird's-eye view', did you know the ostrich is the world's largest bird and can grow to be up to nine feet tall? It typically weighs around two-hundred and fifty pounds. People can actually ride an ostrich, but it's not recommended cuz they are dangerous."

David just stared at me.

"They are fast too—over 40 miles per hour, covering over sixteen feet with every stride. Think of that—sixteen feet!"

I made a sweeping motion, hoping he was measuring out sixteen feet within his mind.

More staring.

"Also, despite popular lore, ostriches don't actually stick their heads in the sand when scared—they flop on the ground and 'play dead'."

I shook my head at that mental picture. I wasn't sure, but I thought I

180

saw a twinge of interest for a moment from David at that last comment. So, I plowed on.

"The ostrich is one of the largest omnivore animals, feeding on both plants and small animals. Because of this diet, they actually have three stomachs—one stomach couldn't process this variety of food. And their intestines are over twice as long as human beings—about forty-six feet compared to our twenty feet."

David's eyes were starting to glaze over, so I went for the eggs.

"They also have the largest eggs of all bird species—almost six inches long, and they can weigh over three pounds. One ostrich egg can make over eleven average sized omelets. Their eggs are so big that it takes an hour to boil their egg to a soft state—and get comfortable if you want a hard-boiled egg—that will cost you an hour and a half."

Hmmm. Maybe since we'd just eaten, his interest wasn't that high on the eggs.

"Ostriches also have exceptional eyesight and hearing, and the biggest eyes in all the animal kingdom—about two inches in diameter. Their eyes are bigger than their brain! Maybe that explains why they think flopping down on the ground and playing dead is a good defensive plan when they're scared."

I was laughing—but I was laughing alone.

I tried one last time.

"An ostrich's long and powerful legs are extremely dangerous to predators—they pack a punch—or I guess a kick! They live almost fifty years and when full-grown, they have the strongest and most advanced immune systems in the world."

I know I said, "one last time", but I had one more thing. Forgive me.

"Also, you'd think that if you ate ostrich meat, of course it would 'taste like chicken', but it doesn't—it tastes like beef and is even cooked the same way!"

I finally stopped and stared back at the staring detective.

"Are you done?" asked Detective Lee finally.

I thought about it, then nodded and said, "I believe so."

"Could I point something out?" asked David.

"Sure," I said, thinking that perhaps I had neglected to mention some salient fact about ostriches.

"First of all, you used the term "lore"—cut that out."

"Secondly, you began this whole soliloquy on ostriches by using the term 'bird's-eye view', which in your mind, led you to ostriches."

"It did," I said.

"Do you understand that the whole basis for that cliché, is a bird flying up in the sky, looking down and seeing the 'big picture', if you will?"

"I do."

David stared at me for a moment and then slowly delivered his target sentence.

"Ostriches . . . don't . . . fly, Einstein."

OK, that *was* in fact a salient point that I had neglected to note—possibly one of the most salient known facts about ostriches among the general public. However, I'm not sure that adding "Einstein" to the statement was necessary.

But I had to grudgingly admit that he had me there. That one neglected fact seemed to negate the whole point of, what I had thought, was a pretty cool and compelling treatise on ostriches.

Oh well—whatcha gonna do?

CHAPTER
— 69 —

"Why don't we just go have a look in Senator Ashford's office?" said Detective Lee.

It kind of felt like he said that in order to forgo the chance that I might break into another soliloquy, but I really couldn't blame him for that.

"OK, but ostriches are pretty cool, right?" I said, trying to salvage my treatise.

"Sure Blake, ostriches are very cool."

That sounded very much like he was just trying to placate me, but I'll take it.

With that, we moved on.

When we stepped into the late Senator Ashford's office, the first impression was pretty good. It was a longish room with a high ceiling—the room probably a little under forty feet long by about twenty-five feet wide. There was a big window at the far end of the room, covered in nice burgundy drapes, with the walls painted beige and the carpet a plush royal blue.

I wouldn't have thought you could put burgundy with royal blue, but it worked in a regal sort of way.

The senator's polished, solid-wood desk was sitting right in front of the window, facing the room. On either side of the draped window were flags, the American flag, and the California flag.

On the right was a huge fireplace, overlaid with granite or marble in gray and white. Above the fireplace was a huge ornate mirror. To the left, and by his desk, was a door that I assume went to his private bathroom.

Closer to us on the left, was the politician-approved and required "ego wall" of the senator shaking hands with "movers and shakers". There was a long couch under the ego wall for visitors.

Directly in front of us was a seating area with nice chairs surrounding a cherry-wood coffee table where, I assume, Senator Ashford held meetings with multiple people. To our right, running all the way to the pretty fireplace, was what looked like mahogany bookshelves, filled with books and knickknacks of various kinds.

All in all, it was a very nice and pleasant office, which was currently the focus of a crime investigation.

CHAPTER 70

I walked further into the office.

"I'm assuming that both the Capitol Police and the FBI have been through everything in the desk and any files that were in this office as well," I stated, the question implied.

"Yes," replied Detective Lee.

"And they found nothing that was helpful?"

"Nope—and not a thing about ostriches either."

"Hardy-har-har," I said, unable to come up with any other instant quip that would win this particular battle of wits.

Cindy would probably tell me that in a battle of wits, she feared I was often unarmed. I know that's snarky, but that woman just cracks me up.

I walked further into the office and then went around the desk. I pulled out the desk chair and sat in it, just as Senator Ashford would have. I pulled open a couple of the drawers to see how he kept things.

"Were things left in the same basic order that they were found?" I asked.

"Yes, why?"

"I'm just trying to get a feel for what kind of mind Senator Ashford had. Everything I'm seeing here is very organized and in place. If that was the senator's way, then he was fairly disciplined and orderly. That would mean that he had a process for the things he did, which would potentially greatly benefit our investigation."

"How so?" asked David.

"Well, if the senator was organized, and he had a process for the things he did, then he planned things out. My understanding is that his laptop was not uploading to the Cloud?"

"That's correct, unfortunately," replied David.

"I agree, but the fact that he did *not* have the things on his laptop backed up to the Cloud indicates that he was concerned about what he was working on being either hacked or at least discovered."

"But looking around his desk makes me wonder if he didn't build in a contingency. He was an orderly, perhaps even meticulous person. The idea that a person like that would trust that his laptop would never be destroyed or end up presenting with the dreaded "blue screen of death" is just hard to imagine. All his work and investigation would just be lost if that happened."

"A guy like this doesn't operate like that. Someone disorganized or even lazy might, but not this guy."

Detective Lee was clearly thinking this through.

"OK, but how does that help us? Both this office and his reception office have been thoroughly searched. His apartment has been searched as well. We found nothing."

I thought about that.

"Have you asked his wife or maybe a close friend if Todd mentioned anything to them or gave them anything to hold for him?"

David was nodding.

"The FBI took care of that and said nothing came from that inquiry."

"What about a safety deposit box?"

"None that we could find on record, and his wife went and checked theirs at their bank and found nothing in it related to what we were looking for."

Hmmm.

"OK."

I got up and took a quick look behind the door next to the desk. Just like I was guessing, it was a bathroom. I looked in the medicine cabinet and found nothing of note. I lifted the lid off the toilet tank and looked inside.

Nothing.

I felt a little stupid doing this, since I was well aware that all of these places would have been searched multiple times. However, I wasn't sure what else to do.

I walked back out into the office, where Detective Lee was passing the time looking at the ego wall. I went and stood next to him and looked at the pictures for a moment. They were the typical shots you'd find in any politician's office—nothing of note jumped out at me.

I wandered over to the fireplace and looked at the pictures on the mantel. These were of Todd and his family. They were great shots, most of them taken during real life, showing a nice family enjoying each other.

They made me smile sadly.

I walked down the mahogany bookshelves and looked at all the books Todd had there, once again carefully placed. Placed in front of many of the books were knickknacks from various places in California.

One shelf that was just below eye level had a whole team of bobbleheads—it looked like it might be the whole current New York Yankees team, and even many of the great Yankee players from the past.

That made me smile.

I looked over the impressive collection. So, Senator Ashford was a Yankees fan—and not just a fan, it appeared he was a *big* New York Yankees fan.

I touched a couple of the bobbleheads and made them jiggle—then I touched some more. It was a funny sight. I did about ten of them before I realized that I was being immature and needed to move on.

Wow, I must be growing as a person.

I finished the bookshelves, having found nothing helpful, and then walked back over to David.

Detective Lee looked over.

"Anything?"

I shook my head and said, "Nope—you?"

He shook his head.

"Alright," I said, "I've probably used up enough of your day. I'll run you back over to the precinct, and I'll start looking for another line of investigation to chase."

CHAPTER

— 71 —

It was now late afternoon in Washington, D.C., which made it early afternoon in San Francisco. I decided that I'd better make a report to my employer, friend, and favorite billionaire, Mr. Triplehorn.

"Hey, Blake."

"Hey, Mr. T, how are you doing? How are things in San Fran?"

"Um, I assume alright. I'm actually over close to you in New York City."

"Taking over the world, one company at a time, I assume?"

Mr. Triplehorn chuckled.

"Something like that—although sometimes I like to buy them up in groups—it can be more efficient."

I shook my head and laughed.

"I don't doubt it. Do you have a minute for a report?"

"Sure—hit me with it."

"Well, I've made a little progress so far today, but just a little. I met with the Capitol Police Chief, which was a waste of time, but the lead detective—David Lee—has been very cooperative."

"OK, what's the progress part of it?" Mr. T asked.

"I was able to determine that the assassin came into Senator Ashford's apartment from the roof, not the ground, so that was new information the police hadn't found. We found out how he got access to the structure to be able to get on the roof, which was more new information."

"How did he do it?" asked Mr. T.

"He pretended to be their HVAC company calling to get the code, saying their regular guy had a family emergency, and they didn't want to bother him to get the code."

"OK, clever."

"Then I was able to determine that the assassin was most likely left-handed and around thirty to forty years old."

"Do I want to know how you did that?"

"It was the way he hit Todd. The way the marks on his face were placed, I felt pretty sure that he backhanded him as opposed to punching him with his fist. Since the mark was on the left side of his face, backhanding him would mean his dominant hand was left."

"Good catch."

"Yeah, that narrowed the suspect list all the way down from about one-hundred and seventy-million men to a sphincter tightening four or five million."

"Well, that's good to hear—cuz my 'check sphincter light' just came on. Hardly seems like much of a challenge at those numbers."

I had a good laugh at that. I liked Mr. T—he was my kind of guy.

"So, what's your next move?"

I thought about that question.

"I really think that I need to talk with Todd's wife and hopefully his closest friend or friends. I need to make sure I know him well enough to get inside his head to see if I can figure out what he left us as clues."

"Are you pretty sure he left clues?"

"Yeah, I think so. I was in his office today, and he was a very organized and orderly man. While I understand his caution in not backing everything up to the Cloud, I just can't see him rolling the dice that his computer would never be hacked or even die on him, taking all his investigation and plans with it."

"I'm guessing there's something to be found—I just need to get inside Todd's head and find his backup plan."

There was silence for a beat.

"Well, how do you feel about funerals?" asked Mr. Triplehorn.

I resisted the urge to point out that I just about got whiplash with this change of subjects, and then finish strong with something like, "But, who doesn't love a good funeral?"

Wow, maybe I really *was* growing as a person.

"I can take 'em or leave 'em," I said.

OK, maybe I'm not growing *a lot* as a person.

Mr. T chuckled.

"I'm heading back to California tomorrow morning to go to Todd's funeral. His wife and friends will all be there. Why don't I swing by and pick you up and take you with me. I can introduce you to anyone you need to talk to, and you can get a feel for who Todd was."

That was a great plan.

"That works, Mr. T—a funeral can tell me some things about a man. That would be great."

"Alright, where did you fly into?"

"Dulles."

"Hmmm, that's pretty far out if you're at the Waldorf. How about I pick you up at National?"

By that, he meant the Ronald Reagan Washington National Airport, and that was pretty much just across the Potomac River from me.

"OK, that sounds great. What time?"

"Well, the funeral isn't until the afternoon, and we'll be making up three hours in the time change, so I'll just pick you up around 9:00 a.m. That work for you?"

"Sure."

"And Blake, make sure to go to the private plane terminal. I don't want to have to try and find you, just to end up realizing you're sitting over at the American Airline terminal for some unexplainable reason."

"Sir, I am offended! I can assure you I am an accomplished private jet world traveler, ever since I met you," I said, trying to sell it with an indignant tone. "I assure you that I would never make such a pedestrian mistake as that."

"Shut up—meet me there at 9:00 a.m."

I could tell he was laughing when he hung up.

CHAPTER 72

That night, I got to talk to my lovely bride, and the mother to our twins—Cindy Lou Who—Moran.

"Hey, pretty Momma."

"Yet another nickname, Blake—will your clever romance never end?"

"No, my dear, my clever romance will never end."

"Good. How are things in our nation's capital?"

"From what I can see, really messed up—but I'm doing well."

Cindy chuckled.

"How are the boys?" I asked.

That set off a litany of stories about the antics of the twins. Now, using the word "antics" might be a little broad, since they were just babies and most of their "antics" consisted of a surprising smile or coo here and there. However, I was surprised how much I enjoyed each and every simple story.

I gotta say, the one about Lincoln surprising Cindy by peeing straight up during his bath, would certainly classify as an "antic", and we both laughed hard at that one.

That's my boy!

"So, where are you in the investigation?" asked Cindy.

"So far, I've gotten settled, met the Capitol Police detective I'll be working with, visited the apartment building—the scene of Senator Ashford's murder—and looked around his office on Capitol Hill."

"Did you get anything from any of that?"

"Well, I figured out how the assassin got in and out of the Senator's apartment. I also discovered that he was left-handed. I don't have much more than that."

"Well, it's a start. What's next?" asked Cindy.

"It looks like I'll be flying over you tomorrow."

"Seriously—why?"

"Well, I need to talk to the Senator's wife, so when I was updating Mr. Triplehorn on the investigation, it turns out that he's in New York City—you know, taking over the world—and he asked me if he could drop by National tomorrow morning and fly me to the Senator's funeral in California."

"Wow, that should be really helpful for you to get a feel for the man."

"Yep, I think so too. I just wish I could see you and the boys while I'm out that direction."

"Well, maybe you can."

"How?" I asked.

"It turns out that it's somebody's birthday, the day after tomorrow—specifically somebody's fifteenth birthday."

"Oh wow, I completely forgot—Isabella."

"Yep. And in her culture, what does that mean?" asked Cindy.

"It means the very thing you've been planning for weeks—it's her quinceañera."

"That's right. And do you remember where we're having it?"

"Yep, I do."

"That's right, here at 'Casa Moran'—right on our own estate, oh husband of mine."

Blake was thinking.

"I really don't want to miss that. Let me talk to Mr. T and see if he will drop me off in Tucson after the funeral so I can be there for Isabella's quinceañera. Or if he can't, I can get a flight over to Tucson. That is just too important for me to miss."

"Good call, but I'll see you one better."

"What's that?" I asked.

"Mr. Triplehorn was the key player in getting all seven girls you rescued, and their families, settled here in the states. When it came to Isabella and her family, he got them settled here with us. You saw how emotional he got when Isabella thanked him and hugged him and Susan."

"Yeah?"

"So, invite them to join us."

I thought about that.

"That is a really interesting idea. I'll do that."

We talked some more, and I told Mrs. Moran how anxious I was to see her.

"Blake, just a reminder—we're still in that one-month 'abstinence' timeframe."

I just shook my head.

"What is it with you women? I just say I'm anxious to see my wife because of my deep and abiding love for her, and she immediately thinks about *sex*! Why is everything always about sex with you?"

Cindy chuckled.

"Nice try, champ. Not buying it, but you can keep trying to sell it, if you want," replied Cindy.

I smiled.

"Oh well, I thought it was worth a try."

CHAPTER 73

I got to Ronald Reagan Washington National Airport, or "National", around 8:00 a.m. and found out that flying private meant I really didn't need to get there early.

Ah, the life of the wealthy.

I got the red Challenger settled, and took the extra time to call David, or as we know him, Detective Lee.

"Hey detective."

"Hey Blake, what's up?"

"I just wanted to let you know that I would be out of town for a few days. I'm flying to California to attend Senator Ashford's funeral and talk with his wife. I'm then stopping home in Tucson for an important event, and then I'll be back."

"OK. What are you hoping to find by talking to the senator's wife?"

"I honestly don't know. I'll certainly get a feel for the man from the funeral, but I'm hoping that something will jump out at me from talking to his wife and seeing his family in their home setting."

"I usually have to do things like this to get an investigation moving forward. I just keep stirring the pot until something rises to the top."

"OK. Hit me up when you get back, and we'll see what else we can come up with," finished Detective Lee.

"Alright, talk with you later."

Mr. Triplehorn's sixty-million-dollar Gulfstream 650, emblazoned with "Triplehorn Enterprises" on the side, came floating out of the blue sky a little before 9:00 a.m.

There was no denying it—it was an awesome airplane! I read the brochure about it before my first flight aboard it, and I learned a lot.

This bad boy could cruise at Mach 0.85 at an altitude of over fifty-one-thousand feet and has a maximum non-stop range of seven-thousand nautical miles. Also, the maximum specified speed for the G650 is Mach 0.925, which is almost the speed of sound!

Not bad!

The G650 brochure also brags that they use a Rolls-Royce BR725 series engine for what they describe as *"a silent, more economic, as well as powerful, experience."*

That part always cracks me up, cuz after spending the sixty-million-dollars to buy it, you know the big question all the rich dudes are asking is, "Yeah, but is it economical?"

Hey! Billionaires gotta save some pennies where they can, just like the rest of us!

The brochure I read actually said, *"The Gulfstream G650 is a delight for its passengers with hi-tech entertainment features, wireless internet and satellite phones."*

Seriously—it said it was a "delight". As Mr. T's plane settled to the tarmac, I started planning right then and there to be fully "delighted" by my experience.

CHAPTER 74

I got to walk right out to the plane and hand my bag over to the flight attendant—the same one from the last time I flew on "Air Triplehorn".

When I got into the cabin, I was reminded of one of the extras of this plane—its cabin height was six feet, five inches, which meant I could stand straight up, with a whole inch to spare.

Mr. Triplehorn was on the phone when I got on—conquering or purchasing some part of the world, no doubt. He waved, and I sat next to him while he finished.

Since the G650 had a fully functional kitchen and even a dining table, I wasn't surprised when the pretty flight attendant offered me breakfast.

You'll undoubtedly guess that I took her up on her offer and enjoyed a "delightful" breakfast. See, I was already being delighted by my experience.

The brochure did not lie.

Mr. Triplehorn got off the phone about fifteen minutes after we took off.

I was just finishing up breakfast.

"Good morning, Blake."

"Sir. How's my rich buddy doing today?"

Mr. T shook his head and chuckled.

"I'm doing alright. I'm glad you're going to get to meet Todd's wife. She's a great lady who didn't deserve what happened to her family."

"Me too, sir."

"Hey, I was wondering about something—well, truth be told, my wife asked me to ask you something."

"Well then, by all means, ask."

"You remember Isabella—the girl you met at my house last week."

"I do. I may be older, Blake, but I am not senile."

I chuckled.

"Yes sir. Well, tomorrow is her fifteenth birthday. It's a Hispanic custom to have a thing called a quinceañera when a girl turns fifteen. The word is derived from the word for fifteen, and it's to signify a girl becoming a woman. It's a big deal."

"OK."

"We're hosting the party at our home, and Cindy and I were wondering if perhaps you and Susan would want to join us for the celebration."

Mr. Triplehorn thought about it.

"I would love to be there—and I'm certain that Susan would want to be there too—but I'd have to see if I could move some things around to pull that off. Can I get back to you on that?"

"Sure. We realize that it's short notice, so if you can't, we understand."

Mr. T spent much of the rest of the three-hour trip calling his staff and seeing if things could be moved around for him and Susan to join us.

I just sat back and enjoyed the sixty-million-dollar experience and pretended I was a billionaire, and this was my plane.

It was a fun trip—and I just kept thinking, "Ya got me straight trippin', boo!"

(For point of reference, just consider that an "homage" to Eugene Levy who played "Howie" in the movie *"Bringing Down the House"*—he really delivered on that line to Queen Latifah.)

CHAPTER 75

I don't know if you've ever been in this situation, but going to a funeral where you didn't know the person is somewhat awkward. I had a clear reason to be there, but it's still weird to experience the event when you have no skin in the game relationally.

I have to say, it was quite the event. The church was huge, and it was full. There were a number of dignitaries there, including the President of the United States. When a sitting Senator is assassinated, it's not a small thing. That meant that there were TV cameras and various personalities all around, and honestly, that part felt all contrived and artificial.

Until the service started.

There were definitely people there who were wanting face time and exposure—meaning that they were using this funeral to do the "career-enhancing" thing.

However, there were a whole bunch of people who were there because they loved and respected Senator Todd Ashford, and clearly cared about his family.

I was intrigued by how quickly the "keep the camaras on the money" type of people seemed to vanish from view when the *real* stuff started to happen.

Todd Ashford had been the real deal—a wonderful Christian man, a loving husband, and a caring father—that quickly became apparent.

We were both mourning and celebrating the life of a genuinely good and godly man.

Those "posers", in which group I included the President, could not have been more irrelevant when the focus turned to Todd.

I sat there and pondered that. In this auditorium were some of the biggest "movers and shakers" in the world—not just the United States, but in *the world*! This included the man known across the globe as the most powerful man in the world. Yet when the truth about the life of a truly good man took center stage, those powerful people faded into insignificance.

I gotta say, it made me think about a life well-lived, and the simplistic value it provided juxtaposed to what we're often told is important in this world and in life.

The Pastor—Todd's actual pastor, had a lot to say about Todd, but he wasn't the only one. Person after person got up to tell funny, sad, and moving stories about a clearly great man. We all laughed, cried, and were genuinely moved by what we heard.

Honestly, it was the funeral experience that every person would wish could be done in their memory, but rarely is.

Bottom line: you don't just *get* something like this when you die, you gotta *earn* a funeral like this, by living an awesome life that touches and helps lots of people.

Todd had clearly done just that.

In the midst of all the other emotions I was feeling, I was also feeling a deep-seated FURY!

In case you haven't joined me in my other adventures, I work best when I'm somewhat *enraged* at the horrific wrong that has been done. That rage ignites in me a burning desire to right what has been wronged. I feel an intense desire to exact justice.

I know it sounds all "superhero" again, but it really drives me when I can care deeply about those who have been wronged. Just sitting there, listening to what an amazing man Todd had been, and the difference he was making, was lighting a hot fire within me.

And then, to throw gasoline on that already hot fire, I just stared at Todd's widow and his four beautiful children, sitting in the front row, crying. They lost so much and would be scarred by this loss for their entire lives—because somebody, or a group of somebodies, in a position of power, didn't like something Todd was doing.

At least that was my guess.

"Well, we'll just have to see about this," I thought. As I sat there and fumed, I redoubled my efforts, at least in my mind, to find out what had happened to Senator Todd Ashford and figure out who was responsible and needed to pay.

I took a deep breath and thought, "Oh, it's *on*!"

CHAPTER
— 76 —

As he sat in the funeral service, he was thoroughly disgusted. Come on! Nobody was this good. Especially not someone who had been a politician! He figured your odds were better to see bigfoot or discover the Loch Ness Monster—or both!

However, Mercurius had to grudgingly admit that their first move against Ashford was to do a deep dive on him, looking for the inevitable "dirt". They had brought in numerous investigators who had scoured every nook and cranny of this guy's life. And while he wasn't perfect, they were unable to find anything that was actually "dirty", that they could use against him.

Mercurius chuckled to himself.

It was ironic that Ashford's morality and goodness was the thing that got him killed. If only he'd been a normal politician, with skeletons and secrets that he wanted to hide from everyone, they could have controlled him—or at the worst, just made him resign.

But no, he had to be a boy scout. He didn't misappropriate money, he didn't cheat on his wife, he wasn't a drunk, he didn't drink and drive, he didn't party or use drugs—nothing!

The more he thought about it, their investigation probably supported all the things that were being said about Ashford at this service.

Maybe he *was* that good.

And being that good got him killed.

He chuckled as he thought the old adage, "No good deed goes unpunished."

Mercurius looked around toward the family and did a double take when he saw that Triplehorn was there, sitting with them. He guessed it made sense that he would be there—he apparently was tight with Ashford.

He was bored. He looked around to see who had shown up, but when he glanced back behind him and to the left, he had to look back again. He then quickly looked away.

Who was that? He was quite a distance from him, but he felt like he should know him—and it felt like not in a good way.

He looked over casually and stared for a moment.

He was usually pretty good with faces.

His eyes opened wide when it hit him who it was.

He looked away quickly.

It was that investigator—the one who Triplehorn brought in to look into Ashford's murder.

What was *he* doing here?

Last he'd heard, this Moran guy had been somewhere northwest of the White House—that was the best they could do at locating him—and that was just yesterday.

He had been with Detective David Lee, the lead detective on the Ashford case, from the Capitol Police.

And now he was sitting here—in California, at Senator Todd Ashford's funeral.

Mercurius tried to slow his breathing. He assured himself this didn't mean anything. He couldn't imagine why this man would fly across the country to be at this funeral, but it didn't have to mean that he had discovered something.

He just needed to play it cool and avoid coming into contact with this guy.

This Blake Moran was really starting to annoy him. He might have to consider getting the assassin back for a return engagement.

The assassin freaked him out, but this Moran guy could bring the whole house of cards down if he's as good as he'd heard he was.

And that simply could *not* happen!

CHAPTER
— 77 —

Her name was Brooke.

I just called her Mrs. Ashford.

She was a truly beautiful woman, probably in her mid-forties, who was trying to figure out how to cope with the worst of times for anyone.

We were sitting in her lovely home. There were many people in her home at the moment, many who had come from the funeral to the Ashford home in the gated community, to have some food together and talk more about Todd.

Mr. Triplehorn had asked her if she would be willing to sit down with me for a few moments, since I was leaving later tonight. She led me away from the crowd and showed me into what would probably be called a library or a study. There were pictures of the family all over the room—as there were all over the house—and I somewhat dreaded having to talk to this poor woman whose life had recently been destroyed.

But it had to be done.

Once we got settled, I began.

"Mrs. Ashford, I really appreciate you taking a few moments with me, especially on a day like this, and with your home full of guests."

She smiled a weak smile.

"Honestly, I kind of appreciate the break from all the mourners. Everyone means well with their encouragement, but there simply is nothing anyone can say that will make this better. Grief is just hard work, and I know that watching me grieve is hard work for everyone else. But there is nothing else I can do."

Then she chuckled.

"Also, you can call me Brooke—I hear Mrs. Ashford and I start looking around for Todd's mom."

I chuckled with her.

"OK, Brooke. I'm Blake Moran, a private investigator from Arizona, who Mr. Triplehorn hired to try and get some answers on your husband's murder."

She was nodding.

"Good. For all the encouraging words, that's what I need—some answers as to *why* this happened and *who* did it. I'd take *that* encouragement to this any day."

"Have you gotten anywhere yet?" she asked.

I was nodding.

"So far, I've figured out how the murderer got into the seventh floor of the building, and also that he is most probably left-handed."

"Really. Do I want to know how you figured that out?" she asked.

I thought of the photos of her husband and the bruising on his face, and I hoped she wouldn't make me tell her.

I looked at her for a moment.

"I'm reluctant to tell you that, Brooke, but I certainly will if you want me to."

She stared back at me, then nodded.

"Mr. Triplehorn thinks very highly of you, so I will defer to your reluctance, with the caveat that I may want to know at some point."

I nodded.

"Can you tell me a little about Todd?"

She took a deep breath and then sighed.

"You were at the funeral."

I nodded.

"I know how people embellish at most funerals where even contemptible people end up sounding like saints, but that wasn't Todd.

What you heard today was true—he was a genuinely good and godly man—a great husband and father."

"One thing they didn't mention is that he *hated* politics."

"He did?" I asked.

"Yeah. I'm sure it's no surprise to you that many, if not most, politicians are, let's say, less than good human beings. There's a reason most people don't like politicians. Todd was one of those people. He watched men and women sell-out their constituents over and over. Once they got elected to office, they forgot the people they were supposed to serve. He saw such a lack of principle in the 'ruling class' that it made him ill."

"Why did he go into politics then?" I asked.

Brooke looked off and thought.

"Todd was a very successful businessman before he ran for office. We had everything we'd want or need. But he was very concerned about our nation and its direction. He didn't want to leave his kids a wrecked world, and he wasn't sure how to help fix it without stepping into the ring."

She put her head down.

"I sure wish he hadn't done it now," she almost whispered.

CHAPTER 78

I just sat there in the awkward silence while tears fell from Brooke's eyes.

After a moment, she gathered herself, took a deep breath and went on.

"I guess I would have to amend that last statement. Certainly, from our family's perspective, we wish Todd hadn't ever taken this position, but my husband was a great man of principle, with a strong belief in his responsibility. He needed to do this, and the cost was part of the consideration."

"It just never occurred to any of us that the cost could be quite *this* high."

She looked up at me.

"If you don't mind my asking, are you a Christian, Blake?"

"Yes ma'am, I am."

She nodded.

"OK, then you'll get this; Todd firmly believed that God wanted him to step up and help to change this messed up world. In the story of Esther in the Old Testament, her cousin Mordecai told her that she had attained her position of power as the Queen of Persia, *for such a time as this*'—referring to her chance to save the entire Jewish nation from annihilation."

I was nodding. Pastor Brian had taught on this, and it was one of my favorite stories, both from history and from the Bible.

"This was Todd's 'for such a time', Blake," Brooke said, with a catch in her voice.

I knew it would be inappropriate, but I just wanted to hold this poor, suffering woman—she was in such pain.

She looked up at me with tears running down her face.

"Are you good at your job, Blake?"

"Yes ma'am."

She nodded.

"I would like you to consider something. I have no question that Todd was killed because he was a threat to some very powerful people, and their corrupt way of running our country. Todd was clearly doing some very important work, because some very bad people took the ultimate step to stop him."

I was nodding.

"I want you to be very good at your job, Blake, because you may be able to complete Todd's work—his 'for such a time'. Todd lost his life for that work—I lost a husband, and our kids lost a father. I don't want it to be for nothing. I know the world isn't fair—it's so broken—but I hope you'll approach this case as your own 'for such a time', Blake—a chance for you to fulfill *your* calling, and in the process to complete my husband's."

"Do you think you can do that, Blake?"

I just stared at her, then nodded, feeling quite emotional.

"Yes ma'am, I think I can."

Brooke smiled a genuine smile.

"Thank you, Blake. I'll be praying for you."

"I'll take the prayers," I said, and then asked, "If I may, Brooke, did Todd talk to you about the things he was working on?"

She looked up at the ceiling.

"In broad terms—yes. He was putting together a plan to root out the corruption and graft that is thick in Washington, D.C. He told me that he couldn't just expose all the players, because they were all connected to many of the other players. Those 'other players' were the ones who would have to act to fix the corruption, and he knew they wouldn't.

He said they all cover for each other, so he'd have to approach it a different way."

I thought about that.

"You said that your husband had been a successful businessman. It sounds like he was working toward a 'hostile take-over', in a sense."

Brooke chuckled.

"You *are* good—that's exactly how Todd referred to it a number of times."

She turned somber again.

"Listen, we're sitting here today because my husband, who was a very smart man, never considered that these men might *kill* him. He knew there would be fireworks and posturing, but not murder."

Seeming to abruptly change subjects, she asked, "Do you have a family, Blake?"

"Yes, I do. I'm newly married, and we ended up getting pregnant with twins on our honeymoon, so our home is very busy right now."

Brooke was nodding, with a sad smile on her face.

"Then I would be remiss, and even selfish, to not point out that Todd underestimated the lengths to which these evil people would go to maintain their power. So, I'm telling you, Blake, don't underestimate them. If they will kill a sitting Senator of the United States, they won't think twice of crushing you like a bug if they think they need to protect themselves."

She stared at me, then she reiterated, "Treat this as your own 'for such a time', but *don't* let your wife and kids end up sitting where I am now."

"As they say in the military, *'watch your six'.*"

I just nodded back at her.

CHAPTER 79

I knew that she needed to get back to her guests, so I thanked her for her time and started to end the discussion.

"You have a lovely home. I like all the family photos—it looks like your family got to take a lot of trips together."

Brooke looked around at the pictures and nodded.

"Yeah, we took some really fun trips. We even tried the camping thing—in a tent and everything. I quickly discovered that really wasn't for me. It just felt like a lot of extra work, at least for me, so we only did that the one time. The trips to various parts of the world were fun, and we got to see some great things."

She stood up and pointed to a few pictures that showed them in various settings and told me a little about each trip.

I pointed to a picture of them all huddled together outside Yankee Stadium, clearly wet and freezing cold.

Brooke laughed and shook her head. Pointing to the Yankee pennant over the picture, she said, "Yeah, Todd was a diehard Yankee's fan. He took us all to the game on a cold, rainy day. Now that stadium is in the Bronx borough of New York, and it can be miserable weather if it decides to. That day, it decided to be miserable, but look at my husband."

I looked closer.

"He looks positively giddy," I said.

"Yep, you got that right," Brooke said, laughing. "We were all freezing and miserable, and he was like a kid in a candy shop. I think baseball is slow and boring, but my husband could dissect all the things that were happening, like a frog in science class. He loved it."

I smiled.

"I saw all the bobbleheads in his office in D.C."

She laughed and nodded.

"That's right, I forgot he had those. He was always collecting them. That shows you how much he loved the Yankees. I never got it, but he said that the game was complicated and nuanced like chess, if you understood what was going on. I didn't, but it sure made him happy."

I was glad we got to have this conversation. Brooke seemed genuinely happy to be talking about this man whom she loved—it seemed to reenergize her.

"Thank you so much again for taking this time to talk to me. I'll let you get back to your guests."

"I hope I helped, Blake. Please go find out who killed my husband and why—and be careful."

"I'll try to do both, Brooke—I'll try to do both."

CHAPTER
— 80 —

I walked around the spacious home until I spotted Mr. Triplehorn. He was talking to a distinguished looking man when I walked up.

"Blake, did you and Brooke get to have a good talk?"

"We did, sir. She is a wonderful woman; I really feel for her."

Mr. T nodded.

"Blake, this is Tim Nichols, Todd's former business partner and his best friend."

I shook hands with Tim.

"Do you two know each other?" I asked.

That made Tim laugh.

"No, we just met. Todd and I did well, but we never approached the arena that Mr. Triplehorn plays in. Todd told me about Araby, but this is the first I've met him."

I nodded.

"So, you and Todd stayed in touch after he went into the Senate?" I asked.

Tim nodded.

"Yeah. Even though he had to step out of the business, we still hung around here and there when he was back in town and could spare the time. We'd watch a ballgame or get the families together."

Tim looked down and swallowed.

"It was really special."

Trying to lighten the moment, I said, "Rooting for the Yankees, I assume."

Tim laughed.

"Todd would be. I would just go on and on about the Boston Red Sox to watch him get red in the face."

"Seriously?"

"Yeah, he would get livid if I praised the Red Sox, so, as his best friend, I would do it all the time just to tweak him with them. It always worked."

"It was funny," he finished wistfully.

"Did Todd ever discuss what he was working on with you—especially anything recently?"

Tim thought about that.

"We would talk here and there about things, but mostly about how dysfunctional and corrupt D.C. was. Todd really hated that."

"Did you get the idea he had any plans to change that?"

Tim thought again.

"I guess I did. Our conversations would head toward all the ways the mess could be fixed, and I think Todd might have been planning something to do that. I have to say that he would get kind of guarded if we got too deep into that, but I got the idea he was protecting me from knowing too much."

I nodded. It seemed like it was time for me to go.

"It was really nice to meet you, Tim, and I'm sorry for your loss," I said, shaking his hand.

"Thanks. Mr. Triplehorn mentioned what you're doing. Go find the bastards who did this to Todd."

Tim said that with plenty of passion.

I nodded and turned to Mr. T and asked if I could talk to him for a moment.

We walked off to a corner to talk in private.

"I'm going to go ahead and head back to Tucson, sir."

"OK. Did you get anything from this?"

I thought about that question.

"I certainly got a feel for Todd, the man. He was a genuinely good man who was killed, most probably for that fact. His wife told me he was working to uproot the corruption in D.C., but that he missed the memo that these people play for keeps and would kill him to stop him. I was operating on that supposition, but it's good to get some confirmation that he was working on something."

"Past that, I'll have to let everything ruminate. Often, after I let everything sink in, is the time when my brain is sifting and working and then something strikes me and clues me in. So, while I'm at home, I'll let it all sink in and see where it leads me when I get back to D.C."

Mr. Triplehorn was nodding.

"Do you need a ride back to the airport? I can call for a car," said Mr. Triplehorn.

I shook my head.

"No, I called an Uber."

I then smiled, remembering who I was talking to.

"Oh, that's a car service for normal people, where you call them, they get the message on an app, and they come and get you and take you to your destination. You then pay them for their trouble. It's kind of like taxis back in your day."

I got a kick out of needling Mr. T like this.

Mr. Triplehorn just stared at me with a half-smile on his face.

After a pause, he asked, "Are you done yet?"

I pretended to think about it.

"Yep, I guess I'm done."

He nodded.

"Blake, I own over thirty percent of Uber, which gives me the controlling stake. Basically, I'm *'Mr. Uber'*."

I stared back at Mr. T, frantically searching for some way out of my little faux pas—which means "false step" in French—but it was really more like a "face-plant".

Finally, I simply said, "And now, thanks to me, you now know how that company you own works too! You're welcome!"

Mr. T just looked at me, chuckling and shaking his head.

CHAPTER 81

Flying back that night from LAX to Tucson International Airport, I got to think about the case a little more.

I now understood what a great man Todd Ashford had been—one of the really good ones, especially when you factor in that he was in politics.

Since Brooke had confirmed what I was thinking, it seemed more likely now that Todd had clearly stepped on the wrong toes in his plan to root out the corruption in D.C., and that he was having some success with his plan. Someone, or a number of some ones, who were in the corrupt category, had judged Todd to be such a threat, that he had to be neutralized.

A sanitized word for killed—or murdered.

It also made sense that these corrupt people were still out there, and even more motivated than before, since now their corruption extended to murder—assuming it hadn't before.

Brooke's reminder and Cindy's demand of "Don't get dead", took on more significance when all this was factored in.

I had to do this work on the down low, or my family could end up without me too.

I took a deep breath.

I was glad to be heading home for the party—I could use the break from all the D.C. intrigue. I also really didn't want to miss the celebration and wanted to see my precious family.

Mr. Triplehorn told me before I left that he and Susan would be coming to the party. He was flying home tonight to get her and would be at my home tomorrow.

As an afterthought, I asked him if he might consider bringing Thurston Twelvetrees—his butler and my friend, and his French chef, Jon Paul, also my friend.

He said he thought that was a great idea and he would do so.

I insisted that they all stay at our home, and after Araby said that with the party, it would be too much for Cindy, I told him that it would hurt Cindy's feelings if they didn't.

That got him—Cindy was my big trump card with him—and I was pretty sure I was right about Cindy, so I felt safe in saying it.

When I texted Cindy about all this, she texted back excitedly at the news, so I guess I got that little factoid right.

It was going to be a great party. Our little sweetie, Isabella, was turning fifteen, and lots of our close friends would be there to celebrate with us and her.

Since the flight was a little over an hour and a half, I took the rest of the flight to catch a nap.

CHAPTER
— 82 —

Once we landed, I got my carry-on down and rolled it through the airport and to the sidewalk. My lovely wife Cindy insisted on coming to pick me up, which I thought was an awesome idea.

I was looking around for her USSV Rhino GX—which is basically a tank, so it would be hard to miss. I know I mentioned this before, but if you haven't looked it up yet, you really should—it's crazy cool.

The first time I'd ever heard of it was when I found out that my bad guy owned one, so I looked it up. I laughed out loud the first time I saw it. It looked like something you'd expect some dictator in a third-world country to drive.

It had these odd-shaped windows that looked like they had bullet-proof glass in them, huge, knobby tires, and reinforcements all over—your basic "family car".

Seriously, a tank might have been less conspicuous —it looked like you could shoot a cannon at it, and it would survive—but you couldn't beat it for the safety of your precious family.

The three-hundred-thousand-dollar price tag had been a lot, but we had the money now, so it seemed worth it to us.

So, I'm looking for the Rhino, and up drives my beautiful bride in my ZR1, Sebring Orange, C7 Corvette!

I laughed out loud.

My bride jumped out of the car and ran and literally jumped on me. Seriously, I was standing, holding my wife in my arms, while her legs were wrapped around me, and we were kissing. It was quite the Public Display of Affection, or PDA, and we didn't care in the least.

It was a nice welcome home.

Once I came up for air, I said, "Mrs. Moran, I believe we're creating quite the spectacle."

Cindy laughed and looked around.

"Why, Mr. Moran, I believe you are correct. Perhaps we should display a higher degree of decorum."

We both laughed, ignored everyone else and kissed some more. We were both convinced everyone thought it was adorable, whether they did or not.

I finally put her down and got my carry-on into the back of the Corvette. I then got her settled in the passenger seat and got myself settled into the driver's seat.

The interior of a Corvette is designed with the idea of an airplane cockpit in mind. It's no wonder that lots of pilots and military personnel drive a Corvette.

Mmmm. I settled in and this was nice! I had my fine and foxy babe ensconced next to me, with the supercharged power of the seven-hundred and fifty-five "horsies" of my ZR1 Corvette, with a 0-60 time of only 2.85 seconds, and a top speed over two-hundred and ten miles per hour. Let me be clear—I could get in a LOT of trouble right now. I looked into the rear-view mirror at the impressive "wing" that was meant to keep me pressed down on the road so I wouldn't end up inadvertently "flying" this beast, and then off we went.

I drove and was content to listen to Cindy tell me every aspect about all the preparations for Isabella's quinceañera. I couldn't help but note that this little party was going to cost me a fortune, but I didn't mention that, since I knew Cindy would just remind me that I was now a multi-millionaire and could afford it.

It was her "go-to" line.

So, instead of commenting, I just turned on the onramp to I-10 west, and stomped on it—you know, so that I could safely merge with traffic. We ended up going one-hundred and eighty-two miles per hour to "safely merge with traffic", which earned me the evil eye from my lovely, former Tucson Police Department detective bride.

I carefully and dutifully allowed the speed to reduce to a pedestrian level, as all the other motorists stared with appropriate respect—and quite a few thumbs up.

It was a nice moment.

CHAPTER 83

When we got home, the place was pure bedlam! Our home had been replaced by venders and caterers working late to prepare for a blowout event. I saw that the whole Iglesias family was heavily immersed in all the preparation and seemed to be reveling in it.

Isabella was practically glowing as she ran from one job to another, laughing with Cindy as they worked together to make the next day very special.

Isabella, her mom Consuelo, and Cindy all stopped what they were doing when Isabella's father, José, who was also my estate manager, arrived with the dress.

He carried it into one of our family rooms, and the pride in Isabella's parents' eyes was palpable. To think that they almost lost their precious little girl to human trafficking and sex slavery was unthinkable—and at this moment, no one was thinking about that.

Isabella's quinceañera was the focus right now, and it was going to be a blowout!

—◆—

Later that night, Cindy and, what I thought of as, the "party brigade", called it a day, and I actually got to see my wife alone.

We were in our bedroom suite. I had taken some time to enjoy our fancy shower, including the steam feature, since I was clearly not needed—except to pay for everything.

We snuggled together in our big bed. As I started to kiss her, she came up for air and said, "Just a reminder, stud, no hanky-panky for a little while longer."

I just shook my head at her.

"It's always about sex with you, isn't it? Sex, sex, sex! A boy could really start to feel objectified with you! You know, girl, I have a mind too!"

"Are you done yet?" asked Cindy sourly.

I thought about it.

"I could probably go on, but what would be the point? You already know my whole schtick."

Cindy laughed.

"Yes, I do—which is why I quickly reminded you that we can't have sex yet, Mr. Objectified."

I laughed.

"However," Cindy continued, "If you want to, we could *talk* about sex."

That was like yelling "squirrel" to a dog, I was all ears!

"If you insist, I suppose we could."

Cindy rolled her eyes.

"I'm guessing you'll be disappointed, but I'm talking about figuring out how we are going to approach birth control."

She was right—I *was* disappointed. Not exactly the "naughty talk" I was hoping for.

"Oh," was the best I could muster.

"Oh my gosh, Blake, don't look like a kid who just had his candy taken away from him—we can do your other sexy talk afterwards."

"Oh!" I replied, with much more "muster" this time, and even a little "relish" tossed on top.

Cindy started.

"I thought we should decide what we're going to do about future birth control, if anything, before the big event of 'I'm preggers' ends up presenting itself again."

"It's so great to have Nicholas and Lincoln, but we both got caught off guard with our little "oops" on our honeymoon—or maybe "oopses"."

I thought about that.

"Yeah, that was quite the surprise, but as it turns out, what a great surprise!"

Cindy nodded.

"I agree. So, what are you thinking about kids? From your perspective, are we wanting more, are we done, are we wanting more but wanting to wait for a while—what's the plan in your mind?"

I sat back.

"Well, I would love to have tons of kids with you, but I realize that you're the one who is doing all the hard work—well, besides the 'fun work' I get to do," I added, wiggling my eyebrows at Cindy.

She just shook her head at me, so I went on.

"As far as when and how many to have, Nic and Linc are awesome, a couple of real 'keepers'—and we certainly have no financial limit to consider anymore. But to be completely honest with you, I haven't really thought about this side of it, just the sex side of it—so to sum up, I guess I don't have a plan."

Cindy nodded at me.

"That's quite obvious given how quickly you knocked me up, stud."

I laughed and made her actually high-five me as she just shook her head at me.

CHAPTER
— 84 —

"OK, let's try this from a different perspective that you can relate to," said Cindy.

"What's that?"

"Investigation. You're a private investigator. You have to look for facts and try and put together the truth based on what you find."

I was nodding.

"Well, that's what I decided to do. I figured I should investigate this area of birth control so we could decide what we wanted to do, based on some facts."

"OK, that sounds like a plan," I said.

"Great. Let me tell you what I found out. I should probably tell you right up front that I was pretty shocked about how much I *didn't* know, and how much I was *never told* growing up. And I'm not alone in this—it is shocking how little our world actually knows about this very important area of birth control."

I looked at my wife.

"Well, color me intrigued. Please, my dear, educate me."

Cindy nodded and proceeded to do just that.

"First of all, I ended up coming across a book by Dr. Sarah Hill called, *'This is Your Brain on Birth Control'* that was absolutely fascinating. After that, I found some other studies that were helpful as I did my research."

I settled in to listen and learn.

"Hormones are a big deal to the human race—God designed us so that without them, we cannot survive."

"And that's not just for women. The power of hormones is what makes men, 'men'—but for men, it is more related to testosterone. Studies show that men's testosterone fluctuates based on the time of day, relationship status, having a child, seeing beautiful women, having their favorite sports team or political candidate winning or losing, and even being in the presence of guns or weapons."

"Wait, are you saying that just my being around 'Molly' creates a rise in my testosterone level?"

"Yep."

I nodded and tried to get her to high-five me again, but this time she refused.

So, I figured I had to insert a "Tim the Toolman Taylor" patented grunt here. Actually, I did.

Cindy just shook her head but couldn't help but laugh too. She thinks I'm adorable.

Oh, in case you haven't been with me on my previous adventures, that last reference may be lost on you. You may actually think that I had gone the "seeing beautiful women" track of Cindy's comments by citing some woman named, "Molly". As opposed to my requested "high five", you would therefore also be wondering why Cindy didn't just kick me in my "no-nos" for making a comment like that.

Well, in actuality, "Molly" is just what I call my gun—don't know why, I just do. Now, I have a Smith and Wesson 9mm I can carry, but for sheer stopping power I just think the Glock 40 is better. My 9mm is great for target practice since the rounds are so much cheaper and the recoil is a little lighter, but when I'm getting serious, I carry what a lot of police departments do—my Glock—and again, I named her "Molly". Maybe it's just psychological, but that little extra "umph" makes me feel more confident. I also use Hydra-Shok® expanding rounds so that if I need to stop someone, I don't have to ask nicely. When things suddenly get serious, I can't afford to be polite.

So, there you go—you are officially up to speed, and I am *not* a sexist pig! Well, except with my wife.

We now return to our regularly scheduled program, already in progress—said progress being Cindy continuing to educate me after shaking her head at my quite on the mark "Tim the Toolman Taylor" grunt—if I do say so myself.

Cindy continued educating me.

"Getting back to our subject, from a position of logic, the very concept of synthetic, hormonal birth control should strike us as problematic. If you think about it, we are purposely *stopping* the body from what it was designed to do by God—and we are changing our God-given hormone cycle to do so. At its very foundation, this should cause us to take a pause and ask some questions."

"Research has been done for three to four decades on this issue, and the results are conclusive. Hormonal changes have been shown to affect the structure and function of the brain. For women, this is primarily from the introduction of estrogen and progesterone."

"During the time in a woman's ovulatory cycle when the hormone estradiol is high, typically day 9 and on, listen to how this affects a woman. The woman shows an increased interest in sex; she feels more sexy. Randomized studies have shown that she even walks with a sexier gate, dresses differently, and even has a different smell to her body. She is more energetic, has a significantly increased interest in masculine men specifically, and even shows an increased interest in music."

"Really," I said shocked, the question implied.

"Yep—let's call that the 'up' part of a woman's cycle. This is the time when women are fertile and can conceive, so this response seems hardwired by God into women for the purpose of aiding her to conceive."

"However, twenty-four hours *after* a woman releases an egg, her body releases progesterone, which creates significantly *different* reactions in her body. This part of the cycle typically lasts ten to fourteen days and it appears designed to increase the probability of implantation. Because of this, the woman has almost 'nesting' responses. She becomes sleepier and hungrier, she has a decreased interest in men and sex, and even in masculinity in general, and she often becomes moody or grouchy—the classically known 'PMS', or premenstrual syndrome feelings. I think it's fair to call this the 'down' part of the woman's cycle."

"Yeah—not a fun part of the cycle," I observed.

"No, it is not—but hold that thought, cuz it factors *huge* into the rest of this discussion," Cindy replied.

CHAPTER
— 85 —

Cindy went on.

"When a woman takes hormonal birth control, she is given a relatively high level of progesterone with a low level of estrogen, which tells her body to basically *not* produce eggs. This mimics that second part of the "cycle" for women, the 'not fun part' as you called it. It's actually called the "luteal phase", right after the egg is released, and it *keeps* the woman there, preventing ovulation, therefore preventing pregnancy."

Cindy paused and let that sink in.

"Wait. When you say that hormonal birth control mimics that 'not fun part' of a woman's cycle and *keeps* her there, are you saying that women on birth control *live* in that yucky phase?"

"Oh Blake, you are a poet among men. But yeah, it keeps them in 'that yucky phase'—*basically for life.* Women on birth control are placed in the worst part of being a woman—that PMS, grouchy, no sex drive, progesterone cycle. It creates a lack of motivation, no desire to exercise, being overly tired, and what many women describe as kind of 'being in a fog' existence."

"Whoa. What a horrible way to live."

Cindy was nodding.

"It's interesting that age fifteen is the average age for girls to go on hormonal birth control, because we've seen a shocking rise in anti-depressants being prescribed to young women, which is thought to be a result of trying to combat the 'funk' that hormonal birth control creates in women."

Cindy and I sat there for a moment while she gave me some time to try to digest what she had told me so far.

Cindy then picked back up on the depression issue.

"Research over the last decade has also come to show that depression and anxiety are much more pronounced for women who are on hormonal birth control, and this is especially true for adolescent women at *three times* the risk—and this includes a heightened risk of suicide. And here's the kicker; even after these young women go *off* birth control later in life, they remain at a *significantly* higher risk of developing a major depressive disorder in their subsequent years, they believe because of how the altered hormones from birth control affected their developing brains."

"Whoa, that's an intense consequence. So, very real mental health issues later in life is what you're telling me?"

"That's exactly what I'm telling you. And I have to say that it seems almost criminal to me—and to a number of the researchers I read—that hormonal birth control is prescribed so frequently to young girls for things like cramps, period irregularity, or acne, when we're talking about changing the hormones in a young girl with a developing brain. Simple logic would seem to dictate that we should really rethink that."

I nodded and then asked, "So, since birth control locks women into the worst part of their cycle—the part where she is feeling down—are you saying that to counter that, more antidepressant drugs are prescribed?"

"Yep, that seems to be the case," replied Cindy.

I thought about that, as Cindy continued.

"Just think of the impact of having so many women walking around on hormonal birth control. Since they're stuck in the second, implantation, in a 'funk' stage, that would mean these women in general would tend to be more accepting of unmasculine men, even feminized men, which could lead to them even being more accepting of homosexual and transgender ideology—which women surprisingly accept much more than men."

Now I thought about that.

"Whoa. And the heavy use of hormonal birth control around the college age might explain the more accepting attitude toward these behaviors in college," I said.

"Yep. And this one will blow your mind; a number of studies have shown that quite a few women who thought they were bisexual, after coming off hormonal birth control, discovered that they were now interested only in men."

"What?" I asked, fairly shocked.

"Yep, but if you think about it, it makes sense. These women said that they found that they were drawn to men at times and women at other times. Can you guess which was which?"

I thought about it, then took a shot at it.

"Whoa. When their body was trying to ovulate, so estrogen rising somewhat, they were drawn to masculinity—so men. But when their body quit trying to get pregnant, and went into the implantation part, giving into the progesterone, they were drawn away from masculinity—so in their case, women. Is that second stage when they thought they were bisexual?"

"Yep, during the luteal phase, they thought they were bisexual, since they weren't drawn to men. How crazy is that?"

I had to sit and ponder that for a moment.

CHAPTER 86

I had a thought.

"Do you think the focus on what they call, 'toxic masculinity', starts to make sense when you have a bulk of women, especially college-aged women, on hormonal birth control at the same time?"

Cindy thought about that.

"I hadn't considered that, but it would seem to follow that women, who are all stuck in the luteal, or 'down' phase, could develop a distain for all that is man or manly. And it is true that the whole 'toxic masculinity' both started and is huge on college campuses. That is a really interesting idea."

Cindy went on.

"Studies have shown that hormonal birth control even impacts *which men* the same women are attracted to—primarily in terms of masculinity. A woman leans toward the more masculine men during the fertile, or 'up' part of their cycle, and less masculine men—or possibly even women, as we discussed—during the implantation, or 'down' part of their cycle. It's almost like they feel like they're kind of hanging out with 'one of the girls' in one respect."

"They've also shown that women tend to choose men based on attractiveness and masculinity during the fertile part of their cycle, while tending toward choosing a good earner and emotional stability in men during the implantation part of the cycle."

"So, more 'what a hunk' in the 'up' part of the cycle, and a more practical 'what does this dude bring to the table' in the 'down' part of the cycle?" I asked.

Cindy thought about that.

"Yeah, that's probably pretty close."

"The research is also clear that by being on hormonal birth control, there are dramatic changes, not only in the women themselves, but also in how others relate to them—this stuff is that powerful."

"For instance, consider this; one of the major cues that leads to more testosterone *in men* is when they are around *ovulating women*. Now most people are aware that men today have *only about half* of the testosterone that men decades ago had—there has been a serious decline, and *lots* of concern over that reality. While a number of issues might contribute to this problem, it seems to beg the question that perhaps with so many women who are on hormonal birth control, thus stifling ovulation and not providing the usual estrogen cues for men, this could potentially be a contributing factor to the lower testosterone in men today compared to decades ago."

Cindy looked at me.

"For the record, single *women* got access to hormonal birth control in the late 1960s, and testosterone levels *in men* have been going down significantly ever since."

CHAPTER 87

I thought about that hypothesis, then I had a question.

"Speaking of the change in men in the last decades, let me ask you about changes in behavior that would logically be brought about through the use of hormonal birth control."

"OK," Cindy replied.

"When you mentioned the 1960s, I couldn't help but think of the radical changes in morality that happened during that time. Just the impact of Woodstock and the "Make Love Not War" idea that became so huge changed so much. A lack of morality exploded in society."

"Did your research point to how this introduction of the hormonal birth control in the 1960s changed the moral norms relating to both men and women's behavior?"

Cindy was nodding.

"It did. They first of all noted the incredible power that women hold over men, relative to deciding when they will allow engagement in sexual activity."

I laughed.

"Wow, it's hardly even sexy when you put it that way," I said.

Cindy laughed.

"I was actually cleaning up the way the researchers described it. I believe their specific words were, *'men will do whatever is required of them to get into a woman's pants'.*"

My eyes widened a bit.

"Wow, they didn't sugarcoat that at all, did they?"

"No, they did not," laughed Cindy, shaking her head.

"However, they focused on the 'what is required of them' part. They noted that *before* hormonal birth control, women approached sex in a distinctly woman-way of thinking. Since each sexual act at that time could very well lead to having a baby, they seriously considered whether the guy was a 'good guy', whether he would potentially be a good father to a possible future child, and whether he would be a good provider for their family."

"Basically, 'what was required of them' was a pretty high bar. In light of this, the researchers also noted that for many, sex was therefore saved for marriage—the final requirement. Sex before marriage was much more rare."

"Got it—the infamous 'if you like it, you should put a ring on it' requirement," I added.

Cindy laughed.

"Yep. However, they then noted what happened to women's 'requirements' when hormonal birth control arrived. Women changed and began to approach sex now in a distinctly man-way."

"How so?"

"Now that sex most probably would *not* lead to having a baby, the researchers described the new 'what is required of them', or the new norm, to be simply this; be at the *right club* or *party* at the *right time*."

"Whoa, that's quite a change in requirements!"

"Yeah," Cindy said. "To call this a lowering of the standard would be an insult to the word 'understatement'."

"The researchers even went on to speculate about the change we've seen *in men* during this timeframe."

"Change in men? What changed?"

"Well, going back to that whole 'incredible power that women hold over men' by deciding when sex can occur . . ."

I broke in.

"Wait a minute, I'm confused—do you mean what is required of men to get into a woman's pants?"

Cindy shook her head and laughed.

"I had a feeling you might latch onto their description."

"I just want to make sure things are clear."

"Yeah, sure you do, stud."

"Anyway, they speculated on the change in men during this time—a change that has *not* been good. Not only is there the decreasing testosterone issue, but there is also the change in men not being motivated or even lazy. Less men pursued higher education or higher paying jobs, and more men lived with their parents longer, and more."

"They described it as more men sitting in their mom's basement, playing video games, instead of growing up and moving forward in life."

I thought about that.

"You mean that there may be some correlation to men on the whole not growing up and behaving like men, because the requirements of women no longer demanded that they grow up and act like men to get sex?"

Cindy was nodding her head.

"Given the great power women have over men in this area, that is *exactly* what they were speculating. Men may, in part, continue to behave in a juvenile way in their life, simply because they are no longer required by women to grow up and be strong men to have sex with them."

"You mean to 'get in their pants'."

"Would you stop!"

"I would if I could, but I can't, so I shan't. Plus, you said we could do some 'sexy talk'," I replied laughing.

Cindy just rolled her eyes and shook her head.

I knew she loved it, so I just ignored it.

CHAPTER 88

Cindy seemed to join me in my ignoring, by simply ignoring me too, and just kept talking.

"So, the introduction of hormonal birth control for women may well have significantly altered the development and growth of young men since the 1960s as well."

"Wow, you are *really not* painting a pretty picture of hormonal birth control," I said.

"I know, but there's no pretty picture to paint, I'm afraid. Wait till you hear the 'side-effects list' from the pamphlet that's included with the birth control pills. Their side effects include *bleeding, headaches, weight gain, nausea, increased blood pressure, breast tenderness, low libido, acne, mood swings, heightened stroke and heart attack risk, blood clots, liver disorders, vaginal discomfort, depression, abdominal swelling, dizziness, vomiting, exhaustion, body hair changes, loss of vision, numbness in the extremities, increased vulnerability to sunlight, increased risk of suicide, increased risk of cancer, death,* and more."

I was horrified and said so.

"That sounds like a woman's equivalent to their own journey through *Dante's Inferno*—basically their own living Hell!"

Cindy nodded soberly and then brought all this back to what started this discussion.

"Now, instead of hormonal birth control, there is the option that we can just pay attention to my cycle, where I can know when I'm ovulating and when I'm 'safe', if you will, and make decisions about sex based on that."

"Decisions?" I asked.

"Just being extra careful, maybe using condoms when I'm in my 'unsafe' time—things like that."

"Hmmm. What's the downside to that—it seems like that could work," I said.

Cindy chuckled.

"Well, my OBGYN said that there tends to be a name for people who choose that method of family planning."

"What's that?" I asked.

"Parents," said Cindy smiling.

"Oh."

"You see, the problem is that we'd be taking a very exciting, emotional, and passionate act, and trying to apply some measure of control to it. And since the ovulation time of my cycle is when I'm exceptionally interested in my own 'masculine man'—that being you, *ya big stud*—the most *dangerous* time is also the most *passionate* time. It's the time your girl, being me, will most often want to just 'throw caution to the wind'."

Hmmm, I thought.

"So, big fella, are you open to my avoiding all the mess and danger of hormonal birth control, while we just try and be careful, knowing that we might just end up popping out puppies like there's no tomorrow?"

I laughed.

"Like I said when we started this conversation, I would love to have tons of kids with you, so I'm more than open to that. Also, I have to admit that when you pointed out that hormonal birth control basically locks you into the worst elements and feelings of being a woman, I can tell you that I would *never* want you to have to live life that way."

"And honestly, the kicker was when you said that part of being locked in that 'worst' part is that it would lock you into not wanting to have much sex. I would never want that for you or me! I was already tapping out right there. My wife not wanting to have sex with me for *any* reason is an *immediate* 'deal killer'! It just doesn't work for me."

Cindy just shook her head at me.

"Men."

I honestly couldn't argue with her accurate and ironclad evaluation of those of us with the XY chromosomes, so I just acquiesced.

"Yep," I said, nodding . . . "men," finishing with my best "Tim, the Toolman Taylor" grunt.

CHAPTER
— 89 —

When I woke up the next morning, Cindy was already up and gone. I wasn't surprised about that—she had been heavily involved in the planning of Isabella's quinceañera, and today was the big day.

I did all my morning ritual stuff and then went looking for some breakfast. People were everywhere, and everyone seemed to be in a hurry.

I was *not* one of those people in a hurry, since my whole contribution to this event was to be cleaned up and in a suit by three o'clock—oh and pay for the whole quinceañera shebang—there was that too.

Cindy and I really wanted to do this for Isabella. She was like a little sister to Cindy—and I suppose to me too.

I had discovered that an event like this was not cheap—at least not the way Cindy was doing it. I was spending well over $10,000 on this party, and that number just seemed to continue to rise. Isabella's dress alone was almost $2,000! Start adding in the catering, the DJ, and the decorations, and it starts to sound like some real money!

Honestly, I just quit paying attention and keeping score on that front. Cindy was doing her thing, and I was just staying out of it. Thankfully, we had the money now, and I didn't need to worry about it.

I walked through the house, watching all the people frantically doing their part to make this a great day for Isabella and her family. I know Cindy felt that since the Iglesias family had to flee Cancún, Mexico, for their lives, she wanted to make this celebration extra wonderful for them.

After I got my breakfast—and found Cindy and got an absent-minded kiss and "good morning" from her—I headed back to our bedroom suite.

I watched a little Sports Center and then jumped into the shower. I had convinced Mr. Triplehorn to let me pick him up at the airport, along with Susan, Thurston, and Jon Paul. They were getting in at 10:00 a.m., so I needed to get moving. I got my shower and got dressed—no suit yet, just casual until I had to get "gussied up".

Tucson International Airport was only about thirty minutes away, so a little before 9:30 a.m. I said "adios" to Cindy—in the spirit of the day—jumped into Cindy's USSV Rhino GX and headed for the Tucson International Airport.

I quickly decided "the beast" actually drove pretty well—for a tank. You certainly could count on lots of stares and people pointing—it was not a vehicle meant for a "stealthy" activity.

I got to the airport and drove past the regular terminals and over to the private airplane arrival area. I got out and walked into the private terminal which, no surprise, was quite nice. I glanced at my watch and saw that I was five minutes early.

I wandered around and watched planes arrive and depart. About fifteen minutes later, I saw Mr. T's plane descending with "Triplehorn Enterprises" scrawled across the fuselage.

I'd secured permission to drive out to the plane, so I got into the Rhino, waited for the plane to park, and then was let onto the tarmac through the gate.

I drove up to "Air Triplehorn".

Mr. Triplehorn and Susan deplaned, followed by Thurston and Jon Paul.

There were hugs all around, and then I looked up and saw the pilot, co-pilot, and the flight attendant—the same ones I had flown with.

I waved.

I turned to Mr. T.

"Hey, this party is going to be huge—lots of room for everyone—any chance your flight crew would want to join us? After all, they were the ones who were transporting the Iglesias family and all the girls' families who we rescued from the Los Zetas Cartel. I kind of feel like they should celebrate with us—they were part of the whole process too."

Mr. Triplehorn was nodding.

"If you have room for them, I think that's a great idea. They're just going to be waiting around in a hotel room for us to return tomorrow morning."

I was shaking my head.

"How about they come and stay with us? We have plenty of room, and I'm sure it will be much more comfortable than the Super-8 you're undoubtedly putting them up in—ya cheapskate."

We all cracked up at that. Susan especially thought it was funny.

She obviously had a keen awareness of great humor.

"Alright, let's do it," said Mr. Triplehorn.

I went to the flight crew and told them about the change of plans. They seemed genuinely touched at being included in the celebration.

Mr. T told them that Thurston would arrange a limousine to transport them once they finished with the plane. Thurston was already heading to the private jet terminal to do the honors.

I turned to put their bags in the Rhino.

Susan just had to weigh in.

"I see that you have continued to enjoy your choice of driving understated, non-attention-grabbing vehicles, just like you did while you were in San Francisco with us."

"Why, Miss Susan, if I didn't know better, I'd think you were sarcastically needling me."

We all laughed.

"What is this?" asked Mr. Triplehorn.

"It's a USSV Rhino GX, basically a tank. My wife got the idea after I showed her Santiago Mendoza's Rhino, right before I burned it up in his onsite garage at his strip club. She thought it would be safer for Nic and Linc since people periodically have tried to kill me in the past—for some inexplicable reason."

He looked around at it as Thurston returned.

"'Inexplicable' you say? She may have a point."

CHAPTER
— 90 —

The trip back to the estate was a blast, just getting caught up with everyone. Thurston was just as proper as always, and Jon Paul was just looking around at the landscape. He had never seen the southwest "high desert", so he was quite intrigued. I'm guessing he would label it all "magnifique"!

Once we got home, Cindy welcomed everyone like they were long-lost family, which they kind of were, and then showed everyone to their rooms.

I told Cindy about the flight crew, and she agreed that they should be at the quinceañera—they had played a big role in the saving of the seven girls and their families.

An hour later, the flight crew arrived, and Cindy welcomed them and quickly got them settled in some of the bedrooms.

The estate was almost throbbing with activity—people coming and going everywhere. Susan jumped right in to help Cindy. Thurston was walking around, watching to make sure everything was getting done satisfactorily, he just couldn't help himself—it was in his DNA. Jon Paul was interacting with the caterers, quite intrigued by the Mexican food that was being brought in, asking questions, and tasting the various offerings.

Since things were crazy everywhere else, I asked Mr. Triplehorn to join me down by the pool—it was the least crazy place around the estate at the moment.

We just watched the organized chaos from a distance. Mr. Triplehorn took in the house and the Catalina Mountains rising up to the east.

"You have a lovely home here, Blake. You did well."

I thanked him.

"It's quite small at fifteen-thousand-square-feet compared to Triplehorn Mansion, but Cindy and I are learning how not to stumble over each other. I guess we could call it a good starter home."

Mr. T chuckled, and then changed the subject.

"Since we have a moment, where are you now on the investigation? Was it helpful to go to the funeral and talk to Brooke?"

I nodded.

"I think it was. I feel like I have a really good view of Senator Todd Ashford, the man. He was really a good man, wasn't he?"

"He really was—which makes it so wrong what they, whomever 'they' are, did to him."

"Do you have any plans to move forward?"

I looked at Mr. T.

"I would love to tell you 'yes', sir, but I have to say that at the moment, I don't. However, don't let that discourage you."

"Why not," he asked.

I took a deep breath and let it out.

"History, sir. I've learned over the years that my mind collects data, and then starts shuffling it around, trying to find how the puzzle fits. Often, this happens in the background of my thinking process, like during a party like this. Typically, after getting all that data, something will happen—a piece of the puzzle will drop into place—and suddenly the case goes from 'I got nothing' to 'get out of the way, cuz it's go-time' in an instant. I can't assure you of this, sir, but I'm guessing that something is going to break, based on what I've learned so far—I just have to keep looking while my mind keeps shuffling."

Mr. Triplehorn was nodding.

"OK," was all he said, clearly trusting my process.

CHAPTER
—91—

Isabella's quinceañera was a *huge* success!

Typically, a quinceañera actually starts with a Catholic mass. Being a Hispanic tradition, based on the deep roots of Catholicism in that culture, it makes sense that it would typically include Catholicism. However, Isabella and her whole family had visited Desert Christian Church with us when they arrived here, and had fallen in love with it, including Pastor Brian and Kristi. They had even gone through the process of 'getting right with God' as DCC called it.

So, at 3:00 p.m. in the afternoon, sans Catholicism, we just started with the party, and many of the hundreds of people who were there were from Desert Christian.

When Isabella walked out in her dress, I could see why it cost me almost $2,000. It was a beautiful pink fabric, that spread into bell-shaped folds, flowing down to the ground. The color was perfect against her dark skin, and Isabella was breath-taking. Her hair and makeup were perfect, and even the large, gaudy necklace, along with the earrings and bracelets worked like a charm.

She was extraordinarily beautiful and radiant.

I got a little misty looking at her, as did Mr. T. Cindy and Susan just decided to skip right past the "little misty" altogether and just flat out cried tears of joy.

I don't think any of us could help but think of what had almost happened to this radiant young woman. If we had not saved her, she would have been trapped in sex slavery by the Los Zetas Cartel—her life ruined.

That reality was really brought home by what happened next.

Isabella's dad, José, had just done what is called the "shoe exchange", which was a classic tradition of this event, with great significance. Isabella showed up with tennis shoes on under her dress when she walked in, obviously an odd and out-of-place choice for such an expensive, glamorous dress and event. This was purposeful, since her dad then came forward with some beautiful, spiked heels, signifying her moving from a girl to a woman.

Unfortunately, Isabella knew how to walk in spiked heels quite well because she had been forced to do so nightly at the "King's Club"—the primary strip club of Santiago Mendoza, one of the three strip clubs of his that I torched.

For the record, I say that last part with great pride.

However, please don't mention that fact to anyone, cuz we have to keep up the façade that the Cartel Jalisco New Generation were the actual culprits. That's the only way to keep everyone safe from retribution from the Los Zetas Cartel.

So, mums the word!

Any-who . . .

Isabella stood on the beautiful, spiked heels as the Mexican music ramped up.

Suddenly, there was movement from over by the house, and we all, including Isabella, turned to see what the commotion was.

Two beautiful young ladies in lovely, elaborate gowns, were holding hands and walking down the long walkway toward the crowd and Isabella. It took a moment for it to sink in, but finally I realized what I was seeing.

It was Rosa and Alejandra!

In case you missed my last adventure, Rosa and Alejandra were two of the seven girls we rescued from the Los Zetas Cartel—the two girls whom Isabella had been closest to in Dallas, and even specifically asked me to also rescue when I rescued her.

Mr. Triplehorn had used his many connections to get them settled in various parts of the country, and then he employed the fathers in his own businesses to provide for them.

I don't know how Cindy did it, but she had flown the girls in as a surprise for Isabella's quinceañera.

It was quite a surprise!

Isabella *ran* on those spiked heels to hug the girls. At this point, none of us were going for the "misty" anymore, there were full on tears running down the faces of everyone who knew the back-story. Besides our immediate family and friends, that included Mr. T, Susan, Thurston, Jon Paul, and the whole flight crew who had transported the families.

There was no denying it, it was an *awesome* moment.

And the party was on! There was music, dancing, food, and lots of laughter.

At one point, some of the younger boys pushed some other boys into the pool, which then created a free-for-all of boys jumping into the pool.

It was a party for the ages that lasted well into the wee hours of the next morning.

Well done, Cindy Lou, well done!

CHAPTER 92

After seeing everyone off the next morning, it was time for me to get back to Washington, D.C. I kissed and hugged Nic and Linc, and planted a big ole smoochie on Cindy, telling her again what a great job she did on the quinceañera.

I then laughingly asked her if she could quit spending so much money now.

As she considered my request for future frugality, she said she wasn't sure she could make such a rash commitment right here on the spur of the moment. She said she'd have to get back to me on that request.

"Rash commitment"—what a smart aleck!

I grabbed my bags and jumped into the Uber for the ride back to Tucson International Airport to catch my flight. I had to fly into National this time, again, short for Ronald Reagan Washington National Airport, since that's where my red Challenger was parked and waiting for me.

The flight, again in first class, gave me some time to get my head back into the case, now that both the funeral and the quinceañera were over.

What I said to Mr. Triplehorn about my brain taking in the data and shuffling it around to figure out how all the pieces fit together was accurate. However, this was also one of the most stressful times in any case.

I was heading back to Washington, D.C. with literally *no idea* as to what I was going to do next. I had already seen the crime scene—Todd's apartment. I'd done everything I knew to do there. I'd also seen the senator's office, and I really didn't get much out of that.

I could revisit those sites, now that I had a better feel for Senator Ashford, but I don't know if that would yield any more results or not.

The fact that his widow, Brooke, had told me about Todd's plan to root out the corruption and graft in D.C., made it even more likely that this was why Todd was murdered. However, if he was planning this "hostile take-over", he knew he couldn't really trust anyone to not be in on the corruption. That meant I needed to know what he had found and was planning to use, so I would know who was threatened by this.

Threatened enough to hire an assassin to kill a sitting senator of the United States of America.

I need to know what Todd knew!

I thought some more.

Todd had been a very successful businessman before he became a senator. The fact that he knew how to do business, and do it well, seemed to mean that I could guess some things.

While Todd was being understandably secretive about what he had learned, and the "dirt" he had on various powerful people, I just could not imagine that he would trust hard copy paper and just his laptop with the information.

I just couldn't believe he would do that—and my thinking process just continued to come back to that fact.

As I pointed out before, paper can get misplaced or destroyed. Laptops can get fried or suddenly present you with the blue screen of death. Anything important would *have* to be backed up somewhere!

But where?

I understood his refusing to put all this stuff on the "Cloud". When you're playing in this league, with this kind of power, the bad people can get to "stuff", even if it's supposedly "secure". They probably have their own personal hacker on speed dial in their phone.

But wouldn't he at least keep a flash drive or something? Something you could access if the "burn the whole thing down" scenario took place?

"I know I would," thought Blake.

I'm just really hoping Todd would too.

CHAPTER
— 93 —

Once we landed at National, it didn't take me long to get to the Challenger and head back out toward the center of Washington, D.C. I got onto George Washington Memorial Parkway, and then crossed over the Potomac River on 395.

While I had planned to head back to the five-star Waldorf Astoria to see if I could score my seventh-floor room back—and consequentially start charging Mr. Triplehorn $1,275 a night again—I figured that I may as well use this drive to let Detective Lee know that I was back in town.

So, I put the call through the car phone system.

"Hey Blake, are you back in town yet?"

"Yeah, I just flew into National, and I'm driving back your way."

"How did the funeral go? I caught some of it on TV. It looked like quite the display of dignitaries—even the President. Did you learn anything?"

"Well, I learned that Todd was an awesome man—not just in the way people make it up at funerals, but he was honestly a good man. Which was shocking, cuz, let's face it, he was a politician."

David chuckled.

"Well, I work with and am around these guys all the time, and I would have to wholeheartedly agree—that is as shocking as you think it is, and he really was a good man."

I laughed.

"So, what's next?" asked the detective.

"Well, I was going to get settled, but now that I think about it, if you have the time—and since it's close, would you be willing to get me back into Senator Ashford's office?"

There was a pause on the other end of the line.

"Um, I can, but I'd have to just get you in and leave—I have some meetings I have to attend. Could you make sure everything is locked up tight when you leave?"

"Sure, I'd be happy to. Thanks."

"What are you looking for?" asked David Lee.

"Honestly, I don't know. I'm at that moment in the investigation where I need something to jump out and grab me by the throat. I'm just hoping that's what will happen—and soon."

"OK, I get that."

Something occurred to me, based on what Brooke had told me about what Todd was doing.

"Can I ask you an awkward question?" I asked.

There was a pause.

"I guess, but I can't promise I'll answer it. Also, if it references ostriches in any way, I'm hanging up!"

I chuckled.

"Fair enough. I've been made aware that the senator was working on a plan to weed out corruption and graft in the power centers of Washington, D.C. When I referred to it as a 'hostile take-over', like one might do in the business world, I was told that was accurately the way Senator Ashford thought about it—he even referred to his plan that way at times."

"Wow, that's a big deal—and honestly, around here, I can totally see how that could get a guy killed. The literal *lust* for power is constant, and frankly, nauseating."

I was nodding.

"OK, so here is my question; you know the people and the organization you work for and with—if I end up finding something really important, that can lead me to the punks who had Todd murdered—can you *assure* me that my letting you know this information will be safe? That it won't get back to the bad guys, or even end up getting me, and maybe you, killed? Let's face it, these dudes play for keeps."

The pause this time was so long that I finally took a quick glance at my phone to make sure we were still connected.

"Hello? David? Are you there?"

"Yeah, I'm here. You used the word 'assure'."

He took a deep breath.

"I would have to be honest with you and tell you that I *can't assure* you that your information would be safe—and therefore that both you and I would be safe. Washington, D.C. is a small, close-knit community. I wish I could tell you that everyone at the Capitol Police is as pure and clean as the wind-driven snow . . . but I can't."

Well, *that* was sobering—then he went on.

"Honestly, given the level of power and corruption that we're talking about here, I'd be surprised if the bad guys *didn't* have some tentacles into our department."

"So, long story short—and I can't believe that I'm saying this to a member of the general public—but if you find something that significant, I would suggest you think long and hard about revealing it to anyone in the Washington, D.C. realm. I don't know exactly how you proceed with the case without help, but whatever you tell anyone, including me, becomes part of the official record."

"A record that can be discovered or leaked."

"The fact that you have such 'juice' behind you means that you can do things other people can't, so you may consider approaching this in a more unorthodox way. If you follow the normal channels, you and others might actually end up dead."

I took all that in, pondering that "unorthodox" may as well be my middle name—if it wasn't actually "Winchester".

"Detective Lee, I really do appreciate your honesty on this. Should I discover something significant, I will proceed with the caution you suggest."

"OK, great Blake. I'll meet you at the senator's office in about," he paused to look at his watch, "fifteen minutes."

"Great, see you then."

CHAPTER 94

It ended up taking me just under twenty minutes to get to the Dirksen Senate Building, where Senator Ashford's office was located. Detective David Lee was already there, waiting for me.

I shook his hand.

"I really appreciate your doing this, and I especially appreciate your candid comments about the reality of the power structure around this city. I'm sure that 'there may be a leak in my department' is a tough truth to admit, but it might actually save one or both of our lives, so thanks."

Detective Lee nodded.

"I have a family too. I'd just as soon stay above ground kicking as opposed to six-feet-under—same as you."

He led me through the corridors again to get to the senator's office. He then unlocked the door, and we both stepped through the crime scene tape across the door.

"OK, this is where I hand you the keys and walk away to yet another useless meeting. I have another set, so just get them back to me the next time you see me."

"Great. Thanks detective."

He nodded and shut the door behind him as he left.

I locked the door and took a deep breath, looking around the reception office. I couldn't imagine anything out here in the common area would be of much help—I knew I wouldn't hide vital information out here where it could be stumbled on, so I headed into Senator Ashford's private office.

It was just like before—a nice, large office, a big desk, and a big window, with the California and American flags on either side of them.

I pulled out the senator's chair and sat at the desk. I looked around, kind of begging the senator to talk to me somehow.

Nope. No voices from the dead.

I opened and shut the drawers like before, not knowing what I was looking for, and knowing that if there had been something to find in the drawers, the cops and investigators would have already found it. Just in case, I opened each drawer and felt the top of each to make sure nothing was taped there.

Nope.

I looked over at the huge fireplace, all done up in marble, with the huge mirror hanging over it. Across from it was the "ego wall", with all the shaking hands photos.

I got up and walked over to the fireplace. I reached in and felt along the top and found nothing yet again. Todd had multiple family pictures. After staring at them for a moment, since Todd was such a committed family man, on a whim, I took each of the pictures apart and looked to make sure he didn't leave a clue or message on the back of one of them.

Again, nothing.

I looked at the seating area with the cherry-wood coffee table and the mahogany bookshelves filled with books.

I walked over to the seating area and stared at the books. I suppose I could go through each book and see if there was a clue in one of them.

I'd do that if I couldn't think of anything else.

I sat down on the loveseat across from the bookshelves as the silence enveloped me, and I just thought.

I just couldn't believe that a man as thorough as Todd would do all this work on such an important project, and not have a contingency plan.

As I looked around, I saw the shelf that was dedicated to the whole team of New York Yankees' bobbleheads. Now that I was sitting down, they were almost at eye level. It really was an impressive collection.

I thought back to what both Brooke, his widow, and Tim, his best friend, had said about his obsession with the Yankees. Even what Brooke had told me about baseball being like playing chess to Todd. She said that Todd felt that if you knew how all the elements worked, how to know and plan using all the stats of each player you faced—the slowness of the game just became an element of the strategy.

I admit that I did not understand baseball that way, but I knew some guys who did. They could sling stats around like nobody's business. Who hit well against which pitcher, how often they had faced each pitcher, how they fared against lefties, even in which inning, and on and on. What seemed tiresome to most was like fighting a major strategy war to these diehard fans.

I got up and touched a couple of the bobbleheads and made their heads jiggle—just like I did before. I had to admit that it was fun. I started looking at the various players he'd assembled.

It looked like he had the whole current team represented, but he had some of the greats from the past there too.

Lou Gehrig was there—so great and so sad how he died, with Lou Gehrig's disease.

There was Mickey Mantle, one of the best center fielders in MLB history. And he was a switch-hitter, which made him doubly dangerous.

Joe DiMaggio was there, a three-time MVP with the MLB record for the most consecutive games with a hit—fifty-six. He had some great stats, and that was with World War II taking him away from the game for three years during his prime!

He had Derek Jeter, who spent nineteen years with the Yankees, winning five World Series titles in that time. Jeter, or "The Captain" basically *was* baseball during his career.

Yeah, this was quite the collection.

CHAPTER 95

I felt like I should probably start doing something a little more productive with my time, like start looking through Todd's books, but I had to admit this was fun.

I looked through the bobbleheads a little more and found the one I had been looking for. There was the "Great Bambino" himself, Babe Ruth, considered by many to be the greatest baseball player ever. But be careful, saying something like that around some fans could land you in a bar fight. Opinions run really hot among diehard baseball fans!

However, everyone agrees that the "Babe" was one of the best baseball players ever. After all, he was the "Sultan of Swat", the "Colossus of Clout", the "King of Crash", along with lots of other nicknames. If you want a great list, just watch the awesome movie, "The Sandlot"—*so funny*!

For the record, George's real name was George Herman Ruth, but "Babe" worked better.

And he was quite the showman, well-known for "calling his shot"—meaning he simply pointed his bat toward where he was about to crush it out of the park, and then proceeded to do just that!

Can you imagine how *terrified* the pitchers would be when he would do that?

Something hit me as I stared at the Babe Ruth bobblehead—Babe Ruth played twenty-two seasons in the MLB, but for his first *six* seasons, he played for the—cue the *ominous music*—Boston Red Sox!

"Oh, the *HORRORS*," I thought, on Todd's behalf.

I laughed out loud. I wondered if Todd harbored any resentment toward the Great Bambino for starting with the hated Red Sox team.

The story of that whole thing is legendary. Babe Ruth started out as a star left-handed pitcher for the Red Sox, twice winning twenty-three games in a season and being a member of three World Series Championship teams with the Sox.

Ruth even hit long home runs during this time, which was unheard of during what was called, the "dead ball era", simply meaning that the scores were significantly lower before 1921. Baseball historians are honestly not sure just *why* this change happened in 1921. Many think it appears to be just a simple change in strategy in how the game was played.

Even though he had been so successful as a left-handed pitcher, pitchers didn't get to play in every game. So, Babe decided that he wanted to make the move to play in the outfield, so he could have "at bats" in every game.

Soon after that, in 1920, Red Sox owner, Harry Frazee, refused to pay Ruth his desired salary increase. He instead decided to trade Ruth to the Yankees for $100,000, amid *a lot* of controversy. That trade ended up making the Yankees one of the best baseball franchises ever, and fueled Boston's subsequent eighty-six-year championship drought, popularizing the Boston Red Sox "Curse of the Bambino" superstition.

I chuckled again. Todd probably liked that—*a lot!*

Babe Ruth's career hitting numbers are *absurd*. The Great Bambino went on to hit over 700 home runs over the course of his career, while leading the sport in just about every offensive category, multiple times, and was clearly the deadliest power hitter of his generation.

The Yankees won the World Series four times with Babe Ruth, and he was also one of the "first five" inaugural members inducted into the baseball Hall of Fame in 1936.

Babe Ruth changed the face and direction of baseball. His big swing led to large home run totals and his showmanship drew more fans in to both watch and learn to love the sport.

I'm guessing that from reading all of this, you now have a pretty good idea why there is such a rivalry between the New York Yankees and the Boston Red Sox.

I sat back down on the loveseat and stared at the bobbleheads while I tried to think. As I pondered everything, I realized I was seeing lots of red, blue, and gray in the Yankee uniforms. As I kept staring and thinking, all of a sudden, my eye caught a bit of a different color scheme all the way in the back. It was more of a red, navy blue, and white, that didn't match the other bobbleheads.

"Well, that's *weird*," I thought, cocking my head, doing my best imitation of a puppy hearing his name.

I got back up and walked over to the bookcase. I leaned down to try and see the bobblehead way in the back. I then reached in to grab it, knocking over a few of the bobbleheads in the front in the process. I finally got the one I wanted from the back, and then quickly set the ones back up that I'd knocked over.

I then looked down at what I had retrieved.

It was a bobblehead of the "Sultan of Swat", the "Colossus of Clout", the "King of Crash"—yes, the "Great Bambino" himself . . . *in a Boston Red Sox uniform!*

CHAPTER
—— 96 ——

I sat back down with a thud on the loveseat, staring at the bobblehead, trying to work through what I was holding.

I thought back to what both Brooke and Tim had told me about Todd—the man *hated* the Boston Red Sox—they were the *enemy*. To hear them talk, you would think that if Todd ever even *touched* this bobblehead, it might *burn him*!

Yet, tucked way back in his collection, Todd had included a bobblehead of that hated team. Sure, it was a bobblehead of the Great Bambino, but it was still a Boston Red Sox bobblehead.

How could this be?

I sat there pondering all this. I looked back up at all the bobbleheads on the bookshelf—there must be forty or fifty of them, all of them Yankees.

And then there was this *one*!

Did Todd have some closet love of the Red Sox that he didn't tell anyone? It was clearly hidden in the back, so it wouldn't be seen by most people—it clearly was being concealed by Todd. Or could it be that just because it was the great Babe Ruth, he'd made an exception?

I just kept looking at what I was holding, then looking up at the shelf of Yankee bobbleheads.

It just didn't *compute*!

From all the people who knew and loved him, who were around him the most, the Boston Red Sox were the *enemy*, and sports hatred is a real and serious thing in the sports world.

Yet look at what I am holding in my hand.

I just kept pondering it.

One word kept coming back to my mind.

Enemy.

I thought about that.

Not just *an enemy*, but Babe Ruth was one of the most powerful and scary "enemies" in the history of baseball.

If he was on the *other team.*

I was holding a bobblehead representing a scary and powerful adversary, who at this time was an "enemy" because he was on the hated opposing "team".

Todd should *hate* this bobblehead.

Suddenly, my eyes went wide.

Maybe he *did*!

I quickly looked down at the bobblehead in my hands. I began to examine it more closely. I shook it to see if I heard anything rattle.

I didn't.

I moved the bobble "head" itself over to try and see if it was removable.

I didn't seem to be, plus the neck part was too small for anything to be squeezed in there.

I carefully looked over the surface.

I didn't find anything.

I turned it over and looked at the base.

I noticed a line where the base appeared to have been cut open. I tried to move it, but I couldn't budge it.

I sat the bobblehead down on the coffee table and jumped up, hustling over to Todd's desk. Inside, I found what I was looking for—a small utility knife.

I ran back to the coffee table, sat down, and picked up the bobblehead. Turning it over, I took the utility knife and started picking at the line on the base.

I'm really hoping Brooke will be OK with this since I'm going to have to destroy this bobblehead, at least a little, to get it open.

But I don't have to. The piece ended up popping right off, and I can see it was just held on with a small drop of glue.

I look inside.

Jammed into the evil bobblehead of the hated enemy, opposing Boston Red Sox team, is a *flash drive*.

CHAPTER
— 97 —

As I stare at the flash drive in my hand that I had just extracted from the rogue Boston Red Sox bobblehead, I think I was getting Todd's reasoning.

He needed to back up his research. This item worked effectively to accomplish this, being virtually undetectable by anyone else.

Even in the event of his demise, if he actually did consider that, at some point, someone, probably Brooke, would get his things and come across this bobblehead. Seeing it in his collection would literally *baffle* anyone close to him, hopefully causing them to investigate and discover the treasure he'd left for them.

The reason it was held with just a dab of glue was because he had to retrieve it whenever he needed to update the evidence on his computer.

At least I sure hoped the evidence that had been on his destroyed laptop was what was on this drive.

First thing I'd better do is find out what's actually on this drive.

I got up and looked around. No desk computer in this office—it's probably in some police evidence locker somewhere.

Maybe there's one in the outer office, so I ran out there.

Nope. And a computer would probably need a password to access it anyway.

My car.

I had just come from the airport, so I had all my stuff with me, which included my laptop.

I put the flash drive in my pocket and then carefully put the Boston

Red Sox bobblehead back in its place, behind all the other Yankee bobbleheads.

I then made sure that everything was put back, which caused me to see the utility knife sitting on the coffee table.

Well, *that* would've been a big mistake!

I put that back and then checked everything else. I turned off all the lights, stepped through the crime scene tape and locked the door.

I walked down the hallway and out to the Challenger, trying to stay cool, look like I belonged, and trying not to run.

I got into the car, locked the doors, and reached around to get my bag. I got my laptop out, opened it, and fired it up.

When it was ready, I said a little prayer and then put the flash drive in the port.

It came up on the screen and asked for the password.

Well, of course it did!

I tried all the obvious ones: I hate the Boston Red Sox, Boston Red Sox Suck, Yankees, Yankees Rule, all the nicknames I knew for Babe Ruth, Brooke's name, and I was running out of ideas. I even tried one, two, three, four—just in case Todd went low-tech. I didn't know their anniversary date or their birthdays. And it could be any number of other things, the worst of all, but the best for safety, being a totally nonsensical, randomized set of letters, numbers, and symbols.

I let go with a heavy sigh.

What was I going to do. I felt like Todd had given me the information I'd been looking for—at least I sure hoped so—but I needed to get this open, and I didn't know how I could do that.

I thought about calling Detective Lee and asking him for help, but I quickly discarded that idea. David had made it clear that he was somewhat insecure about his department—maybe a little, maybe a lot. The last thing I needed was to have this get out—that I had found some potential evidence that could bring down the power structures of the nation. I might find myself enjoying a swim in the Potomac while attached to some lovely, and quite fashionable, concrete blocks!

What was I going to do? This was HUGE, and I needed to figure this out!

Suddenly, the answer hit me.

I needed to go to Fort Pierce, Florida.

CHAPTER
— 98 —

Now, there's a very real possibility that you have *no idea* why I needed to head to Fort Pierce, Florida—at least if you missed out on my awesome adventure there, rescuing twelve-year-old Skylar De Le Croix, from a murdering pervert.

So, the short answer to the question "why"?

Winston.

If you have a computer problem that needs to get solved—or perhaps "busted"—"who ya gonna call?" Call Winston! (I realize that's only funny or even relevant to those who remember the 1984 movie "Ghostbusters", or maybe some of the remakes, but I thought it was worth a shot. So, sue me—well, actually, please don't—I have a lot of money now that I would prefer to not part with.)

Any-who . . . back to Winston.

To tell you about Winston, I should start with FBI Assistant Special Agent in Charge, "Maverick" Holmes. As you might guess, he was the ASAC in Fort Pierce, Florida.

Maverick was about like you would guess with a name like that, but he was a good guy, and he was genuinely appreciative for my successful efforts in rescuing "Sky" from the pervert. He also was appreciative that said "pervert" was currently awaiting an appointment with a lethal needle in a maximum-security prison.

Which begs the question: Why do they sterilize the needles they use for *lethal* injections? Are they worried the death row criminal will get an infection?

Weird.

I'll let you ponder that deep question on your own time so I can move on.

It was ASAC Holmes who introduced me to Winston, his very own, amazing with computers but not so much with people, computer dude. I so dug Winston that he ended up being one of the groomsmen at my wedding.

Last time I saw Winston, he was a good forty pounds over what could be called "svelte" by anyone he met. However, when he was working on his machines, which he called his "babies", he was as happy as a pig in slop, which I just realized does not paint a flattering picture of a guy who I think is awesome.

I tell you all this to explain why I am currently back in my red Challenger, heading, post haste, right back to National airport, from whence I just both arrived, and then departed.

If you're wondering, I'm not sure why I'm talking this way, but it seems that I have become a little whimsically archaic for no apparent reason.

I'll stop.

Forsooth! OK, NOW I'll stop.

Follow my logic on this and see what you think.

I may—and I stress "may", have just found evidence of what Senator Todd Ashford was planning to do in his aforementioned "hostile takeover", to eradicate the corruption and graft that is rife throughout Washington, D.C.

My problem: I was basically told by Detective David Lee that he could not assure me that evidence turned over to him would remain secret—i.e., the bad guys might be made aware of it—they might even *be* in his department.

I have to say that when the fact of one dead United States Senator finds itself at the top of our "Reality List", his inability to "assure" me of safety was *not reassuring*.

In short, I would like to keep breathing.

So, that means I need to take a run at this myself, but some of the things I need done would have to take place through "official channels".

Thus, the conundrum.

Then there's this; since it was a U.S. Senator who was murdered, the FBI holds a level of jurisdiction. However, when I consider the FBI around the beltway—or Washington, D.C., I'm right back to the corruption and graft issue in D.C.—i.e., there's probably personnel in the D.C. FBI office who are dirty too.

End result, once again—I find myself no longer breathing.

However, I know Assistant Special Agent in Charge "Maverick" Holmes and Winston—they are good dudes. Now, don't get me wrong, ASAC Holmes can be a little uptight—I mean, he's in the FBI after all. But he's not so tight that if you shoved a lump of coal up his butt, it would come out as a diamond, you know?

What? Why are you looking at me like that? Too graphic? Too crude? Hang on—let me re-read it.

Tick-tock; tick-tock; tick tock.

Yeah, you're right, that was unnecessarily graphic. I take that back, and let's just not mention that to Cindy—she believes that I'm growing as a person since we got married. I would hate to disappoint her.

Bottom line: Maverick is a good dude.

(Yes, I'm currently chuckling because I just used the word "bottom" in the context of this discussion, but I'm neither confirming nor denying the significance of its use.)

CHAPTER
— 99 —

Hopefully you followed my previous thought progression. I am going to need some things the FBI can provide, but I *can't trust* the FBI office in D.C. to keep me alive. Since I have to do all this on the "down low" to avoid being murdered, I am heading to Fort Pierce, Florida, where I have FBI personnel who I know I can trust.

And they still might tell me they can't help me.

But I'm going to at least try—face to face.

Which explains why I was about to find myself on a second plane today, this time flying from Ronald Reagan Washington National Airport to Orlando International Airport.

I had gone ahead and turned in my red Challenger, since I didn't know how long I'd be gone, or if I'd need to drive something different when I got back.

However, before I "flew the coop", I needed to let Detective Lee know I was leaving yet again.

"Hey Blake, did you finish up in the senator's office?"

"I did. Listen, it turns out that I'm going to have to get out of Dodge for just a little while again."

"Oh, did something personal come up?"

Hmmm. I didn't want to lie to the detective, but I also couldn't tell him anything significant.

"Um . . . no," was all I could think to say.

There was silence on the phone.

"Did something happen relative to the case?" he asked.

This time, there was silence from my side of the conversation.

"Um, I would rather not say at this juncture."

"You would rather not say?"

I took a deep breath.

"Do you remember our conversation about certain 'assurances' you thought you could and could not provide?"

"I do."

"Well, until I have, let's call it, actionable evidence, I would like to table this conversation."

"Actionable evidence."

"Yes."

"Kind of cryptic, wouldn't you say?"

"Are you kidding? I think it is *crazy* cryptic, but I don't know what else to do. I guess I'm asking for you to give me a little rope to do my thing, and if I can make it all come together, then I'll be able to be straight with you."

I paused and waited.

"OK, but just make sure you don't end up hanging yourself on the rope I'm extending you, cuz I might end up hanging right there next to you."

"Got it, Detective. I'll be careful, and I'll be in touch."

I took a deep breath. I was glad to have that conversation over.

CHAPTER
— 100 —

Once I flew into Orlando, I rented yet another car and made the just over one-hundred-mile trip down the east coast of Florida to Fort Pierce.

Now, in case you weren't with me on my Florida adventure, if you rent a car in Florida, you'd better be ready for the "would you like to buy a toll pass with that rental" discussion.

The first time I was asked this, I tried some humor. "What? Is this like the troll waiting under the bridge for the three 'Billy Goats Gruff?'" They didn't even acknowledge my humor—it's like working at the airport rental car agency was not the fun and jocular place that I imagined it would be.

Go figure.

Any-who . . .

Florida operates toll roads all over the state, and if you don't have this pass that you pay for, you'd get hit for tons of tolls—turns out the toll pass is cheaper.

You might wonder, "But do I have to take the toll roads?" which is just the question I asked the first time. Clearly, great minds work alike!

It turns out that all the fastest routes are toll roads, so they pretty much have you.

If you're about to ask, "How do they even know who has the pass and who doesn't?" so did I. (Given your progression of questions, I'm starting to feel quite sympatico with you.)

Anyway, I was told, "They have cameras everywhere that take your picture when you drive on the toll roads, and they also get a pic of your license plate."

So, you hang the pass they give you on your rear-view mirror and that expedites the process.

Not "big brother" at all, right?

To be fair, this is one of the ways Florida gets away with not charging a state income tax—you get 'em when they drive! And this way, a whole bunch of vacationers, who just want your weather at certain times of the year, pay a bunch of the freight!

Long story short—or actually, long story still left long, and going on and on—I got the toll pass. I wasn't about to take the "long way". After all, I was a multi-millionaire now, and Mr. Triplehorn was a multi-billionaire, and he was the one actually paying the freight.

Sure enough, when I got on I-95 south, it was a toll-road and there were all the cameras!

I started making funny faces at "the man" every time I hit a bank of cameras, but even I got bored with that after the first couple—and I'm really immature!

About an hour and a half later, I pulled into the parking lot of the FBI in Fort Pierce, Florida.

I had left Arizona early this morning, stopped off in Washington, D.C. for some excellent sleuthing, and was now in southern Florida in the late afternoon.

CHAPTER

— 101 —

"What do you mean, he landed at National and hours later turned around and flew back out of National?" he yelled. Apparently, the response from the party on the other end of the line was not acceptable, because Mercurius screamed again and just threw his phone across the room.

Lucky for him, it landed on the couch instead of breaking into a number of pieces.

He was pacing back and forth across his large office. He was really getting a bad feeling about this private investigator. He'd been way too successful in past cases, and his actions might be indicating that he was beginning to make headway in this one.

He was also having trouble keeping tabs on him. Usually, he was pretty much able to know about the same amount the authorities knew, but for some reason, there was no information coming from his sources.

Their excuse was that there was no information to give because nothing seemed to be happening—or at least nothing was being reported or recorded.

That last part was the concern.

He walked across the office, sat on the couch, and picked up his phone. He took a deep breath and called a number he hoped to never have to call again.

"Yes?"

"Hello, I was calling about our former business deal. I was wondering if you might be available in the event that I would need you for some follow-up work on that same case."

There was a pause.

"There would be a vig for continued involvement."

Mercurius was confused.

"There would be what?"

There was a sigh from the assassin—he hated dealing with amateurs.

"It comes from the word vigorish and is an additional fee charged for my continued involvement."

"We paid you well the first time to kill a U.S. Senator—why would we have to pay you more than that to kill a lessor mark?"

A deep breath.

"First of all, shut up, you idiot! You're talking about an op over an open phone-line, which makes me want to both hang up on you and come to your office or home and kill you right now. I know that you have family—perhaps I'll kill them too!"

Mercurius' face colored.

"Secondly, each subsequent hit increases the odds that some mistake could be made, and it certainly causes law enforcement to look even harder at the continued killing."

"So, more potential heat equals a sizable vig."

"How sizable?"

"Double."

"What? That's millions of dollars more! Why should I do that?"

"Do I have to remind you that *you* called *me*? Clearly, you already *have* a reason that you should pay me, or we wouldn't be having this conversation."

"Obviously you are not quite ready to bite the bullet and pay up, so you should *not* have called me. If you decide you want this, do not even consider calling me again and trying to jerk me around. If you do so, best-case scenario, my price will be tripled instead of doubled—and worst-case scenario, I will simply come visit you and slit your throat after beating you."

"Either way, I will be *done* with you."

Mercurius' hand was shaking as he realized the assassin had already ended the call.

CHAPTER

— **102** —

The FBI headquarters in Fort Pierce looked like a typical office building, but their view of the Atlantic Ocean, which was just a couple blocks away, was awesome!

Getting out of the car, I have to admit that I thought you'd have a specific question for me, long before this—something down the line of, "Why didn't you just call first instead of flying all the way to Florida?"

Oh, you *did* have that question? Well, come on, you have to speak up.

Here's your answer: some of the things I needed to say to Assistant Special Agent in Charge "Maverick" Holmes and Winston, should really *not* be said over the phone. But the main reason is that it will be much more difficult for ASAC Holmes to turn me down after I've traveled all the way here, compared to really easy to turn me down over the phone.

Manipulative, you say?

Uh huh. But you use the tools you have.

I went into the familiar building and up to the reception counter. The receptionist recognized me immediately, and enthusiastically greeted me. What I did here before kind of gave me superstar status.

I asked for ASAC Holmes, and she said she would check.

She did, and then said I could go right back, since I knew my way.

That's kind of funny. You see, the first time I showed up here, ole "Maverick" kept me waiting for forty-five minutes to "put me in my place" and remind me who "the big dog" was. There really should be a manual someplace with the wait times listed, just to remind everybody who is who.

Hmmm. And I got to go right in this time.

I would start barking, but that might come off to some people as a little strange, and we can't have that.

Maverick's receptionist waved me to go in, and when I turned into his office, ASAC Holmes greeted me *warmly*.

"What do you want, Moran, and why are you here? Oh, and let me just ask the obvious question right up front, why me?"

I just shook my head and said, "Ah, ASAC Holmes, it's good to see you too, but I don't really have time for all your sentimental interaction. And frankly, as a man, all this 'mush' is just a little embarrassing and off-putting."

You might think that I'd get a smile or a chuckle from the ASAC, but that would only be because you don't really know him. He's not an especially "jocular" sort of guy.

Assistant Special Agent in Charge Maverick Holmes was a big dude, probably about six feet, four inches—which was my height—and about two-hundred-fifty pounds, which was a good seventy pounds more than me, and not a lot of his weight seemed to be going to fat.

ASAC Holmes just looked at me.

"May I?" I asked, pointing to the chairs in front of his desk.

"Must you?" he asked.

I chuckled and sat down.

I got settled, folded my hands, and began.

"I can clearly tell that you've missed me, but I want to get right into my current case. I'm working on a case that has huge national security issues, potentially involving numerous members of both the U.S. Senate and the House of Representatives, perhaps even going all the way to the top, yep, right up to the White House."

We can stop at this juncture, because I have to believe that you're wondering, "When did all *this* happen?"

Well, it didn't. However, it *could* be true. The only problem with what I just said is that I had absolutely *no evidence* for any of it. Other than that, it was all accurate.

Here was the deal; I needed Maverick's help, and to get him to even consider what I needed him to do, I had to "sell" what I had—even if I didn't officially "have" it as far as I knew.

ASAC Holmes responded.

"That basically tells me nothing and I'm pretty sure I'm getting a hint of the distinct smell of bullshit coming across this desk."

Whoa, don't sugarcoat your feelings, Maverick! I thought.

I tried another tack.

"OK. I was responsible for one of the biggest and most popular busts ever in the history of this office. The bringing down of a serial rapist and murderer of young girls, would not have happened for a long time, if at all, without my intervention."

"So, I'm cashing in a chit. You owe me, Holmes, and we both know it, and I need your help."

ASAC Holmes just looked at me. He knew what I just said was true, and deep down, he was really grateful for what I had done. The problem was that he was law enforcement, and even deeper down, it really ticked him off that I was able to accomplish what scores of law enforcement had not been able to do.

All I could think was, "Well, sorry Sherlock—put on your big boy pants—it's not my problem that I'm that good. Life's tough, get a helmet. I need your help and I'm calling in a debt."

(Please don't miss that I said "Sherlock". Do you get it? He is ASAC "Holmes", and I called him "Sherlock" in my mind. I'm going to give you a moment to ponder that, and then to crack up, and finally, to quit laughing, and then we'll move on.)

Tick-tock, tick-tock, tick-tock.

Are you done yet? Well, sorry, finish laughing on your own time, I have to get back to the story.

Finally, ASAC Holmes responded.

"Fine, I owe you. What do you want?"

"A phone call," I said.

CHAPTER
— **103** —

Maverick was clearly confused.

"Like, you want to make a phone call?"

"Not exactly. I need a video-conference call with you, me, and Winston in this room."

"Who are we videoconferencing with?"

"My wife, Cindy Moran."

ASAC Holmes just stared at me.

"What are we talking about?"

"I'll tell you that when we do it, sir."

He stared some more.

"That's all you're going to tell me?"

"That's the 'chit' I'm cashing, sir. I need you to trust me, based on my past performance and success."

"I'm also assuming you heard what I ended up doing with the *'See Me Killer'* in San Fran?"

Maverick stared at me.

"Yes, I did—and that was damn good work, Moran. We actually now use it as a case study at Quantico."

He said that with grudging respect.

That was pretty cool to hear. In case you didn't get the memo, Quantico is a campus that houses the FBI Academy, the FBI Laboratory Division, the Operational Technology Division, and the Hostage Rescue Team. It's located on the U.S. Marine Corps Base, Quantico, thirty-six miles outside Washington, D.C. Quantico is where all FBI employees receive training and experience to prepare them for real-life situations in the field.

And apparently, I'm like one of their *professors* now!

I can hardly wait to tell Cindy! Knowing myself, this might make me a little hard to live with for a while! I wonder if Cindy would be willing to *call* me "professor"?

"Hello! We're losing daylight here!" said ASAC Holmes, snapping his fingers at me.

Oh, my inner monologue got me in trouble again.

"Oh, sorry, my bad. Anyway, all these successful cases should give me all the gravatas I need to ask for this favor. What do you say, ASAC Holmes?"

He eyed me for a moment.

"Fine," he said grudgingly.

He leaned across his desk, pushed the intercom button and said, "Please have Winston from IT join us."

"Yes sir," is all that came back.

I briefly pondered if there might be another "Winston" in the building from a different department, but I decided to just keep that to myself.

CHAPTER
— 104 —

While we waited for Winston to join us, ASAC Holmes and I caught up about our families and our lives since we had worked together.

Psych! Or the more slang, *Sike!*—depending on which one you prefer. Did I get you? Seriously, do you think two dudes like us were having sweet tea together? Sharing our feelings? What? Did you picture us wearing summer frocks?

Nope! Maverick was actually eager to know the inside scoop on the *"See Me Killer"*, so I told him.

Then Winston showed up.

When Winston knocked and walked into ASAC Holmes' office, he was *shocked* to see me standing there. Do you know how I know that? His right eyebrow rose slightly, and as you might remember—for Winston, that's huge!

I hadn't seen him since he stood up with me at my wedding, so I got up and gave him a big hug. The fact that with one hand, he patted me on the back, letting me know that we could stop now, just showed how much he had missed me.

"How are you, my man?"

Winston just nodded—but spoke volumes in the process.

OK, now with all that sentimentality out of the way, ASAC Holmes' earlier comment that we were "losing daylight" was accurate, so I got down to business.

I asked Winston to sit, and then said, "Hang on just a moment guys," as I FaceTimed my bride.

"Hey, stud! How's my man doing in our nation's capital saving the world?"

I grinned from ear to ear, cuz I knew my wife was about to be horrified and embarrassed when she realized she had just said that in front of the Assistant Special Agent in Charge of the Fort Pierce office of the FBI.

So, as the good husband that I am, I said, "Hey, babe, I'm here with the Assistant Special Agent in Charge of the Fort Pierce, Florida, office of the FBI—and Winston!"

Her face *froze*. Oh, if looks could kill!

I turned the phone to show Maverick and Winston, then turned it back to me.

"You could have told me that earlier."

"I suppose I could've, but you were so anxious to call me 'stud', that I hesitated to get in your way."

Another look—this one a bit exasperated.

"What do you *want*, Blake? And why are you in Florida instead of Washington, D.C.?"

Oh, I guess all the sugar was gone and we were getting right down to business.

I smiled.

"I'm really not calling you just to punk you—although I'd be lying if I didn't admit it was quite the *perk*!" I said laughing.

It turned out that I was laughing alone, so I went on.

"Listen, babe—I honestly need your professional take on something from all your years as a detective with the Tucson Police Department. I need a local police officer's take to help me proceed."

That seemed to soften her some.

"Answer the other question though, Blake. You left early this morning for Washington, D.C. *Why* are you in Fort Pierce, Florida, now?"

"Yeah, it's been a busy day, and I will answer that question, my dear."

I looked over at Winston.

"My man, could you take my phone and get it to project onto ASAC Holmes huge wall screen?"

Winston nodded once, took my phone, leaned over ASAC Holmes' computer, typed a few commands to turn the screen on, then worked some magic on my phone and there was Cindy on the wall—huge!

"Whoa, look at that *resolution*! You guys really do have all the neat toys, don't you?"

Maverick just stared at me.

"Can you see everybody now, Cindy?" I asked.

Cindy looked around the room and said, "Yes".

"OK. Now, I need to tell you three a story."

CHAPTER
— **105** —

To say that I had their attention would be a gross understatement—so, let's just call it "undivided".

"Cindy, you and Winston both know Mr. Triplehorn."

I turned toward Winston.

"Remember, you met him at the wedding—he's my favorite billionaire?"

Winston nodded.

I turned toward ASAC Holmes.

"Mr. Araby Triplehorn is the one who hired me to go after the *'See Me Killer'* in San Francisco. He's the twenty-third richest man in the world, and he and his daughter Susan have become close friends of our family."

ASAC Holmes was nodding.

"Wasn't Susan Triplehorn the one you saved from the killer?" asked Maverick, being quite familiar with the famous story.

"Well, she was one of them—we saved another girl from him too. That's actually the reason the killer took Susan—to get back at me, and Mr. Triplehorn, for bringing me into the investigation."

"Anyway, Mr. T hired me to investigate the murder of his friend, Todd Ashford—U.S. Senator Todd Ashford."

ASAC Holmes sat up a little straighter, and his eyes widened when he heard that. He had some questions.

"You're investigating the Senator's murder? That's what this is about?"

"Yes."

Maverick looked visibly uncomfortable.

"I don't know how I feel about continuing this conversation. There's an FBI team that's working this case out of Washington D.C.—why aren't you talking to them?"

"If you'll hear me out, I'll explain."

ASAC Holmes stared, thought for a moment, probably chalked this up to that "chit" thing again, and then nodded for me to go ahead.

"OK. I've been working with Detective David Lee of the Capitol Police. He seems like a good guy and a good cop. I've discovered a number of things about the case that the police had not, and they have been helpful to the case so far. He seems to genuinely appreciate my help."

"So, here's the deal. Mr. Triplehorn had me join him to attend Senator Ashford's funeral two days ago. He wanted me to get a feel for the man, which I did. Todd was the real deal, an actual good man, fighting for what was right. I don't have to tell you how rare that is in general, but for a politician, it's like seeing Bigfoot."

Both Cindy and Maverick were nodding. Winston just sat there, but that was just Winston.

"After the funeral, I got to meet with Senator Ashford's widow, Brooke—another genuinely good person. She told me that Todd had been working on a plan to root out the corruption and graft in the federal government, and she felt strongly that he was killed because of that. Since he had been a successful businessman, when I referred to it as a type of 'hostile takeover', she agreed with that assessment."

"I also got to talk to Todd's best friend, Tim. With Brooke and Tim, they both ended up mentioning Todd's love of the New York Yankees, and subsequently his hatred for the Boston Red Sox—a not uncommon conflict in the baseball world, given the long, ongoing rivalry between the two teams."

"After being home for a day for a special party, I landed back at

National this morning and decided to start by returning to Senator Ashford's office. I wanted to look around and think things through, based on the additional things I now knew about the man."

I looked up at the screen at my beautiful wife.

"Cindy, this is the part where I'm going to need your expertise as a local cop."

"OK," she said.

"As I was driving from the airport to Todd's office, without knowing that I would find something, I called Detective Lee and asked him a question. I simply wanted to know—given what his wife said Todd was working on—if he could *assure* me that if I found something and turned it over to him, it would be safe and remain unknown by the bad guys."

"I explained to him that our lives were on the line here, cuz if these people were willing to take out a sitting U.S. Senator to further their control—they wouldn't think twice about taking out a private investigator and a cop."

"Detective Lee had to really think about that question, then he was honest with me and said that he could *not* assure me of that. He even said that I should evaluate how to proceed with anything I found with that in mind."

"Wow," said Cindy.

"I know, right? Keep that in mind, babe; we'll come back to that."

CHAPTER
— 106 —

I continued the narrative.

"So, Detective Lee let me back into Senator Ashford's office—and based on what ended up happening—thankfully he had some meetings he had to attend and had to leave. That left me on my own in the senator's office."

"I wandered around a bit, and then sat down in the meeting area part of his office. As I sat there, I was reminded of what Brooke and Tim had said about Todd's love of the Yankees, because I was staring at an entire shelf in the bookcase, given over to a 'team' of Yankee bobble-heads. It's an impressive collection."

Apparently, my story was not quite as riveting as I thought, cuz ASAC Holmes cut in after looking at his watch.

"Is there an off-ramp to this tail somewhere in our future? Contrary to what some people think, I do have a life outside of this job."

I smiled.

"I know it's getting late, and I promise, I'm almost done."

He nodded for me to continue.

"I sat on that couch and thought about Senator Ashford. If you saw his office, it was obvious that he was orderly and well-organized. He'd been an extremely successful businessman, so he knew how to do things right. I completely understood why he wouldn't want to keep all this research and his plan on the 'Cloud'—it's just too penetrable."

Winston, our computer wizard nodded knowingly, which was a shocking interjection for him—the dude is quite low key.

"But the idea that he wouldn't back up the notes he had on paper and on his laptop—both of which the killer destroyed—to protect it from getting lost, just did not compute—that's just *bad* business, yet nobody had found any backup."

"As I stared at the bobblehead team and thought about this, all of a sudden, I realized that among the dozens of bobbleheads, I saw some slightly different colors of a uniform on one of the bobbleheads, way in the back. I got up and looked closer, and sure enough, it was different."

"I had to reach all the way to the back to retrieve it, but when I did, this bobblehead turned out to be Babe Ruth, the 'Great Bambino' himself, but in a Boston Red Sox uniform, instead of the one in the New York Yankee uniform, that was sitting in the front of the display."

"I have to admit that I was stunned. Both Brooke and Tim brought up Todd's loathing of the Red Sox without my asking—it was that much a part of Todd. Even though this was the great Babe Ruth, it was before he joined the Yankees, when he was playing for the team Todd viewed as the 'enemy'."

I looked around the room and up at Cindy.

"That was when it hit me. In these forty or fifty bobbleheads, there was only one that was different—but not just different, but one of a hated and dangerous adversary—one that clearly represented the 'enemy'."

I paused to let that sink in.

"I still don't get it", said Cindy.

I looked up at her.

"Think of it as a wife. If the people Todd loved started to box up his precious bobblehead collection, they would be *shocked* to find that one there—it would make *no sense* considering the man they knew. This 'enemy', hiding in plain sight, if you will, could very well represent the enemy he was fighting. It might just trigger his loved ones to look a little closer."

Cindy was nodding now, getting it.

"Wait," said Maverick, "are you saying the backup *was* the bobblehead?"

"Close. I looked it all over and found that the base had been cut open and then held back together with a drop of glue. Jammed inside the bobblehead was *this*."

I stood up, took the flash drive out of my pocket, and placed it right in the middle of Assistant Special Agent in Charge Maverick Holmes' desk.

Everyone stared at it like it was a *bomb*!

CHAPTER
— 107 —

The room went completely silent.

Finally, ASAC Holmes tore his eyes from the flash drive, looked up at me and asked, almost angrily, "What is on that?"

I took a deep breath.

"I don't know sir. It is password protected, and I don't know enough about Todd Ashford to even guess what the password would be after I gave it a few tries."

I looked around the room.

"To be fair, it is entirely possible that there is nothing of significance related to this case on that flash drive—unlikely, in my opinion, but entirely possible. If that is the case, I apologize in advance for wasting all your time—and a fair chunk of Mr. Triplehorn's money flying down here."

"However, since we are currently unaware of the contents of that flash drive, as I'm guessing you're all aware, we find ourselves at a bit of a crossroad."

ASAC Holmes looked up.

"Yeah, like I could arrest you right now for the felonious removal of evidence from the site of an ongoing FBI investigation, and for transporting it across state lines."

"Sure, there's that," I said, waving my hand at him dismissively.

"However, before you arrest me, I would like the three of you to listen to me, and then we can decide where to go with this," I said, gesturing toward the flash drive.

"Speak," said ASAC Holmes, all ears and all business, apparently less concerned about getting to his aforementioned "life outside of this job".

"As you can imagine, I found myself in a difficult position. Todd had gone well out of his way to protect the information he was gathering—not even trusting the 'Cloud'. He clearly knew that many of those around Washington, D.C. could not be trusted—I found out he wasn't even letting his *own staff* help with this project."

"This man knew the swamp much better than I ever could, so I thought that wisdom would dictate that I should defer to Todd's paranoia."

"I then asked Detective Lee his opinion about whether he could assure me that if I ended up finding information they had not, that giving it to him would keep the information—and us, safe."

"Again, he said he could *not* give me that 'assurance'."

I turned and looked directly at ASAC Holmes.

"Can you *assure* me right now ASAC Holmes, that if I had turned this information over to the FBI headquarters in Washington, D.C., that one; the flash drive and I would have been safe, and two; the information on this drive would have *ever* seen the light of day?"

The clock ticked as everyone turned and looked at ASAC Holmes, waiting for his answer.

Maverick had that "deer in the headlights" look on his face. He seemed genuinely uncomfortable as he pondered the question.

Finally, he simply said, "No, I cannot."

I nodded once to basically say both, "there was my problem" and "I appreciate your honestly," at the same time.

"So, what is it you want from me?" asked ASAC Holmes.

"Well, since we are currently in the dark as to whether there is even anything on this drive that relates to what the senator was working on and was killed for, I would like you to grant me access to my friend Winston's extraordinary technical abilities to find out what we are dealing with."

"And then?" asked ASAC Holmes.

"If we find that the information on that drive has what is needed to stop the rampant corruption and graft in our federal government,

I would hope that we would use it to do just that—formulating a plan to do so, just like Senator Ashford had planned."

Cindy had a question.

"Senator Ashford was in a powerful position to pull off whatever plan he was going to put in place, but how would we do the same without his power?"

I smiled, knowing the answer.

"I have grown to appreciate the power of one, Mr. Triplehorn. When he was paving the way for me to work on this case, he simply picked up his phone and called the President of the United States on the 'Commander in Chief's' personal line. He literally had the Pres on speed dial. Mr. T can provide all the 'umph' we would need to execute our plan."

"I did have a question for you, Cindy."

"Yeah?"

"Since they are the local guys who have the job of protecting Congress, how do you think the Capitol Police will be with all this? Are they going to try and get in the way and gum up the project, or will they get with the program?"

Cindy gave a heavy sigh and looked up toward the ceiling back home in Tucson.

"Well, Detective Lee was right to tell you he couldn't assure that you, or the information, would be safe if he reported it. There's politics in every department and in all of law enforcement—local, state, and federal."

ASAC Holmes was nodding.

"The real question comes down to whether the department is trying to do what is right and good, or whether certain members of the team, often the brass at the top, have decided to 'play ball' and are sellouts."

"The answer to that question varies from department to department."

Cindy held up her finger to say one more thing.

"I have to say though that Detective Lee must be one of the good ones, trying to do the right thing, if he was willing to admit this uncomfortable fact to you."

ASAC Holmes was nodding again.

"He told you the truth so you could go the right way, but he also put his career at risk by doing so. Huge props to his integrity."

CHAPTER
— 108 —

I looked at ASAC Holmes and took a deep breath.

"So, that's my story. What do you think?"

Maverick stared at me for a moment.

"I really do want to help, and I do see the dilemma you were placed in when you found the flash drive. I can't commit any further to what I'll do after we see what's on the drive, but I will let Winston work his magic, so we can know what we're actually dealing with here."

I nodded.

"Thank you, sir."

I looked over at Winston.

He stood up and walked to the desk and picked up the flash drive. He waved to Cindy in his goofy way, and she waved back. He then headed for his blue "fortress of solitude" where I had spent many an hour working with him to catch a serial rapist and murderer here in Florida.

I looked up at Cindy.

"This will probably take a while, and it's . . .", I looked at my watch, ". . . already moving toward seven o'clock here. How about I call you in the morning once we have something to look at?"

"OK. I love you," she said.

"I love you too. Kiss the boys for me."

"I will."

Cindy disappeared.

ASAC Holmes looked over.

"You have a *very* beautiful wife, Blake."

That was a surprise to hear from Maverick, and it crossed my mind that he seemed a little surprised that was the case.

"Thank you, sir, I think so too."

"And either you have a really weird marriage, saying, 'kiss the boys for me', or you two have babies."

I laughed.

"Yes sir, twin boys, who were two 'oopses' we conceived on our honeymoon—Nic and Linc."

ASAC Holmes smiled and nodded.

"Good for you—you're going to have a lot of fun with those boys in the future."

Who *was* this guy? He was almost acting like a normal dude. I figured I'd better end on a high note here and cut and run.

"Well, I'm going to go find a hotel, sir. It's been a long day since Tucson this morning."

"OK, see you tomorrow," replied ASAC Holmes.

And I was outta there!

CHAPTER
— 109 —

I grabbed some fast food and then drove over to a La Quinta Inn and Suites over on Crossroads Parkway. I figured I could "slum" for just one night and pay $150 instead of the $1,275 I was paying a night for the Waldorf Astoria—I mean Mr. T was paying.

Wouldn't Mr. Triplehorn be proud of me?

So, I got a suite for the night, which ended up being pretty nice, and I settled in to chow-down on my food.

I sat my phone up at a good angle and FaceTimed Cindy, to have some real husband-wife conversation with her. Since I had sprung the whole, "I need your professional help" phone call on her, I figured we could use some personal time together.

She still wasn't terribly amused that she had called out, "Hey stud," in front of the Assistant Special Agent in Charge, Maverick Holmes, and she made me aware of that fact a couple of times.

However, I *was* extremely amused by the event—and I kept chuckling every time she mentioned it. And as you know, I'm adorable, so my bride finally forgave me, and we were good.

I thought it was funny that she wasn't the least bit worried about Winston witnessing her outburst.

But what can I say? He's just "Winston", and he's always had a bit of a shy, schoolboy crush on Cindy, so she could do no wrong in his book.

We decided not to spend time speculating about what might be on the flash drive, even though we were both so intrigued to find out. We knew we'd be talking about that tomorrow, once we actually knew what was on it, so why waste the time.

So, I got to hear the recap of how much fun the quinceañera had been, and some of the funny things that had happened that I didn't know about.

"I have to give you credit for the little surprise you sprung on everybody of having Rosa and Alejandra show up—that was quite a powerful and emotional moment."

"You think?" replied Cindy. "And you missed quite the moment a little later."

"What was that?" I asked, surprised I'd missed something.

Cindy just shook her head.

"I wish you could have been there. After the party moved on, Rosa and Alejandra sought out Mr. Triplehorn and Susan. They were sitting together, talking with all our friends, now their new friends. Pastor Brian and Kristi were there, along with lots of people from Desert Christian."

I was intrigued, cuz Cindy was clearly starting to get emotional telling me the story.

"Blake—Rosa and Alejandra approached Araby and Susan like they were rockstars. There they were, gorgeous young women in those amazing gowns, and they knelt—*actually knelt*, in front of Araby and Susan and hugged and hugged them."

"Whoa."

"Yeah 'whoa'. There was a huge language barrier, but no one there needed words to know what was happening. Everyone was crying, and then I stepped in and translated their thanks for saving them, and the tears just came on stronger."

"It was an amazing moment. For all the moments Araby must have from all the good stuff he does, I have to believe this one was especially personal. Both he and Susan were shedding tears over this one."

"That is so cool—I wish I could have seen it."

Cindy was nodding.

"Oh, and by the way, maybe as a little payback for letting me call you 'stud' in front of everyone, here's another fun 'little surprise' for you—you paid for Rosa and Alejandra's expensive dresses too!"

I just stared at her, as Cindy was clearly enjoying my shock and horror.

"Now *I* feel on the edge of tears," I said.

"Oh, stop the theatrics—you're *loaded*."

I just slowly shook my head at her.

"So you keep telling me, my dear—so you keep telling me. However, you seem quite determined to 'unload' me of the burden of all our money."

Cindy just grinned back at me with a very satisfied smile.

CHAPTER
— 110 —

The next morning, I was up early, and actually went out and ran a few miles. The weather was awesome here in Florida, and I didn't know how soon I would be able to get some more exercise.

I came back in and showered in a normal shower for a change. I know what you're thinking; I'm courageous and brave; you know it, and I know it—let's both just acknowledge the fact and move on.

I then headed down to the free breakfast buffet and had waffles, eggs, sausage, orange juice, and coffee—a lot of it! I even finished it off with a cherry Danish—kind of like breakfast dessert. It was really good!

On my way back to my suite, I had to ponder why the Waldorf Astoria wasn't offering this awesome free food. I just decided to move on—I'm guessing their wealthy clientele didn't mind paying for their own food.

Even having done all that this morning, I still made it back to the FBI headquarters by 9:00 a.m., not too bad!

When I walked into the reception area, the receptionist directed me back to ASAC Holmes office.

When I got to his waiting area, there sat Winston, waiting to go in as well—so in we went.

Winston sat down and I shook ASAC Holmes' hand. I got my phone out and FaceTimed Cindy. Since it was now the first weeks of November, the whole "Daylight Savings Time" had happened across the country, meaning most of the country had "fallen back" an hour and messed up their own "body clock".

That meant that Cindy was only two hours behind us, so it was a little after 7:00 a.m. in Tucson. With two twin boys in the house, I knew Cindy was *not* asleep—it was Nic and Linc's *job* to make sure that *never* happened, and I knew I could count on my boys to do their job!

As a side note, I gotta say that one of the good things about living in Arizona is that we don't observe this whole "time to change your clocks" thing. Because of its desert climate, Arizona figured that there wasn't a good reason to adjust clocks to make sunset occur an hour *later* during the hottest months of the year.

Allow me to say a profound, "Well, duh!" here.

Hawaii is the other state that does not observe daylight savings time, because of its proximity to the equator. There's just not a lot of variation between hours of daylight during the year on the islands.

Any-who . . .

I got Cindy on the phone, and she looked as lovely and awake as I thought she would.

I handed my phone to Winston, and he jumped up and did his magic, and there she was on the big screen.

I looked over at Winston after he sat back down.

"I have to say, Winston, you look really good and well-rested for a man who was up all night."

Winston just stared back at me.

"You *were* up all night, right?"

Winston just shook his head, signifying, "no".

"Were you able to get into the flash drive?" asked ASAC Holmes.

Winston looked at him and nodded "yes".

Wow, this was going to take "a minute", as they say, with my speaking adverse friend here.

"Winston," Cindy said.

He looked up at my bride—schoolboy crush intact.

She smiled that beatific smile of hers and asked, "Could you please tell us what happened last night with the flash drive?"

He nodded once to her.

Oh sure, leave it to a beautiful woman to get the mute to speak!

The "oh so muted one" became "unmuted" and began to speak.

"I first of all got all the information I needed about the senator and his life and tried all the obvious passwords based on that. Birthdays, anniversaries, hobbies, vehicles, addresses, nicknames, etc. I then hacked into some of his accounts and tried all the passwords he used in those accounts."

OK, that was *not at all concerning* that Winston could do *that*!

"I was surprised when none of those things worked, so I designed a program that would work to break in using random passwords, including applying random letters, numbers, and symbols—which are the best passwords, but hard to remember. They usually have to be written down somewhere because they are so random."

Winston looked over at me.

"Given the length and random nature of the password, I'll bet that somewhere in his office, it is taped under something or hidden in a book."

Hmmm. I probably should have found that. I had checked that "under something" idea, but that "searching through his books" idea that I'd had, might have helped after all.

My bad.

"I was impressed that this form of password is what Senator Ashford used for this flash drive—very smart, because it's very safe."

Says the guy who broke into all the senator's personal accounts, and clearly had broken this passcode as well.

"I set my program to run through the night, and the log said that at 4:27 a.m., it found the right combination and opened the flash drive."

Ah, that explains why Winston wasn't extra tired and had not been up all night "cracking the code", as it were. (Insert "Mission Impossible" theme song here.)

He just directed one of his "babies" to do it and got himself some shut eye.

"That's great, Winston," said ASAC Holmes, "but what did you find on the flash drive?"

We all turned and looked intently at my little computer nerd of a friend.

CHAPTER
— 111 —

Winston just looked back at ASAC Holmes and shrugged his shoulders.

"I didn't find anything on it, sir," he said.

What happened in that room when Winston said that, could *not* be described as "deflated"—that would be too subtle. It was more like the cops had deployed some of their spike strips and we hit it going fast, our tires basically exploding all at once and going *immediately* flat—yeah, that's more like it.

The sheer disappointment in the room was palpable.

"You didn't find anything on it?" I asked. "It was blank?"

Winston looked over at me.

"No, I didn't look at it at all."

I'm not sure, but I think every one of us in the room, including Cindy on the big screen, did that thing where you cock your head sideways and squint, trying to understand something that is really confusing to you. Since Cindy was so huge up on the screen, it was really pronounced with her. It was kind of funny and would've made a good YouTube clip.

You know what is really good at doing this—*dogs*. They do it all the time when you say something to them. You can even say something like, "You're so stupid" in a sweet voice and they still cock their head and wag their tail. So cute.

Finally, Cindy cut through the silence and asked, "Winston, *why* didn't you look at the flash drive?"

He looked up at her and there was a long pause. Winston is really good at this. It goes on so long that you think he must have missed the question, and then about the time you get ready to jump in and try again, he answers.

ASAC Holmes was just opening his mouth to try the question again when Winston spoke.

"Given what Blake said might be on it, I didn't think I should look at it until you were all present."

Oh—OK, that made sense. Don't ask me why Winston couldn't have just said that in the first place and saved us all that "spike strip" moment. All I can say is, he's Winston.

And for the record, given the gravity of the potential information on the flash drive, he *wasn't* wrong.

I weighed in.

"So, no one has looked, but we can look right now?"

Winston nodded once.

I could tell that ASAC Holmes was a little frustrated with his computer nerd, but he knew better than to show it. This little dude was worth his weight in gold with what he could pull off with his little "babies".

Case in point—he "designed a program" last night before going home—and entire program—that cracked a sophisticated code and gave us access to the flash drive.

Genius. Weird as the day is long—and I love him for that—but still, "genius".

CHAPTER

— 112 —

Looking around the room, I said, "OK, well, *that* was fun—could you go ahead and open it up for us?" I asked.

Winston looked over at ASAC Holmes, his boss. Maverick nodded and Winston got up and took the flash drive out of his pocket.

"Seriously? He had the drive in his *pocket*?" I thought. However, I then remembered that I had carried it in my pocket too, so I declined to make the comment.

To be fair, I saw that it was now in a secure case, but still—in his *pocket*?

Before Winston inserted the drive, he looked over at ASAC Holmes.

"I think I should disable any connection to the internet before we open this," he said.

ASAC Holmes nodded his agreement.

Winston then looked up at Cindy.

"I can route Cindy to run only through Blake's phone, so that even the Bluetooth will be secure."

ASAC Holmes nodded, and Winston went to work. It took him all of about a minute and a half to shut us off from the world so we could view the flash drive information in secret.

Cindy's screen flashed off and then on again for a moment, as Winston rerouted it. Then, across the room on another large screen, a huge icon of a simple folder appeared.

The folder was titled, "Cabal Conspiracy."

It felt like an electric shock passed through the whole room, and we all drew in a breath.

We then looked at each other.

"Open it," commanded ASAC Holmes.

Winston did.

Numerous documents began to fill the screen, each one of them titled and dated.

Our eyes all started searching through the titles.

"There," I said pointing up at the screen, "open the one that says 'Summary'."

Winston did.

I have to say that I was surprised to see that Senator Ashford had started the same place I had, by defining his term, Cabal.

Cabal: 1) A cabal is a group of people who are united in some close design, usually to promote their private views or interests in an ideology, a state, or another community, often by intrigue and usually unbeknownst to those who are outside their group. The use of this term usually carries negative connotations of political purpose, conspiracy, and secrecy. It can also refer to a secret plot. 2) The contrived schemes of a group of people secretly united in a plot (as to overturn a government).

Yep, that's what I found too, even to the use of the archaic word, "unbeknownst".

After the definition, Senator Ashford began the summary.

I'm not sure who elected me to the job, but I started reading his words out loud.

"There has always been a battle for control and supremacy, all the way back to before the world was created, when Lucifer tried to dethrone God, and he and his demons were thrown out of heaven."

"In our day and age, around the world, it is a battle of ideologies. One ideology says that the 'elite', or the little people's 'betters', should rule and dictate, usually being the wealthy—which leads to ever larger and more corrupt governments."

"The other ideology believes in the freedom and worth of the individual citizen—that freedom being founded on basic morality—to live as free as possible from the constraints and dictates of a controlling 'government'."

"This second ideology was the unique basis of the founding of America, as set forth by our Founding Fathers."

"I have found that there is a cabal of evil people that is seeking to destroy America as founded."

I stopped reading for a moment and looked around. We all looked a little gob smacked. This was it—what we needed to find—Senator Ashford's research.

I started reading again.

"I have no interest in trying to split hairs between various ideologies or evaluate the merits and flaws of each ideology. If I may simplify the battle, it is the battle of the globalist—the one-world government class, where the 'elite' rule—versus the nationalist, who holds that each nation should govern and live in a way that is best for that nation, which in turn may well benefit the rest of the world."

"Regardless of what title you give it, and the various iterations there are, the 'globalist' thought encompasses ideologies like Fascism, Socialism, and Communism, where government is the key to leading the country."

"In the areas of 'nationalist', and in the specific case that is America, the Founding Fathers established us *not* as a democracy—because they knew that could, and most certainly would, descend into a failed 'majority rules' country. No, they established a 'representative republic', with checks and balances specifically designed to *curb* and *limit* government—which our Founding Fathers saw as a necessary evil to be guarded *against*."

"Both in the Constitution of the United States and in the subsequent 'Bill of Rights', they sought to *limit* the government and *strengthen* the citizens to exercise their rights, *not* conveyed to them by men, but given to them by God, therefore as 'God-given rights'."

I took a break.

CHAPTER

— 113 —

After I took a moment to catch my breath and look up at Cindy, who gave me a nod and reassuring smile, I continued reading.

"Understanding the founding of our country causes us to see just how right and forward-thinking our Founding Fathers were."

"To understand how we got here, we must first begin with the conspiracy that has been ratcheting up since the 1960s to undermine and destroy America and everything it was established to accomplish."

"For the record, I am not using hyperbole here—I am in no way overstating this dangerous reality."

"As a country, we would do well to recognize something: when your enemies tell you how they are going to attack and defeat you—even your enemies from inside your own country—you might want to take a moment and listen to them, take them seriously—and believe them."

I stopped and looked around the room. Everybody had a pretty grim look on their face. I was guessing they were gearing up to listen to our nation's enemies and their plans.

"So, we need to first take a brief look at the recent past when people began to get in line to try and destroy the United States of America—a conspiracy cabal that was started right out in the open."

"Let's start back in 1966 with some hardcore, anti-America Liberal Socialists, Richard Cloward and Frances Fox Piven, who were professors at Columbia University School of Social Work. They developed the Cloward-Piven strategy to overload the American system and collapse America in an eight-step plan."

I had to stop. Did I read that right? They openly created a plan with the sole purpose to "collapse America"? How had I never heard of this before? And who should have seen this in the 1960s and outed them?

I looked around the room. They all seemed equally dumbfounded.

I continued.

"The Cloward-Piven Strategy To Collapse America:"

I just shook my head at what I had just read.

"Healthcare—control healthcare and you control the people."

"Poverty—increase the poverty level as high as possible. Poor people are easier to control and will not fight back if the Government is providing everything for them to live."

I looked up, trying to digest the evil in what I had just read.

I went on.

"Debt—increase the debt to an unsustainable level. That way you are able to increase taxes, and this will produce more poverty."

I took a deep breath—given that America was about *thirty-four-trillion-dollars* in national debt, and again, that was trillion with a "T", I'd have to say they'd accomplished that one.

"Gun Control—remove the ability of the people to defend themselves from the Government. That way you are able to create a police state."

I just shook my head. Messing with my Second Amendment right was taking "Molly" away. That's a no-go!

"Welfare—take control of every aspect of people's lives (Food, Housing, and Income). The ultimate goal was to institute a guaranteed income for each person."

"That's weird," I thought. That "guaranteed income" craziness is being talked about among the "elites" right now, wanting the government to make us all lazy and controlled.

"Education—take control of what people read and listen to, specifically taking control of what children learn in school."

I looked over at Cindy on the big screen.

She weighed in.

"That's a huge fight in the states and the federal government right now, pitting the teacher's union power against the parents having directive power for their own kids. They are saying that teachers and administrators should be able to even help kids go through a transgender process without the parents' knowledge, permission, or involvement."

We all shook our heads at this shocking attempt to undermine the nuclear family.

I looked back up to read the last two of the eight steps.

"Religion—remove the belief in God from the Government and schools."

"Class Warfare—divide the people into the wealthy and the poor. This will cause more discontent, and it will be easier to take from the wealthy through taxation with the support of the poor."

We all just sat there, looking at each other in disbelief!

CHAPTER
— 114 —

Finally, I looked over at ASAC Holmes and asked, "How can these two left-wing nutjobs, not only believe, but teach and even publish their plan to 'collapse America', and get away with it? And as professors at a major American university? Isn't this like treason, or something?"

Maverick was shaking his head.

"I'm afraid this is the cost of us holding fast to the First Amendment, and the 1960s were filled with radicals who wanted to overthrow America. You'd be surprised how open some people were when it came to trying to destroy America. However, most of those people were crazy and their ideas are treated as such by most people."

Cindy weighed in.

"But these guys *were* taken seriously, and their plan has clearly been put into place—and it seems to be working to destroy our country."

ASAC Holmes was nodding. He just said, "Yep."

Blake looked around.

"Senator Ashford goes on—do you want me to continue?"

Winston just nodded.

"We now move to 1969. Bill Ayers was a militant organizer. In 1969, Ayers co-founded the far-left militant organization called the 'Weather Underground', a far-left revolutionary group modeled to overthrow what they viewed as American imperialism."

I glanced up at Maverick and Winston since they should know about this. They both nodded at me, indicating they knew about this guy.

I went on.

"During the 1960s and 1970s, the Weather Underground conducted a campaign of bombing public buildings in opposition to U.S. involvement in the Vietnam War. The FBI described the Weather Underground as a domestic terrorist group. Ayers was hunted as a fugitive for several years, until charges were dropped due to illegal actions by the FBI agents pursuing him and others."

"Ayers went on to become a professor in the College of Education at the University of Illinois at Chicago, holding the titles of Distinguished Professor of Education and Senior University Scholar. During the 2008 U.S. presidential campaign, a controversy arose over his contacts with then-candidate Barack Obama."

I looked at ASAC Holmes and Winston.

"Are you kidding me? This terrorist who bombed public buildings to try and overthrow America, ended up avoiding prosecution and instead became a 'Distinguished Professor' at a major university?"

The implied question, adding a little enraged into the equation, made my position on the subject pretty clear.

ASAC Holmes answered.

"Yeah . . . that was a real black mark for the FBI. These bad guys were clever, so some of the agents crossed some lines to try and get them. We ended up losing our whole case against these obviously guilty perps. They now use it as a case study at Quantico of what *not* to do."

I just shook my head.

"Distinguished Professor and Scholar", I muttered.

CHAPTER
— 115 —

To say this little "history lesson" was sobering would be a gross understatement, but the good senator was not quite done.

I read on.

"Two historically significant things happened in 1971 that continued this attack on America's founding."

"The first started with a premier radical, a committed Socialist, who coined the phrase, 'community-organizer' for himself. His name was Saul Alinsky, and he wrote the book, *Rules for Radicals*.'"

"To understand his impact, it was his influence that led a man named Barry Obama, changed to Barack Obama in 1980, to become a community-organizer."

We all looked at each other.

I read on.

"Barack Obama received a comprehensive course in Saul Alinsky during his years as a community organizer in Chicago. Obama described it as 'the best education he ever had'. Obama went on to teach Alinsky concepts and methods at community organizing workshops and seminars in Southside Chicago."

I stopped, looked around the room, and asked, "The man who became the American President for eight years both accepted and taught others a Socialist's principles from his book called *Rules for Radicals*'?"

No one in the room answered me.

I read more.

"In addition to this, Hillary Clinton stated that she looked up to Alinsky as a hero, even doing her 1969 thesis on him in school."

I just shook my head in disbelief.

"You can begin to get a feel for the tenor of Alinsky's book when you read an epigraph at the beginning of the book: *'Lest we forget at least an over-the-shoulder acknowledgment to the very first radical: from all our legends, mythology, and history (and who is to know where mythology leaves off and history begins—or which is which), the first radical known to man who rebelled against the establishment and did it so effectively that he at least won his own kingdom—Lucifer'.*"

Cindy commented.

"Did Alinsky just applaud *Satan* for trying—and failing, I might add—to overthrow God and for getting thrown out of heaven?"

I nodded.

"Yeah, he sure did."

We were all shaking our heads.

I started reading again.

"Some of Alinsky's rules of attack in *'Rules for Radicals'* were like warfare, where those with different ideas or ideology than them were considered the 'enemy'. Here are some of the rules:"

"Power is not only what you have but what the enemy *thinks* you have."

"Ridicule is man's most potent weapon. There is no defense. It is almost impossible to counterattack ridicule. Also, it infuriates the opposition, who then react to your advantage."

"Keep the pressure on."

"The *threat* is usually more terrifying than the thing itself."

"The major premise for tactics is the development of operations that will maintain a constant pressure upon the opposition."

"Pick the target, freeze it, personalize it, and polarize it."

I stopped.

"Wow, these people were just ruthless in their attack strategy to destroy America."

CHAPTER
— 116 —

I picked up my reading from where I had ended.

"The second significant thing from 1971 had to do with a German man named Klaus Schwab. He took six-thousand-dollars in seed money in 1971 and started the European Management Forum, which was later named the World Economic Forum, or WEF, to reflect their desire for global control and dominance. It has gone from a humble gathering of academics into the most exclusive club in the world, now raking in three-hundred and ninety-million-dollars, annually."

I was shaking my head again.

"What is it with all these narcissists who are so hellbent on controlling and taking over the world?"

No one answered—since it was kind of meant to be an outraged rhetorical question—so I continued.

"The annual meeting of the 'elite', jet-setting billionaires, who want to control the world and everything and everyone in it, meets in a tiny Alpine skiing town of Davos, Switzerland, to literally plot together how to take over and control the world."

"The market capitalization of WEF's top members—corporate giants like Apple, Microsoft, Amazon, Meta, Google, Comcast, and Pfizer—tops ten-trillion-dollars. Double that if you include the ten-trillion-dollar asset manager, BlackRock, whose founder and CEO, Larry Fink, is a WEF board member. So, with more than twenty-trillion-dollars—greater than the Gross Domestic Product (GDP) of every nation in the world except that of the United States—it is easy to grasp why the

WEF is able to exert such extraordinary influence over every aspect of our world."

"The many ways in which the WEF is plotting to control society's future are bone-chilling. Key items on the agenda include the globalist takeover of not just finance, but also energy, food, health, personal information, and technology."

"And what is strange is that they admit and pursue it, right out in the open, trusting that their significant wealth and capital means that the 'little people' can't do anything to stop their aspirations of global dominance and a one-world government—led by them, of course."

"As you can imagine, America and her founding principles, which are counter to *everything* the World Economic Forum stands for, are considered a troubling problem to be attacked and removed by the WEF."

"Klaus Schwab declared what he called a *'Great Reset'* during the mess of COVID-19, starting in 2020. This demonstrated that the WEF was intent on using the pandemic to influence the present and command the future. With control over critical industries and infrastructure, the WEF wants to link arms with the United Nations (UN), the World Bank, and the World Health Organization (WHO) to have unprecedented control over every aspect of the lives of the people in the world."

"Here are some of the ways they are working to accomplish this control: financially, they are working to roll out central bank digital currencies (CBDCs). Why? They say because these offer 'total control' over the money supply. With a CBDC, the globalist financial system could financially cancel (or "de-bank") an individual, a corporation, a whole town, or even an entire country."

I had to stop and ponder that for a moment. The idea that these wannabe dictators could easily take away my newly acquired millions if I displeased them, leaving my family without anything, made me angry.

Just who do they think they are?

Senator Ashford went on, so I did too.

"They are working hard toward energy control—specifically trying to ban oil, gas and coal-based energy, including vehicles powered this way, and trying to take control of each person's thermostats in their homes and work settings."

Cindy was shaking her head incredulously and said, "These fools are trying to stop any of us from being able to travel any significant distance and demanding that they get to decide where we keep the temperature in our own homes. All the while, they are all traveling around the globe in their private jets!"

We all shook our heads at that. I went on.

"The WEF is currently working on forcing people to live in what they call *'Fifteen Minute Cities'*. These cities are designed so that people don't drive vehicles and are fifteen minutes from their home at any given time. They are expected to stay within that distance, so they don't use fossil fuels."

I looked up at Cindy on the screen.

"Yep, you were right—they are trying to restrict *us* from traveling virtually anywhere, while *they* travel everywhere and anywhere they want."

CHAPTER
— 117 —

I went on with Senator Ashford's narrative.

"They are working to control our food supply too. By using the false, man-made 'climate change' hoax, they are seeking to ban traditional fertilizers, placing harsh restrictions that regulate farmers out of existence, and end protein sources like cattle, chickens, pigs, and sheep."

"Another tactic they are beginning to use is that these multibillionaires are using their great wealth to buy up farmland around the globe so that they can control how much food is available. Bill Gates now owns two-hundred and forty-two-thousand acres of farmland in America, *more than any other individual in America.* Just deciding not to farm that land would create food shortages."

We all looked at each other in disbelief.

"As they *create* this food shortage problem, to 'solve' it, WEF members are working with corporations like Bayer-Monsanto, Beyond Meats, and Impossible Foods. They are also working with insect-based protein groups to have the world eat insects.

"And the problem of 'food shortage' isn't seen as a problem from the 'elite's' perspective. They all talk about the importance of *reducing* the human population, which takes us back to the Nazi statements that called those of us in the masses, *'useless eaters'.*"

"If you think these people are kidding, the well-known billionaires who are heavily investing in this 'alternate food' sector include Bill Gates, Jeff Bezos, Mark Zuckerberg, and Virgin Galactic's Richard Branson."

Blake looked over at Maverick and then Winston.

THE CONSPIRACY CABAL

"They are trying to destroy our population *and* take our grill food away from us and give us *insects* to eat instead!"

The anger at that afront was palpable.

I have to admit that thinking about our "grill food" made me a little hungry, but I soldiered on.

"This is especially concerning, because many of these billionaires agree with Klaus Schwab that the world's population needs to be 'reduced'—a sanitized way of stating that some of the world's population simply needs to die. Some of them even refer to the human race as an 'infestation' that needs to be eradicated. They justify this viewpoint based on the fraudulent 'overpopulation' lie."

Senator Ashford then added a little caveat.

"Consider this—we currently have many major countries that are in danger of extinction as a country, because they are not having *enough* children—it's actually *most* countries! The standard 'replacement rate' for population stability is 2.1 children per woman. If the rate for a country falls below this number, the nation is in danger of collapsing on itself—it will not be able to sustain itself as a nation."

"So, with that in mind, consider this; the United States of America is currently at only a 1.78 replacement rate. China is at 1.7. Italy is at 1.3. Canada is at 1.38. As a matter of fact, *most* nations in the world are under the replacement rate for their population."

"This is a significant problem for the continuation of nations, but as you can imagine, it's part of the goal of the 'elite' who want to 'reduce' the number of people by crying out 'overpopulation'. This is why all the 'elites' are so adamant about abortion—killing future generations in their mother's womb."

"They are also taking over healthcare because this is so powerful in controlling people. This was why President Obama was so insistent on 'Obamacare', even though it has clearly proven to be a significant failure—drastically reducing coverage, while boasting skyrocketing premiums. Obama lied that 'if you like your doctor, you can keep your doctor', and that 'every family will save $2,500 per year on healthcare', both of which were shown to be patently untrue, and yet the failed program continues. It was all about controlling the populace."

"WEF partners, including the UN and the Gates Foundation, are pushing to require digital ID systems across 50 countries within five years. This push has increased once these globalists saw what they were able to get away with during the COVID-19 pandemic to force compliance of the masses."

Cindy spoke up.

"Wow, if they see what happened in the COVID-19 debacle as a success, that pretty much tells you everything you need to know about these people. Virtually everything the government told us we had to do ended up being useless, dangerous, and just flat out wrong. Clearly, they don't care about people, but rather just getting power and control."

We all agreed, and I read on.

"Their move into controlling technology seeks to upend the entire human experience. WEF celebrities like Israeli historian Yuval Noah Harari, boldly tout innovations like brain microchips, happy pill-style complacency drugs to keep the masses docile, and eugenics-style gene editing to cull out the 'inferior people'."

"Harari believes that the entire human body can and will be 'hacked'. He says that in the future, 'we need to monitor what's happening under people's skin'. Subdermal microchips are only the beginning. The entire human body, when it comes to the masses, is the canvas for a bizarre globalist experimentation."

"Harari also states that 'death was the great equalizer', seeing it as a useful element in control. This is why what they call the *Fourth Industrial Revolution* will give birth to a new caste system in which poor people still die, but rich people will 'in addition to all the other things they get, also get an exemption from death'."

"They are saying that in their plan, 'elites' will be able to purchase immortality through biotechnological upgrades—to transcend the human condition itself—into transhumanism."

We were all silent for a moment.

"Who are these jerks," asked ASAC Holmes, "a bunch of Dr. Frankensteins?"

I nodded.

"They're like the new Hitler, but with technology to actually get the job done!"

CHAPTER

— 118 —

Senator Ashford's notes went on to a new subject.

"The attack on America also came from a moral perspective, related to sexuality, to destroy the nuclear family. Back in 1987, a then little-known article was written called, *'The Overhauling of Straight America'*. It was written by two homosexual activists named Marshall Kirk and Hunter Madsen who were deeply committed to winning this social, sexual, and moral war. The plan they laid out has been followed to a 'T' and has worked out exactly as they planned. Their article was later expanded into an entire book called, *'After the Ball'*, which was published in 1990. In the book, they sketch out an all-out attack on what they called 'Straight America' to pressure, manipulate, lie and 'trick' Americans into first accepting and then embracing all forms of non-traditional sexuality."

"Like all the attacks we've seen so far, they also listed the 'how to' rules to accomplish this attack. Some of these rules were—talk about gays and gayness as loudly and as often as possible—portray gays as victims, not as aggressive challengers—make gays look good—make those who oppose us look bad."

"Following these rules, the LGBT activists have bombarded the American population, to turn them from traditional, family-based sexuality, toward deviant, anti-family sexuality—and it has worked quite effectively."

"As you can imagine, the 'elites' we talked about are quite in favor of this move away from traditional morality, because removing or destroying the family structure is a major key in destabilizing any nation. In addition to this, it stops more children from being born, which is a major goal for them."

"When we look at all this history, and all those who consider themselves to be 'elite' setting out to attack everything America was founded to stand for, can anyone be surprised that we find ourselves in the mess that our country has currently become?"

"Suddenly, many of the things that might have seemed like miscalculations or errors in judgement, are exposed as having been quite calculated to undermine the American system."

"So, if I may sum up; look at what is happening in our country now. We have the constant political attacks of Bond-villain type billionaire, George Soros, spending hundreds of millions of dollars to undermine our politics and our elections. He works to destroy our criminal justice system by funding District Attorneys and Prosecutors who simply ignore the laws our legislators put in place and just refuse to prosecute criminals. The resulting rise in crime in Democrat-controlled cities across our nation is part of the chaos that these 'elites' are seeking to create. Now that George Soros is ninety-three years old, he is passing his own personal flame-thrower to his son Alex, who promises the world he'll be even worse in his attacks."

"Mark Zuckerburg, founder of Facebook, now Meta, produced the same destruction by attacking our 2020 election, through his hundreds of millions of dollars of 'Zuck-buck' manipulation, for 'progressive' candidates."

"Add to that the deep state that just keeps working to undermine our elected officials through regulations."

"The liberals in our nation demanded support of Black Lives Matter—which is an admitted Marxist organization, while they engaged in rampant rioting, burning, and looting in our cities. There is the constant drive to destroy the family, while liberals scream that everything else conservatives stand for and believe is just 'racist', with the hope this will put an end to the argument. They also continue the destruction of the inner city, with abortion disproportionately wiping out the black family. Then there's the unrelenting drive to get rid of any real morality, and the demanded acceptance of pornography and 'sex work' as somehow a good thing."

"Add to that the denial of truth, the drive to get rid of God, and even the erasure of obvious common sense. There's the celebration of homosexual, bisexual, and transgender behavior, the decimation of the birth rate so that we aren't even at replacement rate anymore, repeating of population growth lies, and destabilization."

"Add to that vote cheating and manipulation in elections, along with huge amounts of outside money to change the outcome. We have corrupt, activist judges, instead of lady justice wearing the blindfold so that justice is fair for all, because 'justice is blind'—at least, it's supposed to be."

"Then there's wide open national borders. This is desired by the 'chamber of commerce' class for cheap labor, and the Democrats as replacement votes to re-supply those who see their failures and don't want to vote for them anymore. This is the 'uniparty' working together. In addition to this, all the illegal aliens create chaos, poverty, division, and more crime—all elements the 'elites' desire because they believe and even say, you should 'never let a crisis go to waste'."

"There's the fascist connection to big tech and other large corporations, who are doing the government's bidding, when government finds itself forbidden to do so by our Constitution. Look at all the lies we were told during COVID-19, and how all the supposed 'conspiracy theories' the people had, quickly became provable truth."

"They needed to get rid of freedom of speech because the 'elites' can't allow debate and truth to take place, because the facts always destroy their position. So, they work to control and manipulate all information, under the guise of what the 'elites' declare to be 'disinformation'."

"The deep state weaponizes 'lawfare' against their political rivals—trying to put them in jail—something usually done only in third-world countries."

"There's the constant drumbeat to get rid of the Second Amendment, since the people can't be armed if the government is to run roughshod over them, even though that was the *point* of the Second Amendment in the first place. So, every time criminals shoot up a location, the 'elites' quickly try to put gun laws on *law-abiding citizens*—who statistically have a lower rate of gun crime than even active duty police officers—all the while knowing that bad guys will just ignore any 'gun laws' the politicians create and get guns for crimes anyway. The real goal is to take the guns away from the law-abiding citizens."

I stopped.

Wow, that was quite a list—quite an accurate list.

CHAPTER
— 119 —

"He flew where?"
"Orlando," came the voice from the other end of the conversation.

It had taken most of the day, but his source had finally gotten the information he required.

Mercurius searched his brain for something in Orlando that related to their operation.

He couldn't come up with anything.

"What is he doing in Orlando?" he asked.

"I was able to find out that he rented a car, but beyond that, I don't have a way of knowing if he is just doing things around Orlando, or if he is driving somewhere else in Florida."

Mercurius thought about all of Florida. There were a few people there who were a part of what they were doing, but most of them had expensive, coastal homes further south in Florida, places like West Palm Beach, Miami, and Tampa. He couldn't imagine why this P.I. would fly into central Florida if he was looking at any of those people.

This just didn't add up! If this guy was as good as they say, why would he stop right in the middle of an investigation and make some random trip to Orlando? Was he just spending a few days at Disney World? No, it just had to relate to his operation. But for the life of him, he could not imagine what it could be.

"OK, listen," he said, "I want you to try all your law enforcement contacts around D.C., and see if they know anything, or have heard anything, about what this P.I. could be doing. I'll reach out to my sources too and see if they can tell me anything."

"As soon as you know something, let me know. I don't like how this is moving, and I may need to step in and put an end to all this."

Mercurius ended the call. He specifically said that last part because he was feeling a little weakened by how the assassin had threatened him. He wasn't used to getting threats—he was used to giving them. He wished he could make the assassin pay for treating him like this, but there are certain people who are so lethal, you simply don't mess with them—this guy was definitely at the top of *that list*!

He took a deep breath and let it out.

He needed to find this Blake Moran and discover what he was up to—and he needed to do it quickly.

The next time he called the hitter, it would just be to point him toward the mark and have him take Moran off the board.

He was already dreading having to talk to the assassin again. He seemed to be running out of chits with this guy, and the killer seemed almost anxious to kill him.

Not good.

CHAPTER
— 120 —

That was the end of Senator Ashford's "look back" at history to see how we got here. He now moved on to what he had discovered since coming to Washington, D.C.

I began reading that section out loud.

"After coming to Washington, D.C., I began to notice a pattern of certain individuals and groups of people, seeming to all move in concert, or the same direction on legislation. I especially watched as the 'deep state', or unelected bureaucrats in various bureaucracies, continued to formulate legislation that would clearly move our country directly toward many of the 'destroy America' goals that had been planned toward in the past."

"They were Cloward-Piven, Bill Ayers, Saul Alinsky's *'Rules for Radicals'*, Klaus Schwab's World Economic Forum, the United Nations, and the LGBT+ cult, all rolled up into a tsunami of legislation. Every time I turned around, I was having to fight these attempts by government officials, to overwhelm and destroy America at her core."

"It happened so frequently, that I began to become suspicious that it was more than meets the eye. These things were not random—they seemed calculated, and even more than that—they seemed *orchestrated*."

"I finally started to wonder if I was witnessing a conspiracy both within and outside our government, that was bent on destroying America as founded."

"It was at that moment that I began to look for a group, or 'Cabal', that was trying to accomplish this, without others knowing what they were attempting to do."

"I found it."

I stopped reading. That was quite a statement. Senator Ashford was saying that he had discovered a group of people who were secretly, and yet actively, working to overturn the United States of America as we know it.

I read on.

"By simply doing a study of the voting pattern of individual members of Congress—both Senate and House, I was able to easily compile a list of potential 'likely' members of the Cabal. From there, I began working to see connections between both members and specific deep-state people who were active in preparing legislation for Congress to consider."

"I then cross-checked members with their clubs and affiliations—and specifically their donors, to see if there was any correlation."

"I found that there was."

"Every person on the list that follows has some connection to one or more of these ideological groups that have openly set out to undermine and overthrow the United States of America. While it might not be true that every single person on this list is actively a part of this conspiracy cabal, I can state with certainty that by far, most are."

"These cabal members are having money, and power, and positions, given to them by the 'puppet masters' who are orchestrating this conspiracy."

"These puppet masters are the multibillionaires who have so much money, that at this point money has now become 'passe' to them. They crave something more—total power and control over the world, and that is what they are orchestrating."

"The list below shows the names and positions of the officials who *could* be in this Cabal. The ones who are specifically highlighted are the people whom I have confirmed *are* in this Cabal. As is easy to see, the confirmed list is quite extensive and includes very powerful people."

"My real quandary has been how to deal with this. I could try and use the judicial system and take these people to court, but the problem is that many of the judges and law enforcement are a part of this Cabal, as you can see. I have no reason to trust that path."

"I have decided to begin contacting the various powerful members on this list and inform them that they can either resign or I will expose their involvement in this conspiracy cabal."

"My intention is to then put in place elements of policy that will deter such actions in the future. That plan is located after the following list."

I stopped and looked around the room and said, "And instead of them resigning, they just decided to kill him."

CHAPTER
— 121 —

I didn't start reading the list—we all just started looking through the names on our own. Since there are four-hundred and thirty-five Representatives in the House and one-hundred Senators in the Senate, it took a while to look through the list, which was hundreds of names long.

Each of us gasped at different times as we saw the names, especially when Senator Ashford had noted that he had confirmed they were in the Cabal. These names included the Senate Majority Leader and the House Minority Leader, both Democrats. It also included members, and sometimes leaders of, powerful committees in both the Senate and House. Committees like "Energy and Commerce", "Appropriations", "Foreign Affairs", "Ways and Means", "Education and the Workforce", "Agriculture", "Homeland Security", and more.

After what we had just learned about the goals and plans of this Cabal to overwhelm and overthrow America, the idea that members of this Cabal had infiltrated such key and powerful committees was horrifying!

But the horror just grew.

Senator Ashford listed powerful members of the military who were in the Cabal. He then included those in the alphabet clubs of federal law enforcement—the FBI, CIA, DOJ, NSA, DEA—hundreds of names.

He then went on and listed those in the administrative branch—the unelected bureaucrats who used regulations to determine the direction of our country. That was thousands of names long, but the confirmed names were hundreds.

What we all found ourselves staring at was his list of the Executive Branch. The members of the President's Cabinet who were both *listed* and *confirmed* to be a part of the Cabal, included the Director of National Intelligence, the Administrator of the Environmental Protection Agency, the Secretary of Education, the Secretary of Energy, the Secretary of Housing, the Secretary of Health, the Secretary of Agriculture, the Attorney General, the Secretary of the Treasury, and the Secretary of State.

But what we all just stared at were the top two.

The Vice-President of the United States and the President of the United States were both *listed* and *confirmed*.

There were thousands of names listed and hundreds of confirmed names, but we all just sat there staring at those two.

I'm not sure, but I think what we were all feeling had to do with the proverbial saying of—how can I say this politely? Hmmm. OK. We felt like native Americans, up a river of excrement, without a means of propulsion.

Yeah. That pretty much summed it up.

CHAPTER
— 122 —

I looked around the room.

I was sensing a lot of angst, so I tried for a little levity mingled with a "glass half full" mindset.

"Well, on the good side, we now have the list of who probably hired the assassin to kill Senator Ashford, down to only hundreds of people."

I got nothing back.

Tough crowd.

I took a deep breath and let it out.

I thought for a moment about our dilemma.

"I don't know how familiar you all are with what happens when we sleep and dream, but it may have relevance here."

That caused all three of them to look over at me, and Cindy was already shaking her head at me.

"No babe, hear me out."

She stopped shaking and gestured for me to continue.

"When we sleep, usually about ninety minutes after falling asleep, we all go into REM sleep—or the Rapid Eye Movement phase. During this time, the brain is very active, and our dreams are the most intense."

"That presents a problem—because our dreams are so intense and they seem so real, that our body would naturally act out the dreams."

By this time, ASAC Holmes is looking at me with a confused expression. Even my typically expressionless friend, Winston, has raised his right eyebrow, which is like a shocked-faced emoji for him.

Cindy, on the other hand, just looked on with a neutral expression, being used to my insight and wisdom, and the way my fertile mind works.

At least that's what I choose to believe her expression means.

I went on.

"As you can imagine, we would be a great danger to ourselves if we actually acted out our dreams while asleep, so God designed a solution for us."

"During the most dream-filled phase of sleep, our muscles become paralyzed, preventing the body from acting out what's going on in the brain. This is accomplished by the release of certain chemicals into our system. So, the voluntary muscles of the body—arms, legs, fingers, anything that's under conscious control—are virtually paralyzed."

"This paralysis keeps people still and unmoving, even as their brains are acting out often crazy and very active dreams. It's also the reason people sometimes experience sleep paralysis, or the experience of waking up while their muscles are still frozen."

They all continued to just stare at me.

A befuddled ASAC Holmes finally asked, "I don't suppose that little story of yours had *any* relevance to the hideous problem we were just confronted with—a group of extremely powerful, wealthy, and connected people who are trying to overthrow the United States of America?

I smiled at him.

"You'd think not but follow me on this."

"Our enemies—the members of this conspiracy cabal—have basically snuck up on our country while we were all asleep. The elements of this conspiracy that Senator Ashford pointed to in past history didn't register with many people, because we all assumed that everything was going along just fine."

"We were asleep at the wheel—if you will. We had set the cruise control and were just motoring happily down the road."

"We were driving down the road while asleep?" asked Cindy.

I looked up at her.

"OK, so maybe it's not a perfect metaphor—although the crash our nation is heading toward might make the metaphor more accurate than we'd like."

"So, as we went merrily on with our lives, things were happening—changes were taking place—and not good things in our society."

"We would have normally reacted to stop these changes, but this ongoing Cabal continued to release 'certain chemicals' into our system. Those 'chemicals' were them telling us over and over that these changes were 'no big deal', there was no 'slippery slope' to be concerned about, they were 'progressive' changes, as though they were good, and to disagree with them would make us a 'racist', a 'bigot', or a 'hater'."

"Well, nobody wanted to be that!"

"These were just the dreams. They seemed so real, because in this case, they were—but the Cabal continued to whisper in our ear to ignore them and not worry about them—they were only dreams, after all. They told us reality was really only just harmless dreams. They put our extremities to sleep, so we wouldn't react."

"Then, all the sudden, Senator Ashford 'wakes up' and looks around at the conspiracy and sees the truth of what they are trying to do. He has now informed the four of us through these facts that he preserved."

I looked around at the other three.

"What we decide to do from here on out will determine whether we are stuck in that 'sleep paralysis' as a nation—and our nation as founded comes to an end—or whether we can wake up and shake off the 'chemicals' of lies and deceit they've used to paralyze us, and instead overwhelm and overthrow them."

"To win, we have to turn the script on them, and 'freeze' them."

CHAPTER
— 123 —

Cindy spoke first.

"I'm going to have to give you an 'atta boy', because that illustration *almost* fit the situation."

I nodded my thanks to her.

"I will accept the 'atta boy', while ignoring the extra commentary, my dear."

"I would expect no less from you, my love," she replied.

I looked over at ASAC Holmes and Winston.

"So, we have a battle to fight here—are you two in?"

There was silence for a moment.

Finally, ASAC Holmes spoke.

"Blake, I'm appalled at what we just read. I see the progression that Senator Ashford laid out and how we got here. I agree that our nation is teetering on the brink, and apparently this 'Cabal' is trying to push her over the edge."

"However, you just listed some of the most powerful and connected people within our government—most of whom would be considered my direct bosses!"

"How could I possibly justify getting into a counter-battle with this Cabal? It would seem to contradict what I vowed to uphold in my position."

I looked at Maverick for a moment, a man who I knew to be a good man and a fellow patriot.

"Could you recite your oath for us, ASAC Holmes?"

"Could I what?"

"Could you recite your oath please?"

"Why?"

"You said to help us battle this Cabal would 'contradict' what you vowed. I'd just like to hear what you vowed."

"So, could you just humor me?"

After a big sigh, Assistant Special Agent in Charge, Maverick Holmes, began his oath.

"I Maverick Lincoln Holmes do solemnly swear that I will support and defend the Constitution of the United States against all enemies, foreign and domestic; that I will bear true faith and allegiance to the same; that I take this obligation freely, without any mental reservation or purpose of evasion; and that I will well and faithfully discharge the duties of the office on which I am about to enter. So help me God."

I let the echo of his voice fade as I let what he had said sink in.

I looked right at him.

"First of all, your first name really is 'Maverick'? Like, on your birth certificate, and everything?"

"Yes."

"And your middle name is Lincoln?"

"Yes."

I looked up at Cindy and smiled.

"Apparently, we named one of our sons after ASAC Holmes without knowing it."

Cindy smiled.

I looked back at Maverick 'Lincoln'.

"So, did you hear it?"

"Hear what?"

"You swore to 'support and defend the Constitution of the United States against all enemies, *foreign* and *domestic*' and that your 'true faith and allegiance' would be to the Constitution."

He stared at me.

"Sir, would you agree that this Cabal is working to overthrow our

Constitution and the government of the United States of America as founded?"

He said, "Yes," without hesitation.

"Based on your oath, wouldn't you agree that it does not change anything that the threat is coming from both inside and outside the government—or even your 'bosses'—but that your oath to fight 'all enemies' both 'foreign and domestic' would *demand* that you fight this cancer—even though much of the cancer we will be fighting would also be considered your 'bosses'?"

ASAC Holmes held my stare for a few moments.

Finally, he nodded once.

"OK, I'm in—*let's give 'em hell!*"

CHAPTER
—124—

Cindy had to run and feed the twins, so we all took a break to use the bathroom and grab some food.

ASAC Holmes had some things he needed to take care of to clear his schedule, since this was clearly going to take "a minute", as they say.

I would've been a little nervous of Maverick "taking care of some things", given what we had just seen from Senator Ashford's notes, but as you can imagine, I scoured the list for any mention of one specific name—and ASAC Holmes was not one of them.

I don't mean to be paranoid, but one must watch one's back, mustn't one? (Wow, three "ones" in one sentence. Oh, there's another one. And another one. OK, I'll stop now.)

I got to catch up with Winston some—as much as one can catch up with Winston—he is a man of few words and doesn't have much going on in his life except his work.

But it was still nice to be with my friend again.

When we all got back into ASAC Holmes' office, and Cindy had joined us again after seeing to the twins, it was time for us to formulate a plan.

"OK," I said, "I think we can agree that we have a conspiracy to systematically overwhelm and overthrow the United States of America and destroy everything that has made our country great from the time of our founding."

"And all of this was supposed to be done while, by and large, the nation was sound asleep and unaware of the attacks."

"Is that a fair assessment of the threat?"

Cindy added something.

"To truly describe the depth of the danger, I think we should add that there are agents of this Cabal in virtually *every* important and powerful element of our society who are involved, so they are in the positions where they could actually get away with this."

I nodded.

ASAC Holmes agreed.

"The magnitude of this threat boggles the mind—reaching all the way into the Oval Office and our Commander in Chief. This is literal *treason*."

I looked around.

"So, how do we attack it?"

"Well, you were certainly right to not talk to the law enforcement agencies in Washington, D.C.," replied Maverick. "I'm guessing you all saw, but all the top leaders at virtually every agency in D.C. are in the Cabal."

"I have to say that makes some sense now."

"How so," I asked.

"Well, as you can imagine, I'm primarily aware of the FBI in this. The D.C. post for SAC and ASAC is a prime position, being so close to all the power players in the nation's capital. As I said, if you look at the list, all of the top FBI in Washington are in the Cabal."

"OK, but what do you mean this 'makes some sense now'?"

Maverick proceeded to enlighten us.

"Across the Bureau, there were many top candidates for those positions in D.C.—everybody knew it and knew who the front runners were. For the record, I was on the short list."

"So, you can imagine the surprise across the Bureau when the team that is now there was chosen. No one, and I mean *no one*, even had these guys on their list. They had never been a part of the discussion and seemed remarkably *unqualified* from every perspective to land such a powerful position."

I looked at him.

"So, now you know that the qualifications were quite a bit different than what everybody thought."

ASAC Holmes just nodded.

I thought about that.

"That also gives us some insight about the enemy though, doesn't it?"

"What insight?" asked Cindy.

"Well, based on what ASAC Holmes just said, it would mean that while we are facing a formidable force of leaders, they are *not* especially the 'best and the brightest'—they only have to have the right political view to qualify."

"That's good news for our fight, cuz just maybe they aren't all that good or bright—just powerful."

They all nodded hopefully, realizing that made sense.

"So, if we can't trust virtually anyone in Washington, D.C., I have to ask all of you—will you go to Washington, D.C. with me to fight this battle?"

CHAPTER 125

Cindy cocked her head sideways and was the first to answer.

"Blake, how could I possibly do that with Nic and Linc to take care of? It's just too soon for me to try and handle them on the road."

I nodded.

"Yeah, I know that babe. I wasn't referring to you. We can Skype you in for our planning sessions to get your take—you stay in Arizona. I really don't want you anywhere near the danger—these guys clearly have no compunction about killing anyone who threatens them."

Turning, I said, "I was talking to you two."

ASAC Holmes and Winston looked back at me.

Winston just nodded, but ASAC Holmes had a question—actually, a couple questions.

"How could I possibly explain to my Special Agent in Charge why I am going to Washington, D.C.?"

"I would suggest that you don't," I responded.

"So, I don't tell my boss where I'm going or why?"

"Exactly."

ASAC Holmes just shook his head.

"I know as a private investigator, you don't have to answer to anyone or have a boss, but I don't get to do things like that—I have to follow protocol."

I just looked at him and said, "But what if you didn't have to?"

ASAC Holmes just slowly shook his head at me.

"I don't even know what that means, Blake."

I smiled.

"Neither did I, at least not really, until I met my favorite billionaire, Mr. Araby Triplehorn."

Cindy jumped in.

"Blake, that's a great idea!"

ASAC Holmes was looking back and forth between us, still confused.

"What's a great idea?" he asked.

"I have learned the shocking ability to influence, that men with crazy amounts of money and power actually have. Mr. T has paved the way for me to do everything I'm doing right now. When he hired me for the job, he picked up his phone and called the personal number of the President of the United States to clear the deck for me. The man actually already had the President of the United States' personal number in his phone! And the President *picked up* Araby's call, and magically, I had all the access I needed."

ASAC Holmes still looked confused.

"Wait, we now know that the President is a part of the conspiracy and in the Cabal. Why would he do that?"

"That's exactly what I'm trying to tell you—that's how powerful a man like Mr. Triplehorn is. We now know that the *last* thing the President wanted to allow was some gumshoe poking around Senator Ashford's murder. The Cabal had buried everything and were just waiting for the heat to bleed off. But even 'the Leader of the Free World' couldn't say 'no' to a man as powerful as the twenty-third richest man in the world, so he had no choice."

Maverick thought about that.

"OK, but how does that relate to me?"

"Mr. Triplehorn could make one call—*one call*—to your Special Agent in Charge, and you would be free to work on this case with me. And Mr. T could do this and not even provide information as to why—he's that good."

"Are you sure he can pull this off?"

"Actually, no. But based on what I've seen, I'm guessing that I'm right. Money talks."

"It would take me one call to find out."

ASAC Holmes stared at me.

He finally said, "Make the call."

CHAPTER

— 126 —

I asked Winston to provide an encrypted phone for the call, and to set it up as a Skype call as well.

Since I had Mr. T's personal number (because I'm such an important and connected player—insert laughy face emoji here, and then yell, "Play on, player!"), I knew he wouldn't answer an unknown number, so I texted him from the number first.

The text read, "Mr. T, this is Blake, texting you from an FBI encrypted phone. I am about to Skype you from this phone on an urgent matter regarding operation 'Take 'em Down'. Are you available, sir?"

We waited less than a minute.

I then got this text: "How much did you sell the car I gave you for?"

I chuckled. He was good, asking something only Cindy and I would know to verify it was me.

I texted back.

"Good spy-craft sir. If things don't work out for you in your current field, perhaps you could come and work for me. $11,500,000. By the way, that's what I sold it for, not the salary I'm offering you to come and work for me."

Again, we waited less than a minute.

"I'm in a conference right now in Tokyo, but I'll step out now. Give me five minutes."

I did, and then Winston did his magic and another huge screen lit up in ASAC Holmes' office.

I made the call.

Mr. Triplehorn's face appeared, and he was already laughing.

"Honestly Blake, I knew it was you as soon as you started offering me a job—and for the record, I'd never work for a measly eleven and a half million dollars—how could you expect me to live on that?"

He looked around and saw everyone.

"Well, hello Cindy, how are you and the boys?"

Cindy smiled warmly from her screen.

"We're doing well, Araby, thank you."

He looked some more.

"Is that computer genius, Winston I see, from the wedding?"

Winston just nodded once, but I think I saw his face color a bit at Mr. T's compliment.

I jumped in.

"Thanks for taking some time, Mr. T. The only one in this room who you don't know is Assistant Special Agent in Charge Maverick Holmes, from the Fort Pierce, Florida branch of the FBI."

Mr. Triplehorn nodded.

"Good to meet you ASAC Holmes—I'm loving the first name Maverick, by the way."

He nodded.

"Thank you, sir—good to meet you too."

Was it just me, or did Mr. FBI seem a little flummoxed to be meeting 'the big man'?

Mr. T turned toward me with a smile.

"So, Blake, my first question is, when did you name this operation, 'Take 'em Down'?"

I laughed.

"About ten minutes ago, sir. It was on the fly, and I was just spit balling if you have other ideas."

"Nah, it works."

"So, my second and third questions are, where are we in the investigation and why is my investigator in Fort Pierce, Florida, when all the problems are in Washington, D.C.?"

CHAPTER
— 127 —

"All good questions, sir—especially considering you're paying the freight for all of this—so let me take a pass at them."

"After the funeral, and then Isabella's quinceañera, I flew back to D.C. to do some more investigation this morning. I honestly wasn't sure what to do next, so I got Detective Lee to get me back into Senator Ashford's office to think."

"While I was there, sitting in the meeting area of his office, just thinking about the case, I found myself staring at his extensive collection of New York Yankee bobbleheads."

Mr. Triplehorn chuckled.

"He *did* love the Yankees."

"See, right there! That's what got me—everyone who knew Todd clearly knew that about him. It's what I was told by both his wife, Brooke, and his close friend Tim, after the funeral. It clearly was such a signature part of the senator that it naturally came up in casual conversation about him."

"So, as I sat there, trying to figure out my next move, it surprised me when my eye caught a different color of uniform on a bobblehead in the back—a Boston Red Sox bobblehead."

Mr. T's head went back, and his face showed surprise and disbelief.

"No, that can't be—he *hated* the Red Sox."

"So I've heard. But when I reached to the back and got it out, sure enough, it was a Boston Red Sox bottlehead of Babe Ruth."

"Really," said Mr. T, the question implied.

I nodded.

"Yes sir. I sat there looking at it, trying to figure it out. This represented, what the senator would see as, the *ultimate enemy*."

"That's pretty much when my eyes bugged out."

Mr. Triplehorn's look just turned quizzical, furrowed brows and everything.

"I'm afraid you're going to have to show your work on that equation, Blake."

"OK. Anyone who knew Todd would be shocked to find this bobblehead among his collection. I wondered if it was his clue to all of us, so I examined it closely and found that the base had been cut. I used a utility knife Todd had in his desk and removed the piece . . ."

"Yeah?" interjected Mr. Triplehorn.

". . . and I found a flash drive, sir."

"OK, that's intriguing, what was on it?"

"Well, sir, that's the answer to your third question. I tried to fire it up on my laptop, but the contents were passcode protected. I tried a couple of things, based on my limited knowledge of Todd and his family, but nothing worked."

"As you can imagine, I was reluctant to use any of the Washington, D.C. law enforcement to try to open the flash drive, because one, it would create a paper trail and two, I didn't know who I could trust and who was involved in what we suspected was a cabal."

"So, since I knew I could trust the men I had worked with on the Skylar De Le Croix abduction case in Florida, I drove right back to National Airport and flew to Orlando, then drove down to FBI headquarters in Fort Pierce, Florida."

Mr. T studied me for a moment and then looked over at ASAC Holmes.

"Am I going to have to get my man out of some trouble now for removing evidence from a crime scene, ASAC Holmes?"

Maverick looked uncomfortable.

"Generally speaking, sir, yes—but given the size and scope of what we found, that may be the least of our concerns."

Mr. T nodded once, and I cut back in.

"Our computer wizard, Winston, set his 'babies' to work on the flash drive and broke the passcode around 4:30 this morning. It turned out that Senator Ashford was not messing around with this, because he used a series of random letters, numbers, and symbols—which are the best passcodes, to virtually encrypt this drive. You either had to have the passcode or use a supercomputer to break into the flash drive, as Winston did so effectively."

Winston just nodded to acknowledge my praise.

I looked back at Mr. Triplehorn.

"What we found on the flash drive isn't good, sir."

CHAPTER
—128—

Mr. Triplehorn's brow furrowed again.

"How 'isn't good' are we talking, Blake?"

I took a breath and let my eyes stray to the ceiling.

"Well, I would say a conspiracy cabal involving hundreds of people in powerful positions to destroy America as it was founded 'isn't good' kind of bad, sir."

Mr. Triplehorn just stared at me.

"Spell it out for me, son."

I nodded.

"On the flash drive, we found a summary that we started with. Senator Ashford began with a history of radical revolutionaries whose writings led our nation here. The things they wrote were truly a step-by-step method on how to both overwhelm and overthrow the United States as founded."

"I'm sorry to say that they have followed that plan to a 'T', sir."

"Senator Ashford then listed all the names that he suspected might be in the Cabal—that list numbered in the thousands. He then noted which names he had confirmed were in the Cabal—that list numbered in the hundreds, sir."

Mr. T just continued to listen.

"Just looking at the names of the confirmed cabal members was sobering. It included every major law enforcement agency, most departments in the government, and very familiar names of major players within the government."

Mr. T just looked at me for a moment.

"How familiar, Blake?"

I took a deep breath before I delivered the bad news.

"The members of the President's Cabinet who were both *listed* and *confirmed* to be a part of the Cabal included the Director of National Intelligence, the Administrator of the Environmental Protection Agency, the Secretary of Education, the Secretary of Energy, the Secretary of Housing, the Secretary of Health, the Secretary of Agriculture, the Attorney General, the Secretary of the Treasury, and the Secretary of State."

I let that sink in for a moment before I continued.

"However, sir, what we all just stared at were the top two names: both the Vice-President of the United States and the President of the United States were *listed* and *confirmed*."

Mr. T's face blanched.

"Sir, Senator Ashford had discovered that this treason against the United States of America went all the way to the top—and when he started confronting them about it, they killed him for it."

CHAPTER 129

Araby just stared at me. Finally, he spoke.

"How can you be sure this Cabal killed Todd?"

"Well sir, while I'll admit there's some conjecture on my part, I think I can show you that it's a pretty *logical* conjecture. Also, I'm sitting here with exceptional law enforcement personnel, and they agree with that assessment. Let me read for you how Senator Ashford set out to deal with what he had found."

I found the place and began to read.

"I have decided to begin contacting the various powerful members on this list and inform them that they can either resign or I will expose their involvement in this conspiracy cabal."

"My intention is to then put in place elements of policy that will deter such actions in the future. That plan is located after the following list."

I looked up at Mr. Triplehorn.

"I would surmise from that sir, that Todd began letting some of these members know what he had on them, and what he intended to do. It appears that instead of resigning, they chose a different option, deciding they could continue their conspiracy if they just killed him and destroyed his research."

"They thought they pulled it off by taking his written documents and then destroying his laptop. However, I have to believe they are really on edge at the moment, wondering if they may have missed something."

Mr. T replied.

"Like a Boston Red Sox, Babe Ruth bobblehead."

I just nodded, then added, "And being 'really on edge' does make this whole situation, and them, extremely volatile and dangerous."

Another really deep breath from Mr. Triplehorn.

"OK, Blake. First of all, I don't want to blow past the fact that once again, you're the man. You found the key component to the case that everyone else missed. I can't thank you enough for your work on this case."

"Thank you, sir," I said with a nod of gratitude.

"Now Blake, I need you to have a plan to destroy this Cabal and save our country. Do you?"

I thought about that.

"Well sir, I have an idea, but I'm going to need your help—a lot."

"Hit me with it."

It was my turn to take a deep breath.

"Well sir, as you know, I would very much like to stay alive."

"I would second that sentiment," Cindy interjected.

Mr. T chuckled at that.

"Yes, I'm aware of that, son—and Cindy," he said, looking over and smiling at her.

I went on.

"That means that, as much as possible, everything we do from here forward needs to be stealthy—virtually untraceable."

"OK, I would agree," said Mr. Triplehorn.

"With something this big, powerful, and convoluted, I believe that we need to assemble a team in the belly of the beast—Washington, D.C."

"Are you familiar with the 'Trojan Horse', used by the Greeks in the Trojan War, sir?"

"Somewhat."

I looked around the room.

"OK. Here's how that played out. After the failure of a ten-year siege of the city of Troy during the Trojan War, the Greeks built a huge wooden horse, leaving it outside the gate of Troy, telling the leaders of

Troy that it was an offering to their goddess, Athena. The fact that a horse was the symbol of Troy helped sell the deception."

"The Greeks then burned their own tents and pretended to sail away, as though they were abandoning the war and heading home."

"Against the concerns of a number of leaders, including Helen of Troy, the leaders opened the gate of Troy and brought the wooden horse into the city as a victory trophy."

"Unfortunately for the city of Troy, the architect of the scam, a soldier named Odysseus, was inside the wooden horse, along with a select force of fighting men."

"The Greeks also left one warrior there named Sinon, who pretended he had been abandoned. Once Sinon saw that the wooden horse had been taken inside the city, he signaled the Greek army, which had sailed back under the cover of darkness and waited off the coast, by lighting a torch."

"Late that night, the Greeks inside climbed out of the wooden horse and opened the gates of the city for the waiting Greek army. The Greek army entered through the open gates and destroyed the city, ending the Trojan War."

I looked around the room.

"As formidable as the city of Troy had been during *a ten-year siege*, they lost everything because they fell for a deception."

"Metaphorically, a 'Trojan Horse' has come to mean any trick or strategy where a target invites their enemy into a secure or protected place."

We were all startled when Winston spoke.

"A malicious computer program that tricks users into willingly running it is also called a 'Trojan Horse' or simply a 'Trojan'. Laymen often call it spam or phishing."

I just stared at Winston. This constituted an all-out "oration" from my little friend.

Will wonders never cease?

CHAPTER 130

After we'd all recovered a bit from Winston's *crazed* outburst, Mr. Triplehorn had a question—a question that I'm guessing everyone in the room had too.

"OK, Blake, what is the point of your Trojan War soliloquy?"

I nodded, now recovered from Winston's outburst.

"Sir, what has happened from this conspiracy cabal is nothing more than a proverbial 'Trojan Horse'. Many of these people were elected, funded by billionaires like George Soros, Bill Gates, Mark Zuckerburg, and the like. They were welcomed into the gates by leftists and are now in a position to systematically destroy America as founded."

I looked around the room.

"We need to flip the script on them, sir—we need to become that 'Trojan Horse'."

"OK. And how do we do that?"

I took a deep breath and thought.

"First of all, can you arrange for Assistant Special Agent in Charge Holmes and Winston to be free to travel with me to Washington, D.C.?"

"Certainly, no problem."

Internally, I just shook my head. Mr. Triplehorn didn't even have to think about it. If he wanted it done, moving two FBI assets from Fort Pierce, Florida, to wherever he wanted them, even without explanation, was just another day at the office. I glanced over at ASAC Holmes with an "I told you so" look on my face.

"OK, great. Now, we all need to 'Trojan Horse' this plan, so will you also charter us a private plane from a more obscure airfield that will not include our names on the manifest?"

"I can have that done. I'll get Thurston on it. Let me know where you want to fly from and fly to and it will be done."

"Great. We'll be flying into National, and we'll get you the departing airfield information momentarily."

I said that nodding at Winston, who took out his laptop and started working on it.

"Now sir, I will need you to get us rooms back at the Waldorf Astoria for us to work out of, but it's got to be without your fingerprints on it, so the Cabal can't trace it back to you. Oh, that goes for the private plane too. I'm certain the Cabal is keeping an eye on you, especially since you're the one who called the President to get my investigation started."

Mr. Triplehorn was nodding—I was speaking his language now.

"OK, I can do all that—I'll get Thurston on that too."

"Thanks."

I looked at ASAC Holmes and Winston.

"I don't mean to be presumptuous here, but I guess I am being just that. Are you two willing to come to Washington, D.C. with me and battle this Cabal?"

They looked back at me and then nodded.

"OK. Mr. T, please have Thurston arrange some way that we don't have to go through a concierge or check-in desk, since we are going to need to avoid being too obvious when we get there."

"Got it."

And then I thought, "And now for the *pièce de résistance*."

"Finally, sir, I need you there with us in D.C. too."

Mr. T looked surprised.

"You what?"

"Sir, to put the 'Trojan Horse' in your terms, we are trying to *stop* a 'hostile takeover' of our country by *executing* a "hostile takeover' of the Cabal ourselves."

Mr. Triplehorn nodded.

"I think you will be invaluable to both our planning and execution, since, at least at times, a 'hostile takeover' is just what you do—and you are *very good* at it."

"There will be things we need to accomplish and access that only you can easily provide—we can't. And when it's time to pile out of the horse and execute our attack, we're going to need all your clout to make it work."

"I know you said you're in Tokyo, sir, I'm sure involved in very important and high-level meetings, but I need you—and your country needs you, in Washington, D.C.—now."

Mr. Triplehorn just stared.

"You're good, son—really good." Mr. T took a deep breath and said, "I'll wrap this meeting in the next hour and be on my way to D.C."

"Thank you, sir—we'll see you there."

CHAPTER

— 131 —

As you might imagine, after we finished the impromptu teleconference, and I said goodbye to Mr. Triplehorn and Cindy, then things started happening pretty fast.

Winston had found a more obscure airfield for us to fly out of very easily. It turned out that Fort Pierce had its own small airfield—Saint Lucie County Airport and even Saint Lucie County International Airport. The airport was only about thirty-minutes from the FBI headquarters. ASAC Holmes arranged for one of his agents to drive us in my rental car to the private airfield part of the airport, and then take care of returning the car for me, keeping me off any of the general airport terminal cameras.

I texted the airport information to Thurston, and he texted back that he would get me the departure flight time "momentarily".

That's Thurston for you—in his world, virtually everything will take place "momentarily".

I had a question for Winston.

"Hey. Is there any way that you could get the information on the flash drive and send it to Mr. Triplehorn to study? He's going to have some time when he's not sleeping on his way back from Tokyo that he could familiarize himself with what we're facing."

Winston looked at me for a moment, clearly thinking, and then he nodded once and set to work. He put all the information on the flash drive into a folder, and then encrypted it with a random passcode, just like Senator Ashford had done.

"It's ready," he said to me.

"OK."

I texted Mr. Triplehorn on the encrypted phone, telling him what we were sending him. I then nodded to Winston, and he sent the folder.

Winston then took the encrypted phone from me.

"I need to send the passcode separate from the material—it's safer."

I nodded and waited while he sent Mr. T the long, random key combination that would open the documents.

I "momentarily" got the departure time for our flight back from Thurston, and we now seemed to have everything set, and a few hours until departure.

ASAC Holmes raced home to tell his wife and family that he'd be gone for a little while. He purposely didn't tell them where he was headed—he pulled the "it's classified" routine.

Winston wasn't married, so he just went to his home and got his stuff together.

I had all my things with me in a bag in my rental car, so I had a little time on my hands.

If you were with me on my adventure here, rescuing Skylar De Le Croix from the murdering pervert, you may remember that the FBI headquarters in Fort Pierce was only a couple blocks from the beautiful Atlantic Ocean—it's actually a great view from the back of the building.

With some extra time on my hands, and being steps from the ocean, why not take advantage of that?

So, I jumped into my rental car and drove up South Second Steet to Citrus Avenue, over to Highway One, to a Kentucky Fried Chicken I knew was there. I knew this because Winston and I had gorged ourselves there one time "back in the day", as they say.

I conservatively only got the three-piece chicken big box meal—after all, a newly married man needs to watch his figure! Just three pieces of extra-crispy chicken, mashed potatoes and gravy, coleslaw, a biscuit with butter and honey, and a diet coke.

See, right there with the "diet coke" is me watching my figure.

I drove back to the FBI headquarters, parked, and then hoofed the two blocks over to the beach. For the record, notice that I *walked* over to the beach, adding exercise to my diet coke choice.

I know, I know—you're thinking that Cindy is one lucky lady. Let's just all agree with your assessment and move on—I'm starting to get a little embarrassed.

There was a light breeze coming off the ocean, the waves were crashing on shore, and the sun was warm, but not hot. I kicked off my shoes and pulled off my socks so that I could feel the warm sand on my feet.

I plopped down in the sand and opened my "feast in a bag".

As I sat and ate, looking out at all the tranquility, I contemplated both the attack that was being perpetrated on my country by the Cabal and the things I might have to do to defend my country from them.

Todd Ashford's funeral had helped me be outraged at what they had done to a truly good man and his family. That was helpful, because I work better and more effectively when I am personally *incensed* by the evildoers.

Yes, I just said "evildoers".

Another element of my success is when I get into my superhero mode—saving mom, apple pie, and the American way—and in this case, that description might just be completely and factually accurate!

And I don't know, but maybe I'll save Kentucky Fried Chicken too—dang, this chicken is good!

CHAPTER
— 132 —

We were all at the private plane part of Saint Lucie County Airport a few hours later when the plane Mr. Triplehorn chartered for us came flying in.

It wasn't quite as large or upscale as Mr. Triplehorn's Gulfstream G650, which only cost a cool sixty-million-dollars, but it was nice. It had to transport only three of us, and it seated twelve, so we had plenty of room.

The flight time on a commercial aircraft from Fort Pierce, to Washington, D.C. nonstop, was typically about two and a half hours. However, private planes flew higher and faster than commercial planes, so we were back at Ronald Reagan Washington National Airport in a fair amount of time less than two hours.

I had a credit card number that Thurston had sent me, which wouldn't connect to any of us or Mr. Triplehorn. So, once we arrived, I used it to rent a vehicle. This time I went for a full-size, Chevy Suburban, black, which reminded me of my Dallas trip to save Isabella. It would also blend in well around D.C.—politicians do love their black SUVs!

With the three of us here now, and Mr. Triplehorn arriving soon, I would need lots of room for all of us.

We all piled in and got back across the Potomac River into Washington, D.C.

Once we got to the Waldorf Astoria, I got parked and we got ready to go in. We all put hats on, pulled low over our faces—we were playing it safe and trying to not have our faces get caught on camera.

We went around to the front entrance like Thurston said to, and when we got to the doorman, I just nodded and said, "Thurston Twelvetrees' rooms please".

The doorman nodded and took four packets out of his suit pocket and handed them to me. I thanked him and palmed him a twenty-dollar-bill.

This was good spy-craft again. The doorman was the only connection to our operation at this point, and his only point of reference was someone named "Thurston Twelvetrees". It would take some work to trace him and get back to Mr. Triplehorn, even if someone questioned the random doorman for some reason.

I glanced at the room numbers, did a double-take, and then headed through the lobby toward the elevators.

ASAC Holmes and Winston were trying to play it cool, but I was guessing this place was blowing their minds.

I would bet the farm that the FBI didn't usually spring for places like the Waldorf Astoria for their agents to stay. At least I sure hoped not! I paid over three-million-dollars in federal taxes recently, and I'd just as well prefer it didn't go for five-star accommodations for federal agents.

There was a reason I'd done a "double-take" when I looked at the rooms listed on the packets. Three of them were the beautiful Jr. Suite with the king bed, just like I'd had before, for a mere $1,275 a night each. However, the fourth one was the best the Waldorf had, the Waldorf Townhouse Two Bedroom Bi-level, which I just so happened to know was $25,500 *a night*!

I didn't know why Mr. Triplehorn would need a two-bedroom room, but maybe when you're as rich as him, you just always opted for the top of the line by saying, "Just give me your best"—I would assume in a haughty voice.

Mr. Triplehorn wouldn't arrive until late tonight, or even early tomorrow morning. It's kind of weird that there is a fourteen-hour time difference between Tokyo and Washington, D.C., and the non-stop flight on his faster private G-650 is right around fourteen hours. That means that since Tokyo is ahead of us, he could leave at say noon on a Tuesday and get back to D.C. around noon on that *same Tuesday*!

So weird.

I was kind of looking forward to seeing his two-story room—just to see what $25,500 a night could buy!

We got to our floor and headed to our rooms. They were all right next to each other, which is what I asked Thurston to set up. Should there be any trouble, we would do better if we were all right next to each other to add layers of protection.

"Here's your packet and keys guys."

I looked at my watch.

"You can order room service for dinner, so we don't show our faces any more than we need to—it will all go on Mr. T's tab. Go ahead and take the rest of the night and enjoy the amenities—tomorrow we plan and start the operation."

CHAPTER 133

After I got settled and got something to eat, I Skyped Cindy.

"Hey babe."

"Hey. So, in what city is my handsome, sexy husband now? Cuz last time you surprised me. Oh, in addition to that, is anybody else listening to us right now, cuz if you did that to me again, you are going to be majorly busted!"

I smiled.

"First of all, I approve of all your adjectives referring to me, and want to encourage more of that particular thought process in the future. And no, it's just the two of us this time."

Cindy chuckled low in her throat, knowing full-well what that does to me.

The little tease!

"I'll bet you like those adjectives! So, are you back in Washington, D.C., or are you for some reason in Argentina this time?"

"No, I'm actually back in the Caribbean."

Cindy closed her eyes and sighed.

"Don't tease me like that—I still think about our time in Cancún, especially when the boys decide to be extra demanding. That was an amazing two weeks."

"Yeah, I would say so—especially cuz that's when your 'handsome, sexy husband' knocked you up with those two aforementioned 'extra demanding' boys."

"Yes, you did, stud, yes you did."

I moved the phone around to show her the suite.

"As you can see, we're back at the Waldorf Astoria, toughing it out on Mr. Triplehorn's tab."

"Can I see the boys?"

Cindy smiled.

"Yeah. They are just laying here staring up at their mobiles in amazement. I laugh every time I see Nic and Linc doing that because they have the same look on their face that you get when something grabs your attention."

She turned the phone so I could see the boys lying on their backs, kicking away, and cooing, as they looked at their mobiles.

She was right, I did get that look of wonderment on my face when I was especially intrigued by something, and I had it now, looking at my twin sons.

"Wow. I do love those little farts so much," I said.

Cindy laughed.

"I'm not sure how I feel about you calling our precious twins 'farts', but I have to admit, they are gassy little dudes."

We laughed.

"So, is everybody settled?"

"Yeah. You should have seen the look on Maverick's and Winston's faces when we walked into the Waldorf."

Cindy laughed and said, "Yeah, those of us who have served on the government dime didn't often find ourselves in five-star accommodations like that."

We both laughed.

"Mr. Triplehorn will get here, either late tonight or tomorrow morning, then we'll get started."

"Can you get some help with the boys from Consuela or Isabella, so you can join us?"

"I should be able to. I'll have to cut out periodically to feed them, but other than that, I should be good. You know how much they love taking care of the boys."

"Yeah, they've been awesome."

So, we had everything set.

CHAPTER
— 134 —

Cindy then changed the subject.

"Blake, I was thinking about something relative to the case, and wanted to run it by you."

"OK."

"I was thinking about this whole conspiracy along with the fact that Senator Ashford was who and where he was, and I started wondering if you shouldn't be looking for a specific 'kingpin' who is pulling the strings in D.C."

"How do you mean? Like, the President?"

"No, that would be a mistake, I think," replied Cindy.

"How so?"

"I think we would naturally think of the most powerful person in the world as the one who would be leading this Cabal, but I think he could just as likely be a pawn, a figurehead—as a matter of fact, I think it is more likely that he is."

"Why?"

"Well, first of all, everyone already knows that the President isn't all that sharp—there are clearly other people pulling the strings behind him and making decisions for him—most notably, former President Obama and his advisors."

"Secondly, the demands of being the President would be such that someone else makes more sense—someone who could devote much of his or her time to pursuing this agenda."

"OK, I can see that."

"It could be a powerful lobbyist, I suppose, but it seems to me that it would help if he had significant political power of his own to wield too. Maybe a chief of staff or someone else high in the administration—or even an elected official."

"They would have to have a direct information channel on all things related to the federal government, and the time and power to run things. And by that, I mean to execute the demands and desires of the 'elites' at the top of the Cabal."

"And when I use the term, 'execute', that would also include the power to give the order to 'take someone out', as they did with Senator Ashford."

I was thinking about it.

"I just want to make sure that as we think of this elusive 'Cabal', we don't lose sight of the fact that typically organizations have 'a guy', and that guy calls the shots."

"Taking on an international Cabal could feel overwhelming and intimidating—but taking out the key component that enables it to work, and destroying it that way, is not so overwhelming."

I was thinking.

"Like taking out a key component in a watch that makes the rest of the mechanism useless."

Cindy nodded.

"Exactly. It was just like when you were dealing with the Los Zetas Cartel. It was a huge, international, multifaceted organization, but you figured out when you went to Dallas, that Santiago Mendoza was 'the man', and he needed to be the focus of your attack. Take him down and the organization suffers."

"However, in this case, take the right man, or number of men out, and the Cabal might not just suffer—at least in the United States, you might destroy it."

I sighed.

"I see what you're saying. We read the thousands of names who are possibly in the Cabal, and then saw the hundreds of 'confirmed' names, and we think vast organization, but we don't have to destroy each of them. We just need to find, and focus on, cutting off the head of the snake to start destroying it."

"Yep, that's what I've been wondering about."

"Good take, Cindy Lou—we'll have to talk about that tomorrow."

Cindy and I spent some more time talking, but I won't record that here—cuz it was sexy talk, and my momma raised a gentleman. (Insert wiggling eyebrows emoji here.)

The good news for me in this aforementioned, unreported conversation, was that Cindy was clearly already over this "one-month restriction" herself.

And with that important revelation, I felt myself *becoming* that wiggling eyebrows emoji.

CHAPTER
— 135 —

I had texted Mr. Triplehorn later that night that if he got in before I was up the next morning, the packet to his suite of rooms was just barely visible under the door of my suite.

I knew that a man like Mr. T wouldn't have to worry about getting wherever he needed to, but the plan here was to keep things on the 'down-low'. Having the twenty-third richest man in the world waltz up to the check-in desk in the middle of the night, where he would most certainly be remembered, seemed to me to defeat that purpose.

When I got up the next morning, the packet was gone, so I knew Mr. T was now at the Waldorf. I amused myself by thinking of my favorite billionaire down on his knees, working to coax the packet out from under my door around 3:30 in the morning, but he probably had people he paid to do such things, so it lost a little of its humor.

After getting cleaned up and ordering some room service, I called Cindy.

"Good morning, my sweet—how did you sleep?"

"Well, your progeny decided they were in a playful mood last night, and while they are cute little guys, it's not nearly as cute at 2:00 a.m. and 5:30 a.m. Little stinkers."

"So, all is good on the home front, is what I'm taking from that."

"I'm sure that *is* what you're hearing, Mr. 'I slept all night like a baby all alone in my fancy hotel room'."

I paused.

"Cindy, you *do* realize that title is *way* too long to land—don't you?"

Cindy sighed.

"Yes, I do. I'm just tired and I couldn't come up with a better one off the cuff."

I smiled.

"I really am sorry it was such a long night. Do you think you can get a nap when the boys do?"

"Yeah, and I have Consuela around, who is always wanting to get some extra time with the little guys. So, I'll live."

"Good. I just have a quick question for you. Mr. T got here sometime in the night, and I don't know if ASAC Holmes or Winston are up yet."

"Fire away, Mr. Well-rested."

"OK, see, now *that one* works."

"Ask your question, Blake," said my exasperated bride.

"OK. Since you're our 'local police' expert, what do you think about my asking Detective David Lee to join our efforts? Do you think he would bring enough to the table to justify working with us?"

Cindy thought about that.

"I do think that a local law enforcement person would be helpful because he'll have a lay of the land that none of the rest of us will. Do you think you can trust this guy?"

"Well, he was willing to tell me that I might do well to not make him aware of anything I didn't want to go into a report that would be available around the Capitol Police Department. He admitted that he couldn't ensure that the place was leak-proof."

Cindy thought about that.

"OK, I agree that's quite an admission for him to make, and it does seem to imply that he is seeking justice and right, instead of just his career."

"Did you check the list when we were looking through it? Was his name there?"

"You bet I checked for his name, and it was not there. However, he was right to be concerned about the Capitol Police. With just a cursory look, I saw at least three or four names that were followed by 'CP', including the Chief of Police, Ortez, the first guy I met with."

Cindy thought about that.

"OK. Then I think his input could be very valuable as we begin to strategize and plan. He'll know how Washington, D.C. works—what works and what to avoid, just like any local cop would, just from working the city."

I nodded.

"OK, I'll get in touch with him and have a 'confab' to see if he wants to help us. However, he'll have to be willing to do it 'off the books', or I can't use him."

"Thanks for insight—I hope you get some rest today. Tell the boys their dad says to dial down the adorable, yet annoying, early in the morning 'playfulness'."

"I'm not sure you can tell them that, Blake, since you tend to engage in quite a bit 'playfulness' with me too."

"Hmmm. Tell Nic and Linc that I said, 'Do as I say, not as I do'."

That made my girl laugh.

CHAPTER 136

I texted Detective Lee from my special phone.

The text read, "This is Blake. I'm back in town and was hoping to talk to you. I'm letting you know that I'm calling you from a different phone, so you'll pick up. Let me know when you are in a secure situation where you can talk, and I'll call you."

He texted me a few minutes later with: "I'm still at home, but if walking into my backyard constitutes enough of a 'secure situation', *007*, then you can call me now."

I know he was being a little snarky with the whole *'007'* comment, but I did view myself that way, so I very much approved of the reference. Besides, if he knew what we were really facing, he'd be surprised how accurate his description actually was.

I called. When he answered, I quickly said, "This is *007*. Is the rabbit in the warren?"

Silence.

"What the heck does that mean, Blake?"

"I'm not really sure, but it seemed like I needed to say something like that with the *007* reference," I said laughing.

David laughed too.

"So, welcome back to D.C. Our last conversation was quite 'cryptic' as I remember. Now can you tell me what's going on and where you went?"

"Sorry, that's classified," I answered.

"What? Seriously?"

"Oh, I'm just sticking with the *007* persona, but I'm kind of not kidding—until I can talk to you and ask you some questions, I honestly can't tell you what's going on or where I went."

There was more silence on the phone.

"OK, Blake. Let me ask this—did you discover something about Senator Ashford's case that I should know about?"

"Hmmm", I thought.

"I did find something, but I can't really know if you should know about it until after we have a conversation."

"Isn't 'a conversation' what we're having right now?" David asked with some confusion.

"We are. However, I was wondering if you'd be able to come over to the Waldorf Astoria so we could talk about some things face to face before you decide how much you actually want to know."

A skip of a beat happened while he thought that through and weighed its significance.

"OK, let me get ready, and I'll get over there. However, I also need to observe that working private investigation must be *very different* from government work if you get to stay at the Waldorf."

"Yeah, if you only knew, Detective."

I thought this might be the wrong time to let him know that I was a multimillionaire, who lived on an estate in the Tucson Mountains, and resided in a fifteen-thousand-square-foot home.

What can I say? I am very in tune with the human psyche.

I gave him my room number and a special, encrypted knock to use when he got there, so I would know it was him.

Allow me to pause for a moment.

Did I get you? I think I got you.

I was just joking about the knock—but down deep, in places I can't really admit to other people—I kind of wish I *had* given him one.

You know, being *007* and all.

CHAPTER
— 137 —

Detective David Lee got to my room about forty minutes later. For the record, he did the standard, "knock, knock, knock'. It wasn't encrypted at all.

So disappointing.

I opened the door.

"Hey Blake. I have to ask how you could you be sure it was me without a special, secret agent knock, or something."

Again, the snark. However, now I knew for sure—I should have given him that encrypted knock.

I smiled.

"I'll remember next time."

He came in and looked around.

"Seriously? I have *got* to get out of public service and into the private sector!"

I laughed.

"For the record, it's not often like this. I'm working for the twenty-third richest man on the planet—and he's a good friend too, so the game changes dramatically in that scenario."

He looked around some more.

"I guess so."

We sat down in the seating area that looked out toward the White House.

"OK. What has happened that is so dramatic that I needed to haul myself over to your palatial digs to hear about?"

I took a deep breath and began.

"I have uncovered some things in the investigation. They are significant. I could really use a guy in the local law enforcement arena for the investigation, and that obvious choice would be you since we have some history."

"My wife, Cindy, was in local law enforcement for years, and she thought you could be a real asset to the investigation, cuz you know the ropes around D.C."

"However, to do so would require you to work—let's call it 'independent'—of your department. What you would be doing with the investigation could in no way be shared with any of your 'brothers in blue'—not *any* of it."

"I realize that is a huge decision to make, and not my decision to make for you."

I just looked at him and waited.

He just looked back at me, clearly uncomfortable.

"Can you tell me more about the situation, or what you've discovered, so I have a little more to go on to make the decision?"

I thought about that.

"I clearly can't tell you too much in case you choose not to join us. I don't want to put you in a bad position where you have to report back to your superiors and end up messing us up."

He looked at me.

"Are you saying that reporting back to my bosses at the Capitol Police *would* put the investigation in jeopardy?"

I looked at him, debating with myself how much to say. I finally simply admitted, "I am."

That hit him hard.

"And you have proof of this?"

"I do."

"Wow," was all he said, realizing that he had just been told that some of the people he worked with were dirty. He made it clear earlier that he wondered about this, but confirmation was a different animal altogether.

He tried another question.

"OK, can you help me out this way? Given that you have information that I don't, and given the fact that your wife was in local law enforcement for years, can you give me a *basis* for making a move like this, outside the chain of command?"

I thought about that question.

"Let me ask you this; did you take an oath that included something along the lines of you committing to support and defend the Constitution of the United States against all enemies, *foreign* and *domestic*' and that your 'true faith and allegiance' would be to the Constitution?"

"I did."

"Then that," I simply said.

He just stared at me and then stood up, turned, and walked over to the window, and stared out at the White House, off in the distance.

Finally, he asked, "Are you telling me that you have proof of an attack on our government by bad actors that relates to the murder of a United States Senator?"

I thought about that.

"I am, but if you choose to not join us, I will enjoin the classic, *'I can neither confirm nor deny that fact, Senator'* if an official chooses to grill me on this in a Congressional Hearing at some point in the future."

Detective Lee just stared at me.

"You can assure me that this evidence is ironclad?"

"I can—and we believe it is exactly what got Senator Todd Ashford murdered by the Cabal, so don't take this decision lightly. You have a family, as do I."

David looked back out at the view, probably not seeing it, but seeing his family instead.

He looked back at me.

"Ironclad proof?" he asked again.

I looked at him.

"In the 1800s, that term came first from the knights who were covered in iron armor. It then was used about warships whose hulls were covered by protective iron sheets."

"The proof I have is that clear and sure—and we'll need that level of protection if you join us, given what we'll be up against."

David looked back out the window, then turned back toward me, clearly struggling with the decision.

He then simply nodded and said, "I'm in."

CHAPTER
— 138 —

I had Detective Lee call in and take a personal day—we really couldn't afford to have some of the bad guys from the Capitol Police coming to look for him.

He did so.

I'd ended up ordering too much food, so I asked Detective Lee if he wanted to dig into what was left in the warming trays. It turned out he had hurried over and hadn't eaten breakfast, so that worked out well for him.

I left him in my suite eating while I went and checked on the other guys.

ASAC Holmes had just gotten out of the shower and had food on its way up. Winston had been up, showered, eaten, and was—wait for it—on his computer.

I know, shocker!

I told them both that I was planning on starting at 10:00 a.m. up in Mr. Triplehorn's suite of rooms on the top floor, and that I would come and get them. I hadn't confirmed that with Mr. T yet, but I was guessing he had slept on his plane and would be able to make the meeting.

I got back to my room where Detective Lee was finishing up breakfast.

He was shaking his head.

"Man, that was good. They really do things top notch at places like this, don't they?"

I laughed.

"Yeah, they do, but they really should. Mr. Triplehorn is paying $1,275 a night for this suite."

His mouth dropped open.

"You have *got* to be kidding me!"

"Nope, and you haven't seen anything yet. As nice as this suite is, we're about to head up to Mr. Triplehorn's suite of rooms, the most expensive at the Waldorf, at $25,500 a night."

His eyes bugged out.

"That is just ridiculous! That's close to my mortgage for an entire year!"

"Yes, it is—but when you have over sixty-billion-dollars and growing—and that's with a 'B', apparently you don't have to concern yourself with such trivial things as how much you're paying a night."

David just shook his head in disbelief at this whole other world.

I told him I needed to call Mr. Triplehorn to set up our meeting and walked into the next room.

"Mr. Triplehorn's room, who is calling please?"

"Thurston, is that you?"

"It is, sir, but may I ask with whom I am speaking?"

"You certainly may, my good man," I replied, trying to use my best British accent.

Then I just waited.

Finally, "with whom am I speaking?"

"Whoa, I thought you'd never ask. It's me, Thurston, you're old buddy, bud, buddy, Blake Moran! The Blake-myster, the Blake-orator—or perhaps I should just reply, 'it is I, Blake Moran, esquire, of the Tucson Morans'."

I got nothing back, but I really didn't expect anything back from Thurston—he was wound pretty tight, which was something I really liked about him.

This also explained why Mr. T needed the big suite with the two bedrooms—he brought his butler with him. Of . . . course, he did.

"Any-who . . . is Mr. Triplehorn around?"

"Master is in the shower and will momentarily be taking his breakfast, sir."

Yeah, you heard that right—Thurston Twelvetrees, butler of Mr. T, calls his boss, "Master". And apparently the uber-wealthy don't "eat breakfast", they "take breakfast"—at least according to my little British friend.

Also, if it seemed that everything in Thurston's world would take place "momentarily"—just like I told you before—that's only because that seems to be the case.

I looked at my watch and figured that Mr. T would have plenty of time to finish his shower and "take his breakfast" by 10:00 a.m.

"OK. Could you let him know that I'm planning on starting our group meeting at 10:00 a.m. in his suite? If that is a problem, just have him give me a call, and we can change it."

"Please also let him know that I have recruited, and am including, Capitol Police Detective David Lee as our local law enforcement contact for our operation."

"Certainly, sir. I will call to confirm the meeting momentarily, after speaking with Mr. Triplehorn."

Now, for the record, that's *not* what I said, and it made more work that way, but I had to smile. Thurston was not a steward, or butler, who could bear to do things the easy way. He *would* call to confirm. And as I said, the aforementioned confirmation call will take place when? Come on, you can get it . . . that's right—"momentarily".

And he did just that about fifteen minutes later.

I just love that little dude.

CHAPTER
— 139 —

I walked back to the other room where Detective Lee was finishing up breakfast. He seemed quite happy to be living the "lifestyle of the rich and famous"—OK, maybe not so famous, but he was living his own version of the rich life.

That made me laugh. I had a bit of a flashback to when I was young, and my parents would watch a British guy named Robin Leach as he would show us the "Lifestyles of the Rich and Famous". It was back in the 1980s and 90s, and I can still remember when his British accent would fill our home, inviting us to join him.

I briefly wondered if Thurston knew Robin Leach.

I just shook my head and smiled. Who would've guessed that there would have come a day when I would be hanging out with number twenty-three in the world based on wealth—and that I'd even gotten to stay at his mansion in San Francisco?

Life is funny.

I looked over at David, and he was just staring at me with a look of concern on his face. I realized I'd been standing there for a little too long—laughing, shaking my head, and thinking my inner monologue—for no apparent reason.

I tried to think quickly to come up with some cover story, but I came up dry. So, I just let him think I was weird.

Cuz I am. Happily so.

"Mr. T said that 10:00 a.m. is a go. He's good with us meeting in his suite, which I'm glad about, cuz I want to see it."

Detective Lee and I talked about our lives and families a little bit, to use up the time, and then headed out of the room a little before 10:00 a.m. to get the guys and head up to the top floor for the meeting.

ASAC Holmes seemed well-rested, but surprised when I was standing at his door with a Capitol Police officer.

I introduced Maverick and David and told Maverick I would explain David's presence when we got to the meeting.

Winston didn't respond much to my little addition, but Winston is not big on facial responses. He is much more comfortable in what I affectionately call his blue-tinted "inner sanctum" with all his "babies", meaning his powerful computers. I briefly toyed with the idea of calling it his "fortress of solitude" when I was working with him at the Fort Pierce FBI headquarters—as a hat-tip to Superman, but I finally landed on "inner sanctum".

After all, since "sanctum" means a sacred place, that's pretty much how my buddy Winston sees his computer room.

And anyway—who doesn't love a great "sanctum"?

CHAPTER
— 140 —

We got to Mr. Triplehorn's bi-level suite of rooms right at 10:00 a.m. I've always valued promptness—I think it shows respect.

Thurston Twelvetrees answered our knock, and I just had to grab him and give him a big hug. As you can imagine, that threw off his whole "dignified butler from the old country" routine, but I just couldn't help it—I just love this little guy.

One might ponder the juxtaposition of my two beliefs that punctuality conveys respect, but invading a dignified man's personal space simply can't be helped.

I'm going to have to ask you *not* to ponder that, cuz for the life of me, I simply have no justification or explanation for the second, and I really don't want to change my behavior—so let's just move on.

After my little friend had "comported himself" once again, he led us into the huge space that a mere $25,500 a night can purchase for a very rich man.

We all just stopped and stared.

Mr. Triplehorn got up to welcome us.

"Gentlemen . . ."

I just held up my hand for him to stop.

"Sir, I know that you live like this all the time—I've lived in your mansion, after all—but none of us have experienced a place like this. Would you be willing to give us a moment to look around at these lovely rooms, and then we'll get to the meeting?"

Mr. T just chuckled, shaking his head, probably expecting nothing less from me, a man he had come to love.

So, my friend just nodded, stepped back, motioned with a sweep of his hand, and said, "Have at it, boys".

And we did just that.

We were like kids on Christmas morning. Even my, "no expression Winston" was showing some movement on his face.

We were at the top of the Waldorf, so the view was magnificent. Not only did this suite house two bedrooms, but it was bi-level, so the ceiling was over twenty feet above us.

The meeting area was huge, with a large, ornate dining table that could seat twelve people. The seating area was filled with luxurious couches and chairs, with the large windows looking over the city, and could seat an additional twelve people.

The main bedroom had a bed that was canopied, with curtains all around it, all looking out through more large windows at the city, which could be shuttered with the push of a button.

The second bedroom was something, in that it was open to a second story library above it that had a railing all around the library walkway.

The bathrooms were huge and filled with fancy fixtures. The walk-in shower, the fancy whirlpool tub, the multiple sinks, and mirrors, and even a bidet in each.

I'll need to remember to mention that to Cindy—she loves bidets. She saw the one in my suite of rooms at Mr. T's mansion and squealed—and that's why we have a number of them at our home in Tucson now.

Having completed our tour, we reassembled back in the seating area. Mr. Triplehorn sat down his computer that he'd been working on and stood up again.

I began.

"I believe you started with, 'Gentlemen . . .', sir."

CHAPTER
—141—

Mr. Triplehorn just chuckled as he shook his head.

I introduced each of the men formally this time, since he had already seen ASAC Holmes and Winston on our Skype visit yesterday.

When I came to Detective Lee, I began this way.

"Guys, this is Detective David Lee from the Capitol Police. I'd like to explain why I asked him to be here, but before I do that, I'd like to Skype Cindy in again."

I looked over at Winston and he held out his hand. I gave him the encrypted phone he had provided for me earlier.

We all watched in silence.

Winston went over to the huge, flat-screen TV and turned it on. He went into the settings and disabled the Internet connection. He then did a couple more tricks and then handed me the phone to call Cindy's number.

"Thanks Winston."

He nodded.

When my beautiful wife answered, she was on the huge screen TV.

"Hey babe. We're all here in Mr. Triplehorn's suite ready to meet. You know most everybody here—oh, and Thurston's here too!"

Cindy looked over and provided a beautiful smile.

"Hello Thurston, it's so good to see you. How are you?"

Thurston nodded.

"I am well, Lady Cindy, thank you for asking. I trust you are well?"

Cindy smiled her beautiful smile.

"I'm a little tired from the twins, but all in all, I'm doing well."

"Quite, quite," came Thurston's patented reply.

That made Cindy smile again.

I think Thurston's insistence on calling Cindy, "Lady Cindy" always gave her a tickle too.

I stepped in.

"OK Cindy, the one you don't know yet is Detective David Lee of the Capitol Police—the man who we discussed last night."

"Detective," said Cindy, with a nod.

"Ma'am."

I looked around the room.

"Since Cindy was involved in local law enforcement for many years as a detective for the Tucson Police Department, I asked her last night about the benefit of having someone in this capacity working with us."

Cindy picked it up from there.

"Being able to have someone local, who knows the ropes, and the pitfalls of an area—or in this case even an entire federal bureaucracy—could prove vital to making sure that our operation doesn't fail simply because we did something stupid and entirely avoidable."

She looked right at David.

"That would be your job, Detective."

He nodded, but then asked a question.

"But exactly what is this operation?"

I nodded at him and looked around the room.

"As you can tell, I haven't briefed Detective Lee yet, deciding to wait to do that here with all of you."

Turning to Detective Lee, I said, "Let me give you the 'Cliff Notes' summary of what we're doing here."

I looked around the room.

"Just so you all know; I made sure that David was not on the list of thousands or the list of confirmed hundreds of the Cabal. However, some of his colleagues in the Capitol Police are, including his superiors."

"What list?" asked Detective Lee, the concern evident in his voice.

Holding up my hand, I said, "I'm going to tell you."

I looked back at the room.

"I want you all to know that Detective Lee has agreed to listen to what we have to say, but to be fair to him, he'll have to decide *after* he hears the basic story whether he will join us. To do this, and still protect our operation, I will need to be a little vague."

I turned to Detective Lee.

"I'm going to tell you a *hypothetical* story."

"Hypothetical?"

"Yeah, maybe it happened, maybe it didn't. Basically, if you choose to *not* join our operation, I'm just weaving a tale—an interesting, whimsical yarn."

Detective Lee looked confused.

"I'm just giving you and us plausible deniability, should we end up not working together. *Capiche?*"

I stopped. What was that? Did I just become an Italian mob boss from the 1940s?

Cindy was just shaking her head at me.

CHAPTER 142

I looked around the room.

"OK, here's the skinny."

"Let's say that I hypothetically found something in Senator Ashford's office when you let me in a few days ago."

Detective Lee sat forward, asking, "What?"

I waved him back.

"Let's say that it was exactly what I'd been looking for this whole time. But since it was encrypted and needed a passcode, I couldn't open it, so I went to see my friends from the FBI in Florida."

I gestured to ASAC Holmes and Winston.

"Let's say that my friend here is a computer genius—which he is—and he got in. Imagine if what we found was a detailed investigation into a cabal that was involved in a conspiracy to overwhelm and overthrow the United States as founded."

David's eyes were getting bigger.

"Let's imagine that Senator Ashford had a list of thousands of names of possible cabal members and a confirmed list of hundreds of members."

"What if the senator had included a history of radicals from the past, who had led our nation to this point, along with the current players who were actively trying to take down this nation as we know it?"

Detective Lee was starting to look a little green around the gills.

"And imagine if the names on the confirmed list included the highest officials in our governmental system—all bent on taking down the United States as founded—while calling it 'transforming' our nation."

I looked at Detective Lee.

"I'm guessing you've already jumped to the fact that it makes the most sense that it would be someone from that 'confirmed list' who we would expect to be the murderer of a sitting United States Senator—or at least the one who ordered the hit."

David nodded slowly.

"So, that's the short story version. If that were all true, it would seem that someone—or a group of 'some ones'—should step up and stop the destruction of our country—not 'transformation', but literal *destruction*."

"The question is whether you want to be one of those 'some ones'?"

Detective Lee just stared at me.

"How confident are you in these facts?"

"I would have to say that for a fabricated, hypothetical story, the facts are ironclad. Case in point—the Cabal killed Senator Ashford."

"Hypothetically speaking," I added.

Detective Lee was wrestling with himself.

He looked up.

"And you're sure that there are members of the Capitol Police who are on that list? People I work with?"

"Yes, I hypothetically counted four members of the Capitol Police on the confirmed list, all high up in the department."

I stared at him and thought as he mulled that over. I then decided to take one more big step.

"OK David, hypothetically speaking, your own Chief of the Capitol Police himself, Raymond Ortez—the guy I met with when I first came to your headquarters—is on the confirmed list."

I looked at him.

"Again, hypothetically speaking."

Detective Lee stared back.

"Do you remember that I asked you, Detective, about your oath, regarding enemies, foreign and domestic?"

"I do."

I pointed at Maverick.

"ASAC Holmes is here because he took the same basic oath. So, I gotta know—is this story about to get real for you, or does it just remain hypothetical, and you simply head out and go back to your day job?"

David paused for a moment and thought.

"I'm in."

I nodded.

"Welcome aboard."

CHAPTER 143

"I just got a call from our source at the Capitol Police."

"Well, it's about time you found something out—I was starting to wonder why I pay you all that money. Tell me something good."

"Well, Detective Lee called in a little while ago and took a 'personal day'."

"Hmmm. That's random and sudden. What are they thinking?"

"To start with, our source is a little confused. He checked on the detective's phone location, and for some reason, Detective Lee's cell phone is placing him at the Waldorf Astoria, on Pennsylvania Avenue."

That threw Mercurius a little too.

"That's weird. What on earth would a police detective be doing at such an elaborate, high-end hotel? Is he having an affair? If he is, why would he go there mid-morning when that is in the 'check-out time' category, not the 'side-piece time' category? And how can this guy afford such a swanky hotel? Is there some corruption with this guy that we've missed?"

"That's where all the confusion is coming from—we can't make any sense out of it. The Chief doesn't have any idea why his detective would be there."

Mercurius thought about that.

"Well, why doesn't he just call him in on the carpet and demand to know?"

There was a pause.

"We could have him do that, but as soon as he does, Detective Lee will know we're tracking him—either by following him or by his cell phone."

Mercurius went quiet. That was a dumb thing for him to suggest. He should have realized that would compromise their surveillance. Having his underling investigator needing to explain that to him, was a really bad look. He couldn't let this employee of his see him as weak.

What was wrong with him? He clearly was freaking out over this possible additional investigation, and their inability to even locate this Blake Moran. It was like he had just dropped off the planet after going to Florida for some reason.

And why Florida? What connection did Senator Ashford's murder have with the state of Florida? He was racking his brain, but he just couldn't find the connection.

Mercurius realized that his investigator was waiting, so he made a decision.

"OK, since this detective is our only possible link to this Moran guy, I want you to get over to the Waldorf and wait for him to appear. Make sure that he doesn't make you—we can't afford for him to know we're monitoring him. And before you go over there, have the Chief make sure that his phone is still showing him there, so you don't waste time waiting for him."

"So, do I follow him when he leaves?"

"Now why would you do that? If we can just track him with his cell phone, it would be a waste of time for you to do the same."

Mercurius was secretly glad his investigator had inadvertently given him an opening to belittle him for not thinking well. It overshadowed his own blunder moments ago.

"No, once you see him, I want you to try and discover why he is there. We need to find out if this is just some stupid affair or if it somehow relates to the Ashford investigation."

"Right, OK, I see that now. I'll try to look around and ask around to see what I can find, and I'll get back to you once I find something."

"Let me know either way. We need to find this Moran fellow. Having him out there and not knowing what he's doing is not good for our cause."

Mercurius had another question.

"I assume you're still not finding anything out from Florida?"

"Well, that was the second thing I wanted to tell you. I tried tracking his rental car through their toll road system, which is extensive down there. I was able to track him from Orlando to Fort Pierce, which is south and east of Orlando, right on the Atlantic coast."

"OK, that's something. What's in Fort Pierce, Florida?"

"Well, that's the thing—not much—at least nothing I could put together with our case. Then, two days later, so yesterday, Moran's rental car was returned to the Saint Lucie County Airport in Fort Pierce."

"OK," said Mercurius, getting excited, "so where did he fly?"

"That's the thing—there's no record that he flew anywhere. No credit card, no flight manifest, nothing. It was like he drove to the airport, gave them the keys, and just walked away from the airport."

"Well, that makes no sense."

"I agree, but it really is like he just vaporized."

Mercurius thought.

"So, we don't know why Fort Pierce is even in play, nor do we know where Moran ended up or where he is right now."

"Yes sir, unfortunately that is accurate."

"Hmmm. Alright, I'll think more about that. You get over to the Waldorf and see if you can find out what our little detective is up to."

"Yes sir."

CHAPTER 144

"Alright, now that we're all in, I can stop doing my 'hypothetical' schtick."

Detective Lee nodded.

"What did you find and where did you find it. I gotta say, both the FBI and the Capitol Police scoured that office."

I told him my story of the bobbleheads, and the moment I saw a bobblehead of Babe Ruth in the back, but this one was Babe Ruth as a Boston Red Sox.

That furrowed Detective Lee's brow.

"Long story short, as I thought about this apparent contradiction of everything I heard about Todd, and his attitude toward the Red Sox, I realized that this bobblehead would represent to him the ultimate 'enemy', which is what he was fighting with the Cabal."

Realization sprang to Detective Lee's face.

"Oh my gosh, there was something inside the bobblehead!"

I nodded.

"Yep, a flash drive that gave us all his research, history, names of possible and confirmed 'evildoers', and even a plan to stop them and put our Representative Republic back in place afterwards."

"Wow, can I see it?"

"Sure."

I turned to Winston.

"Any ideas on how we could do this?"

Winston stared at me and then nodded once.

He got up and just said, "Follow me."

So, I did.

He led me into the dining area, where for some reason there was another large, flat-screen TV.

Now, in the hotels where I usually stay, the TVs are always bolted to something, to make sure the riffraff don't steal them. The "riffraff" in this scenario is apparently me, their faithful customer.

However, at the Waldorf, this big, expensive TV was *not* bolted to the table.

I'm guessing the management of the Waldorf doesn't believe that the "riffraff", who can afford to pay $25,500 a night for their accommodations, don't need to steal their TVs, so they don't insult their high-end clientele by bolting their TVs down.

Winston unhooked everything and we carried the TV into the seating area, setting it on a low table. Winston hooked it up and attached his laptop to it. He had downloaded the flash drive to his laptop, so he just opened up the file on the big screen and looked over at me, waiting for me to tell him which part I wanted to see.

I thought about that.

I figured I could either fill David in on all the history later or he could read it for himself. I was guessing I knew what part he really needed to see first.

"Let's start by showing Detective Lee the hundreds of names that Senator Ashford was able to confirm were a part of the Cabal."

Winston nodded once and navigated to the list.

Detective Lee just stared as the names scrolled.

His eyes opened wide when he saw the names from his own department. He even gasped a little when he saw the top name was Capitol Police Chief of Police, Raymond Ortez—his top boss.

The same guy to whom he was supposed to be reporting all the progress of his investigation into Senator Ashford's murder, as he worked with Arizona private investigator, Blake Moran.

Detective David Lee felt a little sick.

CHAPTER 145

Detective Lee took a deep breath and soldiered on.

"Can I see the list from Congress—the men and women whom we're tasked to protect?"

Winston nodded once and scrolled to that part of the list.

Detective Lee was shocked and horrified at all the members of Congress, both in the Senate and the House, who were confirmed members of the Cabal.

"Wow, this is really, really bad," he said, shaking his head, staring at the list. "So many of them—even the Senate Majority Leader, Brooks."

"Yeah, it is bad, which makes our planning here that much more important. We need to get this right."

David just looked at me.

"Couldn't we just go to the administration and out all these people?"

I looked over at Winston.

"Show him."

Winston did.

There at the top of the confirmed list were both the President and the Vice-President of the United States.

Detective Lee just deflated.

"You have *got* to be kidding me!" he said, shaking his head slowly.

I just shook my head.

"I think you can now see the gravity of the problem and why we have to get this right the first time."

"How could you possibly hope to fix this?"

I simply pointed over to Mr. Triplehorn.

"My main man here is the twenty-third richest man in the world. His ability to get anything he wants done is mind blowing. He can get to anyone he needs to, and we're going to use his power to map out a plan to take down this attack. We're going to flip the script on them."

Detective Lee looked hopefully from Mr. T to me.

"And how are we going to do that?"

"I have absolutely no idea," I responded, grinning from ear to ear.

Detective Lee visibly deflated again.

It was Cindy who spoke up.

"Don't let that comment concern you detective. My husband rarely knows what he's doing at any given time, but if you just give him some time, he really is remarkable."

"Why, thank you, my love," I said with a nod.

Cindy chuckled.

"Seriously, this isn't just blind love talking—I've never seen anything quite like it. Just consider his finding the flash drive. Your whole department and the FBI looked everywhere and didn't find it, but he just listened and learned, then let his mind percolate, and now we have it."

Mr. Triplehorn weighed in.

"Blake took down the *'See Me Killer'* in San Fransisco the same way. Nobody else saw it—Blake did. And he saved my daughter's life in the process."

Mr. T got a little misty at that last statement.

ASAC Holmes spoke up.

"I have to admit that Blake put together the facts to take down a serial rapist and murderer of underaged girls. We didn't even know the cases were connected till Blake connected them."

Winston nodded his agreement.

Cindy jumped back in.

"And I met this big lug when he came to Tucson and solved a murder that our Tucson Police Department had already had to move to the 'cold case' pile."

"And for the record," added Mr. Triplehorn, "that murderer was someone I had actually backed to be the future President of the United States. That's how I knew about Blake and brought him to San Francisco."

I looked around the room.

"Wow, you guys are awesome—thank you."

"I guess we'd better get busy figuring all this out, since I still have absolutely no idea how we're going to do it. After all you just said, it sounds like I got a rep to protect!"

CHAPTER
— 146 —

"So," I said, rubbing my hands together and looking around the room, "how do we rescue the United States of America from this conspiracy cabal and not all end up dead?"

There was a lot of thoughtful staring.

"OK, how about this?" I said. "One observation I had by going to Senator Ashford's funeral and then talking to those who were closest to him, was that he was a genuinely good and godly man. I respect him for that."

"Secondly, just going through this information shows that he was extremely aware and intelligent, able to compile information, see patterns from the past, track down and document the 'evildoers', and even have some great, tangible plans as to how to restore the United States as the Representative Republic it was founded to be."

Everybody was nodding.

"Thirdly, and finally, the man had absolutely NO STREET SMARTS!"

That took everybody back—they certainly weren't expecting that. There was a little of the whole, "we don't speak ill of the dead" vibe going on.

I looked around the room and decided to address it.

"Please understand that I'm not trying to talk smack about Todd—the senator was an awesome man. I'm just trying to learn from his actions. I know the whole, 'don't speak ill of the dead' thing, but that is my whole point. Todd was awesome in so many ways, but when it came to dealing with bad guys, he was naïve—a novice, and he didn't know how quickly bad guys can do bad things to further what they want."

"I can honestly say I would bet the farm it never occurred to Senator Ashford that they might just kill him and be done with the problem."

I looked around the room and up at Cindy.

"If any of you had the information that Todd had and were trying to accomplish what he was trying to accomplish, would it have occurred to you and *seriously* been on your mind that your life was in danger?"

I looked at each person—all of whom were nodding, except Mr. Triplehorn.

"So, all of us who work in this 'industry', if you will, FBI, Capitol Police, Cindy for TPD in Tucson, and me dealing with bad guys as a private investigator, all understand and even expect the danger."

"I'm guessing it never crossed the senator's mind. Like I said, naïve—a novice."

I looked at Mr. T.

"Sir, I know from where you sit, the idea that someone would try and take your life is unfathomable—you're just too rich and powerful. But you do understand the cutthroat world of business and some of the hideous things people will do for money and power. I need you to understand that with this Cabal, if they will take the chance of killing a sitting United States Senator, the idea they might orchestrate a malfunction on your sixty-million-dollar Gulfstream G650 that causes a crash, is a very real possibility."

"And those same people will go to your funeral and say, 'The world has lost a great man and philanthropist today', while they laugh and spit on your grave."

Mr. Triplehorn looked at me for a moment and then nodded his head once. He got it.

I was guessing he was also reminding himself to have Thurston beef up security around his plane. The fact that he simply glanced at

Thurston, who then walked out of the room making a call, confirmed my suspicion.

"So, Senator Ashford has given us all the material we need to begin this operation, even providing a framework to fix the problems that have been created."

"But he has also unfortunately shown us what *not* to do—so, let's talk about what he did."

CHAPTER
— 147 —

"If you guys remember, Todd actually recorded what he set out to do."

I looked over at Winston.

"Can you find that place for us again."

Winston nodded once and then began to scroll. I wasn't sure how he could see the words that quickly—I finally had to look away cuz I was getting dizzy.

He found the paragraph.

I read it for them as I had back in Fort Pierce, not to remind them, but to enlighten Detective Lee, since he had yet to hear it.

"I have decided to begin contacting the various powerful members on this list and inform them that they can either resign or I will expose their involvement in this conspiracy cabal."

I then looked around the room.

"And that sentence got him killed."

They all nodded.

"He believed that his position insulated him from harm, but the bad guys had no such illusion. If Todd had just noticed how many positions of power they controlled, he might have realized that they could just kill him, and then control the investigation until it came to an end."

"So, we clearly know what *not* to do.

I looked around the room.

"Let's talk about my 'Trojan Horse" soliloquy."

I turned toward Detective Lee.

"Are you familiar with the Trojan War?"

403

"Oh yeah, the Greek's historic fake-out of the citizens of Troy after a ten-year failure of a siege in the thirteenth century B.C.? That was an amazing piece of military strategy."

OK . . . so Detective Lee clearly knew his history. Good.

"Alright. I surmised that the Cabal has pulled off their own 'Trojan Horse' move, by inserting hundreds of people into powerful positions, maybe more, including our President and Vice-President."

"For us to win this battle, we're going to need to 'flip the script' on them and do our own 'Trojan Horse' move."

"What does that mean?" asked ASAC Holmes.

"I don't know yet," I admitted. "But I think we can figure it out."

"What was the weakness of Senator Ashford's plan?"

We all thought about that.

Cindy weighed in.

"He was only one man—a powerful man, but still only one man. Take him out and the whole threat evaporated."

I nodded and responded.

"Using your illustration, he jumped out of the wooden horse all alone, with no Greek army on its way, and wasn't much of a threat—they could just cut him down and the battle was over. Honestly, in that scenario, the whole city of Troy would have laughed hard at him, right before they ceremonially slit his throat."

We all nodded.

Mr. Triplehorn wanted to add his two cents—or in his case, over sixty-billion-dollars' worth of "cents", which was a lot to add.

"I think his failure was wed to his fear that if anyone else but himself was included in this effort—and it got out—it could rock our nation, perhaps even toppling major financial institutions and government related institutions."

"I'll bet that's why he was proceeding person by person instead of just exposing the whole Cabal."

Mr. T looked around the room.

"If I may weigh in as a major leader in worldwide financial markets and as the owner of many large conglomerates—Todd wasn't wrong. The information we have could be used to topple our nation, and if the United States of America falls, there are plenty of 'bad actors' out there who would relish the chance to take over."

"Russia, China, Iran and many Islamic countries come to mind."

He looked around the room.

"If I can speak from my expertise gentlemen, which is extensive—we need to be careful that in our attempt to 'save America', we don't end up taking America down as the moral, financial, and military leader of the world."

"All of the alternatives to America's leadership of the world would be a vast downgrade, to put it nicely."

He decided to *not* put it "nicely" or leave what he was saying, open to interpretation.

"They would all lead the world into a hellish Fascist, Socialist, Communist, or Theocratic rule that would degrade all nations and life as we know it—it could easily take our world back to the Middle Ages."

We all looked with wide eyes at Mr. Triplehorn.

Finally, I offered, "Come on, Mr. T; don't sugarcoat it for us. Tell us what you really think!"

CHAPTER
— 148 —

"OK," I said with emphasis, lifting my eyebrows, "apparently one of our goals here needs to be that we *don't* commit global Armageddon—noted."

Mr. Triplehorn smiled.

Cindy jumped in.

"I think the mistake Todd made was that they could just kill him, and that was the end of it. If we go back to your 'Trojan Horse' illustration, Blake, like you said, Todd's mistake was being the only warrior inside, going up against so many—when that one dude jumps out, the other army just laughs—they aren't scared. So, it would seem to me that we need to 'flip the script' by becoming so many warriors or threats, that they can't simply just take one of us out. We have to create so many threats, making the fire so big and overwhelming, that there's just no simple way to 'put it out'."

Mr. Triplehorn was nodding.

"I think you're right Cindy. I just had a thought that could get us moving in the right direction; what if I had my lawyers put together a situation that goes something like this for each one of us? If any of us are killed, all of Senator Ashford's information will automatically be forwarded to all conservative news organizations. That would force all the other news organizations to cover it as well."

He looked over at Winston.

"You'd have to put all of Todd's information into an easily readable and understandable format that people could comprehend quickly. Could you do that?"

Winston nodded.

ASAC Holmes had a question.

"If we had to release the information, couldn't the Cabal just shut it all down using their members in the mainstream—basically governmental news organizations—or at least just explain it away? They control so much of what is allowed to be seen through social media, print media, and news media, couldn't they just choke it out under their fake labels of 'mis' or 'disinformation'?"

Mr. Triplehorn was nodding.

"That would be a problem, except I own or have a controlling interest in many of those media outlets too, so I can demand controls to make sure they don't get to choke it."

Everyone was nodding.

Detective Lee had an idea.

"Maybe we could even build in a procedure where if one of us doesn't call every day, or on the hour with a code, the information automatically gets released. That could negate them taking one of us hostage and holding the rest of us hostage with that person's life."

More nods around the room.

"I could add voice recognition software for them too so that they could be sure it was us," added Winston.

Everyone stopped for a moment of surprise at Winston speaking.

I looked around the room.

"OK, those are great ideas, and they increase our number of warriors or threats, like Cindy said, so Mr. T, that goes on your 'to-do list' for when we're done here."

"We need to make sure that this part of the plan is a deterrent, not just a result *after* they kill us. It can only be a deterrent to killing us if we make sure the cabal members we deal with know the facts of what happens if they mess with us. Let's not miss that important fact."

Detective Lee spoke up.

"I think we'd all have to agree that none of these cabal members can be allowed to stay in office—ideally, they would all be put in prison for treason, if not for the murder of Senator Ashford, as well. However, to do this and not topple the entire government, we would have to have a plan in place to immediately replace the cabal members—at least the most vital ones."

I thought about that.

"Wow, how are we going to do that?"

"Well, because of my job in the Capitol Police, we are well-versed in the procedure of succession—it's kind of what we do—so, I can give you all an idea of the law behind this."

I nodded.

"Please do."

CHAPTER
— 149 —

Detective David Lee looked around the room, took a deep breath, and then began.

"The U.S. Constitution lays out a presidential line of succession in the case of the elected President's death, resignation, removal from office, or incapacity."

"Most people are aware that the first in the line of succession for president is the Vice-President. This is the one case where the next in line assumes the actual office of the presidency itself."

"Since 1789, the Vice-President has succeeded to the presidency intra-term on nine occasions: eight times due to the incumbent's death, and once due to resignation."

I jumped in.

"Yeah, but since both the President and the Vice-President are in on this conspiracy, we have a real problem now, don't we?"

Detective Lee nodded.

"Well, we have a different problem, but the Constitution allows for this too. However, I will tell you that it's *never* happened in America's history—we've never gone past the Vice-President."

I thought about that.

"So, you're saying this would be 'un-precedented'?" I said with a smile on my face.

I looked around the room and just got stares, Cindy shaking her head at me.

"Get it? It sounds like president. Un-pre-ce-dent-ed," I said, one syllable at a time.

Still nothing.

Whoa, tough crowd.

David looked up at Cindy and asked, "Remarkable, you say?"

Cindy just shrugged, so David went on.

"If the Vice-President is also out of the question, the powers and duties of the presidency pass to the Speaker of the House of Representatives, then to the president pro-tempore of the Senate, and then Cabinet secretaries, starting with the Secretary of State, then Treasury, then Defense, then the Attorney General."

He paused.

"It goes on from there, but I already saw that the Democrat president pro tempore of the Senate and a number of the fifteen Cabinet secretaries were on the 'confirmed list' of being in the Cabal—so many of them are out of the question too."

Detective Lee looked around the room.

"That brings us back to the Speaker of the House. Since the Republicans hold the majority, the Speaker is a Republican, which means there would be a party change from the President's and Vice-President's Democrat party. I can promise you that will cause quite a ruckus among the political class, but it's the Constitutional succession plan, so that's just how it is."

"It'll be the first time it's ever been used past the Vice-President in the history of our nation, but again, it *is* the process."

"Given what we have to do here, we are going to need a great leader to give the country some stability when the country is going to feel very betrayed by all these people. From that standpoint, a switch from the party that was doing the betraying might be just what the country needs. The political class and pundits will scream and moan, but the citizenry would probably welcome it."

I spoke up.

"OK, I'm sure I'm supposed to know this, but who is the Speaker of the House?"

Mr. Triplehorn answered my question.

"His name is Abernathy Wright, and he's from the state of Alabama."

"Abernathy?" I asked, feeling a joke coming on.

Mr. T laughed.

"Yeah, everybody just calls him 'Abe'."

"Well, I would hope so!" I interjected.

"I know him personally, and everything I've seen indicates he is a good man and a patriot—some people even call him 'Honest Abe' as a throwback to President Abraham Lincoln. It's also interesting that when I was reading through Todd's notes before I got here, Todd actually referred to Abe Wright as a great leader of the House of Representatives."

I looked back and forth between Detective Lee and Mr. Triplehorn.

"So, you're telling me that Abernathy Wright is the next one in line for the Presidency."

David spoke up.

"No—not actually to *be* the President, but he's the next in line to have the powers and duties of the presidency passed on to him until a new President could be elected."

"I can also tell you that Abe Wright is highly thought of by those of us who are tasked with protecting him, just like Senator Ashford was."

He looked around the room and shook his head.

"As I'm sure you can imagine, I'm afraid that can't be said about the majority of people in Congress who we protect."

CHAPTER
—150—

A plan was starting to form in my head.

"So, Mr. Triplehorn, you say you know this guy?"

"I do. I've talked with him a number of times and have had a few meetings with him when my business interests intersected with government interests."

I looked at my favorite billionaire and thought.

"I'm guessing that you have resources to get all the information you need about virtually anyone within hours—am I right sir?"

Mr. T nodded.

"Can you call whatever investigator you use and have him get everything he can on the Speaker of the House—like yesterday?"

Mr. T thought about it and then said, "Yes."

He looked over at Thurston and simply nodded, and my little friend immediately walked out of the room and called the investigator.

I had another thought, so I called Thurston back.

"Thurston, can you ask the investigator to specifically get all the 'oppo research' on Wright that the Democrats try and use against him? That will be our quickest way to discover if there are any legitimate concerns, or if they had to fabricate stuff to attack him."

Thurston looked over at Mr. T, and he just nodded.

"Now, assuming that report is favorable, do you think you have the clout to convince Speaker Wright to meet you here in your suite tonight?"

Mr. Triplehorn furrowed his brow.

"I honestly don't know—but I would imagine so, as long as he's not otherwise engaged."

I thought about making a comment about who on earth uses terms like "otherwise engaged" in general conversation besides Thurston and BBC television, but I decided to be more mature than that.

I know, weird, huh? I'll need to check my temperature later.

"But the real question sir, is can you get him to come here *without* his security team?"

"Why?" said both Mr. Triplehorn and Detective Lee at the same time, probably because the Capitol Police would *be* the security team.

I looked over at Detective Lee.

"If his security team were to come here, would they have to report the visit to their superiors?"

Realization hit David's face.

"Oh—yeah."

"Would they also have to report *your presence* at our meeting, along with everyone else who participated?"

"Yeah," David said, nodding.

"And would all that information immediately go to Chief of Police Ortez, a confirmed member of the Cabal?"

David just nodded slowly, waving the white flag.

"We can't have prying eyes and whispering lips on this—and I imagine Washington, D.C. is full of *both*!"

Detective David Lee nodded his wholehearted agreement to *that* statement.

Mr. Triplehorn was nodding as well.

"Alright, after we get the facts on Abe, if we're still good to go, I'll call him and ask for an emergency—and private meeting tonight."

CHAPTER
— 151 —

Cindy had to run off and tend to the twins, so we all decided to take a break and get some lunch.

Thurston called to get room service, and we all hit the bathrooms and got some drinks out of the refrigerator.

The food arrived surprisingly fast—I guess that's just what happens when you pay $25,500 a night for their best suite of rooms.

We all dug in and, no surprise, the food was excellent. We all got to talk and laugh, which was a nice break from all the serious things we were contemplating.

Once we finished up and visited the facilities, we all sat back down to start strategizing again. Winston got Cindy back on the big screen, and we were off.

ASAC Holmes had a question.

"I get that Speaker Wright is next in the line of succession to the presidency, well, to the powers and duties of the office." He said that quickly before Detective Lee could correct him. "However, I have to ask what exactly your plan is when you get him here? What are you going to say to him?"

I thought about that.

"Well, we'll have to first of all make him aware of the Cabal and the conspiracy they are perpetrating on our country."

"Blake," said Cindy, "did you just use the word 'perpetrating'?"

I laughed.

"Yes dear—I got caught up in all the intrigue—I apologize."

She laughed, nodded her forgiveness, and then added her thoughts.

"I think that's a good start, but honestly, if we don't have a 'so, here's what we need to do' plan, this whole thing could go sideways really quickly."

"I agree," said Detective Lee. "The kneejerk reaction would be for Speaker Wright to report all this, which would mean the Cabal would just ratchet up their machine and squelch this."

Mr. Triplehorn leaned forward.

"Did you guys get to read through Senator Ashford's plan to restore our Representative Republic?"

Things had been so crazy for all of us just getting back to D.C. that we hadn't. Mr. Triplehorn's flight back from Tokyo had given him time to read the whole thing.

So, we all shook our heads 'no'.

"Well, I did—I studied it carefully. While Todd's idea to try to singlehandedly take down all the bad guys without a fallback plan was a bad idea, what he called his 'Restoration Plan' was really good. Todd knew the Constitution well, and he knew the government. He also had a very good business mind. His ideas to fix the problems of our nation could work."

He looked around at all of us.

"What do you think about using those to give Speaker Wright a roadmap to righting the wrongs in our nation? If he's on board, that could be our path forward."

We all looked around at each other. I spoke up.

"OK, first of all, please tell me that in your head, you were spelling the 'righting the wrongs' with the "W", as 'Wrighting the wrongs', since that's Abe's last name."

Mr. T just shook his head at me. I was used to that, so I went on.

"Secondly, we're all novices in this area of running a nation, and you say Senator Ashford knew his stuff. So, tell us Mr. T, what were some of his ideas that you think we could present to Abernathy Wright as a way forward?"

CHAPTER
—152—

Mr. Triplehorn nodded, took a look at the notes he'd taken on his phone, and began.

"Senator Ashford provided a fairly detailed proposal of changes that would affect nearly every aspect of government—honestly way too much to present to the Speaker all at once. However, there were some major proposals we could present that I think would provide almost a U-turn as a nation, to get us going in the right direction again—primarily because they are just common sense, which D.C. tends to be extremely short of."

We all nodded, and he went on.

"Well, one of the key elements that Senator Ashford noted as an underlying problem of our government was that the representatives of the people are no longer *around* the people they are supposed to represent very much."

That made sense to all of us.

"Because they spend too much time in Washington, D.C., he pointed out that our officials get caught up in the 'beltway contagion', as he called it, speaking of D.C., where they think that the things the liberal pundits and media tell them on CNN and MSNBC, are actually the things they should care about."

"In addition, he pointed out the jobs of being a Representative or a Senator were *not* supposed to be full-time—and they weren't in the beginning. The officials were supposed go to Washington, D.C. to do their work, then go back home and be around the people they represented."

"He noted that being home kept them honest and knowledgeable about what the people really cared about—therefore, they could accurately represent them."

"He also pointed out all the lobbyists and political action committees, or PACs, that bring so much money to the table for their campaigns, that those entities end up being the people they serve, not the citizens who elected them."

We were all nodding at the common sense of this.

"He talked at length about the bureaucracy that has been established in D.C.—the unelected bureaucrats who write the laws and restrictions that end up governing our whole country. He pointed out that Congress has allowed this monster that many call the 'deep state', or recently, the 'swamp', to become the de-facto law makers of America."

"He decried the power and reach of these pencil-pushers to control every aspect of the lives of our citizens."

Mr. Triplehorn looked around the room, while I pondered whether to comment on him using the word "decried" in that last sentence. Since Mr. T seemed to be on a roll, I decided against it—I would "decry" my objection later.

"So, let's start there. Todd emphasized the founders believed in and created 'limited government' for very limited purposes. He also noted they saw government as a necessary evil and an ongoing danger to our nation. The whole purpose of the addition of the 'Bill of Rights' was to *limit* government even more and *strengthen* the individual citizen against the government."

Mr. T shook his head and laughed.

"He cited President Ronald Reagan being right on the money when he said, *'The nine most terrifying words in the English language are—I'm from the government, and I'm here to help'.*"

We all laughed at *that* truism.

"So, to make America do a U-turn back, we have to significantly change and limit the size and scope of the federal government."

We were all nodding that we were following him.

CHAPTER
— 153 —

Mr. Triplehorn nodded back and resumed.

"He said to do this, it can't initially be done with a scalpel—the problem is simply too malignant—it'll have to be done with 'rough cut'—like a chainsaw."

Mr. Triplehorn took a deep breath and looked down again at the notes on his phone.

"He said the first step is to do a random, mass 'lay-off' of bureaucrats in the administrative state. Apparently, civil servant protections make it tough to fire them individually, but they could be laid-off in mass as long as it was random—meaning it can't be partisan. He suggested maybe any person whose last digit in their social security number was odd would be gone—totally random."

"To do this, he suggested between fifty to eighty percent of the deep state be laid-off in one fell swoop. He went on to say that the inefficiency of government workers was shocking, in part because they don't think they can lose their job. Because of this, he believed you could get rid of this huge percentage of people and still get everything done that the department is supposed to accomplish."

"After that, he wanted to change the hiring and firing restrictions and begin to make sure to get the best people working there, now being able to use the scalpel approach to find and excise the bad employees in a second mass lay-off and then hire better people."

Mr. T paused and looked up.

"For the record, I've seen this firsthand when some of my corporations have had to deal with the government. The incompetence among the deep state bureaucrats who tell everyone else in the country how they have to live is *shocking*. They are not the caliber of people who I would allow to be hired to work in *any* of my businesses."

He continued.

"So, as you can see, this would greatly reduce government immediately. He suggested the same treatment for what he called the 'Alphabet Agencies', like the FBI, DOJ, CIA, DOE, HUD, SSA, SBA, GSA, USDA, DOT, the VA and others."

Mr. Triplehorn looked at ASAC Holmes, Winston, and Detective Lee.

"I'm certain that you men are very good at what you do, because I know that Blake wouldn't have you here if you weren't—so present company excluded."

ASAC Holmes waved his comment away.

"I'm guessing I can speak for these two that we all see the bloated bureaucracies and incompetence within our own ranks too. I would agree that we could at least use the senator's fifty percent cut figure and still do our job well—actually better, being leaner and meaner."

Both David and Winston nodded their agreement. Mr. T nodded and went on.

"A second step Todd wanted to make was to move major departments of the government *out* of Washington, D.C. and into parts of the country that made more sense—once again getting people closer in contact with the people they are supposed to be serving. For instance, he pointed out that it was crazy for the Department of Agriculture to be in D.C., instead of, say Iowa or Nebraska."

Cindy interjected.

"It's kind of hard to argue against that logic."

Mr. Triplehorn nodded to her and went back to Todd's notes.

"By doing this, we could 'decentralize' the federal government better, and keep the people who work there in better touch with the American people. This would eliminate the 'beltway contagion' that infects people who live in D.C. and begin to 'drain the swamp'."

"He then wanted to term-limit Congress, in the same way the President is. He said there was never a plan by the founders for the 'career politician' we see today—you were supposed to do this simply to serve your country. He believed term limits would lead to higher quality men and women who would serve their country and then go home, not stay and try to profit."

"He pointed out that most politicians—from both sides of the aisle—say they believe in term limits, until they get in office. After that, they talk about all their experience the country desperately needs. Because of this, Todd thought it should be done unilaterally 'for' them."

"For the record, Todd noted that it would take a Constitutional Amendment to do this."

Mr. T looked at his phone again.

"Oh, he also wanted it to at least be considered that only a single term would be allowed for each official, perhaps considering a no 're-election' approach. His reasoning for this was that a politician typically spends one to two years of his term running for reelection instead of doing his job and making America better. He wondered if they simply had their single term to do their thing, and then they were out of office, that it might work better."

"He also proposed limitations in the number of days a representative could be in Washington, D.C. in any given year, so they would be at home most of the time."

"He also wanted to get the big money out of the political system and force candidates to rely on citizen contributions. This would eliminate the billion-dollar campaigns and the funding by Political Action Committees, forcing the politicians to care more about the citizens instead of what he called, the 'money changers'."

"One thing that went along with that was he wanted to make a law that a representative could *not* become a lobbyist after their term in office. This leads to obvious motivations for corruption while *in* office, for the purpose of 'payback'—landing the job after they got out."

CHAPTER 154

Mr. Triplehorn stopped talking, apparently done.

I nodded at him.

"OK, that's a start. I think we can all agree these are common sense solutions, so we'll start there with Speaker Wright and see if he agrees with any of these proposals, assuming your investigator clears him."

Thurston came walking into the room.

We all looked over at him.

"Sorry to disturb, Master, but your investigator just called me to say the information you required is now residing in the inbox of your secured email account."

"Excellent. Thank you, Thurston."

"My pleasure, sir."

I looked over at Cindy on the screen, and we shared a smile. I think she might have even giggled. Thurston was a joy and a treasure to us—we got a real kick out of him.

We all waited for Mr. Triplehorn to scroll through the pages of information.

"OK. Everything I'm seeing here—and that's including the oppo research—is just attacking Speaker Wright for being 'too right', 'too conservative', 'too religious'—and they even threw in the disparagement that Abe is just a white 'Christian Nationalist', which to them is the ultimate denunciation."

I responded dryly.

"So, the best they've got on this guy is that he has very little pigment in his skin, he loves God, he loves his country, and he puts our country's interests first before other countries' interests."

Mr. T nodded his agreement, so I summed up.

"Wow, what a disappointment! We have a *madman* on our hands here! He's white, which is irrelevant, he has a foundation of morality for his life in God, and he's *not* a globalist, which is *exactly* the Cabal we're fighting against!"

"The next horror story we'll hear is that he loves his wife and children! Please, someone *stop* this maniac!"

Mr. Triplehorn laughed out loud.

"Believe it or not, Blake, I just came to the part that attacked him for having a problem with women, because he doesn't meet with women alone who aren't his wife."

"I knew it! This crazed lunatic must be *stopped*!"

We all had a good laugh at that.

Mr. Triplehorn continued to scroll.

"Honestly, everything I'm seeing here basically reminds me of Todd—he was accused of all the same stuff. The left clearly can't come up with any new material or find anything of substance to wage an attack against Abe."

He looked up.

"He seems like he could be our man to help save America from this conspiracy and lead the nation back. I think Todd would have agreed."

CHAPTER
— 155 —

I nodded and looked around the room.

"OK, are we in agreement to try and pursue Abernathy?"

There were some chuckles at the use of his full name, which was exactly why I used it—gotta go for the laugh when you can.

We all agreed he was the one, so I went on.

"Great, let's talk about how to pull this off. I'm thinking that Mr. Triplehorn will give him a call and use all his clout and position to convince the Speaker to join us here and meet with us. The question is how we can get him here without anyone knowing."

"Can't he just ditch his security team and drive here?" asked Mr. Triplehorn.

All of the law enforcement personnel sitting there, including Winston, and Cindy on the big screen, started shaking their heads "no".

Detective Lee spoke up.

"He could ditch his security team by saying that he's going to go to his room early, but he wouldn't be able to then get to his car and use it to drive away. His detail is trained to monitor his vehicles as well as him. If he drives away, they'll know it. Also, we don't want 'the next in line' for presidential powers to be unsecured—ever. Imagine if we had him do that and something happened to him. We could be criminally prosecuted."

ASAC Holmes jumped in.

"And if they know it, they'll find out what he's doing, or at least where he's going, and our whole plan is outed."

We all thought about that.

Cindy chimed in.

"Blake, what vehicle are you driving?"

"A Chevy Suburban."

She thought.

"Did you rent it in a way so it couldn't be traced back to you?"

"Of course I did."

"OK. What if you, ASAC Holmes, and Detective Lee were to set it up so that you wait at the back of his house, and he just comes to you and jumps in. We could have our law enforcement guys be his 'Uber' drivers."

I thought about that while I resisted the urge to tell Cindy, and everybody else there, that Mr. T held the controlling interest of Uber.

"That's not a bad idea. That way, he doesn't have to make any extraordinary effort, and we can function as his security team while he's with us."

I looked at ASAC Holmes.

"Did you bring your heat?"

He nodded and said, "Always."

"Me too. OK, I like that."

"Blake," said Cindy, "do what you did in Dallas and smear just enough mud on your license plate so that it's not quite readable—just in case."

I nodded.

"Good call. We might as well play it safe."

I looked around the room.

"What do you guys think?"

The law enforcement guys all nodded.

Winston started typing frantically on his laptop, which got our attention. I leaned over and saw that he was looking at a bird's eye view of Speaker Wright's home.

Winston started narrating.

"He has a high-walled backyard with a gate which would of course be locked. There is an alley outside that gate where you could pick him up, and then leave him when you take him back."

He looked up and nodded.

"If you give him a definite time you'll be there, the extraction should be fairly straight-forward."

After we all got over the fact that Winston had just spoken a full paragraph to us, I just nodded and said, "Thank you, Winston."

CHAPTER
—156—

"OK," I said, turning back to the group, "it looks like we can do this, but how do we get Speaker Wright to go along with it?" Mr. Triplehorn answered.

"I think he'll listen to me because of who I am, but I'm not sure I can convince him to do what we're asking. I try to imagine how I would be persuaded to do this if it were me—I'm having trouble getting there."

I was thinking about that.

"You need to first of all get him to have a private conversation with you—he needs to go somewhere that he won't be overheard."

Mr. T nodded.

Detective Lee spoke up.

"I think you tell him as little as possible, but as much as necessary to get him to come here."

ASAC Holmes was nodding, and then added, "Yeah. For instance, I would tell him this all relates to the murder of Senator Ashford, but don't tell him that the President and Vice-President are complicit. That could feel like a bridge too far at the outset."

Cindy was nodding.

"I think you could talk in general about a cabal that your investigator has uncovered but try and be sparce on details until you can get him here and can show him."

I had a thought.

"You know, perhaps if you point out briefly that his 'Uber drivers' are all qualified law enforcement who can and will guard him well, he may feel better about taking the chance to talk to us."

I looked at my watch—it was mid-afternoon.

"Let's also get some darkness on our side, so let's pick him up at 6:30 p.m.—if he goes for it."

I looked around.

"We all good with all that?"

There were nods all the way around.

Mr. Triplehorn took out his phone.

"Would you be comfortable putting it on speaker, sir, so that we could start to get a feel for the man," I asked.

"Sure."

He looked up Speaker Abe Wright's personal cell phone number, which his investigator had included with his information and dialed it.

It rang three times before it was answered with a tentative and questioning, "Hello?"

"Hello, Abe, this is Araby Triplehorn—I hope I haven't caught you at a bad time."

"Oh, no Mr. Triplehorn, I'm just between meetings and winding down for the day. What can I do for you?"

"May I first ask if you're in a secure situation where you can talk freely?"

There was a pause.

"Um, I'm in my office, but let me go close the door."

We all waited and heard him tell his secretary not to disturb him and then the sound of the door closing.

"I'm back Araby. Can I ask why all the cloak and dagger?"

Araby laughed.

"Sure. I need to talk to you about something that no one else can know about—kind of a DEFCON 1 situation."

Abe laughed.

"Well, actually, DEFCON 1 is the highest alert level, for something like nuclear war. DEFCON 5 is the safest, we're at peace, level. People get those confused all the time and say it backwards."

"I'm not confused, Abe—I have the right DEFCON."

Araby let that set there for a moment and it certainly got the Speaker's attention.

"Is this something regarding one of your corporations?"

"No, it's not, it's about the nation. I can tell you that it is regarding the murder of Senator Ashford, and information my investigator has uncovered."

There was nothing but stunned silence.

Finally, the Speaker spoke.

"I remember getting the call from the President about your investigator and then I called and asked Chief Ortez to cooperate with him. But Araby, while I appreciate you calling me to let me know any developments, you really should contact the authorities and give them whatever information you have."

Mr. Triplehorn took a deep breath and sighed.

"Abe, I wish I could do that, but the information I have makes it clear that's the *last* thing I should do."

Mr. T let that sink in.

"Why are you calling me, Mr. Triplehorn? I'm really not in any position to offer you help in a murder investigation."

"Abe, I'm going to ask you to listen to me, but I'm also going to ask you to remember who I am and what I represent. I am a truthful and honest businessman, and one of the wealthiest men in the world. I love my country and only want the best for it."

"Do you agree with that description?"

Speaker Wright thought.

"I do."

"OK. I want to cash in on my reputation and redeem every chit I have to ask you to do something for me."

We all waited in silence for the Speaker to respond.

CHAPTER
— 157 —

"What is that?" the Speaker finally asked warily.

"I would like you to meet with me tonight at my suite at the Waldorf Astoria. I have information that I need to show you that is pertinent to the health and future of our nation. I can promise you I am not overstating the case here, and I am not misrepresenting myself."

"You won't be sorry that you took the time to see me."

There was quiet on the phone while the Speaker considered Araby's words.

"I suppose I could have my team drive me over if you're sure this is that important."

"That brings me to the second part of my request Abe—it is imperative that no one knows you are coming here to see me."

"Yeah, I got that, it'll just be my security team and me."

"No, Abe, I'm saying that your security team can't know about it or be with you either."

Another pause.

"Alright, at the risk of offending a very important man, Araby, *what exactly is going on here?*" Abe asked angrily.

"Speaker Wright, I promise I can make it all very clear when you get here, and I assure you it will all make sense at that time. You trusting me on this is what I meant by that 'cashing in on my reputation and redeeming every chit I have' comment."

Araby looked around the room, and we all nodded that he was doing a good job.

"So, I'm just supposed to jump into my car and drive over to the Waldorf and see you."

"Actually, no Abe. I don't want you to be unprotected during any of this process, so I want to send some trusted law enforcement personnel to bring you here and take you home."

"What are you talking about? Why would I leave my own security team home, just to be transported by a different security team?"

Araby took a deep breath.

"Because your security team can't know where you're going or that you're gone, Abe. I need you to ditch them."

You could almost hear the Speaker shaking his head through the phone.

After a heavy sigh, Speaker Wright asked, "Why would I do that, Araby?"

Mr. Triplehorn looked around the room and shrugged—he had to say more.

"Abe, if your security team brings you here or even knows you came here, they will have to report that to their superiors. If my team brings you here, this can all happen without that report being made."

"Why does it matter if they report it if this is all on the up and up?" asked Abe.

Another deep breath by Araby.

"Because I have proof that the upper leadership of the Capitol Police is one of the elements that have been compromised. If they got this information, some very bad things could take place."

More silence.

"Are you saying the Capitol Police—the men and women who are tasked with protecting the Congress—are responsible for the death of Senator Ashford?"

"I am not, Abe. But there are compromised parties at the Capitol Police and throughout Washington, D.C., and they cannot become aware of this meeting."

"It's a meeting, Abe, just a meeting—but probably the most important meeting of any of our lives. Again, think of who you're talking to here—I need you to trust me on this."

He was clearly thinking about it.

"How would I even ditch my security detail?"

"You would tell them that you're going to go upstairs early to work and that you'll see them tomorrow. You can then go out your back gate, into the alley at 6:30 p.m., and my team will be waiting for you in a black Suburban."

"How do you know that I have an upstairs, and about my gate and my alley?"

"Abe, remember who you're talking to—I have a team."

"So, at 6:30 p.m. my team will bring you to the Waldorf, and we'll talk. My team consists of my investigator, Blake Moran, Assistant Special Agent in Charge Maverick Holmes of the FBI in Florida, and Detective David Lee of the Capitol Police."

"Wait, I know of Detective Lee. Why is it OK for him to know about this meeting if my detail can't?"

"Because based on the facts, Detective Lee is not part of the compromised Capitol Police and has agreed to work independent of his department on this operation. You'll understand why once we talk."

There was a deep breath on the other end of the line.

"You know I was going to watch the football game tonight? You're ruining that."

Araby laughed.

"They'll be another game, Abe—or maybe I'll just buy an NFL team and let you come watch with me from the owner's box."

That got a laugh from both sides of the call.

CHAPTER
—158—

After Speaker Wright agreed to the plan and the time, Mr. Triplehorn got off the call.

I ran over to him and high-fived him and then ran around the room, high-fiving everyone.

What can I say, I'm immature—and all that football talk at the end got me into a sports enthusiasm high.

I even went to the TV and held my hand up to 'five' Cindy.

She just looked at me.

"Come on, babe—don't leave your man hanging!"

She just shook her head and slowly put her hand up for an "air-five", which I immediately gave her.

My girl laughed.

I like to make my girl laugh.

Now that we had the meeting scheduled for later tonight, we had just a couple of hours before we had to pick up Abernathy.

Sorry, I just can't help enjoying his full name.

Cindy let us know that she needed to go and be a mom, and the rest of us split up to take a bit of a break.

Mr. Triplehorn immediately opened his laptop, checked a few stock prices, and then started calling around the world and doing some of the business he had missed while working with us to save that world.

Billionaires. Whatcha gonna do?

The other four of us headed back to our rooms for a little "R & R" time. Thurston had informed us that Mr. Triplehorn was having dinner brought into his suite at 5:00 p.m., so we could eat and then head out for our clandestine mission of absconding with the Speaker of the United States House of Representatives, stealing him right out from under the noses of his security team.

Thurston didn't actually say it quite like that, but I'm improvising with you to give it a more *007* feel.

So, we had about a two-hour break.

I don't know what ASAC Holmes, Detective Lee, and Winston did with their time, but being the consummate professional that I am, I stayed *laser-focused* on the case and prepared for *every* facet of what we might encounter tonight.

In other words, I took a nap.

CHAPTER
—159—

Now at the top of my game after tirelessly pursuing excellence—you know, not tired now cuz of my nap—we all walked back up to Mr. Triplehorn's suite at 5:00 p.m.

When Thurston welcomed us in, the rooms smelled magnificent! The bounty of food available for us was surprising. We all looked at each other and shook our heads—this is how a billionaire does it, apparently.

There, set out in the dining room, was tri-tip steak, prime rib, sides of ribs in barbeque sauce, orange roughy in melted garlic butter, shrimp, lobster, and even barbequed chicken. Along with that were all the sides we could imagine, and a few that we couldn't.

Mr. Triplehorn came walking in.

"You really expect us to eat this slop?" I asked.

Mr. T chuckled.

"Yeah, I didn't know what you guys might like, so I had Thurston get a little of everything."

"I *little* of everything?" I asked, looking around at the spread. "Is there an NFL football team joining us that we don't know about."

Mr. Triplehorn looked around.

"I guess we might have gone a little overboard," he said, nodding.

"Ya think?" laughed Detective Lee.

Having said all that, we weren't complaining. Each of us got a plate and piled it high with the amazing food. Mr. T had Thurston put the pre-game on the big screen, and we all got to forget the op for a little while and just gorge ourselves and talk about football.

It was a lot of fun.

I knew Mr. Triplehorn really well, but these other guys didn't, so it was interesting for me to watch them be shocked at what a normal, down-to-earth guy Mr. T was. He was laughing with us, giving his take on the upcoming game, arguing with us about which quarterbacks should be considered in the top five of all time and why. He was totally just one-of-the-guys . . . until you remembered that he had more money than the Gross Domestic Product of most countries.

But other than *that*—just one-of-the-guys.

We finished our food and practically dove into the desserts. I had to admit that we weren't exactly preparing ourselves well for our op by gorging ourselves on all this amazing food—but come on! You just don't turn down a feast like this.

A little before 6:00 p.m., the three of us who were now upgraded "Uber drivers" got up and headed out for our op. I was glad to see that we had all worn black for our little adventure—we were professionals after all.

The others wished us luck, and we headed down to the lobby in the elevator. Once we were in the lobby, it was just a short walk around the corner to head into the parking garage.

I had brought a bottle of water with me. Once we got out to the garage, I walked right outside the garage, poured some water onto the ground, waited a moment for it to sink in, and then pulled up a handful of mud.

We finished the walk to the Suburban. It was dark now, so it was easy for me to casually do what I needed to do without being too obvious about it.

Fun fact: Washington, D.C. passed its first motor vehicle registration law back in 1903, which is kind of funny, given that Henry Ford established the Ford Motor Company in 1903, and then *five years later* the company rolled out the first Model T.

So, there just wasn't all that much to "register" until 1908.

After Ford introduced his revolutionary new mass-production methods, including large production plants, the use of standardized, interchangeable parts, and the world's first moving assembly line for cars, *that* was when more cars started showing up.

Initially, Washington, D.C. residents actually had to provide their own plates—you have to wonder what *those* looked like.

However, the city began supplying official plates in 1907, probably about the time a bunch more cars were starting to hit the roads.

Any-who . . .

You may be wondering what any of this has to do with our story, let alone the price of eggs at a New York bodega.

Well, to answer your question, it has absolutely nothing to do with the price of eggs at a New York bodega, so we can put *that one* to rest right now!

However, if we may return to our story—and me with the muddy hands—since passing that first motor vehicle registration law back in 1903, Washington, D.C. has required that vehicles have license plates on both the front and back of the vehicle.

So, I had to treat both license plates—front and back—with my mud concoction to obscure the numbers.

What? Why are you looking at me like that?

Yeah, that last part—mud on front and back—was the *whole reason* I told you all that stuff about the D.C. registration law back in 1903.

Too much? OK—noted. I'll try to do better next time. (But we all know I won't do better, so let's just move on.)

I then poured some more water on my hands and wiped them with the hotel towel I brought with me for this very purpose. I had a feeling the Waldorf Astoria would not be amused by my use of their extremely high-thread-count, soft and fluffy towel to wipe off my dirty hands.

Well, they can just use some of the $1,275 a night to wash it well, or even just buy a *new* towel—right?

We were ready to go, so we jumped in, fired her up and drove out of the garage.

So far, so good.

Or so I thought.

CHAPTER

— 160 —

Sometimes he *hated* this job.

The waiting was the worst.

He had been sitting around the Waldorf Astoria all day. He had checked with his source a couple of times, and Detective Lee's cellphone said he was here, he just didn't know where.

What was this guy doing? If this was an affair, this was one marathon session!

He had to keep moving around and looking like he was doing something, or he knew someone from the hotel staff would eventually approach him and ask him what his business was here. This wasn't a Holiday Inn after all.

Mercurius had called him after just a couple hours and demanded to know if he had found Detective Lee. He pointed out that he had already asked at the desk if they could get a message to Detective Lee's room, and they informed him that they didn't have a "Detective David Lee" registered at the hotel.

That ended his chance to just find him in a room.

If he was having an affair, he would've probably used a different name, so that wasn't all that surprising.

When Mercurius demanded that he just start "going through the hotel" and find him, he pointed out that you really couldn't just start wandering through a high-priced hotel like this, knocking on doors and seeing who answered.

To say that "management would frown on such things" would be a gross understatement.

He just shook his head—sometimes the employers he had to deal with could be real imbeciles.

Mercurius had kept calling him each hour, but he had just let it go to voicemail. He'd texted him twice that he would let him know if and when he found something—the unspoken message being, "Leave me alone, and let me do my job!"

Evening had arrived, and he had just taken about his seventh position and started acting like he was working on his phone. He was starting to think about where he could get some food he could actually afford, when a group of three men stepped out of the elevator and turned to walk toward the parking garage.

One of the men was Detective David Lee.

He'd marked him!

His heart rate jumped up significantly as he quickly stood up and walked as fast as he could without drawing attention or looking suspicious. He was a distance behind them, but that was OK—he didn't want them to mark him.

He looked at the other two men from a distance. He didn't recognize one of them for sure, but when he looked closer at the other guy, he realized it was the Arizona investigator they had been both trying and failing to find.

Blake Moran.

This was great! He'd found Detective Lee and the investigator—his employer was going to be very happy about this!

After they disappeared into the parking garage, he gave them a moment, and then walked out with his head down but his eyes searching for them.

He saw them over at the far end, doing something around a black Suburban.

When he saw them start to get in, he quickly exited the garage and then ran to his vehicle, which he had parked on the street.

He started his car and watched for them to exit. He quickly grabbed his phone and sent a text to Mercurius, using voice to text.

He just said, "Marked Lee and he is with the Arizona investigator, Moran, so I have them both. There is a third man, but I don't recognize him. They are driving away, so I will follow them. I will text updates when I have them."

He hit send as the black Suburban exited the parking garage. He tossed his phone into the passenger's seat, threw his car into drive, and began the tail.

CHAPTER
— 161 —

As we drove out of the parking garage, we started talking about nothing, the way you do when you're confined in a small space with people you know, but not all that well.

I had some music on—I figured country music would probably work for everybody.

As I went into the left-turn lane to head west on Pennsylvania Avenue, NW, my eye caught a car from the side of the road suddenly shooting onto 12th Street, NW and then getting into the left-turn lane a few cars behind us.

I have to say that my "Spidey-sense" started humming, something I have learned to pay attention to.

While the guys talked, I turned left and started looking for a gas station. I didn't need gas, but I needed information.

In less than half a mile, I pulled into a station.

"Seriously," asked ASAC Holmes laughing, "you didn't think to fill up with gas? Come on, Blake, you're better than that!"

I didn't say anything, which got Maverick and David's attention. I just sat at the pump and watched as the car I had marked pulled into a business parking lot a couple hundred feet behind us.

Keeping my eye on the car, I said, "Listen, there is a non-descript sedan about two-hundred feet behind us which just pulled into that business parking lot, but those businesses are all closed for the night. It's dark, so you can look. I'm going to go in and pretend to buy something, you guys watch the car."

The mood inside the SUV had turned markedly more serious immediately.

With that, I jumped out of the Suburban, walked around the front and into the quick mart, purposely not looking over at the car. I wasted a minute in there and then came walking out like I had something.

When I got back in the car, the talk was now all business.

"Is it still there?" I asked.

"Yeah, it hasn't moved," said Detective Lee.

"OK, you two monitor it and let's see if it tails us when we leave. If it does, we're being followed."

I started up the Suburban and slowly pulled out into traffic.

"Well?" I asked.

"Not yet," said ASAC Holmes, "wait, yeah, here he comes."

I hit the steering wheel in frustration.

"I don't understand this. We covered all our tracks. There is *no way* they could've found us."

"Oh no," said Detective Lee.

My eyes went to the rearview mirror to look at him.

"What?"

"Blake, I am so sorry."

"What?" I asked with greater urgency, wondering if I'd been played and David was a part of the Cabal.

CHAPTER
— 162 —

I kept glancing in the rearview mirror, waiting for David's answer. "I just realized that after you left for Florida and I was back on the job, I had to turn my phone's location service back on—you know, the one you had me turn off when we went to Senator Ashford's apartment? I never thought to turn it back off this morning when you called me to come over."

I closed my eyes slowly, but briefly—I was driving after all. By this time, we were passing just south of the White House, which was on our right.

"So, they tracked your phone to us," I said, bummed.

"Blake, I'm so sorry. Does it help that I just turned it off now?"

I shook my head and took a deep breath.

"It's OK—stuff happens. I just need to think fast because we need to get to Speaker Wright on time or he could bail on us, but we can't take this tail with us to his house. That's a good way to get a bunch of us killed."

I thought, and then I had an idea.

"Alright, I'm going to lead him along with us for a little while—I don't want him to know he's been played after I'm done—but then I'm going to execute some evasive maneuvers, and you guys keep 'eyes-on' him while I do, so we'll know for sure if we lost him. Got it?"

They both nodded in the affirmative.

I turned right on 17th Street, NW and went west of the White House. I then turned left again onto another section of Pennsylvania Avenue, NW.

I was heading for the Washington Circle Park roundabout.

Do you remember how I told you that Washington, D.C. was designed in a "spoke and wheel" fashion? Well, since our founders came from Europe, the "wheel" part meant there were various circular "roundabouts" across the city—those maddening, seemingly dangerous circles with lots of roads, or "spokes" to turn off on as you go around the circle.

This particular roundabout was right around the George Washington University campus—and we were coming up on it now.

"OK guys, eyes on the target. I'll try and make this look as normal as I can, but you'll need to hang on."

The tail was about four vehicles behind us, so that gave me some room to work. I was thrilled when we started to merge onto the roundabout cuz it was packed, and there were already a fair number of black SUVs in the pack.

This is Washington, D.C. after all—again, politicians love their black SUVs.

I saw an opening and moved two lanes over, getting one horn in the process. I sped up and passed the turnoffs for New Hampshire Ave, NW, 23rd Street, NW, and Pennsylvania Avenue, NW, which is the street I eventually wanted to get back on to.

The tail was fighting traffic to get into the smallest part of the circle, the far-left lane I was in.

However, after he was committed to that lane change, I suddenly moved back over to the far-right lane. When I got to the southern leg of New Hampshire Avenue, NW, I turned right quickly and gunned the big engine.

"Tell me how we're doing guys!" I yelled.

"I don't see him," they both agreed.

I raced to the next intersection of 24th Street, NW and made the awkward turn back right, taking us north again. I then drove normally, so as not to attract unwanted attention, while we all watched behind us until I got to Pennsylvania Avenue, NW again and turned left.

Like an Arizona lizard, we'd lost our tail—not a good thing for a dog or a cat, but a very good thing for us.

"Blake, I am so sorry," Detective Lee said again as they drove, now apparently safe from the tail.

"It's OK. You both know that in any operation, circumstances change, and you have to adjust. We'll need to factor in that they know about the Waldorf now, but probably not where we are in the hotel and nothing about Mr. Triplehorn. We've hid all that well, but they will be watching the hotel now."

CHAPTER
— **163** —

"What is this dude doing?" he wondered.
When he saw the investigator was pulling into a gas station, he quickly looked around and saw a parking lot he could pull into, which he did.

Since it was dark, he could stare at the SUV and see what was happening.

It turned out that the P.I. just went into the convenience store for a minute—probably just got a soda or something.

When they pulled out, he gave them a moment to start moving, and then pulled out and positioned himself about four cars back.

This was going well.

He followed them as they drove south of the White House, and then up the west side of it. Once they got back onto Pennsylvania Avenue, NW, he relaxed and just planned to follow them to see where they were headed.

His text chime sounded, and he was pretty sure it would be Mercurius. This guy was *so* annoying! He told him he would text him when he had an update, but he seemed to not be able to stop himself from being a jerk.

They were coming up on the Washington Circle Park roundabout. He really didn't care for these European style circles, but he had gotten used to them over the years.

As the SUV merged into the roundabout, it pulled over a couple of lanes, so when he merged, he tried to move over, but just got some horns and fingers for his trouble.

He finally was able to get over, but now he couldn't see the black SUV—it had gotten too far around the circle. He felt some perspiration under his arms and on his forehead as he started to feel a little frantic. He hit the gas and tried to maneuver through the traffic to get closer.

He still couldn't see it.

He was almost halfway around the roundabout and still hadn't found the SUV. It didn't help that black SUVs were the favorite choice of politicians to tool around D.C., and that there were a number of them on the roundabout. He glanced down New Hampshire Avenue, NW as he passed it and just caught the back of an SUV heading south, but he was already past the turnoff.

He wasn't even sure if that was the black Suburban he had been chasing, it was too far down the road to tell, so he sped up and wove back and forth through the traffic, looking for the SUV.

Once he had done a complete 360-degree trip, he decided his only choice was to try the street he saw an SUV on and hope that was them.

Once he could turn onto New Hampshire Avenue, NW, he gunned the car and sped southwest, slowing, and looking down each street he passed. When he got to Virginia Avenue, NW, he turned right and then turned left into the parking lot of the Watergate Hotel, which overlooked the Potomac River.

He sat there, staring at the Potomac, fuming and uttering some choice words. They could be anywhere by now, and he had lost them. It seemed fitting that he was sitting at the Watergate—the site of a cataclysmic failure of the Nixon administration.

He was going to have to call his annoying jerk boss and tell him that he lost the tail—without mentioning that they apparently weren't even trying to lose him.

This was a classic screw-up, and it was on him.

Not that he was about to let Mercurius know that.

CHAPTER

— 164 —

Speaker Wright lived in an expensive area in Georgetown, in a nice brownstone. I glanced at my watch, and we were still going to arrive a few minutes before our 6:30 p.m. time. That was why I had to lose that tail fast, because we'd only built about fifteen minutes of buffer into the plan.

I pulled into the alley and down to his back gate and left the Suburban running so that he would hear it and know we were there, even before opening the gate.

After sitting there for a little while, I looked at my watch, which was now showing 6:33 p.m., not time to panic, but it was still concerning that he wasn't here yet.

A minute later, the gate barely opened, and Speaker Wright looked out and then slid carefully out the small opening. He carefully and quietly closed the gate and then headed for us.

ASAC Holmes jumped out of the front seat and opened the back door for the Speaker, who got in with a nod of thanks.

I pulled the SUV down the alley and headed back out of Georgetown toward the Waldorf.

ASAC Holmes started.

"Speaker Wright, I am Assistant Special Agent in Charge Maverick Holmes from the Fort Pierce, Florida headquarters. I believe you said you knew of Detective David Lee of the Capitol Police, sitting next to you."

They both nodded to each other, then I spoke up.

"And I'm Blake Moran, Mr. Triplehorn's investigator. You might know of me from the investigation and stopping of the *'See Me Killer'* in San Francisco."

Speaker Wright stared at me.

"That was you?" he asked, clearly impressed.

"Yes sir. Also, you must know about the taking down of Nicholas Whitlock for murder, since he was on the fast track for the White House?"

"Of course."

"Me again."

He just stared.

"I only tell you this because we need you to know that Mr. Triplehorn has quite a high-end team assembled here, sir. We are not hacks; we are top in our field."

"OK," he said.

"I tell you this because we're about to do some clandestine stuff, and I need you to trust us and work with us."

"What clandestine stuff?" he asked suspiciously.

"Well sir, someone tried to follow us here to pick you up tonight. I lost the tail, but we now know that they are aware of us being at the Waldorf Astoria."

"Who was it that tried to follow you?"

I looked at the other two guys.

"While you'll know exactly who it was when we can talk in Mr. Triplehorn's suite, right now, let's just say generically that the 'bad guys' tried to follow us."

"Because of this, our entrance into the Waldorf is going to be a little unconventional, sir."

"Unconventional how?" the Speaker asked.

"I'm going to need you to go in disguised as a waiter in full uniform, sir, carrying a food tray."

"What?"

I laughed.

"I was just messing with you, sir—but I am going to need you to go with ASAC Holmes and Detective Lee when I drop you three off, and you'll need to proceed upstairs using the service elevator. I scoped it out earlier, and if I drop you off at the back of the Waldorf, it will be right to your left when you enter the service area."

"Where are you going?" asked Detective Lee.

"Well, I can't park the car in the parking garage now—they might find it—maybe even put a tracker on it. So, I'll do a quick stop and you three jump out, and David, you get Speaker Wright up to Mr. Triplehorn's suite."

"OK."

"Maverick, I need you to do something else."

"What's that?"

"We know that whoever marked us knows what Detective Lee looks like. It's also probable that he knows what I look like too, since someone at the Capitol Police would've told them about my working the case. However, there is no way they know you. The dude would have no choice after losing the tail, but to come back to the hotel and wait for us."

ASAC Holmes was nodding.

"You want me to scope out the lobby and see if I can mark the dude who spotted us," said Maverick, getting the direction I was heading.

"Exactly. You can walk freely around and look." I thought about that. "On second thought, there's an outside chance he saw enough of you with us to recognize you, so don't be too obvious about it."

I looked around the car.

"Listen, I have a hat back there. Wear the hat and untuck your shirt to try and alter your appearance a little."

ASAC Holmes started to do that.

"You know what to look for—the guy who is trying to look nonchalant, hanging around the lobby, but is clearly staking out the hotel."

"And if you can, try to get some pics of the guy."

"Got it."

"I'll go find someplace to park the SUV while Speaker Wright is here, and then I'll hoof it back to the service elevator and meet you all in the suite."

"Everybody clear?" I asked.

Everybody said, "Clear," including Speaker Wright. I wasn't sure, but I think he was enjoying the intrigue and getting a kick out of the cloak and dagger drama.

CHAPTER

— 165 —

When we got to the Waldorf, I turned right off Pennsylvania Avenue, NW onto 12th Street, NW and drove down the west side of the hotel. When I got past the hotel, I did a quick left turn into the back service area that included the loading dock.

I pointed to the back service area entrance.

"That's the door. The service elevator is just to the left. Go!"

They all three jumped out of the Suburban and headed for the door.

As I got ready to go and try and find some place to park, I realized that just to my right was the huge Internal Revenue Service Building, right behind the Waldorf. Since it was nighttime, it was mostly empty for the evening.

"Well, *that's* convenient," I thought.

Right in front of me, there was some IRS service parking which was just southeast of the rear of the Waldorf, so I tucked the SUV there for now and headed into the hotel.

That was a lot easier than I thought it would be, and I didn't even have to hoof it back for distance—God forbid I should get anymore exercise!

I went in the back service area and started over to the service elevator, and then thought better of it. Instead, I headed through the service areas and toward the lobby.

When I got to the place where I would be heading out into the lobby, I stopped and carefully looked out before stepping out into view. I scoped out some "hidey-hole" spots around the lobby, where I would be unseen.

I took one more look and then headed toward the first one with my head down like I was looking at my phone.

I got situated where I was, now secluded behind a bunch of foliage, so I carefully peered out to see if I could find Maverick. The lobby was huge, so it took me a moment to locate him.

When I found him, he had my hat pulled low on his head and over his face, and the untucked shirt changed his appearance just enough to be "incognito".

He was leaning on an unmanned desk, acting like he was scrolling through his phone, while he was really scoping out the lobby from under the bill of my hat.

Good spy-craft, ASAC Holmes! I gave him a mental "tip of the hat".

I was getting ready to start my own visual search of the lobby when I saw Maverick's eyes stop searching and fixate on a target. I quickly looked where he was looking, and I agreed with his evaluation.

It's hard to explain, but something about the guy just didn't fit. He was a "non-descript" looking guy and was pulling the hat disguise trick too. However, as people were coming and going around him, he was trying just a little too hard to look relaxed and disinterested. He wasn't being stealthy enough as he searched almost frantically for his target—which I was guessing was us.

Clearly, losing the tail had really messed with his head.

As I watched, Maverick walked over toward him, still looking at his phone, and undoubtedly was taking pictures of the dude as he walked past.

Maverick then sat down some distance away from the guy and messed with his phone. He had to be zooming in on his camera, cuz he then put his elbows on his knees and just looked like he was scrolling through something on his phone. However, the phone was pointed right at the dude, so I knew he was getting some good shots.

Well done, Maverick!

I could see ASAC Holmes had things well in hand, so I carefully made my way back to the service area and took the service elevator up to the top floor and Mr. Triplehorn's suite.

CHAPTER
— 166 —

This was getting bad—really, really bad!

He kept looking around, just hoping he would see Detective Lee or the Arizona private investigator walking through the lobby.

He couldn't put off calling Mercurius too much longer. Last he told him, he was following their vehicle. Mercurius had tried to call him three times since then and had texted him twice.

The texts were quite clear.

"Call me with an update," was the first one, while the second one was a bit of a step up.

"CALL ME WITH AN UPDATE!!!"

So, now he was yelling at him—and in case he didn't get the memo, Mercurius added *three* exclamation points to make it clear.

This was bad—really, really bad!

He couldn't stand the prick he worked for, but the dude had juice—he had the power to ruin his life if he decided to—and he just might decide to when he found out how this little adventure had gone.

He decided he couldn't put it off any longer, so he placed the call.

"What the hell is going on over there?" yelled Mercurius.

"I'm back at the Waldorf. I followed Detective Lee, Moran, and the other guy across the city until we got to Washington Circle, NW. The traffic was heavy, and I got boxed in, so when they turned down New Hampshire Avenue, NW, heading south, it looked like they were just heading to get some dinner, so I came back to the hotel to wait for them to return."

He tried to play it off as nonchalantly as he could so he wouldn't have to admit that he had lost the tail. He failed to mention that the route they had taken to get there made absolutely no sense at all, so the route change was suspect to the whole "get some dinner" theory.

Mercurius was quiet on the other end of the call.

"You didn't think you should keep following them to make sure that was all they were doing?"

He almost laughed out loud. This dude might have a lot of power, but he just wasn't the sharpest knife in the drawer.

"No, now that I marked them at the Waldorf, coming back here and waiting for them will give me the best chance of following them when they get back, so I can figure out what room they're in."

He wasn't sure where *that* idea had come from, but it actually made some sense. He just waited while Mercurius thought about it.

"OK. Let me know when you see them again and see if you can get a picture of the third guy. I can see if I know who he is, or even ask around to try and identify him."

"OK, will do sir."

He ended the call and breathed a sigh of relief.

That could've gone a *lot* worse.

CHAPTER

— 167 —

When I got up to Mr. Triplehorn's suite of rooms, Mr. T and Speaker Wright were talking about things and people that I knew nothing about, while the Speaker was helping himself to some of the delicious food we'd enjoyed for dinner.

The football game was only in the first quarter, so since I didn't have anything else to do, I got some more dessert and settled in with Winston to watch the game. Maybe I should have tried to "hoof it" for a little more exercise after all.

Detective Lee joined us as we watched.

Fifteen minutes later, ASAC Holmes came walking in, clearly jacked up from his little adventure. He joined me, Winston, and Detective Lee, sitting down next to us to show us the pictures he had taken.

"I'd forgotten what a rush it is to be in the field," he said, clearly relishing the experience. He looked over at me. "Remember the op taking down Crispo, Blake?"

I smiled and nodded as he continued.

"That was one of the best moments of my career. We dropped that dirtbag and saved that little girl—and even cleared four other murders."

He looked over at me.

"You did some great work on that one, Moran, great work."

I was starting to fear Maverick was going to hug me.

"Did you hear they are also going to include that operation in the training at Quantico?"

I shook my head "no".

He nodded.

"Yeah, they are—that gives you a couple of them now. The first time they do, they've even asked me to fly up and be a guest lecturer."

I smiled—he was really excited about this.

"I'm glad for you—make sure you amaze them. Now, let's see those pictures."

All four of us got around his phone as he scrolled through the pics. Detective Lee thought he looked a little familiar but couldn't quite place him.

Winston took ASAC Holmes' phone and did a couple of things, sending the photos to his phone so that he could add them to our growing list of facts.

We all ended up watching some of the game and eating until Thurston came in and said that Mr. Triplehorn and the Speaker were ready for us.

Showtime!

CHAPTER
—168—

Mr. Triplehorn started.

"Abe, I appreciate you coming here for this impromptu, quite unorthodox meeting. You've met the men who picked you up already. This is my butler, Thurston, and that is Winston, an FBI computer specialist from the Fort Pierce, Florida FBI office."

Each man nodded to the Speaker. The Speaker was clearly and understandably confused about why the FBI agents were from Florida, but he held his tongue and waited.

"On the screen, Abe, is Blake's wife, Cindy Moran, a former detective with the Tucson Police Department, who has been providing some very helpful local law enforcement expertise for us."

Cindy nodded and the Speaker said, "Hello".

"Blake, you've been point-man in getting us to this stage, so why don't you begin?"

I nodded and began.

"OK. Speaker Wright, everything that has led us to this moment has flowed from the murder of Senator Todd Ashford. Did you know Todd, sir?"

The Speaker nodded his head sadly.

"I knew Todd fairly well. He was a great man, and we found that our views on the nation and the Constitution were very similar. We had numerous times where we got to compare notes—if you will."

I was really happy to hear that, as I'm sure everyone in the meeting was.

"Excellent. Well sir, while we don't know the specific person who killed, or ordered the killing of Senator Ashford, we are aware of the entity that is responsible."

"And what '*entity*' is that?" he asked.

"Sir, I discovered a flash drive hidden in Senator Ashford's office that revealed proof of a global conspiracy cabal that is working to overthrow the Representative Republic of the United States of America."

"That Cabal, and Todd's discovery and proof of them—and finally, his intention to expose and eradicate them—is what got him killed."

I let that sink in.

Speaker Wright stared at me.

"What kind of proof are we talking about?"

I looked over at Winston.

"Go ahead and put it up on the screen."

Winston did, and I began to narrate.

"There is a lot of information that you can go through here, sir, but what you are seeing is the history of the Cabal—the cancerous roots from where it started to grow back in the 1960s—moving into a description of what they are currently trying to do."

Winston kept scrolling.

"What you see here are over a thousand names of both elected and unelected officials working in the government who *may* be a part of the Cabal—and I stress 'may' here because Senator Ashford stressed that."

"However, as you begin to look at this list, you are now seeing the names of the co-conspirators who Senator Ashford was able to *confirm* were a part of the Cabal."

Blake let Winston continue to scroll through the hundreds of names until he came to a key page where Blake asked him to stop.

There, the names of major cabinet leaders, the Majority Leader of the Senate, the Vice-President, and the President of the United States were clearly labelled in the "confirmed" category.

Blake looked over at Speaker Abe Wright's widened eyes as he stared at the screen.

"As you can see here sir, we have a *very big* problem."

CHAPTER
—169—

After staring at the screen for some time, Speaker Wright turned to look angrily around the room at all of us.

"You realize that accusing such a large group of our sitting government officials of such an organized cabal—all the way up to our President—would be considered treasonous, don't you?"

Mr. Triplehorn stepped in; his brow furrowed.

"Abe, that would be true, only if what we were saying was *untrue*. Let's back up and think about this—neither Senator Ashford, nor any of us, are committing treason. We are not 'accusing'—we're saying that we have it as a fact. The treasonous actions of these officials are what we are trying to *stop*. Remember, this Cabal is responsible for the murder of a sitting United States Senator. Now, this Cabal is engaging in treason, trying to overwhelm and overthrow our Representative Republic form of government, wanting to replace it with a globalist, socialist one."

"We're the good guys here, Abe, just trying to stop the evildoers."

It probably could go without saying, but I did appreciate Mr. T's use of the term "evildoers".

The Speaker took all that in, still staring at the screen in disbelief.

ASAC Holmes jumped in.

"Sir, I am here only because I took an oath to 'support and defend the Constitution of the United States against all enemies, foreign and domestic'. Haven't you also taken a similar oath? And wouldn't you agree that what you are seeing here are 'domestic enemies' fighting against our country and her founding?"

Abe thought about that, then nodded, and looked around at all of us.

"But why am *I* here? Why did you bring *me* here?"

Mr. Triplehorn weighed in again.

"I would like to answer that question for you, Abe, but can I first of all ask you a few things?"

After a pause, Speaker Wright nodded.

"I should first of all make you aware that I had another investigator that I use look into you, your family, your history, and your professional life, specifically looking at the 'oppo research' on you to see the worst the other side could hit you with."

Speaker Wright looked at Araby.

"I didn't know I was up for some new job, but how did I do?"

Mr. Triplehorn laughed.

"Well, you are apparently a misogynist since you won't meet with women alone who are not your wife," Araby said with a smile, "but other than foolishness like that, you passed with flying colors."

"OK. So, what are the 'few things' you say you want to ask me?"

"Well, Todd not only saw the problem, but he also put together a path to provide a solution to save our Representative Republic. Allow me to list off some of what he pointed to, because we'd all like to know what you think."

The Speaker nodded.

"Todd, like President Ronald Reagan, believed that government was the problem, not the solution, so he was laser-focused on small, limited government, as our founders were. He wanted to decentralize the federal government away from D.C., hoping to get rid of the 'beltway contagion', as he called it, of politicians not knowing what real people thought or wanted."

Speaker Wright was nodding.

"He wanted to term-limit both the House and the Senate, and even limit how many days a year a representative could be in Washington, D.C. He noted this would take a Constitutional Amendment."

Speaker Wright nodded his agreement with that assessment.

"He believed this problem of government would require a 'chainsaw' approach, not a scalpel, so he wanted there to be mass layoffs of government workers—he said fifty to eighty percent to start. He included the 'Alphabet Agencies', like the FBI, DOJ, CIA, DOE, HUD, SSA, SBA, GSA, USDA, DOT, the VA and others in these layoffs."

Speaker Wright's eyebrows went up as he nodded—he seemed to be both intrigued by, and like that idea.

"He wanted to then move these now smaller departments *out* of Washington, D.C., into the real world of our nation—meaning *not* D.C., keeping them in touch with the real America—so more decentralization."

"He wanted to stop the 'deep state' of unelected bureaucrats from being allowed to basically write laws and control the nation through regulations, in turn making the Senate and the House of Representatives actually do the job of Congress by making law."

"He also wanted to outlaw all the big money from Political Action Committees and the influence of lobbyists and make it so only individual citizens could support their candidates, once again getting the focus back on the people while also taking away the obvious temptation for graft and corruption."

Mr. Triplehorn looked around at everyone.

"There's more he talked about, but that gives you a flavor of what Todd saw as a path back to our founding."

"What do you think about all that, Speaker Wright?"

Abe smiled.

"It just reminds me of the times Todd and I would get together and talk. We had very similar views and solutions—we were just unsure about how to make them all happen."

Mr. Triplehorn held Abe's gaze for a moment.

"We're all glad to hear you say that, Abe. We think we know of a way to at least begin to move our country in the right direction."

CHAPTER
— 170 —

Mr. T looked at me and said, "Blake, you take it now."
I nodded back.
"Mr. Speaker, as I'm sure you know, you are third in line for the presidency; not the office, but the power and duties of the office."

That comment led to pure *alarm* on Abe's face.

"Yeah, what's your point?"

"Sir, would you not agree that given this Cabal's attempted coup of our Representative Republic, that these confirmed cabal members cannot be allowed to remain in office, at the very least, and may well need to be imprisoned—at least if we lived in a perfect world?"

The Speaker took a deep breath and then sighed, clearly extremely conflicted about such a catastrophic decision, so I added something else.

"I would remind you of the 1970s Watergate scandal and President Richard Nixon. Nixon was forced to resign for simply covering up a break-in of the Democratic National Committee offices at the Watergate Office Building. He didn't *do it* or *order it,* but he did cover it up—and he was forced to resign just because of that."

"Those in this Cabal are accomplices to the *murder* of a sitting United States Senator, and complicit in the attempted overthrow of our Representative Republic form of government."

I paused.

"Wouldn't you agree that their actions and attempted actions are *much worse* than *anything* President Nixon did or even thought about doing?"

The Speaker sat and stared at me, then nodded.

"So, I ask you again, sir, do you agree that these confirmed cabal members cannot be allowed to remain in office, at the very least, and may well need to be imprisoned?"

The Speaker paused.

"In theory, yes, of course. However, one would have to weigh the safety and security of the nation, and the world at large, with the unlawful acts of this Cabal before proceeding."

I nodded, everyone in the room being happy to hear how Abe was thinking.

"Assuming all that could be managed though, would you agree they have to be removed?"

The Speaker waited a beat and then admitted, "Yes, they would have to be held accountable for both Todd's murder and for this conspiracy."

I agreed.

"But how?" he asked.

"May I ask if you're familiar with the Trojan War, sir?"

Abe laughed, seemingly relieved to be able to.

"Well, I have to admit that I'm a bit of a history nerd, so yes, I'm very aware—almost embarrassingly so."

He went on.

"I don't know if you know, but we have the Troy Trojans from Troy University in southeast Alabama—a town appropriately named Troy. Their basketball team actually set the NCAA record score against DeVry Institute back in 1992 with a score of 258 to 141."

I stared at him.

"How is that *possible?*" I asked in an astonished voice.

The Speaker laughed.

"I'd have to guess a lot of offense and really, *really bad* defense."

"I guess so," I said, then went on.

"Anyway, those of us familiar with law enforcement, which is most of us in the room, believe that we could formulate a 'Trojan Horse' scenario, whereby we walk right into the heart of government, alleviate the cabal members of their jobs, and replace them with good people."

"That's where you come in, sir."

"How so?"

"First of all, the key to this is having a strong President—in your case with the powers and duties, but not the office. This will project power and strength to our nation and the world. This will provide stability during this time."

"Secondly, we need you to pour over these names and decide which positions need to be immediately filled for the sake of the nation's health, and which ones can remain vacant for the time being."

"Thirdly, we need you to identify the specific people you would choose for each position you believe needs to be filled, for the nation to function well right out of the blocks."

"If you think you can do these things, we believe we can construct a 'Trojan Horse' op that will stop the Cabal, while protecting the nation and the world."

Araby weighed in.

"If you were given the power and duties of the presidency, are these things we've discussed, part of what you believe are key to returning to our Representative Republic?"

After a pause for thought, Abe nodded and simply said, "Yes."

CHAPTER
— 171 —

Mercurius had been thinking about the situation since his investigator called him. The fact that Detective Lee and Blake Moran were together was at least problematic—and at worst, possibly "pull the plug" detrimental.

He was struggling with a decision, but he finally came to it. He had been trying to play it safe since the murder of Senator Ashford had turned up the heat, but that approach seemed to be failing. He was guessing that Moran and Triplehorn were going to just keep coming at them, and given Moran's past success, he didn't think he could bet against him.

"Enough already," he said out loud and dialed the number.

The assassin answered.

"I hope you remember our last conversation. In case you don't, if this call is anything other than telling me the job you want me to do, at my required price, I may well just slit your throat after I make you watch me kill your family."

"You don't have to threaten me, I remember. The situation has progressed, and I'm afraid that I'm going to need you to eliminate a couple of threats."

The assassin weighed in again.

"You do remember that my fee will include a vig that doubles the cost?"

"I do. I will pay that price if you can get on this right away. I'm afraid this case has gotten away from my investigator, and I need this taken care of."

"Who and where?"

"The marks are at the Waldorf Astoria on Pennsylvania Avenue, NW. My investigator is there watching for them, but I can have him leave. I'll send you his picture just in case."

"The marks are Detective David Lee of the Capitol Police and an Arizona private investigator, Blake Moran. I'll send their pictures to your phone. Moran was hired by billionaire Araby Triplehorn to investigate this case, and Detective Lee ended up being put on the case to help him. He is just the wrong guy at the wrong place at the wrong time."

"They are at the Waldorf with some other guy—we've been unable to discover who he is or what room they are all staying in. I'll leave that to you."

The assassin weighed all that.

"If you are including me killing a law enforcement officer, the vig rises another half—so it's double and a half. Killing a cop is going to bring additional heat."

"No, I have contacts at the Capitol Police who I control—I can keep the heat off you."

The assassin went silent and simmered.

Mercurius could almost feel his silent anger coming through the phone as clearly his life was being threatened.

"OK . . . fine, double and a half. When can you do it?"

There was a pause as the assassin thought.

"Since it's late and they will probably be in their rooms for the night, I'll go over to the Waldorf tomorrow morning. I should be able to complete the project by tomorrow night."

Mercurius nodded and said, "Good."

He then realized that the assassin had already hung up.

He sent all the pictures to the assassin and immediately felt better—this man was a professional, a scary professional—but one who would get the job done.

Mercurius decided to have an expensive brandy and Cuban cigar to celebrate. He felt better than he had in quite a while—their plan was back on track.

CHAPTER
—172—

After Speaker Abernathy Wright had said that he was all in to save the country, there were some things that they needed to get done very quickly.

Mr. Triplehorn nodded to Speaker Wright.

"Abe, the guys will run you home, but I'll need you to clear your schedule tomorrow so you can get your part done."

Abe nodded.

"Winston will give you a copy of Senator Ashford's information. We'll need you to go over it and decide which positions vacated by cabal members are necessary and must be filled immediately, and which ones can wait. Obviously, someone to stand as interim Vice-President and Speaker of the House in your position will be necessary to protect the succession line temporarily."

"You'll then need to decide who will fill the necessary positions going forward. Once you have that list, you'll need a trusted team to assemble all of them for a meeting that will occur right before our 'Trojan Horse' operation, so they will be ready to step in immediately."

"Can you do all that?"

Speaker Wright was thinking.

"I'll obviously look closer, but based on what I saw so far, I can probably do what we need with less than twenty people in the most vital places."

"But yes, I can do it."

"Excellent." Mr. Triplehorn nodded to me.

I turned to Maverick.

"ASAC Holmes, I'll need you to prepare a list of trusted law enforcement personnel who can be shown Senator Ashford's information and brought in to help. This will include FBI, DOJ, and Secret Service personnel."

I looked over at Detective Lee.

"Can you help with the Secret Service part? You must interact with each other regularly."

"I can. I can also provide some Capitol Police personnel to help."

I nodded to him.

"That would be great. We're going to need a fair number of uniforms to arrest cabal members without any forewarning—we'll just walk in and march them out. And these are powerful people who are used to getting their way, so your personnel cannot be intimidated by them."

Both ASAC Holmes and Detective Lee nodded.

I then turned to Winston.

"Winston, I need you to rig both motion sensors and cameras in the hallway and stairwell, that will run to your laptop and will ping whenever there is movement. Since they know we're here somewhere, we have to be ready in case they find us and then attack to try and stop us."

"Can you do that?"

Winston just nodded once.

"OK. Here's the 'Trojan Horse' part. We are going to decide what places our forces need to invade, and we will then synchronize our invasion to happen simultaneously at all the vital points around Washington, D.C. We don't have to arrest all the members of the Cabal at once, but we need to cut the head off the snake, so the rest are just left flailing. So, we know that the President, Vice-President, and Majority Leader in the Senate will be one primary group."

I turned to Mr. Triplehorn.

"When we know what the vital targets are, sir, we will need your clout to call them and ask for an emergency meeting in the various locations—which will all take place at the exact same time."

I looked at the group.

"When that time comes, each of our groups will 'attend' the meeting, arresting the cabal members. Speaker Wright's chosen replacements will then step into their positions."

I turned to Speaker Wright.

"Immediately after that happens, you will need to do a live, nationwide broadcast from the Oval Office. You will briefly explain that the Cabal is responsible for Senator Ashford's death, and they have been both discovered and are being arrested. You will also give them the unfortunate news that the Cabal included the Vice-President and the President. So, pursuant to the line of succession laid out in our Constitution, you will be assuming the powers and duties of the presidency until an election can be held."

"So, you'll need to write that speech. Also, I know you guys often use teleprompters, but we won't have that luxury since this is a bit of a 'shock and awe' approach. Can you pretty much learn the speech and just look into the camera, and do it? It would be much more powerful if you could sound like a person instead of a politician."

Speaker Wright nodded and said, "I think I can."

I turned back to Mr. Triplehorn.

"Mr. T, I assume with everything you own, you can set up the national broadcast through your companies?"

"Yep, I'll get on it as soon as I know when it will be."

"Well sir, it kind of needs to be a last minute, breaking news, sort of thing. These are journalists and investigators—if we give them *any* lead time to investigate, we could lose the whole 'Trojan Horse' effect."

"Can you pull it off relatively last minute?"

Mr. Triplehorn thought about it.

"I can if I have one of my companies do the feed and give it to all the other networks and streamers—they will all carry it that way. I know who I can trust to keep it to themselves while they get it all set up."

"Awesome," I said, looking around the group. "OK, we all know what we need to do—just remember that secrecy is paramount."

"Mr. Speaker, it turned out that I was able to park the SUV very close to the back of the hotel, so the three of us will get you back home, and then we'll all get started on our jobs."

CHAPTER
—173—

After we all said goodbye to Cindy, Winston started shutting everything down on the other screen. As he did, a picture flashed up. Speaker Wright saw it briefly and asked, "Wait a minute, who was that a picture of?"

Winston backed it up and said, "This is the guy downstairs who was watching for us, and apparently tried to tail the guys to your house. I was getting ready to try some facial recognition software to see if we could get a name."

Abe stared at the picture.

"You can save your software—I know that guy, or at least I know of him."

We all looked at him and I asked, "Who is it, sir?"

"He's an investigator the Senate uses for various tasks."

The Speaker gave us his name and Winston started typing. He found out some basic information about the man and then started another search. It turns out that he was looking at the man's phone records, specifically during the time he had been at the hotel.

It wasn't concerning *at all* that Winston could do this so easily.

There were multiple calls from a specific number, quite close together, and then a call back to that number by the investigator.

"Can you tell whose phone those calls came from?"

Winston typed.

"It's a burner phone."

He typed some more and waited.

"I just pinged the burner phone, and it is here."

Winston pointed to a location that was among the Senate offices.

Speaker Wright looked at the screen and then thought about the layout of the building.

His eyes then suddenly widened slightly.

"That's Senate Majority Leader Samuel Brooks' office."

They all looked at each other.

They had found the cabal member who was giving the orders—and he was the Senate Majority Leader of the United States of America, Senator Samuel Brooks.

CHAPTER
—174—

Mercurius had told him to stand down.

He rolled his eyes when he used that name. He felt stupid calling Senator Brooks that, but the man insisted.

He had gone home the night before after Brooks called him and told him he was done with the case. However, he was so annoyed at being shooed away like a failed child that he found himself sitting back in the lobby of the Waldorf Astoria the next morning.

He didn't want to quit this job—he wanted to complete the work. He was the one who had found both Detective Lee and Blake Moran when they had disappeared. Instead of rewarding him for his efforts, he was just told he was finished. That just wasn't OK.

It was true that he had blown it when he tried to tail the Suburban, but Mercurius didn't know that. He couldn't imagine why he'd been told to stand down when he was so close.

He'd taken his position again in the lobby, sitting in the perfect place to see all the elevators, while being able to see the main entrance with just a turn of his head. He kept his head on a swivel to cover the whole lobby.

He'd been in place for only about fifteen minutes when he felt, more than heard, someone sit down directly behind him. He resisted the urge to turn around and look—that seemed too obvious—but he planned to slowly, and casually, look around and check out who was behind him. As he started to slowly turn, he heard a voice that stopped him.

"Don't turn around," the voice said to him.

He froze. He then started to turn his head anyway.

"If you turn and look at me, I will have to kill you."

He froze again, believing the cold voice.

"You were told to stand down—you are not supposed to be here. The threat-level had ratcheted up and this investigation has been turned over to me by Mercurius."

"If you value your life, and the lives of your family, you will follow my directions: you will get up and walk over to the concierge's desk, not looking back. After a count of ten, you will then walk out the front door of the hotel, again, without looking back. If you do what I'm telling you, I will not kill you. If you fail at any point, you will leave me no choice—I will kill you and your entire family."

For emphasis, the threatening voice then recited his home address.

"Are we clear on each point?"

The investigator sat there, looking straight ahead, as the threatening voice finished. He could hardly breathe. He thought about what had happened to Senator Ashford and was fairly sure he was listening to the man who had assassinated the senator.

"*I said*, are we clear on each point?" asked the voice with more emphasis.

He took a deep breath and replied, "We're clear."

"Then go," said the voice.

His legs felt like rubber from the threat, but he managed to stand up and walk over to the concierge's desk.

"Good morning, how may I help you?" asked the concierge.

One, two, three, four, five . . .

"Sir, how may I help you?" came the question again.

. . . six, seven, eight, nine, ten.

He then turned and walked away, leaving the concierge at his desk, looking confused. Still having a little trouble breathing, he walked straight toward the front door of the hotel without looking to the left or the right. He exited the hotel and walked down the sidewalk to the west.

After he turned the corner, he promptly threw up in the gutter of the street. He then wiped his mouth, went to his car, and drove straight home to his family.

CHAPTER
—175—

Blake had experienced an interesting night.

After we had marked Senator Samuel Brooks as the leader of the Cabal, we all set about doing our parts of the "Trojan Horse" operation. ASAC Holmes, Detective Lee, and I got Speaker Wright out of the hotel, past the investigator, who was still sitting in the lobby, and then got him home with no more drama.

After we got back to the Waldorf, it was somewhat late, but we were still surprised that the investigator didn't seem to be around anymore. That seemed odd.

The next morning, I got up and around, ate something and then headed downstairs. I took the elevator to the second floor and then took the stairs down to the lobby, not wanting to be seen coming out of the elevator.

I took a quick look at the lobby, then made my way back to the foliage that had concealed me so well the night before.

I looked and saw the investigator sitting in the same place. He was pretending to work on his phone, but his eyes were taking in the elevators. Every minute or so, he would turn his head and check out the rest of the lobby and the front entrance.

All-in-all, not bad spy-craft.

I figured that it might be helpful to monitor him for an hour or so and make sure nothing changed with him. Since everyone else was busy setting up their part of the "Trojan Horse" op, I figured I could burn an hour just keeping an eye on the enemy's investigator.

I'd been watching for about ten minutes when I noticed a guy on the other side of the lobby seemingly doing the same thing I was doing—concealing himself while he watched the investigator.

I leaned back a little further in my "hidey-hole". Since I saw this guy, I wanted to make sure I wasn't making the same mistake, giving myself away to him.

I watched the guy look around the lobby and then back at the investigator, who was sitting with his back toward him. He waited until the investigator did his look over toward the entrance, and then he started walking, somewhat with his head down, over to where the investigator was sitting.

I studied the part of his face I could see, but I didn't recognize him.

He sat down directly behind the investigator, facing the other way, toward the hotel entrance, his back to both the investigator and me.

When he sat down, the investigator clearly sensed it and started to turn to look when all the sudden, he seemed to freeze. He even started to turn again, and then froze again.

It was bizarre.

The new guy was clearly talking to the investigator with his back to him.

The investigator sat there, frozen, not even blinking, but clearly listening. Suddenly, he said something, then got up and walked, somewhat unsteadily, toward the concierge's desk.

My eyes were darting back and forth from our old bad guy, the investigator, to whom I could only guess might be our new bad guy.

I was confused with what was going on.

The concierge was clearly trying to engage the investigator, but the investigator seemed oblivious, just staring straight ahead while seeming to be mumbling something. He suddenly just turned and walked straight toward the hotel's main entrance, walking right out the front door.

The new guy had a clear view of this, and he watched the investigator all the way out the door. He then sat for another five minutes, just staring at the front door.

He then got up, walked around the chairs, and took the same seat where the investigator had been sitting. He began the same process of scanning the lobby with an occasional look toward the front entrance.

Now I could study his face.

It was somewhat nondescriptive but had a good jawline that made a face that some might think to be handsome. It was the eyes that seemed off—they just looked dead, even from this distance.

He was working on his phone while he scanned the lobby. As I studied him, something niggled in the back of my brain—something that was bugging me, but I couldn't quite reach it.

Oh well, usually if I quit working at it so hard, it would eventually jump to the front of my brain.

I carefully took a few pictures with my phone and then backed away when he looked toward the front entrance. I then headed back upstairs, using the stairwell to the second floor, and then taking the elevator.

It looked like we had in fact, a *new* bad guy to deal with.

CHAPTER
— 176 —

I went back to Mr. Triplehorn's suite. Winston was already there, working away on something. It appeared that ASAC Holmes was still in his room, working the phones to set up the teams that would need to be at the various locations when we needed them.

I said good morning to Mr. T, who was apparently working on some of his business ventures—probably on the phone with the king of Siam or something like that.

Fun Fact: the term "Siam" comes from a Sanskrit word meaning "dark brown". Also, there is no official Siam now because the area that was known as Siam is now known as Thailand, having its name changed in 1939.

However, saying "the king of Thailand" just doesn't flow off the tongue like a good cliché should—like "the king of Siam" *does*, so I'm going to stand by my statement.

Any-who . . .

Winston called me over to see what he had done. He showed me his laptop screen, which was now divided into four equal squares. He had placed cameras in the hallway, one pointed in each direction for two of the screens. The other two screens were each showing a view of the stairwell.

"Where are these cameras placed," I asked, pointing to the stairwell cameras.

"I placed one around the fourth floor—so about halfway up the stairwell. The other one is on this floor pointing down the stairs, so we can see any immediate threat to this floor, since it's the top floor."

"I also designed it to 'ping' if there is movement, so we don't have to sit and watch it constantly."

As if to prove that point, his computer 'pinged' and we both looked at the screen. Someone was walking down the stairs and had just passed the camera on the fourth floor.

I was nodding.

"OK, good job. That resolution is surprisingly good. Are you going to stay around your computer so you can let us know if there's movement?"

Winston just stared at me, basically telling me that he *always* stayed around his computer.

I just nodded once and said, "Great, thanks."

I told him about the new guy who I saw replace the Cabal's investigator. I gave him my phone and he quickly sent the pics I took to his computer and said he'd start working on identifying him.

While he did that, I headed back to see if Mr. T was off the phone yet.

He was.

"So, how was 'the king of Siam'?" I asked.

That furrowed my favorite billionaire's brow for a moment, but he was used to me by this point.

"You know that Siam changed its name to Thailand, right?" Mr. T asked.

I laughed.

"I do, as a matter of fact, but I think 'the king of Siam' rolls off the tongue better than 'the king of Thailand', don't you?"

That got me just a head shake and a chuckle.

Mr. Triplehorn went on.

"I talked to Speaker Wright, and he already has over half the names for the positions he says he'll need to fill. He felt he could complete his part of the op by about noon."

"Awesome. I think ASAC Holmes and Detective Lee are both

working the phones to get the law enforcement side of this in place. If we can get those elements ready to go, you could start calling to get meetings at the appropriate places for our 'Trojan Horse'."

"Do you think we could possibly do this tonight if we can get all the elements in place?"

Mr. Triplehorn thought about that.

"If we can green light this by mid-afternoon, I think I can get all the meetings set up and the TV coverage in place to get it done."

"Good," I said. "In an operation like this, the longer you drag it on, the more chance that something is going to get leaked, or some unforeseen counteroffensive happens. I have to believe the Cabal is feeling nervous, especially after seeing me here with Detective Lee. They have to be guessing something is up, and if that makes them jumpy, they may act."

"You mean try to kill one of us?"

"Whoa, Mr. T, you are one 'glass half empty' sort of guy! But yeah—they might try to kill one of us, or more."

"Just so you know, it looks like they put a substitute in for their investigator downstairs. We'll need to keep an eye out for him now. As long as they can't find where we are in the hotel, we should be relatively safe."

"However, that's why we need to move on this as soon as we can. The longer they have to look for us or investigate what we're doing, the more chance they end up stumbling onto something where we lose the element of surprise."

"It's the surprise—and the natural confusion that follows, that makes the 'Trojan Horse' op work."

Mr. Triplehorn nodded his agreement.

CHAPTER
— 177 —

After watching the lobby for a little over an hour, the assassin decided to take some proactive steps. He did a final look around, and then got up and headed toward the service area of the hotel.

As he walked into the service area, a couple of people looked at him like they might question his presence in this area, but his demeanor as he stared at them did not lend itself to them challenging him.

He had long ago perfected his "you don't want to mess with me" persona. Basically, he looked like an understated, yet very scary dude.

He walked into the food service area and went into the back where all the waitstaff jackets were kept. He picked out one of the white jackets with the words, "Waldorf Astoria" emblazoned across the heart area and tried it on. It fit nicely.

He was now surprisingly incognito, given that people tend to see one element that they recognize and then make their assumptions and conclusions based on that. So, they see a waitstaff jacket, they assume and conclude that person is part of the waitstaff.

With his newfound freedom to move around, he walked through the kitchen area until he found what he was looking for—the order desk. He looked both ways, then began to look through the orders from yesterday and today.

He was looking for anything stating an order and room number for either Blake Moran or David Lee, since he knew they had been here for at least yesterday and today, and yet had not been seen out of their rooms much.

Everybody has to eat, after all.

He took a quick look at all the names and neither of the names Moran nor Lee showed up anywhere.

He took a deep breath and read the list over again.

He was about to put the list down and move on to try and figure something else out, when his eye noticed a huge order the night before. Someone ordered thousands of dollars of food that could probably feed an entire NFL football team, all delivered to the Waldorf Townhouse Two Bedroom Bi-level, which he knew was on the top floor of the hotel from the research he'd done.

It didn't say who the resident was who purchased all this, it just had the credit card number to run.

He was shaking his head at all this money spent when he saw a handwritten note, with nothing but the words, "Araby Triplehorn", probably so the waitstaff would personalize their service for this obviously crazy wealthy client.

Something was pinging in his head. He just stared at the name. He knew that name, but he couldn't remember how or why. Then it came to him. Mercurius had mentioned in passing that "billionaire Araby Triplehorn" was the one who hired the Arizona private investigator for this case.

A half-smile crossed the assassin's face. Very clever. They had hidden their presence throughout the hotel, covering their tracks, but some "let's make sure we give the rich guy full-service" manager just outed them to him.

He took another deep breath and put down the list.

He looked around and found what he needed—a silver plated covered serving tray that helped him to complete his "server" look, which would enable him to go anywhere in the hotel without getting a second glance from anyone.

As he walked out of the service area with the serving tray, he was contemplating that he might well have to kill one of the richest men in the world if he was found with Moran and Lee.

He didn't care about the killing, but the fallout from such a kill would be huge. Mercurius would be paying him much more than two and a half vig if that happened.

CHAPTER
— 178 —

I was walking back through the other room, getting ready to go check on ASAC Holmes and Detective Lee, and see what progress they had made for our operation.

Winston was sitting at the huge dining table, working away. He was using facial recognition software on his computer to try and identify the new guy from the pic I gave him, the one who replaced the Cabal's investigator.

I told him I'd be right back and was almost to the door when I heard the "ping". I looked around about the same time Winston yelled, "Blake"!

Now, for the record, Winston *doesn't* yell. Winston barely and rarely talks—but I kid you not, Winston yelled!

I ran back to see what he was looking at, and was shocked to see the replacement bad dude with the dead eyes from the lobby. He was now decked out like a waiter, carrying a silver tray, moving slowly and cautiously toward the camera Winston had placed on the fourth floor.

He was moving more like a cat than a waiter, with caution and looking around, quite alert. And why would this "waiter" be taking the stairs, except to avoid cameras? Thankfully, he hadn't seen Winston's camera.

I sprang into action and yelled at Winston as I ran out of the room, "Call ASAC Holmes and Detective Lee and tell them I need immediate backup in the stairwell on the top floor! And hit 'record' on the feed!"

I ran into the other room to leave out the door, but as I ran past Thurston and Mr. Triplehorn, I yelled, "We have an incoming threat—time to get your ninja on, Thurston."

I knew from the past that Mr. T's butler had some surprising skills that one wouldn't expect from such a small, British steward. I was guessing that Mr. T could probably inflict a little damage too—if he had to; the man was fit.

I ran down the hallway as fast as I could, then I stopped outside the stairway door and took some deep breaths to ready myself.

I checked to make sure that Molly was secure and ready for action in my back holster.

She was.

I crouched down low and opened the door to peer into the stairwell. The perp hadn't made it to the top yet, but as I stopped to listen, I thought I heard him brush up against the wall a couple of floors down.

I moved into the stairwell and quietly shut the door behind me. I then moved down the stairs to the first landing halfway between the lower floor and the top floor.

Then I waited.

Our fake "waiter" was still moving slowly up toward my position.

I decided I'd waited long enough.

"Hey, bad dude. I'm up here waiting for you, but you're taking an awful long time to get here. Come on, man, you're burning daylight!"

The movement below had stopped as he considered his next move, since my appearance clearly wasn't in his plan. He then just walked up the stairs, clearly no longer concerned about the noise.

I was looking down the well between the stairs when I saw him look up at me.

"Keep coming bud, I'm waiting."

His head disappeared, and I was ready to pull Molly out and duck if he came forward with a gun.

He didn't.

He walked casually to the stair landing that was just below me and looked up at me. He then set the silver tray down. As I looked at him, now that I was closer to him, I realized what had been niggling my brain back down in the lobby. The dude had been using his left hand to work on his phone. Before he set it down, he was carrying the silver tray with his left hand. Now, he was leading with his left side and left hand—different from most people in the world—about ninety percent of people in the world, to be exact.

The dude was left-handed, like only ten percent of people in the world—with men being more likely to utilize and display their left-handed dominance.

Does that ring any bells with you? It sure did with me!

I looked into his dead eyes, and I knew. It was a gut instinct, but my gut was finely tuned to stuff like this.

I said, "You're not just a watcher like the other guy, are you? You're left-handed, so I'm guessing you're the assassin—you're the one who killed Senator Ashford."

He just stared at me, clearly a little surprised I had somehow discovered he was left-handed, and that I knew he was the assassin—but I could tell I was right. If I was about to die, I at least got to enjoy the fact that my ascertaining he was left-handed unnerved him a little. He had clearly made a mistake, and that disturbed him.

So, Senator Todd Ashford's murderer was standing right in front of me, on his way to murder more of us—apparently, planning on starting with me.

The Cabal was coming for us again.

The bad guy finally spoke.

"Now that you've seen my face, I'm going to have to kill you," he said, so matter of fact, that he clearly thought it was already a *fait accompli*.

For the record, that's just French for saying the thing was already accomplished and presumably irreversible.

And since *my death* was what he was referring to as already accomplished and presumably irreversible, I took issue with his presumptuous statement, and I took it rather personally.

But just between you, me, and the wall, I have to admit—it was a little intimidating.

CHAPTER
— 179 —

I had just enough time to think, "I could really use my backup guys right about now," when the assassin charged up the stairs at me.

I backed up on the landing and readied my fighting stance.

The assassin wasn't as tall as me—I'm six feet, four inches tall, so I would have him on reach—but he was at least six feet and was more heavily muscled than me.

In addition to that, fighting a "south-paw" was just a whole different beast. That term came from when baseball diamonds were typically laid out with home plate to the west, so a left-handed pitcher was throwing from the south. And just like having to bat against a lefty creates unique issues in baseball, fighting a lefty kind of throws off a normal fighter's rhythm.

We could ponder this a little more, but I'm kind of busy right now, so I need to get back to the bad guy.

When he got to the landing, he surprised me when he didn't stop, but just kept coming and charged right into my breadbasket like an NFL lineman, lifting me off my feet and smashing my body against the block wall.

So much for my "fighting stance"! Apparently, we were *not* going to be governing this fight based on the *Marquess of Queensbury rules*, so sacrosanct in boxing since the 1800s.

Which simply means this was nothing more than a street fight!

I can't believe that nobody bothered to carbon copy me on that! I did *not* see that coming!

His move knocked some of the breath out of me, and then he started hitting me with a barrage of punches, landing most of them.

I was able to push him away enough to land a blow on his head. I was trying for his nose to make his eyes water, but he moved so quickly that I missed.

After just a few blows, I began realizing a *really unfortunate fact*—this guy was a better fighter than me. I had skills which I worked on regularly, but this guy was a machine, a total beast, as he just pummeled me with blow after blow. I tried some different moves, but he seemed to anticipate everything I tried. When I went to hit his solar plexus, he turned just in time, and my fist bounced off of the side of his chest.

When I realized that I was outmatched, I tried for the equalizer—I reached for Molly. But as I brought her around, he did a surprisingly fast kick and knocked her out of my hand, and she bounced down the stairs, now useless to me.

My back was now against the railing, with the stairwell right behind me. The assassin got a look on his face that concerned me. It was that look that said it was now time to end this and get about the rest of his job.

However, "ending this" entailed ending me!

He kicked me in the stomach, which doubled me over for a moment and smacked me against the railing. He then went for the kill shot, probably to knock me out and then just twist my neck and break it—which would be game, set, and match—game over.

As I started to stand, he swung his left fist into a roundhouse with all his weight behind it, straight at my head.

Right as he did that, the door above us to the stairway burst open and ASAC Holmes and Detective Lee rushed onto the landing, guns drawn.

I didn't take note of what was happening above us—I was too busy trying to negate that whole *"fait accompli"* thing and not die—but the assassin did notice it, for just a fraction of a second.

And that was my chance—all I needed.

As the assassin went for the "kill shot", he swung his big left-handed roundhouse at my head with all his weight behind it, counting on the contact with my head to stop him. But in that fraction of a second, when he was momentarily distracted, the back of my brain noted it, and at the last moment, I suddenly ducked under the punch, which threw him completely off-center and brought all his weight directly toward me.

With my butt against the railing, as he swung and missed my head and all his weight came at me, I was effectively under him. So, I used his weight and momentum against him. As he came over the top of me with his swing, I simply caught him in the stomach with my shoulder and hands and lifted up like I was doing a hard squat—as I pushed up with all my might.

Now, I didn't plan what happened next, but it was pretty "beast mode", if I do say so myself. If nothing else, it was much more desirable than that whole "I'm dead" scenario I had quite recently been facing.

The assassin found himself flying. Unfortunately for him, he was "flying" right over the stairwell that was a direct drop, about eighty feet straight down, to a concrete floor.

It felt like time froze as we locked eyes—mine now confident and his full of disbelief, then fear. He started flailing around to try and stop the inevitable, but alas, at least for him, to no avail.

In those last moments, he and Sir Issac Newton found some common ground; for Newton, it was the apple that fell on his head that acquainted him with the realization of gravity. For our friendly, neighborhood assassin, it was falling to his death, possibly *on his head*, that reminded him of the very real fact of gravity.

In light of the life-and-death significance of this moment—i.e., I'm not dead, and he was about to be—I hope you can appreciate, as our assassin clearly did, the *"gravity"* of this moment.

(I know this is a pretty serious moment in our story, but if you want to, you can insert a laughy face emoji here. No pressure—your call.)

CHAPTER
— 180 —

Now, as I'm sure you can imagine, I'm feeling pretty awesome about now, since I'm *not dead*. I'm sure my wife, Cindy, and my sons, Nicholas and Lincoln, would agree—that is, if Nic and Linc even knew they were alive or who on earth I was.

However, this little development was *not* so good for our little "Trojan Horse" operation—a dead guy, eighty feet below in a high-end, extremely expensive hotel, smashed on the concrete floor—is rarely a good thing for a "stealthy" operation.

So, we had some quick thinking that we needed to do.

ASAC Holmes and Detective Lee had rushed down to try to help me, about the time the assassin took flight. We all just stood there and watched as he fell and then hit. I'm guessing we all knew we should look away, but seriously, we just couldn't.

Even though he was the bad guy, we all kind of scrunched up our nose when we saw and heard him hit. It just wasn't a pleasant sight or sound.

However, I have to say, it could *not* have happened to a more deserving guy!

I was still huffing and puffing as we stood there looking down at the dead bad guy. I finally took a deep breath and turned toward the guys.

"Thoughts?" I asked, breathing heavily.

They both turned toward me.

"Are you OK?" asked ASAC Holmes.

I cocked my head as I painfully moved my shoulder and did a quick body check.

"I'm in pain, but I don't think he broke anything."

I moved my torso.

"Ouch. OK, maybe a rib or two, but I'll live."

Detective Lee glanced back down at the perp and then over at me.

"Did you notice you were right? He was left-handed."

I smiled a weak smile and just nodded.

"The good news is that ASAC Holmes and I got here in time to see him attacking you and you simply defending yourself, so I think you'll be in the clear on what happened here."

I nodded again, then added.

"Good. I also told Winston to record what came from that camera," I said, pointing up the stairs. "Most of what happened should be reviewable."

"Oh, great," said Detective Lee, "that makes it even better—should be a slam dunk."

I nodded.

"The problem is that we have a dead body down there, and we need to stay on schedule for the 'Trojan Horse' op. Is there any chance you can get this taken care of on the down-low so we can stay on schedule?"

Detective Lee thought about it, then nodded.

"I'll have a couple of trusted uniforms from the Capitol Police come over and keep people away, and I have contacts in the Metropolitan Police Department of D.C. that I'll bring in. They will handle the crime scene work, and if we can stay on schedule, the investigation and interviews will happen after we complete the 'Trojan Horse' op."

"Honestly, with our testimony, and if Winston also got a good visual of the fight, their talk with you will only amount to them checking it off their list of to-dos."

I looked over at ASAC Holmes.

"Given that this is all related to the big picture of what we are about to do, and this is undoubtedly the killer of Senator Ashford, do you need to get some Feds on this?"

He was nodding.

"I will need to, but I can wait until DCPD does their initial work, and then I'll have some agents step in and inform them of the bigger picture."

"OK. David, why don't you go down and guard the scene and make your calls from down there so there's no contamination to the area. This would be a bad time for some nice family to decide to use the stairs."

"Got it," said Detective Lee as he started down the stairs to guard our dead bad guy.

"Oh Blake, you'll probably want this back," he said as he retrieved Molly from the steps below us and brought her back to me.

"Oh, thanks. I gotta say, that guy was very good. He kicked this outta my hand almost as soon as I tried to bring it around. I sure am glad you two came in when you did—it distracted him just enough, at just the right moment, for me to beat him."

They both nodded.

"OK, you head south David, and Maverick and I will head north back to the Batcave."

They were both so relieved I wasn't dead that they didn't even comment on my use of the "Batcave".

CHAPTER
— 181 —

When we got back to Mr. Triplehorn's suite of rooms, Mr. T gave me a big hug, and even Thurston seemed a little emotional.

Apparently, they had been watching on the computer, and had feared my almost demise. Go figure.

I informed them that the bad guy who most probably killed Senator Ashford was no longer among us in the land of the living, and they all seemed quite happy about that.

We watched the recorded feed of the altercation, and all agreed that it made clear what had happened—primarily that he was trying to kill me, and I was just defending myself.

ASAC Holmes said this recording would satisfy any questions law enforcement might have about what happened, even in a crazy, liberal bastion like Washington, D.C., where they tended to protect criminals, not citizens.

That being the case, we all moved into the living room and started to plan "Trojan Horse".

I started.

"So, we know that the Cabal is scared and is coming after us. At least the killer knew what room we were in—although I have *no idea* how, so we'll have to keep a close eye on security until the operation takes place."

I said this last part looking at Winston.

He nodded.

"Where are we on the law enforcement side?" I asked.

ASAC Holmes spoke up.

"I have been able to secure ample FBI agents for the operation, men and women who I know I can trust. Detective Lee knew the top dog at the Secret Service, so after we looked and made sure he wasn't on the cabal list, David called him, and he actually came here and met with us this morning."

That scared me.

"Did you make it clear to him how important secrecy and surprise is for this op?"

"We did. Once he heard the facts of what the Cabal was planning to do, he was all in. Turns out the Secret Service agents don't like the current administration very much."

"He told me he would provide Secret Service agents for our op, and he would be there personally to deal with the Administration side of things."

"Wow, that's awesome. That will make that part—possibly the most important part—a lot easier."

I looked over at Mr. Triplehorn.

"Have you heard from Speaker Wright yet?"

He shook his head "no".

"Not yet, but I'll call him as soon as we're done here."

I nodded.

"OK, it sounds like we have all the elements in place for the operation, we just need to confirm that final element, being Speaker Wright, and then we can complete the plan."

"After we get the go ahead from him, we'll decide on a time, then Mr. Triplehorn will call and make all the appointments with the major powerful people involved with the Cabal—only one meeting that he'll personally keep—the one with the top two bad guys. You'll also set up the live TV feed for the networks and for streaming."

"Is that all doable?"

Mr. Triplehorn looked at the $70,000 watch on his wrist—the one that I maintain keeps about the same time as the watch I got from Walmart. He then did some calculations in his head.

"It's getting a little close on time to accomplish all that. To get this done, everybody will need to be ready to spring into action as soon as I get the nod from Speaker Wright."

Mr. T had another thought.

"When I do big business deals, I always insist that we put everything we can out for the shareholders to see all the facts about what's happening. I know we're tapping the media, but we know that many of them will try to hide the facts and lie about the Cabal."

"What do you all think about taking an additional step in transparency by publishing Senator Ashford's notes online—perhaps on X, formerly Twitter—so we can show the American people that we're giving them all the facts for them to decide for themselves?"

"It would limit the Cabal's ability to lie about what they did to get us here or about what we know they're going to try to lie about to repair the damage."

I was nodding—I liked it! I added something.

"In the Gettysburg Address in 1863, when America was dealing with the Civil War and the need to get rid of slavery, President Abraham Lincoln pointed out that this is supposed to be a 'government *of* the people, *by* the people, and *for* the people'. Since this is exactly what the Cabal is trying to take away, I agree that letting 'the people' see what the Cabal was trying to do is vital."

I turned to Winston.

"Can you get that ready to post?"

Winston nodded.

Mr. Triplehorn spoke up.

"You'll have to redact all those names that were not on the 'confirmed list' of cabal members. That would be unfair to impugn them if we don't have solid proof yet."

He thought some more.

"And it will make the document shorter too, which is probably a good thing. Think 'Cliff Notes' style."

Winston nodded, and then I concluded.

"OK. Let's have you call and talk with Speaker Wright, Mr. T, and then maybe Detective Lee will be back by the time you're done. We'll then finish the details, and you can make all your calls to set up your Oval Office meeting, all the other fake meetings, and the TV coverage."

We then all put our hands in together and yelled, "Go team!" and we were off.

(Did I get you? I think I got you. In *my head* we actually did this, adding in a stirring rendition of the "Star Spangled Banner", but *not* for realsies!)

CHAPTER
— 182 —

It was now after twelve noon, and Mercurius was getting nervous. He knew the assassin might need more time than this to find Detective Lee and Blake Moran in the Waldorf, but he couldn't help but be on edge while he waited.

He had just been in a Senate Committee meeting where he had pushed hard for the cabal's agenda. He hadn't gotten what he wanted yet, but he would keep pushing. He was thinking about having the President weigh in to see if that would push them across the finish line, but he had to be careful to not go to that well too many times or it might start to lose its effect.

Now that Senator Ashford was out of the way, the threat of exposure was gone, and he could operate more forcefully with other members. Their involvement, and the additional support from mega-rich oligarchs across the globe who wanted to diminish and then end America's domination, gave him immense power and control—and wealth.

Their clandestine Cabal represented the new world order that would control the direction of the world from here on out. The only real obstacle remaining for them was America, and the ridiculous idea found there, that "the people" should be free and self-determinant. Those "Constitutionalists", "right-wingers", "God and Country" crazies were the last wall of opposition they needed to tear down—and tear them down they would!

What a load of crap! People were idiots. Morons who needed an elite group like the Cabal, to tell them what to do, how to live, and what to think.

Enough of this almost 250-year experiment! People were sheep who needed to be led—and the members of the Cabal were the ones to lead them!

Mercurius thought again about the assassin. He wondered how he was going to have to manipulate the story regarding the reality of the bodies of Detective Lee and Moran. He decided he had better start thinking about how to squelch any blowback, should he need to, like he'd had to with Ashford's murder.

He figured he'd go with the reality of how dangerous Washington, D.C. was—one of the most dangerous cities, per capita, in the nation. He might even try and use the murders to talk about and push for gun control again—maybe even go on a tirade about criminal reform too.

That made him laugh.

See how dumb people were? A criminal could commit a murder, and Mercurius could turn around and use *that* to demand that guns be taken away from *law abiding citizens.* So, instead of pointing out that the dead victim could've protected and defended himself if only he *had* a gun at the time of the murder, he would argue that *future* victims should be deprived of their stupid Second Amendment rights!

And the press and the gullible students in the liberal universities would eat it up and applaud the position.

They would agree and demand that their own rights be *taken away from them.*

He just shook his head and laughed again.

People were just so *stupid*!

CHAPTER
— 183 —

We were all back together, early afternoon. I had called Cindy and filled her in on everything, and she was now back on the big screen for this final meeting.

If I may comment on that earlier conversation with Cindy, I have to say that she did not seem at all amused at my recounting of the fight with the assassin. The fact that I had admitted to her that the assassin ended up being a better fighter than me, made her jump to the completely unwarranted conclusion that he could have *killed* me. Here I was, just trying to be an open, transparent, and vulnerable person, trying to learn how to be a man in the twenty-first century, and *that's* the conclusion my bride jumps to?

I pause, shaking my head in disbelief.

I know, mystifying, right? Where did *that* come from? Him—kill me? Come on!

Now that we were parents, the reality of my job was even more concerning to Cindy. I was now a husband and a father, and she revisited the conversation about maybe I should reconsider what I do, because I need to stay safe.

I thought about that, and my mind once again went immediately to a great philosopher and what he said in a similar situation—Rocky Balboa.

So, just like I had said to her back in Arizona, in my best Rocky voice, I said, "I never asked you to stop being a woman, so please, I'm asking you please, don't ask me to stop being a man."

As you might imagine, that was met with stoic silence from my wife, undoubtedly overcome with the depth of insight and wisdom that I had just displayed. She was also probably mesmerized by my spot-on Sylvester Stallone impersonation.

Now, just because she ended that silence with, "You're an *idiot*", does *not* mean that I misread the silence. You know how complex women are, and I just don't think Cindy is as in-touch with her emotions as am I, and that's just her way of saying, "I really, really love you, Blake."

At least, that's how I'm taking it.

CHAPTER
—184—

So, like I said, we were all now back in Mr. Triplehorn's living room to do the final planning, including my seemingly angry wife on the big screen—the kids must be acting up—who can know? Women *are* a mystery!

"How did it go with our dead assassin?" I asked.

Detective Lee shook his head.

"About as good as you'd think since they haven't been able to talk to you about it yet. ASAC Holmes and I both gave our eyewitness accounts of what happened at the end, and then we provided Winston's recording for them to look at—that helped a lot."

"They are processing the scene as we talk, and they're keeping it on the down-low for now. However, when I told them this was most likely Senator Ashford's killer, their eyes lit up. That's a big score for them, and they are not gonna want to sit on it for very long."

"How did you buy me some time with them?"

Detective Lee glanced over at Maverick.

"ASAC Holmes pulled the 'National Security Issue' and they backed off."

I nodded.

"Well, he's not wrong about that."

Cindy chimed in.

"Blake, you really don't want to give the wrong impression to the local cops. You're probably about done with what you need to do after this planning meeting. Why don't you have David give his lead detective a call and tell him you'll be available right after this meeting to give him a statement. You don't want it to look like you're hiding anything here."

Detective Lee looked from Cindy on the screen to me and agreed, saying, "She's not wrong, Blake."

I nodded and said, "OK, make the call."

Detective Lee nodded and walked into the other room to make the call.

I looked over at Mr. Triplehorn.

"What's the news from Speaker Wright?"

"I have to be honest and say that he started off sounding like he was getting 'cold feet', but then I told him about your little adventure with Senator Ashford's assassin, and that seemed to put some steel in his spine."

"He's completed his part of the plan, staffing the positions that have to be filled immediately. As soon as I give him the word from this meeting, he will set up the meeting with the whole group and let them know what's about to happen and their role in the new administration. He said that he'll have each person report to their position, along with the law enforcement personnel, at the time we designate, to facilitate a smooth transition."

I nodded.

"Did you remind him to emphasize this is top secret, and that they can't let anyone know if we're to pull off the whole 'Trojan Horse' plan?"

"I did, and he said he would meet with them right before the op started, so they wouldn't even be able to say something that would mess us up."

I nodded and looked over at ASAC Holmes as Detective Lee returned from his phone call.

"Where are you guys on the muscle?"

ASAC Holmes started.

"I have FBI agents for each location, and David hooked us up with the head of the Secret Service, so that won't be a problem—but we need to do this quickly—too many people for my comfort are becoming aware of the op. We're just asking for a leak."

I agree with him on that.

Detective Lee weighed in.

"I've secured Capitol Police for both the Senate and House members who are being arrested, but Maverick is right—we need to get this done."

I nodded and looked over at Winston.

"Is the whole document ready?"

He nodded.

"I shortened it as much as I could and organized it to read clearly from beginning to end. I also redacted the names that weren't confirmed. It is a fairly straightforward explanation of what the Cabal set out to do and why this 'Trojan Horse' action was necessary."

"OK, great," I said.

I looked around the room and then looked at my Walmart watch.

"Given the time difference across the country, if we set the op to go at 8:00 p.m., with the national address by the then temporary 'President Wright' at 9:00 p.m., that would put the national broadcast at 7:00 p.m. on the west coast. That would seem to work for the whole nation."

"Does that give everybody time to get your part set up?"

Everyone looked around and began to nod.

"Mr. Triplehorn, can you get all your calls made in the next hour or two?"

Mr. T thought about the calls he would need to make to set up the meetings.

"To be safe, I would say I could do it in the next hour or *three*. If I run into officials who are in meetings or need to call me back, it might take a little while, but that would still be within the time parameters, wouldn't it?"

"Yeah, that timing works. You're going to have to insist on these meetings, sir, and if some people can't be there, you'll need to notify

ASAC Holmes and Detective Lee so they can arrange to go find and arrest the other cabal members who don't attend."

Mr. Triplehorn nodded and said, "OK."

I looked around.

"Alright, let's do this!"

CHAPTER
— 185 —

It was a good thing we waited till the last minute to set up all the meetings, because the Washington, D.C. rumor mill lit up like the Times Square ball on New Year's Eve. Detective Lee was plugged in, so he let us know.

Thankfully, we hadn't given them very much time to compare notes, so all they knew was that they were needed to attend a very important meeting.

I took the time to meet with the officers who were conducting the investigation into our dead assassin.

I explained that our team was being watched by an investigator, and I gave them his picture and name. I told them he had been replaced by the assassin, and that I saw it take place—which was why I recognized him on camera, coming up the stairway, pretending to be a waiter.

And that's what led to my decision to confront him.

In some ways, that created more questions than it answered, but I told them we could be more forthcoming soon, and then appealed to "national security" to not answer any further questions.

I took them through the footage and explained what had happened and what had been said at each moment—including when I had both realized and then accused the assassin of being the murderer of Senator Ashford.

The rest of the story spoke for itself as they watched him beat me and then saw the change in momentum in the fight, with his sudden departure from the top floor and subsequently this world, undoubtably right into Hell.

They gave me the obligatory "Don't leave the city" routine, but I expected that. They clearly were quite satisfied with what they had since we had basically done their job for them and had handed them Senator Ashford's murderer.

They thought they were going to break that news later tonight for the 10 o'clock news—their big moment.

I didn't have the heart or the freedom to tell them their thunder was going to be taken at 9:00 p.m. in a national broadcast by the new and temporary, "President Wright".

After I got out of the meeting, something else occurred to me, so I went in search of Mr. Triplehorn.

"Hey Blake, how did the meeting go?"

"It was fine, pretty much what I expected."

"Listen, it occurred to me that one of us should call Brooke and fill her in as to what we've discovered, and what we're planning on doing tonight. It just doesn't seem right that she would watch it all on TV along with the rest of the nation, when it was her husband who made this all possible, and who gave his life to see this happen."

"And then there's the facts that her husband's murderer is now dead and in Hell, and the cabal that is responsible for ordering his murder is about to be eviscerated. It seems she deserves to hear all this personally from someone she trusts—preferably you."

Mr. Triplehorn was nodding.

"You're right, she should hear the facts before the nation does. I'll go ahead and call her and let her know all this before she sees it unfold."

"Great, thanks sir."

CHAPTER
— 186 —

It was time for "Operation Trojan Horse".
You might remember that, on the fly, I had previously told Mr. Triplehorn that the operation was called "Take 'em Down". However, as I noted at the time, it was a working title, and I was just spit balling. This one worked better.

Everyone had completed their tasks and were heading to their respective locations for the surprise moment when we "climbed out of the horse" and revealed the real reason for being there—and then arrested them.

We had chosen just over forty people who needed to be arrested immediately, based on Senator Ashford's notes. Of those forty plus people, only one was too sick to be at this "important meeting". He would be arrested at his home separately—sick or not. The rest of the over 100 people on the confirmed list would be arrested in the coming days.

Mr. Triplehorn was ushered into the Oval Office at 8:00 p.m. The President and the Vice-President both stood to greet him.

And then came the "Trojan Horse".

They were both puzzled as they stood there when other people followed Mr. Triplehorn in—ASAC Holmes leading the way, followed by the Speaker of the House, Abernathy Wright. The President and Vice-President's own Secret Service detail were right behind them, along with other FBI agents. After them came a camara crew with all their equipment, followed by Winston.

They began to put their equipment in place around the Oval Office, getting ready to set up.

The President waited a beat, with his brow furrowed, clearly confused, then turned to Mr. Triplehorn.

"Araby, can I ask what's going on and what this meeting is about?"

"Certainly, Mr. President."

Mr. Triplehorn turned to the camera crew.

"Would you all please excuse us for a moment?"

The crew stopped their set up and filed out of the room.

"Abe," said Mr. Triplehorn, giving the Speaker of the House the floor.

"Mr. President and Madam Vice-President; as you know, Senator Todd Ashford of California was murdered—that investigation has been ongoing. We can report that we have now discovered his assassin, and through some events where we had to defend ourselves, that man is now dead."

"Well, that's excellent news," said the President, trying to play it straight. "So, I'm giving an impromptu statement to the nation about these events?"

Speaker Wright simply shook his head "no".

"Through an investigation initiated by Mr. Triplehorn, we have come into possession of the information that Senator Ashford had collected through his own investigation—the same information that got him killed."

The President and Vice-President continued to try and keep a straight face, but they couldn't keep the fear out of their eyes when the Speaker said that.

"This information details a conspiracy by over one-hundred confirmed members of a Cabal within our government. This Cabal is committed to overwhelming and overthrowing our government and the nation as founded. We are in the process of arresting those members, all over Washington, D.C., as we speak."

"As you know, you both are confirmed members of this conspiracy, and as such, you will both resign your positions immediately."

Both the President and Vice-President began to fume and deny what the Speaker was saying.

"You have no right and no authority to take such an action! I demand that my Secret Service detail take *you* into custody immediately!"

His detail didn't move.

"Mr. President, we not only have all the facts, but we are also going to place all those facts online in less than half an hour. The American people will all be able to see the facts for themselves, and they will demand your resignation at the very least—they may well demand your incarceration."

"We don't believe it would be in the best interest of the nation for the two of you to be incarcerated, but if you refuse to resign, I will have these federal agents arrest both of you right now."

The President was seeing red.

"You all work for me! I am the Commander in Chief!" he yelled.

Speaker Wright took another step forward.

"No sir, they all took an oath to protect our nation and the Constitution against all enemies, foreign and domestic. They have all been shown the facts of your collusion with the globalist oligarchs. You are guilty, sir, and you are finished as President."

"I would remind you of the 1970s Watergate scandal and President Richard Nixon. Nixon was forced to resign for simply covering up a break-in of the Democratic National Committee at the Watergate Office Building."

Speaker Wright paused.

"You both are complicit in much worse. The Cabal you're both a part of has made you accomplices to the murder of a sitting United States Senator, and the attempted murder of at least two other men today, and very possibly a third being the attempted murder of Araby Triplehorn."

Speaker Wright looked almost sad.

"You have both failed in your oath to this country, and your primary hope should be that you're not charged for treason. You will both step down immediately . . ." he gestured toward the camera equipment waiting to be set up, ". . . and I will be addressing the American people and explaining all this to them in a few minutes."

Speaker Wright looked at both the President and the Vice-President, no longer sad—just mad.

"Both of you are done here. We can do this the hard way or the easy way—that's up to you."

CHAPTER
— 187 —

I was still feeling the pain from the beating the assassin had given me this morning.

Mr. Triplehorn had insisted on bringing in a doctor to have me looked over. From what he could tell, it appeared that I had avoided any broken bones, but he couldn't rule out any cracked ribs.

It did hurt when I took a deep breath.

The Doc had wrapped me tight around my torso to keep me from moving too much or doing any more damage, and then gave me some Percocet to help with the pain.

That stuff always made me feel a little loopy (Hey—no rude comments from the peanut gallery), so I was surviving on a combination of ibuprofen and acetaminophen.

I didn't feel great, but I would survive—and I wasn't about to miss the big "Trojan Horse" op!

I knew that Mr. Triplehorn and ASAC Holmes had things covered at the White House, not to mention Speaker Wright. (Question: why do we say, "not to mention", right before we do in fact "mention" someone?)

Any-who . . .

All across the nation's capital tonight, scheduled meetings were turning into arrest parties—the DOJ, FBI, CIA, the Capitol Police, and more. However, since we had identified the D.C. leader of this Cabal to be Majority Leader Samuel Brooks, I decided that I would join Detective Lee at the United States Capitol building for the "festivities".

We had talked Detective Lee into letting Winston take a crack at the assassin's cell phone. Winston had discovered the assassin's identity through this, which was very helpful for the DCPD's investigation, but more importantly for us, he had found Senator Brooks' number in his phone under the name, "Mercurius".

Not only that, but "Mercurius" had called the assassin last night, then had tried to call him three times after the assassin did his swan dive off the top floor of the Waldorf Astoria's stairwell—and went splat.

Hmmm . . . Senator Brooks certainly seemed awfully interested in our friendly, neighborhood assassin.

I looked that name up online and found that "Mercurius" was supposedly a Roman god of commerce, eloquence, travel, cunning, and theft who also served as messenger to the other gods. He is commonly linked with the Greek god Hermes.

I just shook my head—what a *douche*! These cabal members were idiots who just had way too much power. They really believed themselves to be the "masters of the universe". Now you all know that I imagine myself to be a superhero a lot—but I am aware that I am just *imagining*—*pretending*, if you will. I don't really *believe* it!

So, I found myself in the U.S. Capitol building conference center, where both senators and congressmen and women were starting to arrive, clearly excited to be included in such an important meeting—whatever it was. They were all talking and interacting with each other.

I had a funny feeling that the excitement might change a little when they heard Speaker Abernathy Wright on TV—at that point temporarily "President Wright"—begin to explain to the nation about the conspiracy and the Cabal. How long until they look around this room and realize that all the participants weren't just members of their political party, but were also members of the Cabal?

And then would come the time for them to all be arrested and booked.

That's a tough way to end a party.

I sang, "The parties over—it's time to call it a day . . ."

CHAPTER

— 188 —

As he walked through the tunnel between the office buildings and the U.S. Capitol, Mercurius looked at his Rolex GMT-Master II Batman Oystersteel Watch. It had a black face with some blue around the dial and was his pride and joy. It had cost him almost $17,000, but when people saw it—and he worked hard to make sure they did in fact see it—they knew he was a power player.

He was still unsettled that he couldn't get in contact with the assassin, but maybe he had "gone dark" while he was on his mission. Perhaps the old cliché of "no news is good news" would hold true.

That's why he was walking instead of taking the congressional "subway" tonight—he figured the exercise would help him burn off some of the tension he was feeling.

He had checked with his contacts at DCPD and with Capitol Police Chief Ortez. While the Chief was still unaware of Detective Lee's location, since he had taken some personal days, no one seemed to be reporting any murders from the Waldorf Astoria.

He had been tempted to have his investigator go back to the Waldorf to check on the progress. So tempted in fact, that he called him about it. When he broached the issue with him, the investigator said, "Absolutely not."

He wasn't accustomed to being talked to like that.

"What do you mean by that?" he had asked indignantly.

"That freak threatened to kill me and my family—then recited my address to make his intentions clear—if I so much as turned my head and looked at him. If you think I'm going to risk my life to 'go and

516

check' on that lunatic's work, then I'm sorry, you're going to have to get the Senate a new investigator. I draw the line at the murder of me and my family."

Since Mercurius could relate to having the assassin threaten your life, he just told the investigator to forget it, which he believed the investigator promptly did, and then hung up.

He took a deep breath. He was on his way to some important meeting of both Senate and House members of his party, which meant he would be the "big dog".

That was always fun, and he was determined to enjoy it, despite being nervous about other things going on.

He took another look at his expensive watch and stepped up his pace.

CHAPTER
— 189 —

After the President and Vice-President had finally come to the realization that their "reign of terror" was over, they were escorted out of the Oval Office by members of their Secret Service detail and some FBI agents.

Mr. Triplehorn checked his watch again and saw they only had about twenty minutes till "show time", so he cracked the whip to get things moving.

"Let's get the camera set-up people back in here and get Speaker Wright camera-ready," he said loudly.

A very significant and historic event had just taken place that would be discussed and dissected by historians for generations to come—and there was literally no time for them to think about that or ponder its implications.

If they didn't want this whole thing to "face-plant", they needed to do this next part very well.

The camera people were rushing around, running cables, and checking the uplink to make sure everything was connecting with the remote broadcast van that was parked right outside the White House. All the equipment they needed to get this broadcast to the nation and the world was sitting out there on four wheels.

"Seven minutes to show time," shouted Mr. Triplehorn to keep everyone moving quickly.

Araby walked over to Speaker Wright. They were just finishing up his on-air make-up, so he was looking a little orange.

"How are you feeling?" Mr. Triplehorn asked.

After taking a deep breath, with a weak smile, he honestly said, "A little terrified."

Mr. Triplehorn nodded.

"I get that."

Mr. Triplehorn thought for a moment.

"Are you familiar with the story of Queen Esther, the wife of Xerxes, King of Persia around 600 B.C.?"

Speaker Wright smiled.

"Do you mean the Esther from the Bible?"

Mr. Triplehorn nodded.

"Yes, from the Bible, and from history. You might remember that when she was the only one who could save the entire Jewish race from annihilation, she got scared too, and she wasn't going to step up—she decided that just maybe she was going to sit this one out."

"Do you remember what her cousin Mordecai said to her? It's something I think about often when I'm doing important national and international deals."

"Remind me."

"He basically said to her, 'How do you know that you haven't achieved this position for just such a time as this?'"

Mr. Triplehorn looked at Abe.

"Abe, tonight isn't about you, your political career, your power, or your position—and it's not about me—or anyone else involved in this. Our nation is a mess because it has lost its way and allowed bad people to come in and try to take it over. So, don't think about yourself right now—think about the nation, and the people on the other side of that camera who make up this nation. The American experiment has been a colossal *success* when we've stayed true to our founding principles, and a colossal *failure* when we haven't. President Ronald Reagan wasn't wrong when in his farewell address to the nation, he said that we are "the shining city on a hill"—at least that's what we can be, if only we'll stick to our first principles."

Mr. Triplehorn paused for a moment.

"Abe, your part in that is now. You didn't plan on this moment—none of us did, but Senator Ashford gave his life for it, and factors have put us here—and it is an historic moment in world history."

"So, I would like you to consider that just possibly, 'you have achieved this position for just such a time as this'."

"Two minutes to live!" the director shouted.

Mr. Triplehorn saw a new resolve in Speaker Wright's eyes.

"Are you ready for your own, 'for such a time as this'?" asked Mr. Triplehorn.

Abe nodded with conviction.

"You bet I am!"

CHAPTER
— 190 —

The U.S. Capitol conference room was filling up with members from both the House and the Senate. The members were laughing and talking with each other, but I had heard a few comments, wondering why there was no food or drinks.

"This is SO *not* the party you think it is," I thought to myself.

Detective Lee was overseeing everything here, but he had put another trusted Capitol Police officer in charge of keeping track of "attendance", if you will.

I looked at my watch and then walked over to the officer and asked him how we were doing.

He looked at his sheet and then around the room as two more members walked in.

"Those two who just came in mean that the only member who is not here yet is the Senate Majority Leader, Samuel Brooks."

I nodded, not saying it, but concerned that the cabal leader within our government was the one who had yet to show his face. I hoped he hadn't gotten wind of our "Trojan Horse" operation somehow.

"The live broadcast will be starting in just a few minutes. Let's get the TVs on and ready for them all to see what this party is really about," I told the officer.

He nodded and signaled one of the other officers who then started turning on the TVs, causing all the "guests" to take notice.

"Alert your fellow officers to be ready. I don't want anyone getting any funny ideas, thinking they can sneak out of here when they realize that 'the party's over' in a very literal way, if you will."

The officer nodded and keyed his comm device as he walked and alerted the officers to plant themselves around the doors.

The broadcast was to begin in about a minute, which I wanted to watch, but I was focused on our truant member, Majority Leader Samuel Brooks.

He was the dude who was leading this attack on our nation by the "elite" oligarch globalists, but from within our government. He was also the dude who put the hit out on a good and godly man, Senator Todd Ashford, and two other good men I knew—me and Detective David Lee. Maybe even Mr. Triplehorn too.

Suffice it to say, I was not too amused by ole Sammy Brooks, and I wasn't about to let him get away with this.

So, after I looked around to make sure that everything was taken care of in the conference room, I slipped out a side door just as the networks began to cut into their "regularly scheduled programming" for a surprising, unscheduled message from the Oval Office.

CHAPTER

— 191 —

Senator Brooks was almost to the conference room. He had cut it a little close, but another look at his watch told him he would get there right on time.

"Oh well, better to make my grand entrance," he thought, chuckling to himself.

Something had been bugging him for the last ten minutes of his walk though. He was going over the various members of his party who had reached out to him today, either by phone or text, to let him know they would see him at the meeting tonight.

He had just passed the little bodega at the end of the tunnel and moved into the Capitol Building when he slowed as he realized that every person who had contacted him was in the Cabal.

That, added together with the fact that he couldn't get in contact with the assassin, made him pause even more till he stopped, now in sight of the conference room.

"Was something happening here?" he thought, looking around. "Were they outed and being played?"

It was at that moment that the side door to the conference room opened and out stepped the Arizona investigator who was supposed to be dead by now.

The Majority Leader's eyes went wide as their eyes locked. The man started walking toward him.

He froze for a moment, but knew he had to get out of here. However, he needed to stay cool and not overplay his hand. How much could they really know? There was no reason for this man to even know who he was.

This might be completely coincidental, and he could blow it by acting guilty.

He decided he'd just turn nonchalantly and head back down the tunnel, banking on the hope that he was still undiscovered.

That hope was dashed when he heard the investigator yell out, "Oh come on *Mercurius*—don't try and skip out on the party now!"

Senate Majority Leader Samuel Brooks took off at a flat-out run.

CHAPTER
— 192 —

Blake had been praying for Speaker of the House Abe Wright as he stepped out of the room. The pundits on the TV were all talking about this surprise address from the Oval Office, thinking it was coming from the current President, and talking about how curious it was that they weren't given any advanced notice about it.

The speculation was running rampant.

He closed the door quietly and turned toward the tunnel entrance to begin his search for Majority Leader Samuel Brooks—or as he thought of him now, the evil "leader of the pack".

Blake was shocked when he looked up to start the search, only to see ole Sammy-boy standing about a hundred feet away, right at the tunnel entrance.

They locked eyes, and Blake could see the disbelief, and then the fear, in the Majority Leader's eyes. Blake was guessing that the disbelief was because Blake was supposed to be dead—and here he was, still kicking, and now standing at the conference room door where his "important meeting" was taking place.

Blake could see the indecision passing over Sammy's face, as he tried to do the math, trying to discern just how screwed he either was or was not. Blake gave him just a moment to freak out, then decided he'd finish the equation for him by letting him know just how totally and forevermore screwed he actually was.

As Brooks tried to casually and slowly turn away, Blake yelled out, "Oh come on *Mercurius*—don't try and skip out on the party now!"

The Majority Leader's face freaked out when he heard his made-up name come out of Blake's mouth, and he turned and ran back through the tunnel entrance door.

Blake said aloud to himself, "Moran, we got ourselves a runner!"

Blake raced after Mercurius.

CHAPTER 193

"My fellow Americans," began Speaker Abernathy Wright. "Many of you won't know who I am, so please allow me to first introduce myself; I am the Speaker of the United States House of Representatives, Abernathy Wright."

He smiled.

"Don't worry, most people just call me Abe."

Mr. Triplehorn nodded. It was a great start. Araby thought of all the news staff and pundits across the nation and the world, who were now scrambling and screaming for everything they could find on the Speaker of the House.

"I wish we could have gotten acquainted under better circumstances, but I'm afraid that we find ourselves in a dire moment in the history of our great nation, the United States of America."

"As most of you know, we lost a truly great man weeks ago, when Senator Todd Ashford was murdered, here in Washington, D.C. Through the efforts of a great patriot, Araby Triplehorn, and his investigator, Blake Moran, and others of his team, we have discovered the perpetrators of that murder."

"I can inform you that the assassin himself is dead, having fallen to his death at a Washington, D.C. hotel while trying to kill Mr. Moran."

Mr. Triplehorn knew that this was sending shockwaves around the country.

"However, there's much more to the story. We discovered that Senator Ashford had done extensive investigation on a conspiracy that was at work in our nation. This conspiracy was funded by global oligarchs, seeking to undermine and overwhelm our great nation."

"What Senator Ashford discovered, and what ultimately got him killed, was that there was a cabal of officials within our government who were spearheading the efforts to change the very fabric of our Representative Republic. They wanted to change America from a nation that is a 'government *of* the people, *by* the people, and *for* the people', as Abraham Lincoln stated in his Gettysburg Address, into a globalist nation, run by elitist billionaires."

Abe paused and looked deeply into the camera.

"To reach this goal, they were willing to kill."

The Speaker took a deep breath.

"The confirmed members of this evil Cabal are being arrested here in Washington, D.C. as I speak. We will root out all the members of this conspiracy and will seek to restore the principles the founders of our great country gave their lives to implement."

"My desire is to be completely transparent with you, the people of the United States of America. Because of this, as soon as I complete this address, all the facts of this conspiracy and the cabal of people who were behind it will be immediately uploaded online for any or all of you to review. After all, this is *your* nation—we all just work for you—and it's a 'temp-job' at that."

Abe paused again.

"The obvious question that I would imagine every journalist, pundit, and American may well be wondering right now is, 'why is the Speaker of the House telling us this extremely important information—and doing this from the Oval Office'?"

Another deep breath.

"I am sorry to report to you, the American people, that two of the confirmed members of this Cabal were the President and Vice-President of our nation."

The Speaker just looked into the camera, being well aware of the shockwave he had just sent across the nation and the world.

"Because of this fact, both the President and Vice-President have been removed from their position. Based on our Constitution, the Speaker of the House of Representatives is to assume the powers and duties of the office of the presidency—I am doing so now."

"Please understand that I serve only temporarily in this position. In our nation, the American people make the decision as to who will lead them, so I will only serve in this capacity until the next election, which takes place in two years."

"My goal during this time will be to unify our nation around our core principles, established by our founders, to be a sovereign nation under God—that 'shining city on a hill' spoken about by President Ronald Reagan in his farewell speech."

"My fellow Americans, this task will not be easy. We have learned that there are enemies of this vision for America, both within our nation and outside of it. But for the record, there always have been."

Abe's face grew hard.

"So, first of all, to those of you out there who have chosen to make yourselves enemies of the United States of America—you have made a grave mistake. We are not afraid, and you very much should be. We have been tried as a nation, over and over, and we just keep standing. This time will be no different. If you choose to come against us, please know that while we don't start fights, we are shockingly good as a nation at finishing them! I would advise you not to test us. Consider yourselves warned."

Abe's face softened.

"And now to you, the American people; your leaders cannot do this alone—we cannot succeed in making America that great nation again without you. You are designed by the Constitution to be our bosses—you are supposed to be in charge, and you, all of you, are the key to any future success."

"So, please allow me to challenge you tonight. Let's together decide to each do our part for our family, our community, our state, and our nation. Let's decide to be better husbands and wives, better fathers and mothers, better friends and neighbors, and better citizens of the greatest nation on earth—in my humble opinion."

"Our nation has lost her way, but we can find our way back to family and God and country. It'll be a fight, but I hope that you'll agree with me that it's a fight well worth the effort—for our nation and world now, and for future generations."

Speaker Wright paused.

"I know I've laid a lot on you tonight, but I'm going to ask you for one more favor. I'm going to ask that you pray for me, our leaders, our nation, and our future. Some of you may have never prayed, but I'm going to humbly ask you to start. This nation was founded on a basis that God was in it, as the source of our direction and our rights—not the government. Our only hope for the future is that God is still in it."

Abe looked into the camera.

"My name is Abe; I am humbled that you took your precious time to listen tonight. May God bless you and your family, and may God bless, help, and protect the United States of America."

"Thank you and good night."

CHAPTER
— 194 —

Blake hit the tunnel entrance door crash bar on the run and looked to see Mercurius running into the tunnel. He raced after him, trying to keep him in his line of sight. He was really feeling the beating he'd taken from the assassin earlier, but the adrenalin was making up the difference for him.

Blake was surprised that Brooks could keep up this pace for as long as he was—it seemed that abject fear can give a man a second wind. The man was probably in his sixties, and he had a bit of a paunch around his middle—but so far, he was still chugging it out.

"He'd better be careful he doesn't give himself a heart attack," thought Blake as he ran.

Blake, on the other hand was both younger and a runner, so he knew that ole "Mercurius" was a "god" who was going to run out of steam any time now, if he just kept chasing him.

So, he just stayed right with him, calling out to him periodically to freak him out, "I'm still here Mercurius; you're not going to outrun me."

Brooks rounded a curve where Blake couldn't see him for a little bit, so when he came around the corner, he was surprised when he didn't see him in front of him anymore.

Blake stopped and looked around, then said the famous Tommy Lee Jones' quote from the exceptional movie, "The Fugitive".

"We got ourselves a gopher!"

On the curve, over to his left, Blake saw that the tunnel actually sported both a "Subway" sandwich shop and a Dunkin' Donuts. They weren't open at this time of night, but they were there, along with all the tables and chairs in the large seating area.

Go figure.

Now, while Blake was unaware of this fact, Majority Leader Brooks would be well aware of it. And it just so happened that this is where Mercurius disappeared.

So, Blake just tried to still his breathing, walk around quietly, and listen.

And there it was.

The extra years and weight on ole Sammy meant that he couldn't help it—he was huffing and puffing, as quietly as he could, but Blake could hear him.

He was clearly hiding behind the Dunkin' Donuts counter. Given his extra weight, maybe he was noshing a Boston Cream donut while he was hiding.

Blake knew it was odd timing, but that thought made him a little hungry.

CHAPTER
— 195 —

Given that I had no idea what was going on in Samuel Brooks' mind, I moved parallel to the Dunkin' Donuts counter, staying about thirty feet away from Brooks, walking through the tables and chairs.

I decided to try and talk him out.

"Senator Brooks, you need to come out and give yourself up. We know you're Mercurius and the leader of the Cabal within the government."

Nothing.

"Oh, by the way, your hitman is dead—he took a swan dive of about eighty feet onto a concrete floor. There is nowhere for you to go. It's over, man."

I waited, staring at the Dunkin' Donuts counter, which is why, when Majority Leader Samuel Brooks started standing up, I saw the gun in his hand before he started to lift it to point at me.

I reacted before I even realized what I was doing. I dropped down to the floor, and as I fell, I pulled the table over on its side as a barrier. I then crouched as low to the floor as I could while pulling "Molly" out from my back holster.

And it was a good thing that I did.

Majority Leader Brooks clearly had continued to lift the gun and started firing at me. I could hear and feel it hitting the table in front of me.

It's odd what goes through your head when things like this happen. Believe it or not, my *first* thought was that ole Sammy was a pretty good shot. Most of his bullets were hitting the table, and from thirty feet; that's not bad.

My *second* thought was that, given the gun's sound and striking power, I was guessing that Brooks was shooting a 40 caliber—from the sound, possibly a Glock. I had to give Brooks props for that, since this was exactly what "Molly" was.

My *third* thought was that I didn't think Sammy was using the Hydra-Shok® expanding rounds like I did—if he had, the damage to the table would've been more extensive.

My *fourth* thought was to realize I had been subconsciously counting the shots Brooks sent my way. My count was up to seven. The reason that mattered was because, unless Brooks bought an extended magazine—which was unlikely for most people, the standard Glock magazine held only ten bullets.

My *fifth* thought was that I should probably *stop* 'thinking' and do something about this—so I tried to get the shooting to stop.

"Mercurius!"

The shooting stopped.

I took that as a good sign.

"Listen, the Speaker of the House, Abe Wright, is right now making a national address. The President and Vice-President have been removed from office, and Speaker Wright will be acting President until the next election. All of your colleagues from the Cabal are being arrested as we speak. Everyone knows you are the leader of this at the behest of the globalist oligarchs, who will also be pursued by America now."

"It's over Brooks. There's nowhere to run and hide. We have all of Senator Ashford's proof of what you've all been doing."

"Lastly, I'm also holding a gun, and I'm very well-trained and accurate with it. If I come up from behind this table and shoot, *you will die*—I don't often miss. So, clearly we can do this the easy way or the hard way. I hope you won't make me do the equivalent of 'suicide by cop' to you, but I will if you force me to."

"So, I'm asking you to surrender and stay alive. What do you say? How about you just admit the fail, and throw in the towel? You'll probably look great in prison orange!"

There was a pause as Majority Leader Brooks heard and processed everything I had just told him.

Then, with a loud, somewhat unhinged voice, he just screamed, "No!"

I shook my head, took a deep breath, and got ready to end this thing the hard way.

And then I heard a single gunshot.

However, this one did not hit the table.

The room was silent.

I peered around the top of the table briefly and saw nothing. I then ran over to the wall and raced down the side toward the counter, keeping myself low.

I had "Molly" at the ready as I glanced over the counter.

There lay the former Majority Leader, Senator Samuel Brooks, with the top half of his head missing—clearly having decided to "eat his gun".

I just shook my head. After all this jerk had done—killing Todd and trying to kill me and David, after trying to take over and ruin our great country—just like his assassin, it could *not* have happened to a more deserving guy.

CHAPTER
—196—

As you can imagine, I had lots of stuff I had to do with DCPD and the Capitol Police, after former Senate Majority Leader Brooks' suicide. Since people kept dying around me, it was starting to look bad. However, it all went pretty quickly, since they had security camera footage—my account clearly matched the recording.

Being the second "how did this bad guy end up dead" scenario of my day, I was really starting to get the hang of it.

I was able to head back to the Waldorf while someone else had to clean up the mess.

I found that after seeing ole Sammy after the fact, I wasn't craving that donut anymore.

I was craving a talk with my "boo", so I called Cindy.

"Hey babe," I said.

"Hey, how are you?"

"I'm alright. I ended up having to chase the ringleader and stop him. He tried to take me out, but in the end, he decided to eat his gun instead of being taken into custody."

"How was your night?"

That made Cindy laugh.

"Well, I had to change a couple of poopy diapers and Linc peed on me, so I was living the dangerous life too."

I laughed and said, "From the last couple of days I've had, that sounds like 'living the dream'."

We both laughed in agreement.

"I should be able to come home now. Everything is pretty well set up, and now that Speaker Wright is acting President, it's his job to start fixing the mess."

Cindy jumped in.

"Speaker Wright's speech was so good; really, really good. I think we got us a keeper there—and I think Senator Ashford would be happy with him."

"And I'm very anxious for you to get home. Now that my hero has saved the nation and the world, you have a family here that needs you."

Cindy wasn't done.

"And you can forget about that 'wait for a month', no sex rule from the doctor—all this hero stuff where you're saving mom, apple pie, and the American way, has got me wanting my husband in quite the carnal way."

I was surprised, my eyebrows went up, and I laughed.

"Well, well, well," I said. "You might remember little lady, that I predicted in the hospital room you wouldn't be able to keep your hands off me for a full month. I even gave you a little walk, if you remember, so you could view my derrière and feel the seduction."

Cindy chuckled.

"And you might remember, my dear, that the more you talked, the more I said I was sure I could resist you. You might want to heed that warning now."

"Oh, yeah."

So, I quit talking and just accepted the fact that my wife could *not* resist me.

Now, what I could have pointed out was that if the doctor's rule was that *I* had to wait for a month, then the rule was also that *she* had to wait for a month too.

Good luck trying to guess which way I went on *that*!

I'm guessing you'd like to put some serious money on whether I pointed that out or not, right?

If it helps you guess, I was even *more anxious* to get home now than before. As I've told you, and will continue to contend, women just have *way too much power*!

Past that, I can't help you.

I know—we're *all* thinking it. Who can know whether I pointed this out to her, or not? It's *such* a tough call! We might as well face it—I'm simply an *enigma*.

CHAPTER
— 197 —

Mr. Triplehorn, Thurston, and Winston got back to the hotel around midnight. ASAC Holmes and Detective Lee showed up about twenty minutes later.

We all gathered back in the living room and got some of the food that Thurston had ordered to have sent up from the kitchen for us.

We were all pretty exhausted, but hungry too.

"How are you doing, Blake?" asked Mr. Triplehorn.

I thought about that.

"I think I'm getting more and more sore from the assassin who tried to kill me this morning, *but* I don't have any bullet holes in me from the evil, diabolical government leader who tried to kill me tonight."

I paused.

"So, I'm gonna call today *a win*."

Everybody chuckled at the day we'd all had.

I turned to ASAC Holmes and Detective Lee.

"What's the 411 on all our arrested conspiracists?"

They both smiled.

Detective Lee said, "Some are just yelling for their lawyers and threatening us, but quite a number are singing like the proverbial bird. They are incriminating all the other members of the cabal to get a sweeter deal for themselves."

"I have to say that watching the Capitol Police Chief, Raymond Ortez, get handcuffed, was something the whole department kind of enjoyed."

He then added, "The dude was a ginormous nob—nobody liked him."

ASAC Holmes said, "We're seeing the same thing—a bit of a mixed bag, but by and large, the old adage 'there's no honor among thieves' is proving true here."

I nodded, glad to hear that some of the cabal members were providing even more evidence of their crimes.

I turned to Mr. Triplehorn.

"So, what's been the fallout and the public's response?"

He smiled a tired smile.

"Well, 'official Washington' is in an uproar and trying to see if we could even do what we did today legally. I have some of the best attorneys in the country on it, so I don't expect that to go anywhere. The more we are learning about the Cabal, the more it becomes clear that this was a secret coup of our governmental system. These guys are as guilty as it gets."

He then smiled a little bigger.

"But when it comes to the public, that's been *awesome*. People already didn't like how this group of politicians were messing up everything in the country: the economy, more crime, an open border, the attacks on morality, family, faith and God, the transgender garbage, the energy crisis they created and more. They were tired of being told by the government media, 'You're stupid. Don't believe your lying eyes—things are great', but the American people *aren't* stupid—they know how awful these people have made their lives."

"I guess I'm saying they were ready for a change. Did you get to hear Speaker Wright's speech?"

I laughed.

"No, somebody was trying to kill me right about that time—I probably should have recorded the speech. Cindy said it was really good."

Mr. Triplehorn smiled.

"Well, she's right—it *was* excellent. But how old *are* you, Blake?

Record it? Do you want all the kids to 'get off your lawn' too? It's all over the internet, so don't worry, you'll be able to watch it."

"Little snarky, Mr. T," I said.

He laughed.

"Well, Abe nailed it—he struck all the right chords, and he seems like a genuinely good and godly man . . . like Todd was."

A shadow passed over Mr. T's face, and he sat up.

"Gentlemen, a great man actually did give his life for his country, and based on his sacrifice, our country now has a chance to decide if it will be great again. I don't want to ever forget his sacrifice, or that of his family."

He held up his drink.

"Let's raise our glasses to Senator Todd Ashford, a real man, a husband, a father, a godly man, a public servant, and a patriot to his nation—may his sacrifice lead America to once again become that 'shining city on a hill'."

NOTE FROM THE AUTHOR

I'd like to make you a deal:
If you loved this book, please tell *everyone you know*.
If you didn't, let's just keep that *our little secret*.

Davie Mac

The Art of the Steal

— A BLAKE MORAN NOVEL —

A Preview

PROLOGUE

He moved quietly through the hallway. It was the middle of the night, and the museum was closed.

To everyone but him.

He had passed numerous beautiful works of art—items for which his clients would pay seven figures, a couple of them even eight figures.

But he wasn't here, shopping like he was walking around the "we have everything" aisles of a Carrefours or Costco in Paris, trying to decide what he was going to select. He had been chosen and directed to unburden the museum of a specific piece of art—one worth tens of millions of dollars on the open market but considered priceless by the curators at virtually every museum.

He was covered in black, his face included. His hands sported riding gloves that enabled him to both conceal his fingerprint identity and make sure that his purchase on the work of art was secure.

It was never a good idea to accidentally drop a priceless work of art.

He moved across the museum quickly, paying close attention to how quiet he was at the same time. He considered this part of his craft. So many people who engaged in the larcenist endeavors simply had no finesse, no style, no *art* to their work. If there is no panache, no je ne sais quoi—then why even do it? If one does not take a measure of pride in one's work, why labor at the job?

He had to chuckle to himself. He had just thought the phrase, "je ne sais quoi", which was typically taken to mean something having a certain quality or characteristic that makes it special, or interesting, or unique.

PROLOGUE

However, the French phrase, literally translated to English, means, "I am of the not knowing"—so basically gibberish.

It got to its current meaning because when someone was "not knowing" *what* the special quality or characteristic was, but they knew it *was there*, that meant it had that certain "je ne sais quoi".

By the time he had finished that amusing anecdote in his head, he was at the artwork. It wasn't all that large—only about half a meter square—but the brushwork was exquisite. From the fifteenth century of the Italian Renaissance, it was truly *magnifique*!

He carefully removed the priceless painting while detaching the security tag. He then wrapped it in soft cloth and placed it on the floor.

Out of his bag, he took out his own art, art which he cut into steel and prepared for this very display. He mounted it where the painting had been, stepping back and taking a moment to admire it. He then took a number of pictures of his art in place, with the focused show lighting, highlighting its brilliance.

It was time to go, so he placed the priceless painting into his bag and retraced his steps back down the hall, just as quietly and quickly as he had entered.

Before he turned the corner, he stopped to gaze lovingly at his own special work of art.

Then, he was gone into the night, like he'd never been there.

After all, *that* was "the art of the steal".

ACKNOWLEDGMENTS

An author must depend on other people of great skill if he or she is to hope to remain focused on his or her skill—creating a story that people want to be a part of. I continue to thank my oldest son, Jake McAllister, for all of his help in marketing and advertising the Davie Mac books. His passion and effort for their success means the world to me. Also, Nicole Baron, of Nicole Baron Designs, creates the artwork, does the typesetting, and generally walks me through all of the steps of delivering the Davie Mac books to the reading public. Thank you for your always excellent efforts on my behalf. My team of editors; John Fink, Bobbie Jo King, Lorella Ritzel, and Julia Huslig, have done such a great job in finding mistakes in the manuscript, while still being kind when they show me the corrections. They commit their time and expertise out of love for me and my family, and the belief that what we are attempting to do with the Davie Mac franchise actually matters. Thanks to each of you—you matter to me as well.

ABOUT THE AUTHOR

Davie Mac (aka David McAllister) is a resident of Tucson, Arizona, and has always been a big fan of the "whodunit" genre. Davie is currently working on the sixth book in this series and planning for a seventh. Davie is also a song writer—having written over 60 songs to date—he plays the drums in a band and is an avid weightlifter. Professionally, Davie has been in Christian ministry for over 40 years, and founded and has pastored the Bridge Christian Church in Tucson for over 30 years. Davie and his wife Kimberly have seven children and seventeen grandchildren.

For more information about the author visit:
www.daviemacbooks.com

Other books by Davie Mac:

Made in the USA
Las Vegas, NV
27 July 2024